Stone of the Denmol

Shadows of Hiraeth, Volume 1

R.C. Gray

Published by R.C. Gray, 2019.

STONE OF THE DENMOL

First edition. October 6, 2019.

Written by R.C. Gray.

This book is dedicated to all my family and friends.
Without your support, I wouldn't have made it far.

Into the Web

His footsteps were silent as he made his way across the fallen leaves and thick moss that lined the forest floor. The woodland around him stretched out for miles in all directions, and the towering trees dampened the glow of the morning sun that was beginning to break over the horizon. Tall oaks, golden maples, and white pines swayed gently in the cool breeze, covering any sound his light footsteps might make. Several birch trees pushed up through dense rows of brambles and blackberry bushes, their bright white bark contrasting the dark brown tangles of branches that wove tightly around their trunks. Large rocks jutted up like broken teeth between the trees, hiding the mouth of the cave just a stone's throw away.

Crouching to one knee on a small game trail, Skara stopped to check for any signs of movement in the area. Although he had gone into the cave many times, it was never without risk. Brushing the dirt off his palms, he reached for the small pouches that hung tightly on his belt and opened the flaps of each, checking to make sure he had brought his vials of antidote. Feeling the small bottles wrapped in strips of cloth inside, he closed the pouch and slid his hand forward to rest on the hilt of one of the twin daggers he had found long ago deep inside the cave.

The dagger on his belt was nearly the length of his forearm with dark brown leather tightly wrapped over its hilt. Its slightly curved blade was blackened and inscribed with silver runes that ran down its length and was pressed firmly into a leather sheath that hung on his right hip. A second dagger, nearly identical to the first, was attached on his left hip, and a straight-bladed knife hung in a horizontal sheath on the back of his belt. Giving each of his weapons one last touch, Skara rose to his feet in a crouch and slowly moved forward.

His soft deerskin boots padded lightly on the damp earth as he crept between the trees and rough stones that lay scattered around the edges of the trail. His dark green tunic and brown pants blended with the forest around him, but the sharp eyes that were trained to hunt could easily see his movement if they were watching. Pausing at the base of a large tree, he raised his face into the wind, his slightly pointed nose sniffing quickly as his dark yellow eyes darted from side to side across the small clearing that stretched out between his position and the mouth of the cave. Hearing a slight rustle in the canopy above him, his pointed green ears twitched, and his pupils narrowed into slits, scanning the branches that hung high overhead.

The morning light glittered through the brightly colored autumn leaves, making the red, gold, and orange look like flames dancing in the wind against the brightening blue sky. The leaves that had blown free fell lightly into the clearing, painting the dark green patches of moss with bright flecks of color. Skara closed his eyes and took a deep breath, enjoying the smell of the brisk air around him. Shivering slightly, he opened his eyes and focused on the task ahead.

"Must've been the wind," he muttered to himself while scratching at the black arm wraps that covered his mottled, dark green skin. His voice was low and slightly rough as his breath cut sharply through his pointed teeth. Being so close to the caverns always put him on edge; but the chance at finding gold, weapons, or other treasures was worth the effort. Licking his lips nervously, he pulled his long black hair into a tight ponytail and glanced around one last time before darting across the clearing and into the vast, dark mouth of the cave.

Once inside, he scurried behind a large rock near the wall and waited, watching for any movement in the depths beyond. Running his hand lightly along the damp wall, he let his eyes adjust to the darkness, being careful of his footing over the slick, uneven stones scattered across the cavern floor. And although he could see in near-total blackness, one wrong move could draw unwanted attention and put him in a dangerous position.

The cave was nearly forty feet high and twice as wide with massive weavings of webbing covering the walls and portions of the opening that led deeper into the murk of the Surwynd cave. Moving away from the wall and pulling out a small sack that was tucked into his tunic, he rubbed a slick salve on his hands and tugged at several thick strands of web that hung tattered between two large rocks, shoving pieces into his bag.

Above him hung balls of webbing suspended from the cave ceiling, each filled with something that had been unlucky enough to stumble in or be caught and carried here. There weren't many that chose to visit the cave, as its inhabitants and depth kept away most explorers; but occasionally, someone or something would venture here unprepared and get caught up only to meet a horrible fate. And as unfortunate as it was for someone else, it made for easy scavenging that led him to find quite a few valuables that would have otherwise been lost.

Reaching out his hand, his fingers stuck slightly to the rope-like webs attached to the rock in front of him. Pulling out his dagger, he cut lengths of it away, wrapped it into balls, and stuffed them into the open sack on the ground. Cutting several more strands, he shoved them into the bag as he glanced around the cave, looking for anything else that could be useful. Catching sight of a large bundle of web hanging from the ceiling, he picked up his bag and moved over to the slightly swaying mass.

It was wrapped from head to toe in webbing, and only a small opening could be seen around the noticeably human mouth. The cold air in the cave had turned the partially open lips a pale pink, while the stubble and skin around them were damp with moisture from the cave; or from the man forcing his tongue through the web trying to get air. The body hung at an angle with the head slightly lower than the feet, attached to the high ceiling by several thick lines.

"Poor bastard. I hope it was quick," Skara said, jabbing his sharp nail at the side of the hanging body.

The body suddenly let out a loud gasp and began to twist and writhe inside the cocoon, swinging it from side to side. Letting out a startled grunt, Skara stepped backwards, tripping on the stones behind him, his right side scraping down a long, rough stone before he landed hard on his back.

Scrambling back to his feet, he quickly drew a dagger and hid behind a broken boulder, eyes searching the ceiling as he glanced back and forth between the swaying body and the massive white webs.

"Who's out there? Answer me! I know you're there; I can hear you. You have to get me out of here. I've been here all night, and that thing could be back at any minute."

The man began to grunt and jerk frantically at his bindings, causing him to rock unsteadily back and forth. "Can you please help me? You can't just leave me here," the man said as he stopped struggling, letting out a loud roar that echoed off the walls around them.

Moving quickly over to the body, Skara placed his hand over the man's open mouth. "Shut your mouth or you'll get us both killed."

The man stopped squirming, and Skara could hear a muffled groan coming from beneath his hand. Moving his palm away from the man's mouth, he quickly gulped in air.

"What are you doing?" the man said, breathing hard. "Are you trying to kill me? The one opening that I have in this death trap is for my mouth, and you cover it up! Now stop playin' around and cut me outta here. I know you may not want to know this, but this web is really...constricting."

"What?"

"Tight. Around the..." the man paused, thinking about what to say next. "Around the lower region. I think I'm losing circulation! It's like when you've slept on your arm wrong and woke up to a painful, tingly sensation. Think about how that feels, but in your nether region. Now, will you hurry up?"

"I think that's the point. The whole purpose is to keep you in place until the spider can come back, stick its fangs into your squishy torso and suck out your innards. It's not a warm hammock meant to keep you cozy," Skara said as he eyed the man and took hold of one of the lines holding him in place. Hearing the skittering sound of small rocks cascading down a wall farther into the tunnel, he gripped the hilt of his dagger as he scanned the tangles of webs hanging in the distance. "Don't move."

"What is it?" the man said, fear tinging his voice.

"Quiet," Skara said, his sharp eyes peering through the darkness as he ducked below the man's body, watching for any signs of movement but seeing nothing.

The man moved slightly, tugging at his bonds. "Are you still there?"

"Do you know how many spiders there are in here?" Skara said, catching the scent of alcohol as he stood up next to the man. "This cave stretches under the whole of Uthrea, they say. It goes deep underground with openings everywhere. No one really knows what's down there, but I know there's more than spiders! Most likely a few clans of deep dwarves and dark elves; and they're the least of your worries. And you think you can get drunk and come down here..."

"Thanks for the lesson, but that's not what happened. Besides, you've just let me hang here for some time for no reason. Now, if you don't mind, I'd like you to take out a knife, cut these webs, and let me down."

Working quickly, Skara reached out his hand and took hold of the thick strands of webbing and began to saw through them. He made sure to cut the strand nearest to the man's head first so that his body hung at an awkward angle before cutting through the web at the man's feet, letting him fall limply to the ground. The man let out a small groan as he landed hard against the stone. He writhed and strained as Skara cut away the webbing that held his legs in a tight bundle.

"Stop moving, or you'll get cut. It's hard enough to take this off without you wriggling all over like a worm."

"Then, hurry up. I don't like being so close to getting eaten."

"We should be fine if we're quick. The spiders move deeper into the cave to nest before the sun comes up. They don't get out and moving again until close to dark. They're night hunters. I'm sure that's when they got you, stumbling alone out in the dark. They strung you up to finish you off in the evening. Most likely, a little meal for one of the younger ones."

Skara ran his dagger through the white, sticky mass, pulling it open as he went. As he neared the man's chest, cutting his arms free, the man ripped the remaining webbing from his face and sat up. Rubbing his eyes and pushing back his long, dark blonde hair, he winced as he rubbed a bloody bump on his forehead. Moving his hand down to rub the back of his neck, he looked over at Skara, his eyes opening wide in surprise as he looked him up and down.

"So, you're a goblin," the man said, pulling strands of webbing off the tips of his pointed ears. "Not that there's anything wrong with that. Just not what I expected."

"And you're an elf," Skara said, tilting his head to the side and squinting down at the man. "I thought you'd be some little lord-ling out playing the hero. No one else would be fool-ish enough to come in here otherwise. Or maybe you are a lord-ling, although you couldn't tell it from your clothes."

The elf was wearing a dark blue long-sleeved tunic, its top buttons left open to show what looked like a black tattoo on his upper chest. His left sleeve hung down over his wrist, unbuttoned at the cuff, while his right sleeve was rolled up over his elbow. The black pants he wore were dirty and tat-tered and tucked into his black boots that reached halfway up his calf. He wore a plain black belt with several small pouches and what looked like an empty sword and dagger sheath on his left hip.

"Well, let's not forget you're in here too...and I'm about as much of a lord-ling as you are," the elf said, pushing him-self to his feet and brushing the dirt off his pants. "I don't have the luck for that. Although things would be a lot easier if I were. Faine is my name."

The elf slightly bowed, twirling his hand in an exaggerat-ed motion as he bent down.

"Skara."

"Well, Skara, it looks like I owe you one for saving my life. Do you know what it's like to have eight hairy legs wrap-ping around you? I mean, normally I wouldn't mind hav-ing eight legs twisting around me, but not from a massive, gods-damned spider. Now, I think we should stop standing around and get out of here. These spiders could come to tear us apart any second now."

The elf looked from left to right before lightly running towards the brighter end of the cave. Grabbing his bag and following the elf, Skara smirked to himself as he watched

Faine stumble over several of the slick stones that were scattered across the cave floor.

"So, how'd you end up here?" Skara said, following close behind the elf.

Faine shook his head and tried to clear a bit of the fog that still hung there. "It's kind of a long story. Let's just say I got into something that I shouldn't have and ended up in the woods in the wrong place at the wrong time last night."

"You got lucky," Skara said. "They don't always wait to eat what they catch."

"I don't know if I'd say that...but maybe you're right. There's a lot more in these woods that could have gotten me in the dark," Faine said, glancing back over his shoulder at Skara. "But why are you here?"

"For the web."

"What do you mean?"

"I take the webbing down, roll it into balls, and sell it to a merchant in Banrielle. They make it into fabric or use it to make clothing or light armor."

"How can they do anything with it when it's so sticky?" Faine said, running his hand across a small patch of webbing still clinging to his pants. His face twisted in frustration as the white threads stuck to his palm and had to be scraped off onto the jagged edge of a rock.

"It has to soak in a solution to get it clean. The merchants won't touch it if they can't do anything with it."

"So, you just show up here to collect webs? Hardly seems worth the trouble unless the merchants pay good coin for it. But you know when the spiders sleep, so you must come around quite a bit."

"As much as I need to. You never know what might've been dropped by someone else down here."

"You mean someone caught up like an animal? How often do you come across people hanging in here?" Faine said, breathing heavy as made his way up the incline out of the cave and into the light of the clearing. He stopped, leaning over to put his hands on his knees and catch his breath. "Oh, thank the gods...sunlight."

Skara scowled, looking over at Faine. "Not often. But if they're here, they don't have use for what's in their pockets anymore. Coin's no good to the dead."

"True enough. I'd say that I'm sorry about you missing out on possibly getting a few coins from me, but since that means I would have been dead, I'm really not that sorry. And besides, you still have your balls."

Skara looked at him with a puzzled look, his face turning into a slight frown.

"Your balls of web. You know, to sell back in town. Speaking of which, where is it? I know it's north of here, but about how far?"

"About four miles or so."

"You heading there now? I'm a little turned around. There's a gold coin in it for you if you can get me there."

Thinking about how the coin could make up for some of the trouble the elf had put him through down in the cave, Skara slung his bag over his shoulder and motioned for Faine to follow. "Come on, then."

The woods were quiet as the sun rose higher in the sky, its scattered light shining down on the small trail as they walked, Faine talking about several other exploits that he had barely escaped. Only speaking occasionally, Skara kept his eyes on the path, watching for rocks as he moved quickly through the trees, trying to reach the edge of the forest.

The two walked for nearly two miles before Faine suddenly froze, his face going blank. "Skara, stop!"

Skara turned to look at Faine, a worried expression washing over his face. His ears twitched as he heard the branches of the thick tree in front of them creaking under a heavy weight. Small twigs broke and fell around them as they both raised their eyes to look at the branches above. Glaring down from the tree directly above their heads, a massive spider perched, watching them with eight large eyes.

Its grotesque body was nearly the size of a warhorse with a brown abdomen and a spotted grey thorax. Thick, bristly hair covered its spindly legs as it stretched them out towards the pair, picking up their vibrations and scent with the delicate hairs on the tips of its legs as it leaned forward, getting ready to jump.

"Run!" Skara said, taking off in a sprint in one direction while Faine ran in another.

The spider leapt from the tree as it followed behind Faine, moving swiftly across the rough terrain, darting between trees and jumping over open areas to quickly catch up to the fleeing elf. Using its front legs, it slammed into Faine's back, sending him sprawling onto the dew-soaked leaves. The impact of the fall nearly knocked the air out of his lungs, and he struggled to catch his breath as he rolled onto his back, pushing hard with his legs as he tried to escape.

The spider moved over Faine and raised its two front legs, exposing its sharp claws and piercing fangs. Reaching out his hands for anything that could be used as a weapon, he gripped a fist-sized stone in his right hand and threw it as hard as he could manage from his position. The jagged edges of the stone struck the spider above its fangs, directly in one of its dark, glassy eyes, popping it with a sickening, wet sound as liquid fell out onto Faine's face.

The spider let out a high-pitched screech and stepped backwards, its legs stomping at the ground. Faine pushed himself back to move out of the way, trying to put some distance between himself and the great beast in front of him; but the spider was already moving forward, its fangs glistening with thick, dark liquid as it stalked closer.

Faine let out a scream and raised his arms over his face as the spider reared back, preparing to sink its fangs into the flailing elf on the ground in front of it. Just as the spider moved to strike, Skara stepped in front of the massive creature, slamming a sturdy branch onto the creature's head, driving it backwards and away from Faine.

"Get up!" Skara said, quickly pulling a dagger from his belt and letting it fall onto the ground behind him.

Grabbing the dagger, Faine jumped to his feet behind Skara, slashing at the creature's legs as it thrashed wildly to keep the two at bay. Raising the large stick above his head, Skara swung down hard at the creature's eyes, landing a solid blow to one of the spider's legs as it scurried sideways, moving its head out of reach. With a faint snapping sound, the lower segment of the long, left front leg broke in half, causing the beast to shriek and go into a frenzy.

Flinging its legs madly and striking out with its fangs, the creature rushed forward, pushing them back as they stumbled over downed branches and rocks. Catching his right foot on a wet log behind him, Skara slid, nearly falling as he lost his balance. Seizing the moment of opportunity, the spider lunged forward, knocking Faine to the side with one of its scurrying legs while its needle-like fangs darted down at Skara as he stumbled. Still not entirely on his feet, Skara raised his left arm to shield his body just as the sharp, poisonous fangs crashed into him, tearing two bloody slits into his left forearm and filling his blood with poison.

Skara screamed and pulled his injured arm close to his body as he swung the club with his right arm, fighting desperately to fend off the attacking fangs. Rushing in from behind the beast, Faine drove his blade deep into the top of its abdomen, pulling and sawing as he cut jagged gashes in its flesh. The spider wheeled and turned away from Skara, knocking him over with its bulbous abdomen as it turned its attention fully at the elf, dark blood dripping heavily from its open wounds. Stepping back slowly, Faine slashed out with his blade, keeping distance between himself and the creature's rearing fangs.

Skara felt a wave of sickness as pain shot through his arm, spreading quickly into his shoulder and chest as he lurched to his feet and staggered towards the distracted spider. Pulling the straight-bladed dagger from its sheath on the back of his belt, he moved quickly to the spider's side and darted between its stamping legs, hacking down at the narrow piece of flesh connecting the abdomen to the thorax.

The blade struck hard against the pedicel, cutting a deep wound into the soft flesh behind the armored exoskeleton on its thorax. Chopping down again and again in quick, hard strikes, the thin blade cut deeper each time before falling from Skara's grasp as he dropped to his knees, his chest tight as he gasped for breath. The forest spun around him as he crawled away from the spider, bile climbing up his throat as his stomach tightened and waves of pain wracked his body.

The spider shrieked as it jerked from side to side and flailed its legs, crouching low as it prepared to jump onto the branches of a nearby tree. Springing forward, its body twisted unnaturally, the weight of its bulbous abdomen pulling hard on the tattered strands of soft tissue barely holding the creature together. Thick blood splattered across the bright leaves that littered the ground as its abdomen tore away from its thorax, falling with a sickening thump as its upper body flew through the air, its legs slightly twitching as it crashed into the ground twenty paces away.

Skara collapsed onto the ground, his arm clutched tight to his chest. His left arm was bleeding, and black, viscous poison was caked around his wounds. His right arm shook as he reached for the pouches at the back of his belt.

Dropping the dagger, Faine ran over, kneeling next to Skara. "What do I do?" he said, his hands shaking as he held Skara's arm and looked at the deep cuts.

"In my pouch," Skara said, leaning over so that Faine could open them. "Bottles of antidote wrapped in cloth."

Faine reached into the pouches and pulled out several small bundles of cloth, each wet and filled with broken glass.

"Shit, they're broken! You must have landed on them." Thinking quickly, Faine put the bundles of wet cloth together and held them over Skara's mouth. "Open your mouth."

Skara stared off into treetops above him, his eyes beginning to glaze over as a soft, white froth began to gather at the corners of his mouth.

"Nai'eteln!" Faine said, cursing as he grabbed Skara's face, leaned his head back, and squeezed his cheeks to open his mouth. Holding the rags, he squeezed as hard as he could, pressing the liquid-soaked cloth onto Skara's tongue. Feeling the bits of glass breaking and grinding together beneath his grip, he squeezed harder and shook his hand up and down to press every drop he could get out of the fabric.

Skara coughed and took a breath as his body began to tremble slightly. He turned his eyes to look at Faine. "I need to get to a healer. That bit-" he coughed, his body shuddering as his muscles began to stiffen and contract. His fingers curled into his palms as he closed his eyes and gritted his teeth. "Need more antidote."

"Shit! Hold on. I know where to go."

Faine looked at the forest around him. Diffused rays of sunlight shone through a thin veil of grey clouds spreading across the sky, causing the shadows to dance on the ground around him. The spider sat broken and silent in the distance, its body in two sections with a trail of dark blood and entrails strewn on the forest floor between them. Running his hands roughly through his hair, he stood and ran over to retrieve one of Skara's daggers and slid it back into its sheath, hoping he wouldn't run into any more spiders. Gritting his teeth, he knelt next to Skara and grabbed his right arm, sat him up and hoisted him onto his shoulders.

"Just hold on! We're about a mile away, but I'll get you some help...I'll get you there," Faine said, moving through the forest as fast as he could, sweat beading on his forehead as he ran; his breath just as ragged as Skara's.

A Chance Meeting

Faine's breath was sharp in his chest, and his legs burned as he stumbled up to a cabin hidden by a small copse of maple trees surrounded by a loose circle of sycamores. The shelter was made from small logs and clay and had a straw roof with a small stream of smoke rising out of a hole on one side. Several wooden framed windows lined the walls, and a small door made from long branches was left standing open, letting the morning breeze flow into the hut.

"Renna!" Faine said, falling to the ground, letting Skara hit harder than he would have liked. "Renna, get out here and help me!"

A woman appeared in the doorway, wiping her hands on a dark brown apron hanging over a light brown dress with small holes and tears near the bottom. Her dark brown hair held several braids pulled behind her pointed ears, while the rest hung loosely over her shoulders. Her skin was a pale green, and small tusks protruded from under her bottom lip, reaching just slightly over the top of her upper lip. Her smile quickly turned into a look of worry as she dropped her apron and rushed out of the cottage towards Faine.

"Gods, Faine. What happened? Are you alright?" Renna said, her face contorted with worry.

"I'm fine. But Skara was poisoned by a spider. He took a little antidote, but I don't think it was enough. His body is stiff. I think his whole body is cramping."

"Help me get him into the house," Renna said, grabbing Skara by the arm and picking him up most of the way off the ground before Faine could stand to help her.

As the two reached the cottage, the pair moved Skara to the bed and gently placed him on his back. The cottage walls were covered with furs and wool blankets to help shelter it from the cold drafts that came in during the night, and small bookshelves were placed in front of the pelts, each filled with books of varying sizes. The dirt floor was packed smooth, and a stone hearth stood against the back wall, a crackling fire burning inside. On the opposite wall stood a long table covered in books and scrolls. A pestle and mortar sat near the end of the table, surrounded by several vials filled with darkly colored liquids. Bundles of dried plants hung from the ceiling and made the air smell of green herbs and spicy barks and roots.

Renna quickly rummaged through her herbs and vials and began to pour a dark, acrid liquid into a wooden bowl, tossing several handfuls of herbs and strips of cloth inside, swirling it together with a wooden spoon. Taking down a bottle filled with a dull yellow liquid from a shelf above the table, she uncorked it and poured a small amount into a nearby silver tankard. Picking off several serrated leaves from the bunches that hung from her ceiling, she ground them up, brushed them into the cup, and added in a bit of water and honey before stirring it together and bringing it to the bed.

"Skara, can you hear me? I need you to drink this. It won't taste good, and it will make your stomach roll, but it will help to neutralize the poison," Renna said, her voice calm and low.

Skara raised his head slightly and opened his mouth to drink the mixture. It smelled faintly of mint but had a bitter taste that puckered his mouth and burned his throat as he swallowed it. Although his body was tense, he was starting to feel movement in his limbs as his muscles began to relax. He knew that what little antidote he had used would have kept him from death, but it wasn't enough to save him from being paralyzed and deathly sick for several long hours. He would have survived, but he was sure there would have been times in his sickness that death would have been a welcomed release from the agony; so he was willing to take any help that could spare him the pain he would have felt without it.

Renna handed the cup to Faine, and he held it to his nose to smell it before drinking the remainder of the liquid. "Just to be safe." He set the cup on the table and looked over at Renna. "What now?"

"Take the wrapping off his arm. I need to get to the wounds."

Faine began to undo the black wrapping on Skara's arm, tossing it onto the floor and kicking it under the bed when he was finished. Behind him, Renna looked on the shelves beneath the large table that held her vials and pulled out a pot and a jug of water. Hanging the pot over the fire, she filled it with water and swung it over the flames to bring it to a boil. Grabbing a bottle of strong, clear alcohol from a nearby bookshelf, she moved over to Skara and pulled his arm so that it hung off the side of the bed.

"Hold him down," Renna said, looking at Faine. "This isn't going to be very pleasant for him."

Faine reached his hand out for the bottle of alcohol that Renna held, and she handed it to him with a bit of reluctance. Grabbing the bottle, he took a long drink before handing it back to Renna. He then moved his body over the top of Skara's to hold down his arms and chest and to try to keep him from flailing. "Sorry about this, but it has to be done."

Renna examined the two cuts down Skara's arm before moving over to the fire to check the pot of water. The water simmered as she dipped in a strip of clean cloth, pulling it out when it was fully saturated. It steamed as she held it in her left hand and picked up the bottle of alcohol with her right.

Getting a firm grip on Skara's arm, she held in place under her left bicep and began pouring the clear alcohol over his arm and scrubbing with the clean cloth. Skara winced and tried to pull back his arm, but his sore muscles and the weight of Faine on top of him held him in place. He grunted in pain, and his breath came in quick gasps as she poured the alcohol onto his skin, burning and stinging his wound before harshly scrubbing at the open cuts.

Blood began to pour from the gashes in his arm as Renna pushed the flesh around his wounds open, cleaning deeper inside the wounds, trying to get out as much of the poison as she could.

"The poison has crusted and dried in your skin. I have to clean it all out, or the wounds will get infected," Renna said, pouring more alcohol onto his arm.

Skara tried to pull his arm back, but between the pain from the cleaning and the poison, the world around him faded to black, and he fell into unconsciousness. Renna felt his muscles go limp and glanced up to see if he was still breathing. Hearing the quiet hiss of his breath, she quickly finished cleaning he cuts before sitting back onto the floor.

"That should do," Renna said, slightly exhausted from the ordeal. "He shouldn't have to worry about infection, but I still have to try to close the wounds. Do you mind?"

Faine grimaced and released his grip on Skara. He never liked this spell and wasn't thrilled about Renna using it on him. It was good for healing light wounds, but it required someone else's energy to do it.

Sitting up, he held out his hand to Renna, and she took it in her own. Placing her other hand over Skara's injured arm, she began to mutter something under her breath that Faine couldn't make out. He felt Renna's grip tighten on his fingers as his head began to swim. His arms and legs went briefly numb, and he felt as if he had just been beaten and left for dead in the streets. He was already exhausted from running through the forest, so the excess drain of his energy made him feel as if he was about to faint, but the feeling passed quickly, and Renna released her grip on his hand. Faine could see that the wounds on Skara's arm had almost been fully closed as Renna held her palm over his arm. Shaking his head groggily, he took a seat near the fire to rest.

"I'm getting better. His wounds are almost fully healed," Renna said, getting to her feet as she grabbed the poultice she had made and wrapped Skara's arm to protect it from infection. Grabbing two cups from the shelf, she filled them with dried herbs and poured hot water from the simmering pot into them. She handed one to Faine and took a seat next to him, holding the cup to her nose, smelling the herbal tea as it steeped.

"So, what happened?"

Faine stared into the fire and took a slow drink of his tea, grimacing as the hot water burned his lips. "I got lost in the woods and ended up somewhere I didn't want to be."

"And how did you come across Skara?" she said, looking at Faine and leaning back on her plain wooden chair.

Taking another drink of his tea, Faine held his hands out closer to the fire, warming them as he told Renna about what had happened and how Skara had saved him twice.

"Sounds like something was watching out for you," Renna said, raising her eyebrows.

Faine let out a small grunt. "Yeah, Skara. He saved my life. I was stupid enough to let myself get riled up and almost got myself killed. If he hadn't cut me out of that web or fought off that spider, I'd be soup by now. Without him, I don't think I would have made it back."

Renna tapped a finger against one of her small tusks as she looked into the fire. "And does he know about why we're here? You tend to ramble sometimes."

"No. Why would I tell him anything? We talked a bit in the woods, but mostly we just walked. Then we were ambushed and ended up here. He doesn't know anything. But,"

Faine said, glancing up at Renna, "he's pretty handy in a fight and seems to know his way around antidotes. Maybe even thieving. He didn't say too much about it, but he has to have a place to get information or sell what he finds on the bodies in the cave. And he also sells the webbing he takes from the cave—so he might know merchants or a fence in the area. We should talk to him a bit more when he wakes up."

"Maybe," Renna said. "But you don't know anything about him."

"I know he came back to save me when he could have kept running after we were attacked...or just left me in the cave. But he didn't. He came back, and that tells me something."

Renna nodded. "And if he's not interested?"

"I think he will be. Who doesn't like a good adventure now and then? Besides, I know he likes treasure and coin. Why else would he risk his life in the caves?"

The two sat in silence and drank their tea for some time. Skara had awoken shortly after they had sat down but kept his eyes closed and stayed still, listening to what they had to say. From what he could gather, the pair were looking for something or some kind of treasure. Maybe that's why the elf was out in the woods last night, he thought. But who looks for a treasure in the woods at night...when they're drunk? He could smell the alcohol on the elf when he cut him out of the web.

Thoughts rolled around in his head about whether or not he could trust the two that had just helped to heal his wounds and fend off infection. If he had fought the spider alone, or been left paralyzed in the woods, something could have gotten to him before he was able to move and make it home; so, now he had been saved twice. Sighing lightly, he put the thoughts out of his head as drifted back to sleep and let his body heal.

Skara awoke later that evening to the feeling of something crawling up his chest. He blinked his eyes wearily and looked down, careful to move slowly in case it was something that would strike at sudden movements.

Sitting on his chest was a small red squirrel. The tufts on its ears were frazzled and sparse, and its one eye was clouded over as if the creature was blind. Bits of bone and torn muscle could be seen beneath its tattered skin, and almost half of its skull and teeth were visible on its head. Its tail, mostly bone, was barely held together with bits of flesh and even less fur. It let out a slight squeaking noise as it moved closer to his face.

Pushing his head deeper into the pillow, his eyes widened, and he turned his head away as the creature moved up to sniff his face. He blew out several quick breaths onto the animal, hoping that the rush of air would scare it away, but it only blew small pieces of fur off its body and onto his shirt. He was surprised that it didn't stink, given its current state of decay.

"Siangra, no!" Renna said, clapping her hands at the squirrel. "Down."

She moved closer to the red-furred creature, clapping again while she pointed out the window. "Go outside. I'll come see you in a bit."

The squirrel gave one last look at Skara with the one eye left in its head and quickly jumped up onto the window frame and out onto a nearby branch.

"What the hell was that thing?"

"It was a squirrel," Renna said, looking down at Skara. "At least it was at some point, and maybe still is in a way. I'm sorry it woke you. I told the animals to leave you alone, but sometimes they're just curious."

"Where'd that thing come from?"

"I made it. Well, I found it and brought it back to life. It had been dead for a while when I found it, but it's fallen apart a bit more since then."

"You're a necromancer," Skara stated more than asked.

"That's right. Some people have trouble making friends; and as you can see, I don't have to worry about that," Renna said, smiling.

"So, was that thing alive?"

"Yes, and no. Its body moves, and it mostly responds to my commands, but its soul is gone. Right now, it's just a body that's been reanimated with magic. I do the ritual with the intent that it acts like the animal it was, and I bring it back. Eventually, I'll release it, or it will decay, and the magic will drain from its body. So, it's neither alive nor dead; but it's no longer the same animal that it used to be. But don't worry about that right now. You need to concentrate on healing."

Skara sat up and brushed the fur off his shirt and looked down at his wrapped arm. Several bandages covered his wounds and he could smell the strong scent of witch hazel, a bit of oak bark, and several other herbs or roots he couldn't place. Skara watched Renna as she sat down on the bed and took his arm in her hands to make sure the wrapping was tight enough and still soaked through with the herbal mixture.

He could see small scars running up the length of both her arms and several on her face. A small scar rested above each of her tusks where they had cut into her upper lip, and longer, faded scars were visible on her cheeks. Her septum was pierced with a small silver ring, and her ears, which were pointed and slightly longer than most of the elves that he had seen before, were also pierced with several silver hoops running from the bottom to the top. Her right eye was a light grey-green while the other was a deep brown, but both were sharp and bright and stared out at him from beneath wisps of her dark hair.

"Are you an orc?" Skara said, looking at her pale green skin.

"Not fully, no. My father was a half-breed, and my mother was an elf. So, it's easier to just say I'm half-orc, too. It gets tiring explaining it sometimes."

Skara looked down at his own dark green skin and at the jagged scars running up his arms. He thought about all the scuffles that he had been in and wondered what kind of trouble a half-breed might have seen. Just as he was about to ask about what she was doing out here in the woods alone, Faine walked through the door with a dark sack and several rabbits hanging from a rope. Tossing the sack on the ground near the bed, he gestured to it with a pointed finger.

"I went back out and got your daggers and your webs. And I figured everyone would be hungry, so I got some rabbits. I can clean them if you can cook them, Ren," Faine said, opening his eyes wide as he stared at her and waited for a response.

Renna looked at Faine, her eyebrows raised. "And did you reset my traps after you took the rabbits out of them?"

Faine looked at Renna and shrugged his shoulders.

"I'll take that as a no," she said, rising from the bed and smoothing down her brown skirt. "So, here's what we can do. I'll go and reset the traps, and you can cook. I need to gather a few herbs anyway, so this works for both of us. Don't you think?"

Faine looked somewhat defeated as he looked over at Skara.

"Fantastic. I was planning on cooking anyway," Faine said, shaking the rabbits at Renna. "Skara, come help me get these cleaned up. We'll need something to eat before we head into town in the morning."

Skara turned on the mattress and put his feet on the floor and stood. His legs still felt a bit stiff, but he could move easily enough. Heading out the door with Faine, the two moved to a stump a short distance away from the cottage. Tossing the rabbits next to a log, Faine grabbed one, set it on the stump, and began to clean it.

"Why'd you save me?" Skara said, watching Faine open a slit into the rabbit.

"It's simple. You saved me."

"You could have just left me there to die, and no one would have known or cared."

"And you could have done the same to me," Faine said, tossing some entrails on the ground beside the stump. His hand and skinning knife was covered in blood as he pointed at Skara. "And I would have known. You cut me outta the web and fought off a cave spider for me. You could have left me for dead both times. Why didn't you?"

Skara stared down at the rabbit, its grey fur wet and matted with blood. Watching the stream of deep red trace their way down the grooves in the log, he reached out a long finger and scraped his nail across the trickling blood and rubbed it between his finger and thumb. The woods around them were quiet as if waiting for him to answer. The gold, orange, and red leaves danced softly in the slight breeze that carried the scent of woodsmoke across the still forest. "You were still alive and needed help. If I would have left you there..."

Faine looked at him, his eyes dark in the shadows of the trees. His lips were curved down in a slight frown. "How long have you been out here alone?"

"Long enough."

"That's fair," Faine said, pulling the skin off the first rabbit and starting on the other. "And why stay out here?"

Skara paused, looking down at the bloody knife. "Maybe the same reason your friend does. Towns bring lots of problems."

"I get it," Faine said, tossing more bits of rabbit on the ground. "And I'm sure Renna feels the same sometimes. But she also knows being alone all the time can take its toll on someone. And since I'm heading into town tomorrow, I think you should come with me. I know you have a few things to sell and I'd like to buy you a drink. It's the least I can do for you saving my life."

"You don't owe me anything. You carried me here, re-member?" Skara was silent for a moment before continuing. "But since you offered, I'll take that drink."

It had been nearly a month since he'd been to Banrielle to gather supplies, and given that his antidotes were gone, he would need more. Besides, he thought to himself, the elf wasn't such bad company.

Faine finished cleaning the rabbits and turned to head back to the cottage. Just as they were about to enter, Renna walked out and around the corner. She had changed out of her skirt and into a plain white tunic and brown pants and carried a leather satchel over her shoulder. A small axe hung at her hip and she grabbed a walking stick that was leaning against the side of the building. As she began to walk into the forest, she let out a loud whistle, and a raven cawed in the distance as if answering.

Glancing at her as she walked away, Faine stepped into the cottage and stoked the embers of the fire, moving them to one side under a small grate that rested on several rocks. Seasoning the meat with a few of the herbs that hung from the ceiling, he placed it over the hot coals and sat down next to the fire with a small stick and poked at the logs, moving them closer to the sizzling meat.

Walking through the door just as the meat was nearly done, Renna set her bag just inside the door and laid down a small bundle of greens on the table. "Smells good."

"It does. But it always smells better when you just get to eat it and not cook it. Can you grab me a plate?"

Renna passed Faine a wooden plate as he took the meat off the fire, sprinkling it with more herbs before handing it to Skara. Sitting together at the small table, Renna poured three cups of fresh water and pulled a knife from her boot to carve the meat, passing out pieces of the rabbit while the others spread the greens on their plates.

Sitting quietly as he ate, Skara listened to Renna and Faine talk about different towns they had visited and the various foods they had eaten. Some of the foods he had never heard of, aside from stews and wild game cooked over the fire. And although he wasn't sure about everything they described, he thought that if he traveled outside of Banrielle, he would have to try something new.

After dinner, Skara and Faine laid out furs on the ground as Renna shuffled through the many books she had stacked in her bookshelves on the walls. Finding a book that piqued her interest, she crawled into bed and moved a candle closer so that she could read.

"What are you reading this time?" Faine said, straining to read the cover of the book.

"The story of Sigurn and Ingrid," Renna replied, not looking up from the page.

"Again? You read that one all the time."

"I like it. It's a powerful story full of action."

"And love," Faine said, pressing the back of his wrist to his forehead and pretending to swoon.

Renna narrowed her gaze and pursed her lips. "You know it's true, right? You can still go to the Sleeping Mountains and see what happened there. Besides, it's getting closer to Wyldernacht. It's the perfect time to be reading it. There are most likely some nearby towns getting their festivals ready as we speak. I'd love to see a reading this year if I can. That would be amazing."

"Can you read some of it?" Skara said, staring up at the ceiling.

"I can," Renna said, flipping through the pages. "This is a good part. This is a poem that Sigurn wrote for Ingrid before they were called off to fight the Black Dragon of Edinmoore."

Renna sat up on her mattress and turned the book towards the flickering light of the candle, her voice soft as she read aloud.

"The golden morning light pours through the window like honey, and our breath forms clouds above our lips — pale blue, like soft mist resting over the water on a faraway shore. Your beautiful eyes are closed as a gentle light caresses your amber hair and leaves slivers of warmth across your cheek. Your lips curve into a slight smile, and I know behind them lies your silver tongue, which causes me to tremble when you speak and can bend me to your will. It can tame the very forces of nature, just as I have been tamed by you, if only slightly.

"Outside, as the wind blows and shakes the dead leaves from their branches, we rest safely in the shelter of each other's arms. Your heart beats next to mine, steady and slow, and I hear thunder in the west.

"A deep shudder echoes through my body, and my blood runs faster as I lie against you. What brought us together will soon pull us apart, and I fear the days I have seen in my dreams. I fear the day. The day of beauty and love lost, but also the day of such a finality that we may yet find our peace on the golden shores beyond the veil.

"But the fear of the unknown is ever-present. So I must cherish the time we share and strive to know you more deeply and to truly learn what lies in your heart. For all the days to come and for whatever follows, know that I am yours."

Renna slowly shut the book and held it close to her chest and closed her eyes. "Isn't it beautiful? There's so much happening, and she knows that the wars and fighting that brought them together will eventually tear them apart...but they were still dedicated to each other. You can't ask for more than that."

Faine stretched out over his fur, using one hand to poke at the fire with a stick, sending up a burst of sparks as a chunk of wood burst into flame. "Not bad. It could use a bit more action, though. What'd you think, Skara?"

"It was a good story. It's been a long time since I've heard one."

"That's just a small part of it. Would you like to read it?" Renna said, setting the book down next to her bed.

"Maybe someday," Skara said, his fists clenching as he stared into the hearth, the flames dancing in his eyes as he thought about his family, the sound of screaming echoing in his head.

"Then someday it is," Faine said, tossing his poker stick into the fire, snapping Skara out of his thoughts. "But for now, let's get some sleep. We have a busy day tomorrow."

The sun shone through the open window, gently illuminating the room as Skara opened his eyes. Pulling the fur up over his chest, he looked around the room and noticed that Faine and Renna weren't in their beds. Rubbing the sleep out of his eyes, he pushed the blanket down and padded over to the door. He could hear the crackle of the fire outside and the low rumble of voices as he got closer.

Crouching low, he peered out of the door and saw the pair standing next to a small fire. Reaching down, Renna picked up a small kettle sitting just off the heat and poured the hot liquid into a cup and handed it to Faine. He grimaced as he brought the cup to his lips and quickly drank what was inside. Giving the cup back to Renna, he added another log to the fire and continued their conversation.

"I'm just sayin' that I don't know what's going to happen. Be ready in case we have to move."

"I'll be ready. Don't let yourself get sucked into anything with the mercenaries and mind your tongue. It has a way of getting you into trouble. And there's plenty of time for that later."

"You know I can't promise I won't. But I'll be careful. With any luck, we'll find out what they know and be back on the road soon."

Skara moved back away from the door and stood, unsure of what he had overheard. Grabbing his bag of webbing, he stepped out into the morning air and walked towards the fire. The sky was grey and overcast, and the cold breeze that moaned through the trees seemed to cut right through his clothing. The wind blew the leaves off the branches, sending them spiraling down around the pair standing next to the fire.

Faine shifted his weight from one foot to the other, and Skara could see that his sword and dagger now rested in their sheaths on his belt. He rested his hand casually on its black hilt as he adjusted his demi-cloak, swinging the front flap over his shoulder so that his arm could move freely beneath it. His dark grey tunic hung down over black pants that neatly tucked into his mud-stained boots. Beside him was a small leather backpack that looked as if it had seen quite a bit of wear but was still able to hold a good load without breaking.

Renna was also dressed in dark pants with stitching running up the sides of each leg. Her cream-colored tunic was tight and laced at the top near her neckline. She was slender, but Skara could see the muscles in her arms flexing as she poured a cup of tea, and he wondered if it had anything to do with her orcish ancestry.

A small axe sat in a leather loop on her belt, and several small knives were placed around its length. Hanging down from her shoulder was her leather satchel that bulged slightly from the items inside, shifting forward under her wolf skin cloak as she handed him the cup of hot tea.

Holding the cup of tea to his nose, Skara smelled the liquid and pulled his face back as the pungent smell of herbs hit his nose.

"Drink it," Renna said. "It will help with the poison."

Skara looked down at his wound and wondered if the poison was still a threat. Shaking his head, he quickly drank the contents of the cup and handed it back to Renna.

"Are you ready to go?" Faine said, reaching for his pack and sliding his arm through the strap. "It's only a couple miles, but it's cold, and I could use a drink."

"This early?" Renna said, looking over at the elf as he shrugged in reply.

Renna looked at Skara and moved in closer, pulling him into a hug. "Take care of yourself, Skara. I hope we see each other again.

Skara stood with his arms at his side, unsure of what to do in the situation.

It had been a long time since anyone had hugged him, and it made him feel slightly anxious. "I hope we do. And I hope you get to see your play sometime."

Looking back to Faine, he nodded and started walking towards the trail.

"Be safe," Renna said. "The path is twisting ahead of us, but it will take us where we need to be."

Skara didn't know what she meant by that, or what they were talking about by the fire without him, but he was sure he'd find out soon enough.

Strong as Iron

The cart rattled and shifted as it bumped its way down the rutted road towards Banrielle. Braig looked down at the shackles around his hands and ankles and cursed under his breath. The bars of the cage dug into his back, each bump making the iron feel even harder against his already sore muscles. The morning was cold and damp, and a dense fog covered the forest around them. The trees appeared out of the mist as the wagon rolled past, only to be swallowed into nothingness as the wagon and guards pressed on—ten men in front, and ten men bringing up the rear.

Turning his head towards the front of the cart, Braig could see his breath come out in white clouds, and small pieces of ice clung to the dark brown fraying braids in his beard. His mustache was covered in dried blood, and his broad nose was purple and bruised. Scraping his tongue across his teeth, he could taste blood oozing from several that had been knocked loose in the back of his mouth. Red cuts opened on his knuckles as he clenched his fists, trying to keep the blood flowing to his cold fingers. Looking down at his brown tunic and pants, he could see large patches of dirt and rust clinging to the ripped fabric and dried mud caked to his scuffed boots.

"Do you have any water? I need something to drink," Braig said, leaning his face closer to the cage bars at the front of the wagon.

"Onrin, you hear that?" the coachman called out to the man to his right.

"You need a drink, eh," Onrin said, reining in his horse to walk next to the wagon.

"Do you have a waterskin? If I could just have a drink."

Pulling out a waterskin, Onrin took a long drink and stared at Braig. "Here, have a drink," he said, squeezing the waterskin, squirting the cold water onto his face.

Braig recoiled and sat back against the bars, wiping the water off his face and beard, using the water to scrub away a bit of the blood from his mustache.

"A weak trick from an even weaker man," he said, laughing to himself. "I should have known that's what I'd get from a pile of horse shit like you!"

Onrin pulled out a small club and slammed it into the bars, staring fiercely at the caged dwarf. "You think that's funny? Say something like that again, and I'll have you dragged out of that cage and beaten...again."

"I don't know if your men are up for that," Braig said, looking at several of the men with bruised faces riding behind the wagon before looking down at his cut knuckles. "Do you? What d'ya think, boys, up for a little morning scuffle?"

Onrin reached for the keys on his belt as a voice shouted from near the front of the line.

"You pull those keys off your belt, Onrin, and I'll put you off your horse and let you try and teach the dwarf a lesson yourself. Now shut your mouth and fall into line."

Onrin shook with rage as he spat at Braig and spurred his horse forward. Ahead of him to the side of the line was an older man with a short grey beard and closely cropped hair. The man wore a dark red shirt and a black cloak trimmed in blue with a large emblem of a golden flame accented in red embroidered over his left chest. His black riding gloves gripped the reins of his black steed as he moved it back to the front of the line.

Braig knew the man was the commander of the Brothers of the Flame but had only talked with him on several occasions. After arriving in a gulf somewhere southwest of the Surwynd Cave, he was loaded into the cage on the wagon, and the small group of guards taking him north to Banrielle was met by the Brothers of the Flame. The commander of the brothers, Gregor Kiburn, was hired to escort the men and help establish a camp outside of Banrielle that could serve as a base while they looked for the mage stone.

The mage stone, Braig thought, rolling the images he had seen around in his head. He had no idea what the stone was used for, but visions of a black, glass-like shard of stone flashed into his head or crept into his dreams while he slept. He had a vague feeling that there were other stones, but the memory of them was fuzzy and fleeting, like a cloud drifting away in the wind. He had overheard the hooded man that had bought him telling the mercenaries he had matters in Ethilios to attend to, and for them to have answers for him by the time he met them near Banrielle—and to get them by any means necessary.

Braig shuddered as he thought about the lies he told to get here, and what that would mean for him when they realized what they were looking for wasn't here. He had told them that one of the mage stones was buried somewhere outside of a small town near the Surwynd cave; but in truth, he had dreamed about his cage being opened and his shackles being broken. He couldn't see the face of the person that set him free, and he didn't know if he would live through his attempted escape, but he was not a slave. Once his chains were broken, he would kill the men holding him, and find the hooded man that bought and caged him like an animal.

He thought about the beatings he had already endured to try to get answers or invoke a vision, but they couldn't be forced. He had no control over when they came or what he saw. Even the clearest of his visions were hard to understand. They seemed to be only small pieces of a larger puzzle that didn't quite fit together no matter how you looked at them. But it had to mean something, otherwise, what was it that he was seeing? He only wished that he would have been able to foresee the ambush that got him captured. But his visions didn't give him any warning about being trapped, or how anyone found out about what he could do. Wrapping his arms around his knees, trying to stay warm, he wished he had never been born with this curse.

The hours passed by as the cart rumbled down the dirt road. Several times the men had to dismount and push the wagon to free a wheel that had gotten stuck in a rut, or to clear debris from the road. And by the time they had made it to a clearing to set up camp, it was nearly dark. Five of the guards unlocked the cage door and fastened a collar and chains to Braig's neck and led him into the woods to let him relieve himself. As they returned to the small encampment, they chained him to a nearby tree and moved to stand next to one of the three fires that burned around the camp.

Braig huddled against the trunk of the tree, watching as the guards split into groups and began cooking quick meals in small pots or skillets, while several of the men brushed down the horses and checked their hooves for any damage from the long trek. As his eyes scanned the encampment, he noticed Gregor standing near the central fire with his hands held out over the flames, his eyes fixed on directly on him. Pushing himself closer to the tree, Braig sat up straighter, eyeing Gregor as he stepped over the bedrolls being laid out and made his way over to the tree.

Standing over Braig, Gregor looked down, his face as blank as a smooth stone wall. "I think you should make this easier on everyone and tell us what we want to know. I was given instructions to get the information out of you any way I can, and I will do what I need to. Do you understand what I'm saying to you, dwarf?"

"Oh, I understand completely," Braig said, staring up at Gregor.

"And?"

"And I have nothin' to say."

"I want you to remember that I gave you this chance, dwarf. I'll have you whipped and beaten into submission if you don't tell me where the stone my employer seeks is buried."

"I don't know where it's buried. We won't be in Banrielle till tomorrow, and I may not see anything until we get closer."

"But you told your master that the stone could be found there. How can you know the stone is there and not know where it is?"

"He's not my master!" Braig said, spitting on Gregor's boots, "And I said I know it's close to the town. I can't tell you exactly where it is because I don't know. What part of that do you not understand? I thought you brothers were supposed to have wits about ya."

Gregor smiled and crouched to look Braig in the eye. "I've broken many men, dwarf. Stronger men than you. Think about what it is you need to tell us, or I'll make you wish you never crawled out of that stinking hole in the ground you called a home." Slapping Braig's boot, Gregor stood and started walking back to the fire. "Get some rest, dwarf. You're going to need your strength. Oh, and by the way, I thought you'd like to know that your friend Finrid said hello. He's most likely taking a long rest and drinking away the coin he was paid for giving you up. I just thought you'd like to know."

Walking back to the fire, Gregor pulled a boule of bread out of his pack and tossed it over to land in the dirt in front of Braig. Reaching out to pick it up, he took several quick bites and leaned his back against the tree. Braig felt a lump form in the pit of his stomach. How could Finrid sell his secret, and him, for a few coins? They had been friends and business partners, and he betrayed him. But he had to deal with one problem at a time, and that would have to wait.

Looking off into the dark woods around him, he hoped that this would be the night he was set free so that he could show the brothers what it really meant to be broken.

The morning sun broke through the trees to find the men already packing and preparing to move. Loading Braig back into the cage, the wagon set off once again down the long road across the countryside. Closing his eyes and leaning his head against the bars of the cage, Braig tried to sleep to help pass the time, but couldn't get comfortable in the rattling, metal prison.

"Let me out to walk for a ways. I'm in chains, how far do you think I'd get?" Braig said, running his hands through his short hair to rub the lumps on the back of his head from bumping against the cage.

"We've been through this before, dwarf," Gregor called back. "Do you remember what happened the last time we let you walk? You decided it would be a good idea to fight the men and try to get a weapon."

"I remember."

"And you think we'd take that chance again?"

Braig's face grew red, and he started to rattle the bars of the cage, shaking the wagon back and forth and spooking the horses. "Let me out of this gods-damned cage. Open the door and let me walk. Or if your men want a show, I'd be happy to kill that pig-licking prick, Onrin."

"You will sit down and shut up!" Onrin said, moving closer to the cage, his sword drawn.

The coachman drew the wagon to a stop and steadied the horses. "Stop shaking the wagon, or the horses will take off with it, with you still stuck in that cage."

"Let them run. Let them take me away from you miserable bastards. I'm only wantin' to walk and stretch my legs!"

"I'm warning you, dwarf. Sit down and shut your mouth, or we'll make you." Gregor said.

"Oh, I bet you'll try. And you might get me in the end, but not before I take a few of you down with me," Braig said, his eyes darting over to Onrin, "And I'll be comin' for you first, pig-licker."

Onrin jumped off his mount and pulled the cage keys off his belt. "You want a fight; I'll give you one. I'll make you wish that Emin, the defiler, never made you dwarves."

"Do not mention that name to me, you pig-licking, son of a whore. He held us in chains the same way you're holdin' me in 'em. You call yourselves Brothers of the Flame, but you walk in the darkness right beside him."

"Enough!" Gregor said, sliding off his horse and moving to stand next to the cage. "You want to walk, dwarf? Fine, we'll let you walk. Onrin, I want you to scout ahead, and take this filth with you. A little run on the road might be good for him."

"But, sir," Onrin said, glaring at the dwarf, "he -,"

"Be silent, brother. Unlock his cage, put the chains on his cuffs, and run your horse a half-mile up the road and wait for us there. If the dwarf wants to run and stretch his legs, let him run. And if he can't keep up...drag him."

A smile spread over Onrin's face as motioned for the guards to get the collar. Unlocking the cage, he chained Braig to his saddle, giving him one last sneer before spurring his horse forward, jerking him off his feet and dragging him up the dirt road while the men at the wagon watched and laughed.

Braig slid across the bumps and holes, his body rolling back and forth as the shackles pulled at his wrists, forcing him to grip the chains to keep his bones from breaking under the strain. By the time they had made it a half-mile down the road, his body was bruised and cut, and he felt like he had been beaten with heavy sticks. Coughing and spitting out the dirt that the horse had kicked into his mouth, he glared at Onrin through his dust-filled eyes, blinking to try and get him into focus.

"How was your walk, dwarf?" Onrin asked, giving him a hard kick in the stomach, knocking the wind out of him.

Braig sputtered and coughed, folding at the waist. Gasping for breath, he looked up at Onrin and bared his teeth, fresh blood oozing from his mouth, "The view could have been better. All I got to see in front of me was a horse's ass, and the horse he was riding on." Braig let out a small laugh and grimaced in pain as Onrin kicked him again.

"That's enough, Onrin," Gregor called, riding up at the head of the group. "Put him back in his cage and take your position in the line. We need to reach Banrielle by this afternoon, and we've wasted enough time as it is. Now let's move. We don't stop until we make camp tonight."

Two men dismounted and lifted Braig to his feet, pushing him back towards his cage. Grunting as they shoved him inside, he stood and held the bars for support as he looked out into the forest. His eyes strained as he peered through the trees and saw what he thought was a grey wolf watching him from the cover of a twisted bush; and as the cart rambled forward, he could see that it was no ordinary wolf. Its skin was torn and hung off its chest, exposing the red muscle beneath. The bones on its legs showed white through holes in its grey fur, and dark eyes sat sunken in its skull.

Braig watched the wolf as it moved alongside the wagon in the forest, staying out of sight to all but the dwarf.

"I see you, wolf. And I know that your master now sees me," he mumbled under his breath.

Although he didn't know who would be setting him free, he knew that whoever had sent the wolf had something to do with it. Now all he had to do was bide his time, and keep his mouth shut until he was set loose to take his revenge.

BACK AT THE COTTAGE, Renna looked through her belongings, packing herbs and tinctures into a worn, leather traveling bag. Walking by her bookshelves, she ran her fingers over the spines of the books that rested there before pulling out the book *'Magic and its Uses'* and began thumbing through the pages, quietly reading the words aloud. "Water from a spring flows pure and clear. Wisdom and truth, no matter the source, is still wisdom and truth. Magic and the arcane forces are an ever-present, natural force that can be harnessed and manipulated for the user's purpose and is not good or evil by nature; that element is added by the one seeking to use it. And although focusing your intent can sway the forces to flow towards your will, it cannot be fully controlled. There is a wild element inherent in magic, and like any wild thing, it can sometimes cause harm. Remember this: it is easier to dam the flow of a small stream than it is the flow of a raging river. The same is true regarding trying to control the magic you allow to flow through you."

And danger is danger, no matter how it finds you, she thought, putting the book back on the shelf. Although most of the books were fiction, several historical or reference books sat bound between the tales of epic adventures, herbalism, or folklore and legends. Touching the books one more time, she moved to the door and stepped outside, hoping that she wouldn't have to leave the books behind if something were to happen and they had to flee.

Shouldering her leather satchel, she grabbed a walking stick and set off into the woods to take down her game traps and gather roots and herbs. The air was still and cold, and the almost bare branches loomed unmoving above her. The fallen leaves that had dried under the sun crunched under her boots, ringing like a bell in the otherwise silent forest. The overcast sky was dark and grey as the filtered rays of light struggled to break through the thick clouds that hung low, moving slowly towards the horizon. In the distance, she heard the frantic call of a crow and took off in a run towards the sound.

Passing over fallen logs and ducking under low branches, she hurried to follow the cries of the flying crow. She could faintly see its black shape soaring above the treetops, leading her forward. Stopping briefly to catch her breath, she searched the sky, looking for any sign of the large, black bird. Standing still in the forest, a loud cry pierced the silence, sending a shiver down her spine. The bird had found something just ahead of where she stood. Taking a deep breath, she followed the call and rounded a weather-worn outcrop of stone to see the dark opening of a small cave.

Clutching her stick tightly in her hands, she braced herself in case something charged at her from the deep hole. Planting her feet firmly on the ground, she steadied herself and waited for the attack; but nothing could be heard stirring in the cave. Relaxing slightly, she pulled a candle out her bag and placed her fingertip on the tip of the wick. Focusing her energy, smoke began to rise from the braided material until it burst into a small flame. Smiling to herself, she picked up her walking stick and moved into the darkness.

Although she was able to manipulate life energies, she was still learning how to control the elements. But with practice, she had learned to gently move water or create flames, which had been put to use multiple times when she had trouble getting a fire started on damp nights.

Stepping farther into the cave, she could see the brown fur of a creature stirring near the back wall. Pulling out her knife, she approached the animal carefully, whispering to let it know she was coming closer and wasn't a threat. As the light of the candle flickered in the darkness, she could see white spots on the animal's back and recognized it as a fawn, maybe six months old. Renna could see that the animal's torso was severely injured as it tried to stand and hobble around the cave, looking for a way to escape.

Sheathing her knife, she held out her hand and moved slowly towards the deer, speaking gently as she walked. Her words came out almost in a whisper, elvish words drifting across the dark expanse to rest on the injured animal. The fawn blinked slowly as it visibly relaxed and sank back down to its side on the cave floor. Setting the candle down a short distance from the fawn, she moved up beside it and ran her hands down its soft fur, speaking slowly and stroking its neck.

Looking down at the large gashes in the animal's abdomen, she could see that the skin was torn and bloody.

"What happened to you?" she said quietly, examining the wound.

She could see several jagged claw marks running down the animal, and deep puncture wounds from a set of strong jaws on its upper chest. There was a pool of blood under the fawn, and she knew that the injuries were going to kill the creature if she couldn't help.

Despite being skilled in necromancy, she had never learned any real healing magic. She had only learned how to transfer energy between living creatures or to use herbal remedies to heal small wounds, and mending a mortal wound took more power and skill than she had.

But why shouldn't I try, she thought, placing her hands over the deep wounds. Focusing her energy, she pictured the gashes closing in her mind, but when she opened her eyes, the wounds were still open and slick with blood. Closing her eyes once more, she tried again, and again, with no change to the wounds.

"I can't fix you," she said, rubbing the fawn's neck. "Your wounds are too deep."

Not wanting the animal to suffer, she pulled her knife from its sheath and positioned herself over the creature, talking low into its ear. "Be at ease. Go and roam the endless fields and woods in the next life."

Sliding her dagger between the animal's ribs, she pierced its heart, stroking its neck until it closed its eyes one last time. "You'll be at peace now," she said quietly, and she truly believed that.

Taking a moment to say a word of thanks to I'lurian for the life of the fawn, and food to sustain her body, she cut into the deer.

After cleaning the fawn, she hefted it onto her shoulders and began making her way back to her cottage. She was hoping to have the deer skinned and on the fire by the time Faine, and possibly Skara came back to camp. As she made her way through the forest, she could feel a set of eyes watching her from a distance, getting closer as she walked. Quickening her pace, she made her way back to camp and set the deer on the ground near the cottage, and drew her knife and one-handed axe, her eyes darting to any movement around her. Hearing a branch break behind her, she wheeled around, weapons ready.

In front of her stood a large, grey wolf, its skin torn and ragged on its lean body.

"Undriel," she said, her hand over her heart, "you scared me. Why are you sneaking around? I've no time to play now. Maybe I'll give you a piece of meat when I get it skinned, but first things first."

Renna put away her weapons and walked over to the wolf, rubbing its ears as she sat down on the ground in front of it. Placing her hands on the sides of its face, she bowed its head, placing her forehead against his. Taking a deep breath and closing her eyes, she read his thoughts and looked back through his memories. She could see the trees going by in a blur as Undriel ran through the forest, chasing a scent on the light breeze. She saw a group of mercenaries, some with a large emblem of a flame on their chests, chain a dwarf to a horse and pull him up the road as he struggled to keep his head from being smashed into the dirt. She watched as a man kicked the beaten dwarf and have him loaded back into the cage, the iron bars shutting behind him. And she saw the dwarf stare into the eyes of the wolf, a look of surprise and hope on his face as the wagon moved down the road towards Banrielle.

A Bottle of the Finest

Skara and Faine walked for a little over a mile before they reached the end of the woodline and stepped out into a sprawling field of foxtail wheat. The rust-red and cream-colored kernels swayed and rustled with the wind as the two stopped to take in the view. To the east and west of the city, small patches of trees were scattered between the homesteads and farms farther in the distance, with Banrielle to the north straight ahead. The town looked lonely and bleak in the dreary, overcast morning. Its weathered wooden buildings and grey flecked stone wall, collapsed in several places, ran along the border of the city, giving it an unwelcoming look.

A small line of wagons could be seen on the road heading into the city, possibly a caravan selling or delivering supplies. Skara and Faine glanced at each other and made their way out of the field and onto the dirt road leading into town.

The road was deeply rutted, and murky puddles of water filled the holes. Wagon tracks left curved lines in the mud, and the pair had to walk on the grass and pine needles beside the road to avoid getting their boots stuck in the thick muck. Passing through the front gate, several wagons lined the sporadically cobbled streets, setting up tents and getting prepared to sell their wares in the market. Farther into the town, a group of buildings stood around a central square with a stone well in the center. Walking carefully to avoid horse droppings or crowds of people coming to look at the merchant caravans, the two made their way to the center of the square.

Drawing the rope to pull the bucket up from the well, Faine stuck the dipper into the cold water, taking a long drink before he handed it to Skara. Several dirty looks and muttered curse words came their way as people eyed the strange elf and goblin drinking their water. Although goblins were more tolerated here than other towns or cities nearby, they were still generally disliked and avoided by most people.

Seeing the dirty looks as people walked by, Faine took the dipper back from Skara and took another long drink, moving slowly and turning his head so that anyone looking could see him drinking. When he was finished, he pushed the bucket back into the well, not bothering to ease it down with the rope. Hearing the splash, several of the men close by looked at him with scowls showing on their faces. Faine stared back, his green eyes looking through them. Turning his attention towards Skara, he gently hung the dipper back onto a nail in the post. One of the men that had been standing in the group turned and scurried down an alley and out of sight.

"So, where do you need to go first?" Faine said, looking at the buildings around the square. "I mean, you know where I'm heading. Been a lot of excitement lately, and I could use a morning drink."

Skara looked at Faine, a slight frown on his face. "Did you have to draw so much attention? I don't like everyone staring at me."

"They're not staring at you, Skara. They're staring at me. How often do people see a ruggedly handsome elf walk into town?" Faine ran his hand through his hair and leaned against the wooden frame of the small roof covering the well, one arm above his head propping him up.

Skara sighed and looked at the buildings around the square. "I need to go see Javadi. He's the merchant that buys my web."

Faine took his arm off the pole and looked at Skara. "Didn't you say it needed to be soaked in something first because it's sticky?"

"It does, but he has a barrel of it in the back of his shop. I don't do it because if there's any residue left, it could ruin his weaving wheel. And if that happens, it'll be his fault, not mine. So, I made some for him to keep and charged him for it."

"Wait, you made it? How'd you figure out how to do that?"

"A lot of trying. I needed a way to get the web off after going into the caves. I'm sure there's more than one way to do it, but I just use strong alcohol and certain herbs to make it work."

"Aren't you worried he'll figure out what it is?"

"He might. But he still needs someone to get the web. He won't be doing that himself. It takes quite a few things to make the mixture, and unless he can figure it all out by smell, he'll never get it," Skara said, glancing up at Faine.

Faine nodded his head and looked down the square towards the shops. "Then let's go see Javadi. I'd like to see his shop. If he buys web, who knows what else he might have."

Skara and Faine walked to the far end of the square and down an alley leading back behind several of the taller buildings. As they turned the corner, a small shop came into view. The blue paint on its walls had chipped off in small patches and showed the weathered boards underneath. Various sizes of decorative knots were tied onto the wall around the front door, and the windows were covered in a film that made the building look dark inside. Walking up the stairs leading onto the porch, Skara knocked on the door before he opened it and stepped inside with Faine following behind, unaware of a man watching them from around the corner of a nearby building.

The inside of the shop was dimly lit by several glass orbs filled with dirt and glowing mushrooms hanging sporadically from the ceiling. Long shelves lined the walls and were stacked with scrolls, books, small trinkets, and jars filled with clear liquid and what appeared to be spiders and other various creatures that Faine didn't recognize.

Looking down, he could see a dusty leather map stretched out on a table, and he traced his finger around the edge of the continents drawn onto its surface. "Here's where we are," he said, pointing to a small town near the southern end of Uthrea. "See, here's the Surwynd cave."

Skara leaned over and peered at the map, looking at the location Faine was pointing at. "Where are you from?"

"I'm from here, Murwood," Faine said, pointing to a spot east of Banrielle. "Right here, near the forest and the river."

"And where is Sonosa?" Skara said, slightly grinding his teeth.

"A Sonosan man, eh? I thought the accent sounded familiar. It's so faint that it's hard to make out. But it's right here." Faine said, tapping his finger at a spot almost directly north of their location. "It would take a few days of riding to get there, but I guess you already know that if that's where you're from."

Skara straightened himself and walked away from the map towards the front counter. "Javadi, you in here?"

At his call, a short, stocky man emerged from a back room. His thin red tunic was covered in splatters of color, and his brown pants looked wet near the waste. His short, black hair was ruffled, and his dark skin was covered in what was either sweat or water from the dyeing tanks in the back. Wiping his hands on the sides of his pants, he cleared off a section of the counter in front of him and rested his hands on the countertop.

"It's been a while. I was beginnin' to wonder if somethin' happened to you out there. Had a few people askin' 'bout fabric, but I didn't have an answer for 'em."

Skara shifted on his feet and looked around the room, letting his gaze settle on a white banner with a large, orange flame accented in red hanging on the wall. He recognized the symbol and knew that it was used by the Brothers of the Flame in Sonosa. Although they claimed to be followers of Tuvak, they were known for the way they used violence and manipulation to gather people to their cause. Any that opposed them outright were usually taught a lesson. There were several times that he could remember that the brothers led raids among the inhabitants of the lower, poorer districts, and nothing was ever done about it. From his experience, the brothers were a plague on the city, rotting it from the inside out.

Skara clenched his fists, and his face twisted into a sneer as he looked up over the counter at Javadi. "Looking to join up with the brothers, or are you just showing your support?"

Wrenching his hands together, Javadi glanced briefly at the banner and began to tap his finger softly against the counter. "That uh, just recently got dropped in. Hoping I might be able to, uh, get a bit of coin from it. You know how those things go. But, uh...what is that brings you in? Some more webs, I'm hopin'," Javadi said, looking down at the sack in Skara's hand. "I could really use 'em. Been dyeing wool all mornin' and could use another project."

Turning his attention back to the shopkeeper, Skara swung the sack up onto the counter, letting it hit with a hard thud. "I have a few to sell."

Javadi opened the sack, looking at several loose balls of webbing clinging to each other at the bottom. "A fine bunch. People will be rightly pleased with this, I'm sure. Now, it looks like one, two, three, four, five, six bundles of web. That'll be...," Javadi turned his eyes to the ceiling, and his lips moved silently while he calculated the payment in his head. "That'll be four silver, five copper."

"That'll be six silver, eight copper."

Javadi's mouth sagged into a grimace as he looked down at Skara. "That seems a bit steep for six bundles of web. I could-"

"You could pay me what I asked. These are big bundles, and it nearly cost me my life to get them. You made it clear that several people had asked about them, and I know you want to fill the orders. But you can't do that without the spider-silk. Now unless you're going into the cave yourself to get it...,"

Faine looked back and forth between the two, the edges of his lips turning into a slight smile.

"I can't do it. I won't go any higher than what I said."

Skara nodded towards Javadi and quickly grabbed his bag from the counter and flung it over his shoulder, turning to walk towards the door.

"Wait," Javadi said. "Six silver. I can't go any higher. I'd have to sell that web before I could offer more."

Skara stopped and turned around to face the stocky man. "Six silver and that old leather map, and you have a deal."

Javadi sighed and rubbed his chin. "Fine."

Skara brought the sack back to counter and emptied its contents into a metal bin on the floor. Holding out his hand, Javadi handed him six silver coins."

"Pleasure doing business with you," Skara said, placing the coins into a small pouch on his belt. The two turned to leave, grabbing the map before heading out into the crisp air, shutting the door behind them.

As the two walked back up the alley and into the square, Faine stopped and looked at Skara. "You alright? You seemed a bit agitated back there."

"I'm fine. Let's keep moving. I still have to go to the herb shop and get a few things before we have that drink," Skara said, continuing up the path towards the herbalist.

"I'm here if you need me," Faine said, still standing in the alley, a smile spreading wide across his face. "I'm not afraid to be your rock. Skara, can you hear me? Hey..." Faine hurried to catch up, dodging people as he moved swiftly through the crowd.

Several of the buildings were decorated with long ropes covered in deep purple and red banners for the upcoming Wyldernacht celebration. Although it was still weeks away, many homes and shops had already begun to set two candles in their window to represent Sigurn and Ingrid's victory over the darkness and the Black Dragon of Edinmoore. The candles would be burned briefly each night, until finally being left to burn out entirely on the night of the celebration, representing the two heroine's light fading from the world.

Large groups of people were scattered throughout the square, looking through the merchants lined up and down the road leading towards the gate of the town. Women in wool dresses carefully handled yards of colorful linen and wool at a nearby cart, talking and laughing while they each held up cloth up to their chest to get opinions on whether or not it would make a pretty dress. Bards and players stood on corners telling stories and singing songs of long vanquished foes, deeds long past, or the dreadful high elf, Emin, that brought about the shattering and the release of dark magic into the world through his hubris.

Near the west side of the square, a roaring fire was burning, and a three-tiered grate hung over the flames, each holding different meats or vegetables that beckoned people over with their enticing smells.

Faine's stomach growled as he walked by the fire, staring longingly at the cooking food. "Skara, I'll meet you in the shop. I'm too hungry to pass up some hot food," he said, running over the fire.

Stopping on the front stoop of the Greencap apothecary, Skara watched as Faine looked up and down the three levels of roasting foods, pointing to different meats and talking to the people around him. Glancing quickly around the busy streets, he opened the door to the herb shop and stepped inside. The sweet and spicy smell of flowers and herbs wafted through the store as Skara closed the door behind him. The floor was covered with a dark blue rug with images of leaves and trees covering its length. Sconces hung on the walls, each burning a candle scented with various flower extracts. Inhaling deeply, he tried to recognize the different herbs in each one.

Several tables stood against the walls, each with a pestle and mortar, a scale, and several bowls used for holding herbs and ingredients. The counter was sanded to a smooth finish and had been stained dark by using the husks of walnuts. Standing a short distance away, a plump woman stood with her hands on her hips, watching the goblin approach. A long braid of blonde hair hung past her face and over the shoulder of her dark red blouse that Skara thought was cut far too low for this time of year.

"What can I get for you?" The woman said, glaring down at Skara. "But before you answer, know this — I don't have any handouts to give you if that's what you're after. And I've not one bit of interest in seeing you sing, dance or juggle. There's enough of the outside, and I'll not have it in the shop. And if you're here to rob me, I'll cut you down where you stand."

"I don't sing or dance, and I've been here before," Skara said, reaching into his coin pouch. "I'm here to buy, not to rob you. If there's a problem here, go fetch Mary."

"Oh, you're a friend of Mary. Then I do apologize," the woman said, smoothing down her black skirt. "I didn't mean no offense. I only started nearly a month ago, and the mistress is out today trading with the merchants for more goods. She left me to look after the shop while she's away. But with all the travelers passing through, there's been too many half-wits coming through the door -,"

The door to the shop quickly opened as Faine stepped inside and closed the door behind him. "Hey, I got you somethin' to eat." In his hands were two long kabobs of roasted venison and pork, separated by chunks of purple potato and charred carrot. His smile quickly faded as he looked over to the woman behind the counter and saw her eyes wide in shock.

"Out!" the woman shouted. "Get out the shop before you drip meat juices all over the rug."

Faine quickly backed up, running into the door behind him. "I'll just wait for you out here," he said, shifting the kabobs to one hand as he fumbled to find the door handle. Opening the door behind him, he quickly walked out, shutting the door quietly behind him.

"So, I'm here to buy," Skara said again. "I need a few antidotes...and some of the herbs kept in the back room."

"What herbs in the back room? Everything we have is on our shelves."

Skara looked up at the woman and scratched his head, trying to remember what Mary, the owner of the shop, had told him to say if there was ever anyone else tending the shop. Eyes lighting up, he walked closer to the counter and leaned in. "The dark moon rises and shines over deep waters," he said, keeping his voice low.

"Be vigilant, lest they carry you away," the woman said, sliding Skara a piece of paper with the available potions and herbs written on it.

Skara squinted down at the paper and slid it back across the counter. "This is what I need," he said, telling the woman his order, not bothering with the list.

Outside, Faine sat down the step of the building and watched the people walking around the square. Casually eating his kabob, he looked over at the sign to the Bramble Thorn Inn and wondered if any of his clothes were still left in his room. Taking another bite, the door behind him swung open as Skara stepped out. "I got you a kabob," he said, handing the meat over.

Skara reached out and took the kabob from Faine. "How much?"

"It's on me. And I still owe you a drink. Just buy us a second round, and we'll call it even," Faine said, taking a sizeable bite, the juices running down the stubble on his chin.

Skara looked around the busy streets, seeing the scowls and wide eyes of the people that stared at him as they passed. Shifting on his feet, he checked his pouches and daggers and looked over the Bramble Thorn. "Let's get a drink, then. I've already been here too long."

The two cut across the square and into the Inn, weaving between the crowds. Stopping just inside the door, Faine nodded and scratched the tip of his right ear as he looked over at the bartender behind the counter. The bartender ran a finger under his nose as if he had an itch and blinked his eyes twice. Sitting down at an empty table near the corner, Faine called over a barmaid to take their order. "I'll take a Bromoran red ale."

The barmaid looked over at Skara, "And you?"

Skara looked at several of the tables around him, not sure of what drinks they had. "Mossberry mead."

The barmaid turned and headed towards the bar as Faine looked over at Skara. "So, what's next for you?"

"I'll head home. The same thing I always do."

"But don't you think a few things have changed since yesterday?"

The barmaid brought back their drinks and set them on the table, splashing a little mead out onto the side of the cup. "Will there be anything else?"

"Not right now," Faine said, handing her several copper coins. "Check back in just a bit."

"Things always change, but what else is there?"

"You never know what might happen. But you know where Renna is, and I'm usually around here somewhere," Faine said, taking a drink of his ale.

Skara's sharp teeth ripped off a chunk of meat from his kabob. Taking a sip from his cup as he chewed, he looked down at the table. "What are you two in town for? I heard you talking after she healed me. Something about me not knowing anything about whatever it is you two are doing."

Faine clicked his tongue and rubbed the stubble on the side of his face. Looking around the room, he could see that most of the tables were empty, aside from a few people playing dice or cards on the opposite side. The inside of the inn was open in the center and had tables scattered throughout. The bar sat at the far end with a stairwell leading to the second story that stretched out over the kitchen and storerooms of the bar, leaving the main room completely open all the way up to the beams of the ceiling above. The balcony encircled the large, open space on three sides, with several rooms for rent branching off the upper level.

Looking up to the second floor, Faine could see the hallway leading to the door to his room. Tapping his hand on the table, he turned to Skara. "I have a room here. Come upstairs, and I'll fill you in. The walls have eyes and ears in a place like this."

"Is it that secret?"

"It's not that it is, but I don't like everyone knowing my business."

"Then, why would you tell me?"

"Because you saved my life. And I saved yours. You might not think it, but that means something. We're bonded now through a life debt. I would have died without you, and you could have died without me...and Renna."

Skara frowned and picked at the cup with his nail as he thought about the spider. Why had he saved the elf in the first place? What was it about finding someone alive in the web that made him decide to cut him free? Maybe it had to do with his own feelings of being trapped or being alone in the forest for so long. Even after Faine had seen he was a goblin, he didn't try to kill him or put him down. And despite his fatigue, he carried him over a mile to make sure he lived.

Faine sipped his drink and popped a piece of potato into his mouth. "Now I know you've been out there by yourself for, what, years? But maybe that's not where you belong anymore. You came down here from Sonosa, and you managed to survive out there in the woods alone, which is impressive in itself; but is that all you want for yourself, to survive alone?"

"Is there really anything else?"

Faine nodded and finished his ale before standing and motioning for Skara to follow him up the stairs. Opening the door to his room, he stepped inside and went directly to the mattress and waited for Skara to come in and shut the door. Picking up the side of his straw mattress, he reached his hand up inside and pulled out a crinkled note and brought it to the table. "Have a seat."

Skara climbed up into the chair, his small frame barely able to see over the high table.

"This," Faine said, laying the note on the table, "is a note I found in one the mercenary's rooms a few towns back. Take a look."

Skara didn't bother to look at the note. "Just tell me what it says."

"It mentions something about a treasure here around Banrielle. It says that they were hired to guard someone here that could lead them to something important. So, I followed them here."

"And it says treasure?"

"Well, no," Faine said as he grabbed the note. "But why else would they be hired to come here and guard someone that could lead them to something important? Whatever they're looking for, we're gonna find it first."

"Is that what got you into trouble at the cave? How did you end up there, anyway?"

Faine clenched his jaw and rubbed a hand over his mouth. "I ended up there because I was stupid. Instead of waiting for a better moment, a more sober moment, I went into one of their rooms here and started looking around. Then, I got caught. I managed to make my way out the window, but they came around the back of the building and chased me. I thought I could lose them in the woods and go to Renna's place, but I got turned around. I was a bit drunk, heard some noises, pulled my blades..." Faine looked up at the ceiling, laughing to himself and shaking his head, "and I tripped over a rock. Next thing I know, I woke up wrapped in webbing with a headache. And you know the rest from there. So, there it is; my near-death experience brought on by a bad choice."

Skara nodded his head and looked around the sparsely furnished room, glancing at the clothes scattered across the floor before looking up at Faine. "So that's what you do then, look for treasure?"

Faine looked at Skara as if he had just insulted him. "I guess if you really boil it down, yeah. But you make it sound so boring. We, Renna and I, get to travel where we want and make some coin doing it. Have you ever seen the Sanguine Gulf south of here or the Ineren Plains to the north?"

Skara shook his head.

"I have."

"What are they like?" Skara said, sitting up higher in the chair. He had heard stories about the great horse races they held across the plains to the north, or the deep red seaweed that made the water look red to the south but had never had it described to him. He had wanted to travel beyond Sonosa or Banrielle one day, but the thought gradually slipped away, only occasionally creeping back in on sleepless nights when he was alone in the dark. He desired to be free and see the world, but it was his fear of how big the world was that held him back.

Faine leaned forward and rested his arm on the table. "They're amazing. The plains stretch on for hundreds of miles and are rimmed with mountains and rolling hills. Cross between the wide gaps in between, and there are more plains on the other side. Tribes of nomadic people live and hunt there, moving from one place to another with the changing seasons. In the spring, the wind blows across the grasses, and the rain falls on the mountains, making everything smell sweet and new. And sometimes, the storms are so fierce there that the lightning looks like it's ripping the sky in half. The thunder shakes your bones and sends you running for shelter. But when the storm clears, and the sun rises, it's like you feel renewed."

"And the gulf?"

"The gulf," Faine said, leaning back in his chair, "is a lot different than the plains. The land reaches right up to the ocean, and there are long, sandy shores that spread out along the coast. The water out west towards Farengrath is warmer and a bit clearer, but Mivara is still beautiful. The waves sweep across the shore and put shells all along the beach. And farther out, you can see what has to be miles of red seaweed swaying under the water. It looks like drops of blood floating in a basin."

"And what made you decide to leave home and travel? How'd you bring yourself to do it?" Skara said.

"That's a story for another time. But the point is that there's something more out there than risking your life to sell web for a few coins."

"But it sounds like what you do can be just as dangerous."

"You're not wrong there," Faine said, getting up out of his seat to look out the window. "But if it's dangerous no matter where you go or what you do, why stay in one place? I mean, if people are happy where they are, then they should stay and be happy. But if you feel like something's missing, you might just find it out on the road somewhere. We all have to die sometime, and I'd just rather be doing something I want rather than waste away being miserable doing the same thing until I'm too old to do anything else."

Faine's hand rested on the hilt of his sword as he looked out the window, watching the colored flags blowing softly in the wind. His face was blank as he watched several birds land on the swaying rope strung between the buildings. Looking down at the road below, he saw several of the mercenaries he had been trailing making their way towards the inn. "Look, I need to head back down to the common room. There may some trouble headin' my way, so you might wanna get going."

Thoughts about all the things that he should have said and done, but never did, flooded into his mind. He didn't want to keep living the same life, doing the same things until the lonely end. He wanted to see what else was out there, to not be afraid to really live. Feeling a surge of confidence, Skara tightened the leather cord holding his hair before turning to look at Faine. "I didn't get to finish my drink yet," he said, moving to the door and out onto the balcony.

Faine shrugged and followed behind him as they made their way down the stairs and back to their table in the corner. Just as Faine sat down, the door to the inn opened, and a burly, bearded man stepped inside. The man was wearing black pants, and calf-high boots with a dagger tucked in the side. He wore thick, leather armor over his black tunic, and a broad sword hung at his side. Four men entered behind him, similarly dressed, but with various weapons hanging on them in different areas. The man looked around the room, and seeing Faine in the corner, he started walking in his direction.

The man's heavy boots thudded against the floor as he walked over to Faine's table, slamming his hands down on it, causing it to shake and spill the remainder of what was left in Skara's mug. "So, thief, I see you made it back to town. Plannin' to pilfer through our rooms again while we were out?"

"If I were planning on it, I would have already done it...while you were out," Faine said as he looked up at the man leaning over the table. "Isn't that what thieves do?"

The man slammed his hands back down onto the table. "I knew you were a no-good, thieving bastard. And look, you brought a little, green turd along to help you." The man leaned in closer to Skara, giving him a fierce scowl. "Gods, what are you? You can't be no bigger than four feet tall. I've seen piles of horse shit bigger than you," the man said, laughing hard as he looked back at the group of men behind him.

Seeing Skara reaching for one of his daggers under the table, Faine put a hand over his arm to stop him. As much as he would like to watch the goblin stab the man, he knew that they were outmatched in a fight. By the time the first man would be killed, the rest of the group would be on them with weapons drawn.

"He has nothing to do with this," Faine said, interrupting the man's harsh laughter. "He's just someone I was having a drink with."

"Why does that not surprise me? It makes sense that scum like you would sit down with this...thing. But whether he's here or not, we have business. Now," the man said, straightening his back and cracking his knuckles, "this can be settled one of two ways. I can drag you outside by that pretty, blonde hair of yours and beat the shit out of you and leave you bleedin' in the streets. Or, you can take out a knife and cut off one of your fingers as payment for tryin' to rob us."

"Which finger?" Faine said, holding up his hands and wiggling his fingers in front of his face before lowering all of them but the middle one. "This one?"

The man's face turned bright red as he pulled out a serrated knife from his belt and took a step towards Faine. Several of the men also drew daggers and took an offensive stance behind the large, bearded man.

"Wait, I'm sorry. I didn't know if you wanted a specific finger. But I have an option three that I think will be better for all of us."

"And what might that be?" the man said, gritting his teeth and gripping his dagger hard enough that his knuckles were white.

"I think you should let me buy us all a drink."

"You think a drink will make me change my mind about you tryin' to steal from us?"

"I don't, but I think that buying you a drink and giving you a gold coin might," Faine said, looking calmly at the man.

"And what's to stop me from just taking it?"

"Nothing, really. But I know I don't want to get stabbed today. And I'm pretty sure you or any of your men back there don't want to get stabbed either. So, I think you should let me buy us all a bottle of some of the finest wine you'll ever drink and offer you a gold coin for your troubles. It was a mistake, and I was drunk."

"The man sheathed his knife and turned to look at the men behind him. "What do ya' think, lads? Should we have a drink and get paid, or take him outside and take the coin anyway?"

The men shifted and looked at each other before one of the men in the back spoke up. "I say we have a drink and get paid. Lots of people roamin' 'round out there now, and I'd rather not stir up trouble with so many eyes. Besides," he said, looking at Faine, "I'm sure we'll see him around here again."

"There you have it, elf. Looks like we'll be having a drink."

The men pulled up chairs around the table as Faine called the barmaid over to take their order.

"Tell the bartender that I'd like a bottle of Andoran Red and enough mugs for each of us," Faine said, placing several silver coins into her hand.

As the barmaid brought back the wine and mugs, Faine pulled the cork from the bottle and began pouring wine for each of the men, leaving just enough in the bottle for Skara and himself.

"A toast," Faine said, raising his mug in the air, "To many long years ahead."

The men at the table grunted, but each raised their mug to the toast, waiting for Faine and Skara to drink before they finished their wine in one large swig.

As the men set their mugs down on the table, the door to the inn opened, and another mercenary appeared in the doorway and started striding towards the table.

"I have news," the man said, placing his fist over his heart. "The camp is nearly ready outside of town, and the brothers will be arriving before sundown."

Faine tossed down the gold coin on the table and nudged Skara to stand. "Thank you, gentlemen. But this sounds like personal business, so I'll leave you to it. Here's your coin, and I hope you enjoyed the wine. I'll make sure to stay out of your way from now on."

Before the burly man could say anything, Faine and Skara were moving up the stairs towards Faine's room. The messenger eyed them as they left the table, still with his hand over his chest, awaiting orders from the bearded man.

"Make sure that you do!" the man said. "Or next time we may not just settle for coin and a drink."

Faine turned and looked down at the men from the balcony above and nodded before entering his room and shutting his door. Once the door was closed, he began to frantically shove his belongings into a sack and hastily opened the window.

"What are you doing?" Skara said, stepping to the side to move out of Faine's way.

"We have to go. Now!"

"Why, what's going on?

"Well," Faine said, "I just poisoned everyone. Everyone except for the messenger, that is. And he saw our faces. So, we better be leaving."

"You what? Skara said, his eyes wide.

"No time," Faine said, shoving Skara towards the window as muffled screams and loud crashes could be heard coming from the common room below.

Giving one last look around the room, Faine followed behind Skara as they made their way out the window, quickly climbing down the side of the Bramble Thorn Inn; the sounds of frantic yelling echoing in the empty room behind them.

Two in the Bushes

Lowering themselves onto the partially cobbled road below the Bramble Thorn Inn, Skara and Faine stood with their backs pressed against the wall, listening as frantic yelling and footsteps could be heard rushing out of the inn.

"What do you mean you poisoned them?" Skara said, looking up at the elf.

"It really can't mean much else."

"You're going to get us killed. I wanted a drink and maybe an argument, not to get run through because you poisoned everyone."

"And I got you a drink."

"And what about gett-"

"Look, now's not the best time. They were most likely gonna kill us anyway. We can argue about it later."

Shaking his head and clenching his teeth, Skara followed Faine as they moved down the wall, pausing when they heard orders being shouted from the front of the building.

"Dalkuk is dead, and the elf's room is empty. Go back to wait at the camp for the brothers and tell them what happened."

"And what about the elf? He has to be around here somewhere."

"I'll find him. And I'll have his head for what he's done. Go, and I'll meet you back at camp soon."

Keeping their backs against the wall, the two moved to the back corner of the building, peering around the corner and watching as an armored man ran down the road, intent on getting to the camp as fast as possible. Taking one last glance around the corner, the two ran quietly along the backside of the inn, moving from one building to the next. Keeping low behind bushes and piles of broken crates, they made their way towards the front gate, hoping they could hide in the crowds of people looking at the goods the merchants had brought in on their wagons.

"There's the gate," Skara said, pointing out across the crowds towards the high stone archway.

"Move into the crowd and head for it, but don't run. If you run, you'll draw attention to yourself."

"I'll already do that!" Skara said, "I'm the only goblin here."

"Fair point," Faine said, looking around the corner for the armored man. "Let's move. Oh, and Skara," he said, putting a hand on his shoulder, "try and blend in."

Skara tugged his shoulder away and glanced into the crowds before stepping in, dodging between people as he went. Moving around a merchant cart, he could see numerous glass bottles set out in rows across narrow shelves built into its side. Hinged doors, painted green and blue, were thrown open to reveal bunches of dried herbs that hung in the spaces between the shelves.

"Ah, you look like someone who knows what to look for. What can I get for you today?" the merchant said, looking at Faine. "Some blackroot, maybe? Or perhaps some bitter vine, or some sweet cane to chew on while you're on the road?"

Skara looked at all the bottles and back at the merchant. "I'll take some sweet cane and a pouch of broadleaf."

"This isn't the time, Skara," Faine said, looking nervously around the crowd.

"For you, I'll need to get the coin first," the merchant said, scowling as he took the handful of coppers, setting them on a shelf as if they were dirty before handing over the herbs.

Putting the herbs into his pouches, Skara turned and started to nudge his way through the crowd.

"Skara, is that you?" a woman's voice called from behind him.

"You've gotta be joking," Faine said, glaring down at Skara.

Turning around, Skara saw Mary, the owner of the Greencap strolling up to him. Her green dress and black cloak waving behind her as she pushed through the crowd. Her long brown hair, fixed in a single, braid bobbed and swayed over her vibrant red bodice, reaching nearly to her waist. She held a small bag that looked to be stuffed with bright yellow fabric and sweets, and her face wore a smile as she approached. "Out for a bit of shopping today, are ya? Did ya find anything good?"

"A few things," Skara said, looking around the woman several times. "I see you found something."

"I did," Mary said, looking quite pleased with herself. "You know that yellow is my favorite. There's just something about it that brightens my day."

Skara nodded as he looked up at Mary. "I stopped by your shop today and picked up a few things."

"Met the new help, did ya? She's a good worker, but she gets a bit on edge sometimes. But what're ya to do?"

Skara looked at Mary and peered around her again, his eyes darting over the people in the crowd. "I need to be going, but I'll bring you a few mushrooms next I time I come through."

"A few greencaps?" Mary said, raising her eyebrows.

"As many as I can find."

"I'll be looking forward to it. And I should have some new stock for ya to look at when you stop by. I have a new shipment coming in soon. You take care of yourself out there, and don't wait so long to come by next time." Mary smiled and gave a slight nod as she turned, walking briskly through the crowd over to the next wagon.

Faine shook his head, giving Skara a slight push towards the gate as he glanced around the crowd, ducking his head as he spotted one of the men searching for them.

"You there, stop!" a voice shouted above the crowd.

Nearly everyone in the crowd stopped and looked at the armored men running down the road, one with his finger pointed in the direction of Skara and Faine. Each man wore black brigandine armor and carried a short sword and a footman's hammer at their side. Their heavy boots thudded against the hard-packed dirt and cobbles as they ran, pushing small groups of cowering onlookers out of the way, quickly closing the gap between them.

Skara and Faine bolted out of the front gate, running hard down the long dirt road towards the woodline. Slowing to wait for Skara, the two climbed the small hill into the field that led into the forest and stopped to catch their breath. Looking down the hill behind them, they could see the two men still running down the road, their weapons drawn and their faces red with exertion.

Taking deep breaths, Skara and Faine jogged into the forest, breathing hard as they pushed themselves on.

"I don't know how much farther I can go," Skara said, wheezing and kneeling on the ground.

"We're almost to Renna," Faine said, his hands on his knees.

"And then what?"

Faine shrugged. "Three against two."

Skara closed his eyes, breathing deep and wondering why he had let himself get wrapped up in all this in the first place. If he had decided to stay out of the cave that day, none of this would have happened. But, then again, Faine would have died, he would never have met Renna, and he would still be living alone, doing the same routine, just like he had been for years. He didn't know if this was better or worse, but it was definitely more interesting than another day carving runes or boiling water to drink.

Looking up at Faine, Skara held a finger to his lips and motioned for him to hide. Turning his head slightly, he could hear the soft crinkle of leaves somewhere behind them. "We have to move," he said, motioning over his shoulder.

Pushing himself up from the ground, he looked through the trees and saw the two men forcing their way through the underbrush, stabbing their swords into any bush big enough for someone to be hiding in.

"I don't think we'll make it," Faine said, pulling out his sword and a throwing knife from his boot. In fact, I think we can take 'em."

Skara's eyes went wide. "Are you crazy? They're wearing armor."

"There's two of them, and two of us. You just about pulled your knife on Dalkuk, but you don't want to fight these two? You just have to be creative and play to your strengths. If you wanted some adventure, this is it."

Skara shook his head and pulled one of his daggers. He didn't want to be in this situation, but he was. He could either run, taking the chance that someone follows him home, or deal with the problem now. "You're right. Not much choice. Let's go," he said, crouching low and darting off around a big rock and out of sight.

"Didn't think that'd be so easy," Faine said, gripping his sword and moving in the opposite direction.

Stepping slowly over the leaves, Faine watched as one of the men stabbed and swung his sword wildly at the dense bushes, moving farther away from his companion as he searched. When he could barely see the second man through the trees, Faine stood and stepped out from behind the stump he had been hiding behind. "It was a mistake for you to come out here. You should have stayed back in town and cleaned up the mess at the inn.

Startled, the man turned to face Faine, his fingers tightening around the hilt of his sword. "It was a mistake for you to kill any of the Crimson Sword. And I'll have your head for it," he said, charging towards Faine with his sword raised above his head.

"Too easy," Faine muttered to himself, quickly flipping his throwing knife over in his hand before sending it flying towards the man. The blade flew end over end, spinning in the air before smashing into the man's chest, hilt first, before falling harmlessly to the ground.

"Well, shit..." Faine said, frowning and bracing himself.

Stepping back with his left leg, he held his sword out in front of him, keeping it close to his body to guard his face and torso. The man, never slowing his charge, swung down hard, trying to push Faine back with the heavy blow. Parrying the man's blade and sidestepping to his left, Faine dropped to the ground, kicking out his right leg to trip the running man.

Falling hard onto the ground, the man's momentum carried him forward, plunging him face-first onto the fallen leaves. Faine stood still, keeping his sword outstretched in front of him as the man climbed back to his feet and quickly wheeled around. Drawing his hammer, he once again charged, running full speed at the elf, hoping to knock him to the ground with sheer force.

Clenching his jaw, Faine set off in a run at the armored man, his sword raised above his head, ready to strike. Just before the two men collided, Faine dove to the ground directly in front of the man's feet, causing him to trip and fall hard to the ground once again. Rising almost as soon as he fell, the armored man turned and swung wildly at Faine with his sword and hammer, fury overtaking caution.

Struggling to fend off the wild swings, Faine dodged and parried as he was pushed backwards. Keeping an eye on his footing, he stepped around the rocks in his path and used tree trunks to block the man's furious attacks, hoping he would be slowed by roots or downed branches. Only finding occasional openings, Faine struck out with his sword, only to slash at armor, or have his blade parried by the man's sword, followed by a swing of the hammer towards his head. The two men swung high and low, looking for any opening and fighting with everything they had; each knowing that one of them wouldn't make it out of the forest alive.

SKARA HEARD THE RING of the weapons as he watched the second man rush towards the sound of battle. In the distance, he could see Faine blocking attacks and striking out, his silver-bladed sword slashing quickly, trying to find an opening. Creeping, Skara positioned himself behind a boulder that stood directly in line with the second man.

Angry at Faine for getting him into this mess, he briefly considered letting the man pass him by and watch the elf fend for himself; but it was a brief thought, and he quickly pushed it out of his head. Even if he did drag him into this, it wasn't entirely his fault. He could have easily gone out the window at the inn instead of going downstairs, but he didn't. And he didn't save him from the spiders just to let him be killed now. It's like Faine told him earlier — they were both tied to each other, whether he wanted to admit or not.

Holding one of his daggers close to his chest, he leaned back against the rock and listened for the man's footsteps as they quickly approached. Pulling out a handful of herbs out of his pouch, he ground them as best he could in his palm and held them tightly. Just as the man started to run by, Skara leapt out from behind the rocks, slashing at the man's leg with his blade.

The man, startled and in pain, dropped to one knee and clutched the wound on the back of his thigh. Turning his head quickly to scan the forest, the man couldn't see any movement nearby. He could hear his friend shouting curses and the ring of swords echoing off the tall stones nearby, but nothing moved around him.

Skara watched as the man looked around in confusion, a look of worry growing on his face as he watched the blood pushing up between his fingers as he held his wound.

Moving out from behind a fallen tree, Skara crept quietly towards the man as he struggled to get to his feet. Just as the man stabbed his sword into the ground to help him rise, Skara darted in front of him, blowing the crushed herbs into his face. Coughing and rubbing his palms over his face, the man could feel the dried herbs clinging to the moisture in his eyes, stinging and scratching them.

Blinking hard, his eyes began to water, and the woods around him became blurry. The crisp colors of the leaves turned into globs of brown, and everything faded together, like looking through a window covered in a layer of oil. The man could see a small, dark shape moving around him as he held up his sword, his breathing hard and his eyes wide. In the distance, the sounds of fighting had stopped, leaving only silence in the woods around him as he climbed to his feet.

"Put down your sword," Skara said, drawing his second dagger.

"I'll not stand here and let you kill me like you killed the others," the man said as he tried to focus on the blurred figure in front of him.

"You can't change that they're dead, but you can choose to drop your weapon and make it out of here alive," Skara said, his hands tightening on the hilts of his black daggers. "It doesn't have to end like this."

"I think it does, you little demon! I don't need to be able to see you clearly to know that you're a monster. By the light, one of these days all you Fallen will be put back into the ground with the defiler where you belong. And it's already begun," the man said as he pulled back his sword and lunged at Skara.

Sliding sideways to avoid the thrust, Skara rolled forward between the man's legs and slashed open his other calf. Warm blood poured down his leg as he screamed pain and swung his sword around behind him, narrowly missing Skara's chest.

"Skara, move!" Faine said, running through the woods towards him, waving his arms frantically.

Just as Skara turned his head, he saw a large, grey wolf running in his direction, its bone and muscle visible through patches of torn fur. Diving quickly out of the way, the wolf jumped over Skara and onto the man, knocking him to the ground as his fangs sank deep into his neck. Undriel whipped his head as the man's hands punched feebly at the wolf. Gargled moans pushed through spatters of blood spewing from the man's lips as he fought for air, trying to cry out for anyone to help him. Undriel, giving one last pull, tore away the man's throat, leaving a red, gaping hole below the man's chin. The man shuddered as his arms went limp and fell to his sides, his eyes glassy as he stared off into the dull grey sky above.

"Are you two alright?" Renna said, running up to stand beside Skara.

"I'm alright. Although I can't say the same for these two," Faine said as he gestured to the man on the ground in front of him and the other man lying dead a few hundred yards away.

"What about you, Skara," Renna said, looking down at the goblin.

"I'm fine. But no thanks to you," Skara said, looking up at Faine. "What were you thinking, poisoning the men in the tavern? You could've picked a better spot to do it than around all those people. We could have been killed!" Shaking his head, he shoved his daggers back into their sheaths, an angry look crossing his sharp features. "It was in the wine, wasn't it? That means you poisoned me too. How else would you have been able to poison everyone there?"

"You're right, it was in the wine. But that tea you had before we left for town was the antidote. And remember, I drank the wine too. I wouldn't have done it if we could've been poisoned. And I seem to remember you stopping to have a chat with Mary and the merchant when we were trying to leave. We may have been able to make it out before anyone saw us if not for that."

"We wouldn't have had to run if you hadn't poisoned everyone. And I needed some supplies. Not everyone has everything on hand when they need it, or the ease to walk into any town to get it. And Mary sells me things that no one else carries." Skara looked down at the man's body on the ground in front of him, watching the red bubbles gathering around the hole in man's throat. "And she doesn't treat me like the monster most people think I am."

Faine scratched his eyebrows as he looked at Skara. "Look, it's over now. But we can't stay here anymore. They sent a runner to tell the others on their way here about what happened. We have to leave before there're a lot more people out here chasing us."

"No, you have to leave. It may not be safe for now, but I have a home out here, and I'm going back to it. I have a life here, and I can wait it out. It may not be the best one, but it's a life that won't always put me in danger of getting stabbed. Maybe some of us just aren't meant for more." Turning on his heels, Skara kicked a branch out of his way and began walking away through the woods, heading deeper into the forest.

"Skara, wait. This doesn't have to be it for you," Faine said, watching him walk off through the woods. Shrugging his shoulders, he looked over at Renna. "Now what?"

"He's right. It's not safe here. This is what happens when you get ahead of yourself, Faine."

"They would have killed us. You knew that me giving them the poisoned wine was a possibility. That's why you gave us the tea. I know I moved too fast, but what else was I supposed to do, let them cut off my finger and take me into the streets and beat me nearly to death? And then what, let them kill Skara or come after you out here? No, none of those options worked for me. I made a choice, and I stand by it," Faine said, crossing his arms over his chest and leaning against a nearby tree, a scowl growing on his face.

"And I'm not saying you made the wrong one. People die, and I'd rather it be someone else than us. But even with the trouble this may have caused, we can't leave yet. There's a problem coming that we need to take care of."

"What kind of problem?"

"A prisoner on his way here in a cage. Undriel saw him with a group of mercenaries bringing him here. They looked like Brothers of the Flame."

"Brothers of the Flame," Faine said, rubbing his chin. "Ya know, Skara mentioned somethin' about them when we were in town. Well, not really mentioned. It was more of a scowl when he saw their emblem hanging up in a shop there."

"They wouldn't be carrying a prisoner all this way for nothing. It might have something to do with the letter you found a couple towns back. They're guarding him for some reason. I feel like the dwarf has a part to play in all of this, and I mean to break him out of his chains."

"And what about Skara?" Faine said, tilting his head to the side and looking at the wolf sitting quietly next Renna.

"I think we'll see him again. He just needs a bit of time to think. But I have a feeling he'll come around. There are things at work here taking us where we need to be."

Faine let out a grunt and started digging around in the pouches of the dead man on the ground in front of him, pulling out several silver coins and holding them up in front of Renna. "This is what puts people where they need to be. Even the temples pry this from the hands of the people they're supposed to be helping. You know the world is dark. It's about having the will to take what you need from the those that abuse their power."

Renna nodded in agreement and put her hand on Faine's shoulder. "And we will. It's always better to be the wolf than the prey."

THE WAGON JOLTED TO a halt as the Brothers of the Flame pulled into camp just outside of Banrielle. Lowering himself from his horse, Gregor looked back at the wagon and began to shout orders. "We make camp here. Unpack the tents and get them set up before nightfall. Onrin, take several men and survey the area. We're supposed to be meeting up with a group that's been waiting in town, and I'd like to know where they are. I want to know the situation on food, water, and supply deliveries. If we're going to be here a while, we might as well make ourselves comfortable."

Braig laughed to himself as he watched Gregor barking orders. That's right, he thought, enjoy it while you can. It won't be much longer now.

Standing in the cage to stretch his legs, he spotted a man in black armor running up the nearby hill and head straight to Gregor. He strained to hear what the man was saying, but he was too far away to make out anything. But if his expression and gestures told him anything, it was that something had happened in town that needed Gregor's attention.

"Onrin, hold on that order. Men, with me; we have a situation in town. It seems most of the men waiting for us were poisoned. This man says that an elf and goblin were sighted in the inn before this happened, but they're nowhere to be found. Two men went off in pursuit, but they have yet to return. Take to your horses and go get information. If the men were poisoned, we find the means of poisoning." Gregor flung back the edge of his cloak and once more mounted his horse, reining it towards the path into Banrielle. "You two," he said, looking at a pair of guards, "stay here and keep watch over the dwarf. We'll be back before nightfall."

Braig shook the bars of his cage, trying to rattle the door loose as soon as the brothers passed out of sight. "Let me out of this cage, you little worms. I've been in here all day, and I need to step out to piss."

"Then, you might as well just piss yourself. Because you'll be stayin' in there 'til we say you can come out," one of the guards said, straightening his back and flexing his shoulders.

"You mean until you're told you can let me out. You have no say in anything here. You're just Gregor's lapdog," Braig said, tightening his grip on the bars. His broad shoulders and muscular arms looked tense and ready to be flung out through any open space to break any part of the two men that got anywhere near the cage. Eyeing them fiercely, he waited for them to respond or move closer, but both guards turned their backs to him and moved away from the cage and began unpacking the supply cart.

Leaning back against the bars, Braig let himself sink down and closed his eyes. He was tired of waiting for something to happen, tired of being locked up and treated like an animal. But he knew that the door would be opened soon enough, and he would show them just how much of an animal he could be.

GREGOR RODE TALL IN his saddle as he made his way towards Banrielle. As he crossed through the gates near the back wall, men and women were gathered in the streets talking and pointing towards the inn and the approaching brothers. Dismounting, he tied his horse up to a pole near the stable and strode into town, pushing through crowds of people as he walked towards the inn, ignoring their questions. Giving a quick look around the area, he could see the line of merchants leading out towards the main gate, and several established shops positioned around the square. One shop, the Greencap apothecary, caught his attention as he stepped up to the wooden door of the inn and went inside.

The room was empty aside from the barkeep and the barmaid, standing nervously behind the counter. In the back corner of the room, table and chairs were flipped over, and bodies were scattered across the planked floor. Grimacing, Gregor walked up to the man they called Dalkuk and squatted next to him, moving his face from one side to the other. White bubbles frothed out of his mouth, and his eyes were bloodshot and glassy. Blue veins wormed their way over his pale skin, and his tongue was nearly severed from his violent thrashing.

Checking each of the bodies, Gregor noticed a single bottle lying on the floor between them. Bringing it to his nose, he smelled its contents several times before putting it back down. Reaching for one of the mugs, he swirled the last few drops of wine around the bottom and noticed herbal sediment and slight sheen on the wine.

"What's this?" Gregor said, motioning to the barkeep and holding the cup out to him.

Running from around the bar, he took the mug and peered into the bottom. "It's just the herbs that they use when they make the wine, sir. Some wines are filtered, but this batch of Andoran left some in. All the bottles I have are like this."

"And how many bottles do you have?"

"Only about three or four left now," the barkeep said as he set the mug back on the table.

"Tell me, how do you think this happened?"

"I'm sorry, sir. I don't understand."

"Then, let me explain. I was told that a goblin and an elf came here and were seen with these men before they made a hasty retreat from the town right after. So," Gregor said, placing his hand around the back of the barkeep's neck, pulling him closer, "that means that they were either poisoned by the elf and goblin, or by you putting something in the wine."

"I swear, sir," the barkeep said, trembling slightly as he looked at Gregor, "it wasn't me. I just serve drinks to the ones that buy 'em."

"Perhaps you do," Gregor said, loosening his grip on the back of his neck. "But let's try something. Onrin, go to the back and get the bottles of Andoran wine and bring them out."

Smiling, Onrin ran to the back room behind the bar and brought out three bottles of Andoran wine and set them on the table in front of them. "He only had three."

"Just three," Gregor said, looking at the barkeep and smiling. "That's good news for you."

"Good news, sir?"

"Yes. It's good news because," the smile on his face quickly faded and was replaced by a scowl, "it's less you have to drink. Onrin, open the bottles."

Nodding, Onrin pulled the corks from each bottle and set them back on the table.

Motioning to the bottles, the barkeep looked over at Gregor. "You...you want me to drink all three?"

"Yes, unless there's a problem. Is there a problem?" Gregor said, resting his hand on the golden pommel of his long sword.

"No, sir. No problem at all," the barkeep said, grabbing the neck of one of the bottles. Raising it to his lips, he began to drink. Squeezing his eyes closed, the man swallowed drink after drink, only stopping to occasionally take a deep breath. Setting down the first bottle, the man belched and swallowed hard, the color slightly draining from his face.

Sitting down on a nearby chair, Gregor eyed the barkeep. "How are you feeling?"

"Good, sir. It's just strong, and I don't drink that much, is all."

"Well, today is an exception. Because the men and I are going to sit here while you finish the other two bottles."

Onrin reached for another bottle and handed it to the barkeep before picking up a fallen chair and sitting. As the men laughed around him and made bets, he noticed a gold coin on the floor at his feet and bent to pick it up. Looking around to make sure no one was watching, he slid it into his belt pouch and leaned back in his chair, feeling happy about seeing a show and finding a gold. "Don't just stand there. Drink the wine," he said, tossing a cork at the barkeep, laughing and pointing at the man.

Flinching as the cork hit his stomach, the barkeep raised the second bottle and slowly began to drink. As the bottle became emptier, the man's face grew paler and sicklier. "I... I can't do it," the man said. "I think I'm going to be sick."

"Then, be sick," Gregor said, looking sternly at the man. "And then keep drinking."

"Please sir, I already told you," the barkeep stopped, suddenly putting his fist over his mouth to keep from vomiting. The room around him began to spin as he placed a hand on the table to steady himself before he continued, "that I can't finish it."

"Oh, you'll finish it. Or you'll die trying. Now stop talking and drink. The men and I have work to do, and you're keeping us from it. But," Gregor said, turning to the barmaid, "this is making me thirsty. Bring me an ale."

The barmaid poured a mug of ale and brought it Gregor as the barkeep continued to drink. Finishing the second bottle, he dropped it to the ground and fell to his knees, retching on the floor in front of him. The men around him laughed and exchanged coins from the bets they had made on how long he would last before losing the contents of his stomach.

"You," Gregor said, looking back across the room at the barmaid standing near the corner, "are free to go. I don't think that it was you that poisoned the wine, and I think you've seen enough for one day. Let her pass, brother."

A stocky man carrying a two-handed sword on his back stepped to the side as the barmaid ran to leave, stopping to look one last time at the barkeep before running out of the door, tears streaming down her cheeks.

"Now, let's finish this. Men, sit him up."

Several of the brothers moved forward and picked the man up off the floor and propped him on his knees. Handing him the third bottle, the man weakly took it in his hands, taking a small sip before gagging and vomiting down his chin.

"Please, sir, no more. I just want to go home to my family. I just want to go home," he said, his face pale and wet from the tears and sweat.

"And I wish you could. But unfortunately, you helped kill these men. And an assault on the men under our employ is the same as an assault on a Brother of the Flame."

"I'm sorry. I was only told to bring out that bottle for a special occasion. I didn't know it was poisoned. It wasn't me."

"I believe you. I know it wasn't you, at least not directly. But a price must be paid. Onrin, make him drink."

"Please, no," the man said as the bottle was shoved back into his mouth and tilted upwards. The wine poured down the man's throat as he coughed and sputtered, choking as the red liquid poured down his chin, spreading like blood over the front of his white shirt. Trying to reach up and pull the bottle away, two men grabbed his arms and held them behind his back. As the barkeep coughed, the wine spilled from his mouth and splattered on the floor beneath him. Gasping, the barkeep struggled for breath, coughing roughly before his body heaved and went limp.

"Looks like he's not going to finish it after all," Onrin said, tossing the bottle to the floor and signaling the men to let the barkeep go.

The man's body fell to the floor, his face a sickly white with red stains on his cheeks and chin. The inn was silent as the brothers around him looked to Gregor, awaiting their orders.

"This is the way of the flame," Gregor said, peering down at the man. "When you walk in the darkness, the flame will either guide you to the light or burn you. Now let's show them we will not tolerate our men being killed, or the harboring of criminals working against the progression of the light. Burn the Bramble Thorn!"

The Red Banner

S kara walked through the forest, his mind wandering as he absently swung a small stick in the air in front of him. What had Faine been thinking, giving him poison in the wine? Although it wasn't meant to kill him, it could have. What if the antidote hadn't worked? But then, it did work; and Skara had a feeling that Faine and Renna didn't want to see him dead. They had several opportunities if that's what they wanted, but they had saved his life instead.

And what if Faine was right about seeing new places and this not being all there is? But that would mean leaving, and that hadn't crossed his mind in a long time. There are so many places to see out there, but also so many people that would like to see him dead just for being what he is. And after his fight with the mercenary, he wondered if he would have what it takes to kill someone if he needed to? Faine had done it so easily, and it didn't seem to affect him at all. Maybe all it would take is the right reason and the will to do it. But it was a simple choice for Faine to poison everyone because they would have killed them, and not had a second thought about it.

"I don't know what to do," Skara said, throwing his stick to the ground. "Should I just leave everything behind and see where it takes me?"

Skara sighed and walked down the steep hillside that his home what built into. His front wall was the only section of his house that was visible outside of the hill. It was made from long branches standing vertically in the hillside and latched together with rope, with a small door in the center. Stuck in between the gaps in the front wall were clumps of moss and balls of clay that helped to keep out the wind. Unlatching the door, Skara stepped inside and closed his eyes, standing still in the silence around him.

The inside of the hovel was a large rectangle dug deep into the hillside. On the left wall, a small hole for a fire had been carved into the wall and lined with stones that led up through the narrow chimney and out to the top of the hill. A wooden bedframe stood in the corner with a worn-out mattress made from leaves and moss shoved into several lumpy sacks laid out over its length. A small, solid wood table and a single chair chiseled from a stump sat in the opposite corner near the firepit. Several candles and hunks of carved bone and wood littered its surface, along with a few sets of runes in old leather pouches.

Between the bed and the desk was a sturdy looking door that was just big enough for Skara to crouch into. The tunnels behind the door split off into several crawl spaces leading different directions, and each passageway led to a sealed exit a short distance from his home. Ladders stood at the end of each of the tunnels, each leading to a wooden hatch that could be pushed open from the underside for a quick escape. On the surface, the doors were covered with soil and debris to keep them hidden and padded in case anyone happened to walk over them.

Laying his pouches down on the table, Skara walked over to the firepit and set kindling and tinder into its center. Holding a piece of charcloth on the edge of the flint, he struck down with the steel, sending sparks different directions. Striking again, a spark jumped and landed on the charcloth, burning a small corner as it smoldered inwards. Placing the cloth into a bundle of straw, cedar bark, and birch shavings, he blew gently until the ember burst into flames.

Placing the burning bundle into the kindling, he stacked thicker sticks in a circle around it until the flames lit the up the inside of the room, casting dark shadows from his table and lone chair onto the walls around him.

Lying down on his bed, he gnawed at a piece of sweet cane as he looked around the empty room. "And who'd want to leave all this behind? Miles from town, alone in the woods with no one to talk to, and giant, poisonous spiders roaming around." Throwing his piece of sweet cane across the room, he turned over and closed his eyes, thoughts about how there might be something more out there rolling through his head as he drifted off to sleep.

Skara awoke several hours later to a scratching sound at his front wall. The fire had burned down to embers, gently lighting the dark walls in a soft, red glow. Grabbing his daggers and buckling on his belt, he quickly ran his arm over his table, knocking all the bone carvings and runes into a cloth satchel and slung it over his shoulder at an angle across his chest. Backing deeper into the corner, the scratching outside became louder. Rays of sunlight passed through the gaps in the door, and he could see a faint outline of something crouching just outside. A soft whine poured through the wall as the clawing became harder, shaking the door on its rope hinges.

As Skara began to move towards the door to the tunnels, the whining became a ragged howl as his front wall started to shake under the weight pushing against it. This wasn't the first time that something had tried to get in, and like before, he didn't want to stay and find out what it was. Unlatching the door to the tunnels, he climbed inside and shut the door behind him. Looking out through a small gap in the wood, he could see a pair of dirty paws pushing under the wall as the creature frantically began digging a hole under his door.

Turning away, he scampered down the tunnel and climbed the ladder to the first escape hatch. Pushing open the door, he looked around the forest, the evening sun showing dimly through the branches above. Climbing out of the hole and quickly covering it back up, he began to move away when he heard a low howl coming from the front of his house. Shaking his head and hoping he wouldn't regret it, he crawled over the slope of the hill and peered down at the creature standing in front of his door. It was a grey wolf with patches of its fur missing and bits of muscle showing beneath.

"Undriel," Skara said, standing and looking down at the wolf.

The wolf let out a low whimper and ran up the side of the hill and began pacing back and forth in front of Skara.

"I don't know what you want. Why are you here?"

The wolf hunkered down on the ground and crawled towards Skara, turning around to run off in the other direction when he got too close. After seeing the wolf do this several times, Skara began to get irritated.

"What? Why aren't you with Renna? Do you want me to follow you or something?"

Letting out a low howl, the wolf turned and started running in the direction of Banrielle, stopping to look back at Skara, waiting for him to follow. Gritting his teeth, Skara reluctantly began following behind. "This better be worth it."

For nearly two miles, Skara jogged behind the wolf, stopping to walk when his legs became too tired to run. Holding his fingers up to the horizon under the sun, he could see that only a few hours were left before nightfall. The air was crisp, and the scent of fallen leaves and cedar filled the air around him. A slight breeze rustled the leaves, and his eyes darted to any shape he thought he saw moving in the forest. The last thing he needed was to run into another spider and have to deal with that again. Even with Undriel with him, he doubted he had much of a chance. Although, the wolf was already dead so he might be able to make an escape.

A soft bark up ahead of him brought him out of his thoughts, and he instinctively crouched, his hand going to his dagger. Up ahead, he could see two figures sitting behind a bush, whispering to each other. Pushing himself close to a tree, he strained his eyes and could see Faine and Renna talking and glancing up as Undriel approached them. Turning their eyes out towards the forest, Skara could hear them quietly calling his name. Stepping out from behind the tree, he ran over to the pair, keeping low as he went.

"You made it," Faine said, clapping him on the shoulder.

"What was I supposed to do? Your wolf nearly tore through my door trying to get my attention. You could have just come yourselves if you wanted to talk."

"We didn't know the way, and Undriel could follow your sent and doesn't get tired," Renna said, glancing over her shoulder at Skara. "There's something you need to see."

Motioning for Skara to follow, Faine and Renna crept towards the edge of the forest, looking around to make sure no one was nearby before standing and pointing down towards Banrielle.

As Skara moved up beside them and looked towards town, he could see large plumes of smoke billowing up from one of the buildings, black smoke against the grey sky. His eyes widened as he saw specks of orange flicking upwards, climbing higher as the flames spread. Banrielle, it appeared, was burning.

WALKING SILENTLY THROUGH the tall grass just outside of town, Skara kept low against the outer wall that surrounded Banrielle, moving towards a collapsed section that had crumbled to the ground years ago. The air was heavy with the smell of burning oak and cedar, and tendrils of smoke curled their way around the broken stones of the old wall. Following behind, Renna and Faine crouched low and peered into the square beyond. The Bramble Thorn Inn was nearly burned to ash, leaving only sections of charred timbers that reached like skeletal fingers towards the darkening sky.

Men, women, and children cried in the streets, their voices low as they looked around nervously, or held each other for comfort. Above the low murmur of frightened voices, they could hear a man begin to speak, silencing the crowd.

Stepping through the gap in the wall, Skara scurried behind the buildings, darting from shop to shop until he reached a barn near the back gate and stables. Opening the back door, Skara ran inside, leaving it open for Faine and Renna to follow. Sneaking inside, he stopped to listen for any sounds, but the building seemed empty, aside from several horses in their stalls on the lower level. Dashing up the stairs, the three made their way through the hayloft and over to a dirty window that faced out towards the crowds. Peering out, Skara could see the buildings around the square stretched out in front of him.

To the left of the square was the burned inn, the Greencap Apothecary almost directly across the square on the right. Several of the buildings had their doors and windows closed, but Skara noticed that the balcony door to the apothecary shop was open, and a light flickered inside. On the banister of the balcony, between the purple and red flags, a length of rope trailed inside the shop, but he couldn't see anything inside.

Turning his attention to the crowds below, he could see nearly ten men in black cloaks gathered around the inner circle, with two men dressed in faded brown armor over white tunics with silver trim and dark green cloaks. He couldn't tell if they were merchants, or with the guards, but they didn't look as if they were afraid like the onlookers gathered in the square. Leaning forward, Skara listened as the man spoke to the crowd.

"And for those that protect criminals or seek to hinder justice or the light, there can be little mercy. There are those in this town that have been found guilty of treason against the righteousness of the Reverent and have committed the act of murder. Upon questioning, the woman named Mary was turned over, and a search of the Greencap apothecary was conducted. Hidden inside a back room, we have found poisonous herbs, illegal goods, and forged documents. Under the authority granted to me by the High temple of Sonosa, all goods and assets of the guilty are now the property of the Brothers of the Flame," Gregor said, turning in a circle for all to see, his palms raised in the air. His face was grim as he looked over the crowd, their voices rising in concern over the mention of treason and murder.

"Gregor!" Skara said, his body trembling with rage as he gritted his teeth and looked out over the crowd, keeping his eyes fixed on the man.

His hands gripped the handles of his daggers as his body shook, ready to spring out the window to the ground below. His mind raced as he thought about all the years that had passed since he had seen Gregor in Sonosa and had made a blood-oath that he would find him again one day, and finish what he was too young to do before leaving the city and heading south for Banrielle.

Renna and Faine watched Skara as he squeezed the handles of his daggers. The leather wrapping creaked under his twisting hand as he stared out the window. His lips were pulled back into a sneer, his sharp teeth clenched as a low growl rumbled up from his throat. Just as he was about to climb out the window and leap down to the ground, Gregor began to speak.

"Silence," Gregor said, lowering his hands and waiting for the murmur of voices to die down. "Know this, the brothers are here on holy orders, and any who stand in our way or seek to thwart our efforts will be dealt with accordingly. The woman you know as Mary has been judged and sentenced to death. Let this be a lesson to you all—and may the Lords of Light have mercy on her soul.

Waving his hand towards the Greencap, two guards, each wearing a black cloak with the emblem of a flame, forced a struggling woman out onto the balcony. A noose hung tightly around her neck, and her hands were tied behind her back. Her long braid was untwisted and disheveled, and a dark bruise could be seen over her left eye. Her mouth was gagged, and her body trembled with sobs as she tried to pull herself free from the men's grasp. As they pushed her body forward, she planted her feet and tried to fight the men holding her, but they only gripped her arms tighter, lifting her up as they carried her towards the balcony and awaited the order.

At Gregor's nod, the two men gave Mary a sharp push, her body flipping head over heels over the railing to come to a hard stop at the bottom of the rope. Her head twisted unnaturally to the right as her neck snapped, her tongue falling out of her mouth to hang limply over her parted lips. The crowd stared in silence as her body swung lightly in the wind, her bright red bodice swaying like a banner against the deepening shadows of the evening.

Skara stood and began to unlatch the window, trying spring out onto the crowd of people below. Faine's arm struck out and roughly grabbed him, pulling him back inside.

"Let me go," Skara said, struggling to break free of Faine's grasp. "I'm going to gut him where he stands like I should have done before I left Sonosa."

Faine tightened his grip over Skara's chest, keeping his arms away from his sharp, biting teeth. "Not now! If you go down there, you'll die before you ever get close. He has at least twelve men that we can see, maybe more."

"He just killed Mary, and he burned down the inn. He leaves a trail of death wherever he goes," Skara said, writhing and cursing under his breath.

"And you'll get to kill him, but if you want to get the job done, it has to be done right."

"He's right, Skara," Renna said, placing her hand on the goblin to try to calm him. "I know you want blood, and you'll get it. But don't rush in and get yourself killed."

"And what should I do then, let him walk away?" Skara said, a slight tranquil feeling spreading over his body.

"For now. His camp is a short distance from town, and they'll be setting up their tents before nightfall. Strike in the dark when they least expect it. We can go into the camp while they sleep and take them out one by one."

"We...What does this have to do with you two?" Skara said, the anger slowly fading from his voice.

Faine rubbed his hand over his face and looked out towards the ashes of the Bramble Thorn. "Because he burned the inn and most likely killed the barkeep. If he died, it's my fault. I paid him to hold that bottle for me in case I ever needed it. I didn't expect them to burn the inn. But I should have known something bad would happen after I left. I can't sit back and do nothing while his family grieves and their livelihood smolders just outside."

"And besides," Renna said, "a wolf always hunts better in a pack."

Skara nodded his head and shook himself free of Faine's grasp. By the time he stood and looked out the window, Gregor and his men had untied their horses and had started up the trail back to their camp. Looking towards the balcony of the Greencap, he watched as several of the townsfolk hoisted Mary's body up and over the railing and slipped the noose off of her neck, letting it fall to the balcony as they set her body down. Mary's apprentice stood over her body, her face beaten and bloody as she wiped tears out of the corner of her eyes with a blood-stained rag. Leaning down, she covered Mary's body with a piece of bright yellow fabric and helped carry her inside the darkened room, gently closing the door behind them.

Yellow had always been Mary's favorite. But now the bright, vibrant fabric seemed dull and cold.

"Fine," Skara said, clenching his fists into tight balls, "we go after nightfall. But Gregor is mine. He'll die by my hand."

"He'll die by your hand," Faine said, nodding his head. "Now, we should go while everyone's still distracted. We have plans to make and need to scout the area."

Taking one last look out the window, the three moved down the stairs and into the cooling air outside. Staying close to the wall, they made their way back out of the gap, through the fields, and to the woodline above Banrielle.

"I have a few things back at the cottage that I think we can use," Renna said. "It's best if we head back, gather some supplies, and prepare. I have food waiting for us."

The woods seemed hollow to Skara as he thought about Gregor and what he had just seen. It had been over twenty years since he left Sonosa and traveled down to the outskirts of Banrielle to make a new home. Over the years since he'd been gone, he had thought about what happened less and less, but his hatred towards the Brothers of the Flame was still as potent as it had been the day he left; and seeing Gregor brought it all back.

Faine walked beside Skara, glancing down occasionally to see the grim look on his face. "You had this same look when you saw the banner at Javadi's place. Before we go barging into their camp tonight, is there anything you can tell us about 'em since you're from Sonosa."

"They're murderers that use the light as an excuse to do what they want," Skara said, kicking a small stone out of his way. "You saw what they can do. They go anywhere they want and use the power of the temple to make people afraid."

"What can we expect tonight? They look like they're organized and follow the man that was speaking today. What did you say his name was?" Faine said, trying to get Skara to talk about how he knew of the brothers.

"His name is Gregor. He was young when I last saw him, but still had command of a small group of Keepers."

"What's a Keeper?" Renna said, moving up from behind Skara to his walk at his side.

"A Keeper of the Flame. It's what they call themselves before they become brothers."

Faine stepped around a stump in the path, taking a few quick steps to catch back up to the pair, his eyes focused on Skara. "And you knew Gregor before he was a brother?"

"I knew Gregor when he killed my family!" Skara said, growling in frustration. "He would lead raiding parties in the lower city to try to run us out of town. If you weren't human, they thought you were part of the rot in the city. Most of the time, they would just throw some punches and make some threats, but sometimes..."

Renna stopped and put her hand on Skara's shoulder. "Remember what they did, Skara. Bring it back to the front of your memory and let it burn inside you. I know it's hard to think about but use that anger to do what you need to do tonight...let us feel the anger with you."

Skara shook his head as if trying to clear the roar of thoughts that flooded into his mind. "I lived with my family outside of the main town down by the water. It wasn't anything more than a shack, but it was home. We always knew that the Keepers were dangerous, so we had a way out that led under the house and down to the underside of the docks below. They came late that night. They were stumbling around and laughing, throwing bottles at the houses, and stirring up trouble. There were several other broods and goblin clans on the docks that started opening their doors or looking out their windows to see what was going on, and that's when it happened.

"The keepers saw a woman, a goblin, walking back to her house on the far side of the dock. She was keeping her head down and just trying to pass, but they couldn't let her go. They taunted her and pushed her, made threats, and yelled. And that's when the doors opened, and the other clans came out to help. The Keepers saw that some were armed with small metal rods and pots or knives, that was all it took. There was yelling in the street as they started to cut down any goblin with a weapon. They shouted about how the light was going to wash all this filth from the city, and that they were the cleansing hand of flame here to purify it. My family put me through the door in the floor and under the dock.

"My father went out to try to stop the fighting, but it wasn't long before the Keepers were kicking in the door. I heard screaming, and I covered my ears...and then it was over. I could hear the thud of boots on the wooden floor and then the splashes in the water as they threw the bodies in, letting them wash down the river. I sat there and watched the bodies of my mother and father float down until they were out of sight. I stayed there the rest of the night, not knowing what to do. I was angry and alone and had nowhere to go.

"I tried begging, but out of fear, none of the other clans wanted to help; or even could. Eventually, I was forced out of my house by another brood storming their way in. So I took what little I had and left for Banrielle. I knew I would have to go back someday to finish what had been started that night, and now, it'll end here." Skara's hand twisted on the handle of his daggers as he stared at Renna.

He had relived that night over and over in his head, but he had never told anyone about it. Mostly because he had no one to tell, but also because he thought that if he kept it buried inside him that the pain and anger of what happened would fade away; but it was always there, just on the edge of his thoughts, waiting to creep back in and rip at him from the inside. But why had it all happened now? Why had he met Faine and Renna so soon before Gregor came to Banrielle? It had to mean something that everything was happening now. Or maybe it didn't mean anything at all. But whatever the meaning, he knew that he was going to kill Gregor.

Faine was sitting on a rock nearby and stood as Skara began to walk again. He put his hand on his shoulder, giving it a gentle shake. "Don't worry. One way or another, it'll end tonight. You find Gregor and let us deal with the camp."

Walking the rest of the way in silence, they stepped into the cottage and sat together around the table. Beside them, a blackened pot hung from the swing arm over the faintly glowing embers in the firepit. Using a stick to hook the handle, Renna set it on the table and opened the lid. Steam poured from inside, and Skara could see large chunks of meat and several vegetables resting in a dark liquid. A wild, spicy scent filled the room.

"Smells good," Faine said, pulling out a chunk of meat and some vegetables with his knife. "What is it?"

"Braised venison with carrots, potatoes, and leeks," Renna said, spooning out a hearty portion for herself.

Skara eyed the food but didn't move to put any in his bowl.

"Not eating?" Faine said, shoving a cube of meat into his mouth, letting the juice drain down his chin.

"I don't feel like it," Skara said, pushing his bowl away.

"It's your choice. But I think you should have something. It's delicious. And besides, this may be your last meal," Faine said, smiling and looking over to Skara.

Skara shook his head and reached for the pot, pulling out a thick piece of carrot and several chunks of venison.

He wasn't sure if Faine was serious, but the thought had crossed his mind. "So, how does this work?"

"Well," Faine said, a stern look crossing his face, "you use your fork and stab the meat. The knife is used for cutting. Then-"

"We wait until midnight," Renna said, eyeing Faine. "Then we move into the camp."

Faine cleared his throat and pointed his knife towards Renna, then over to Skara. "That's right. We go tent by tent and take out as many as we can while they sleep. But it has to be quick and quiet. If you miss the kill and someone wakes up, they'll yell, and we'll have to fight our way out. You aim for the heart or throat."

Skara took a small bite of his food as he listened to Faine's instructions. "And if they wake up?"

"If there's too many to handle, we run to the forest and hide. It's easier to take them on one at a time in the darkness than if they fall into a formation. If that happens, they're going to have armor and shields, so watch your strikes and don't waste your energy. We don't know how many there are at the camp, so we don't move until we scout it out."

"Are you going in, too?" Skara said, looking over at Renna.

"I'll be there. This isn't my first fight. I know enough to take care of myself and to watch out for you two. Especially you," she said, looking over at Faine.

"Really, you get me out of a couple tricky situations, and you act like I don't know what I'm doing."

"Exactly. Do you remember the time you got caught with one of the chief's daughters? He was going to have you strung up for it," Renna said, laughing.

"I would have gotten out of it. And let's not forget that you were with one, too. You just didn't get caught. But it could have just as easily been me saving you."

Skara watched them both laughing, and a worried look crossed his face. "What's it like?"

"What's what like?" Faine said.

"Killing someone."

Faine let out a deep breath and looked over to Skara. "It's hard at first. But it gets easier each time. And before you know it, you don't even think about it anymore."

Skara looked down at his bowl and spooned another small bite into his mouth. He wasn't sure about how easy it would be, but he was ready to find out.

The Shadow and the Flame

The looming trees cast long shadows on the ground as the three crept towards the camp. Crouching low in a row of bushes just inside the woodline, the three looked out over the clearing. The sky above them was clear, and the two moons hung low, their pale light shining down on the camp that stretched out across the clearing in front of them. Nearly twenty small canvas tents littered the encampment, and several small fires burned in pits between the structures. On the outer edges of the camp, several wagons loaded with supplies sat near a row of short trees that the horses were tied to. Aside from a few murmuring voices and ragged coughs through the camp, there was mostly silence.

"I can only see three guards, but that doesn't mean there aren't more somewhere else. I'd be willing to bet there's at least one in the woodline somewhere," Faine said, looking back at Renna and Skara.

"So, what do we do?" Skara said, glancing back at the tents.

"We move. I'll go around the woods and check for anyone there, then work my way in from the opposite side. We make our way towards the middle, moving tent by tent. Strike fast and be quiet. If you see a guard, avoid them or take them out. We don't want anyone to wake up or see any bodies on the ground and sound the alarm. If that happens, run to the forest and hide and take them out one by one."

"There's the cage," Renna said, craning her neck to look farther into the camp. "That's where I'm heading."

Faine gave her a concerned look. "There's a lot of armed people down there. How are you planning to get him out?"

"I don't know yet, but I'll figure it out. It will most likely involve breaking the lock with a hammer."

"Then give us time before you do. But if the alarm goes up, break the lock and let him loose. I'm sure he'll take out a few of them."

"And what about Gregor?" Skara said, looking at Faine. "He's the reason I'm here."

Faine nodded his head towards his left shoulder, "You see that bigger tent at the end with the banner and guard out front? That's where Gregor will be. But it won't do you much good if you get taken out by twenty guards before you get there, so take out as many as you can first."

Skara looked down at his hands and wiped them on the front of his dark green tunic. His palms were sweating, but he felt strangely calm for what he was about to do. Checking his daggers and pouches to make sure everything was in place, he took a deep breath and watched the flames flickering in the camp below. Seeing a glint of light out of the corner of his eye, he watched as an armored guard passed the fire and began moving in a straight line in their direction.

Motioning to Faine and Renna, the three crouched lower and watched as the guard set down his shield and moved to the bushes only several feet away. Mumbling to himself about being awake for no reason, the guard undid his pants and began to relieve himself.

Putting his finger to his lips, Faine moved closer to the guard, drawing his dagger as he crawled silently over the dirt and leaves. Just as the guard was about to walk away, Renna let out a slight whistle, causing the guard to turn quickly back towards the bushes, alarm showing on his face. As he turned, Faine stood and thrust his dagger under the man's chin and up into his skull. The man's eyes twitched as blood spattered out of his mouth and poured down Faine's arm, dripping into the bush below. Pulling out his dagger, Faine took hold of the guard's body before it fell and pulled him behind the twisted branches. Laying him down quietly, he wiped his blade clean on the man's tunic and looked over at his shoulder.

"I think I got piss on me!" Faine said, brushing his hand over the wet spot and holding it to his nose. "Yeah, right on my shoulder."

"But at least that's one less guard in the camp," Renna said.

"That it is. So, let's move. Stay in the shadows and strike fast. We'll meet in the middle when it's finished." Faine gave Skara a reassuring look before he crept away, disappearing into the shadows of the trees a short distance away. Skara watched as the two broke off in different directions, leaving him alone at the edge of the forest. Steeling himself, he drew one of his daggers and ran into the camp, staying the shadows around him.

Moving close behind an unlit tent, he could hear the faint sound of someone snoring inside. Peering around the corner, he moved the partially open tent flap and slipped inside. The tent was only big enough for one soldier and their gear, with only a little room to stand and move around.

Stopping to listen for any voices or movement, Skara looked down at the sleeping guard, letting his eyes adjust the darkness. The man was covered with a thick, black cloak that bore the emblem of the flame on its shoulder. Raising his dagger above his head, he moved closer to the bed, ready to strike. His hand trembled, and his breath caught in his throat. Thinking about all of the nights he had to live without his family, and Mary being hung in Barielle strengthened his resolve. Letting the dagger strike down in a flash, the blade pierced the man's throat, pushing through his flesh like a hot knife through butter. The man's eyes darted open, but the blade flashed down again, silencing any cries before they were ever made.

Holding the blade out in front of him, Skara touched his thumb to the blood and rubbed it between his fingers. "No different than any other animal," he said quietly to himself, his face grim. He could feel something welling up inside him. It was an anger that had been trapped for years behind fear and uncertainty, and it was now awakening in the cold darkness around him. It was the anger of choices made for him by those that had brought him nothing but self-doubt and fear. And in the still night air, he could feel the fear slipping away.

Wiping his blade on the black cloak, he sheathed his dagger and quickly searched through the man's pouches lying on the floor beside his cot. "And you won't be needing this anymore," he said, pulling out several coins and a set of dice, shoving them into his belt pouch.

Opening the front flap, he looked to the next tent a short distance away. Quickly covering the distance between them, he slid through the opening and drew his dagger, once more killing the man before he had a chance to wake. Taking the few items the man kept in his bags, Skara stopped before sneaking back out into the night. Thinking that it's better to be prepared, he pulled out a small vial of dark liquid and coated the blade of his second dagger before putting them both away. Moving out into the darkness, he caught a glimpse of Renna running behind the wagons, her axe glinting in the light of the two moons.

RENNA MOVED QUICKLY past the tents, stalking the guard that walked in a loop around the perimeter of the camp. Rushing from one hiding place to the next, she watched and waited for the right moment to attack. Looking towards forest beyond the clearing, she could see Faine darting between bushes and boulders across the open space, knowing that if there had been a guard there, he was dead now. Turning her attention back to her target, she eyed him as he turned toward the clearing. The guard's head moved quickly from side to side, and his hand went to his weapon. Renna jumped to her feet and ran across the damp grass, her boots thumping lightly as she went. The guard drew his war hammer and opened his mouth to shout when he heard footsteps creeping up behind him. Turning swiftly to swing his hammer, Renna's axe came smashing down, cleaving his skull before he could cry out or finish the blow. His body fell lifeless to the ground, his weapon falling with a thump beside him. Reaching down, she picked up the hammer, slid it in her belt, and began to drag the body out of sight.

The guard's body was heavy, and his armor grated against the rocks under him, causing a sharp screeching noise as she pulled. Cursing under her breath, she tugged harder, trying to move it under one of the wagons nearby. Hearing footsteps behind her, she wheeled around, her axe ready.

"Whoa, it's just me," Faine said, holding up his hands.

"It's about time. Grab his feet and help me move him."

Grabbing the man's feet, they carried the body and rolled it under one of the wagons still packed with supplies. As Faine and Renna began to move back into camp, the flaps of a nearby tent were flung open, and an unarmored man with a bow moved out in front of the fire, peering in their direction. Seeing the two standing in front of him, he fumbled with his arrow and began to shout. "Everyo-"

His words were cut off as a Undriel leapt out from the darkness and bit down on his neck. The man toppled backwards into the fire, sending a shower of ash and sparks into the air. The wolf tore and tugged at the man, ripping wildly at his throat. Shouts rang out across the camp as guards rushed out of their tents, weapons in hand, shouting and leaping at the shadows as they searched for the intruders.

As two men ran into the clearing near the firepit, the blood-soaked wolf lunged and sank his teeth into the larger man's leg. Screaming at the wolf, the second man cut down hard with his bastard sword, cutting it in half behind its ribs. The wolf released its grip on the man's leg, but its limbs still kicked at the dirt, and its blood-stained maw snarled and bit at the two men that stared down at the creature.

Coming up from behind them, Faine and Renna struck them down and darted away into a nearby tent.

"I'm going after the dwarf," Renna said, opening the tent flap.

"Wait! The plan was to go into the woods and fight."

"I don't think that's the plan anymore. I don't think Skara's going to leave before he kills Gregor—or gets himself killed first."

Faine shook his head. "You're right. Then let's give him some cover. I'll see you in the middle."

Faine waited for two men to pass and took off behind them. His blade struck hard between the segments in the closest man's armor, sending him to the ground holding his left side as dark blood poured out. The second man, wearing nothing but a light shirt and pants, wheeled around and thrust his sword hard at Faine's stomach, driving him back while he deflected the blade.

Switching his sword to his left hand, Faine lunged forward, his left leg in front driving his sword straight at the man's unarmored chest. Stepping back to parry the blow, the man knocked Faine's sword to the side with a quick sweep, leaving his chest open. Darting forward on his right leg, Faine stabbed the man repeatedly in the gut with his dagger. Out of the corner of his eye, he caught a glimpse of a man running full speed at him, sword ready to strike. Pulling the knife out of the man's stomach, he threw it end over end to smash into the approaching guard, burying the blade deep in his chest.

"Glad that worked," he said, running to retrieve his knife and take cover in the shadows.

AS RENNA MADE HER RUN out of the tent, she saw Undriel's split body pulling itself along the ground, a trail on innards dragging behind it. Running up to the wolf, she held out her arm and began to chant. Pulling a small knife from her boot, she made a shallow cut on her arm, dripping her blood onto its fur before flinging some onto the nearby corpse of the man that Undriel had killed. Raising her hands into the air, she drew them close to her body as if pulling a rope, and a dark smoke rose from the wolf and swirled in the air in front of her. Casting her hands down at the corpse, the smoke flew into the man's broken body, sending it into convulsions before it stood, dead eyes looking at Renna. His face and body were burned and charred, and his throat hung open, strings of flesh quivering as he twitched.

"Fight to kill," Renna said, sending it her thoughts to keep her and her companions safe. With a guttural groan, the beast picked up a sword and took off in a sprint, cutting down a startled man that got in its path before chasing down and killing another. Watching the man kill, she pulled the hammer off her belt and bolted towards the cage. She could hear the dwarf yelling and shaking the bars, trying to break them open.

"Open the cage, you cowards. Don't just leave me here," Braig said, kicking the bars.

"Move back," Renna said, running up to the cage and climbing onto the cart. "I said, stand clear!"

Positioning herself in front of the door to the cage, Renna struck down hard with the hammer, busting the lock and sending the cage door swinging open.

"I knew you'd come," Braig said as he stepped out of the cage. "I saw the wolf watching from the woods. Now get these chains off me."

Renna jumped off the wagon with Braig and ran to a nearby stone. "Put the chain on the rock and close your eyes."

"You there, step away from the dwarf," Onrin said, pushing two guards forward, "Or you'll be strung up in a cage next to him."

"Hurry up and break it!" Braig said, rattling the chain as he stared at Onrin.

Renna raised the hammer high above her head and smashed it down onto the links. Bits of iron and rock exploded under the force of the blow as Braig stood up and stretched his arms, his broad shoulders flexing in their freedom.

"Go, girl. I'll catch up with you when I'm finished. These three are mine."

Renna turned and ran back towards the camp, hoping that Faine and Skara were still alive.

BRAIG STEADIED HIMSELF as the two men rushed him, one with a spear, the other with a sword.

"Kill him, you fools!" Onrin shouted from behind them, his sword gripped tightly in both his hands.

The spearman thrust at Braig, aiming for his chest. Sidestepping to the right, he dodged the blow and caught the spear with his left hand. Using the spear, he blocked the downward swing from the second man's sword and kicked him hard in the knee, knocking him backwards. Bringing his right forearm down onto the haft, he broke the spear in half and thrust the splintered wood into the swordsman's throat, pushing him onto the ground and jamming the haft into the dirt with the speartip pointing towards the sky.

The spearman pulled his sword but stood motionless, despite the threats and curses that Onrin shouted at him. Picking up the dead man's weapon, Braig walked towards the spearman, the sword held firmly in his grip. "Are you just gonna stand there, or are you gonna fight me?" Braig said, sprinting forward at the man.

The man swung wildly out of fear at the dwarf. Ducking and stepping to the left, Braig tackled the man to the ground and began crushing his face with heavy blows from the pommel of his sword. The man's face cracked and broke under the force, pushing bits of bone through his torn skin.

Braig was breathing hard, and his face was covered in blood as he stood and looked at Onrin. "Looks like it's just you and me, pig-licker. I hope you prayed to whatever god you follow, cause you're about to meet 'em."

"I'll cut you down, dwarf. By the time I'm done with you, there'll be little left to throw to the dogs."

Cursing under his breath, Onrin ran at Braig. His sword swung down in quick strikes causing Braig to backstep as he tried to parry the blows. Onrin's sword flashed down, again and again, narrowly missing its mark. Braig fought to keep the man at bay, but his thin sword was too fast, and a quick slash cut deep into Braig's left arm. Stepping back, he touched the gash and looked at the blood covering his fingers.

Onrin smiled as he looked down at the dwarf. "You can't win this, you filthy beast. I'll have you neutered and put back in your cage when I'm done with you."

Anger spread over Braig's face as he tightened his grip on the sword. Raising it over his head, he charged at Onrin, swinging down at an angle at his chest. Onrin raised his sword to block the blow, but the force of Braig's swing knocked it out of his grip. Glancing down at Onrin's weapon, Braig kicked it out the way as he rushed forward and slashed down with his sword, cutting off Onrin's hand at the wrist.

Onrin screamed in pain as he clutched at his arm, a look of shock on his face. Throwing down his sword, Braig slammed his fist into Onrin's thigh, bringing him to his knees.

"Please don't kill me. I'll...I'll do anything," Onrin said, bowing his head. "I have a gold coin. It's yours if you let me go. Here, take it," he said, reaching his bloody hand into his pouch to pull out the coin and hand it to Braig.

Braig sighed as he took the coin from Onrin and placed it into the side of his boot.

"Thank you, dwa-"

Braig's fist smashed into Onrin's jaw, breaking the bones and causing his jaw to hang loose on his face. Scowling, he stuck his hand into Onrin's sagging jaw and gripped it tightly. "You talk too much, pig-licker," he said, pulling down sharply, ripping his jaw and a large chunk of skin off of his face and neck.

Onrin's eyes widened as his tongue fell through the large hole where his jaw used to be. As the blood drained from his body and his eyes began to close, Braig picked up his sword, grabbed Onrin's hair, and severed his head with several quick chops.

Closing his eyes and taking a deep breath, Braig walked over to the spearhead pointing out of the ground and slammed Onrin's head onto it, turning it so that it looked out over the hillside. Stopping to take the keys off Onrin's belt, he unlocked the shackles on his wrists and started walking towards the encampment.

CORPSES LAY SCATTERED across the camp as Skara darted from tent to tent. Screams sounded around him as Renna's undead warrior cut its way through the brothers. The rocks were wet with blood as Skara crept around the tents, keeping low in the shadows. Sneaking closer to Gregor's tent, he could see the man standing with his guard near a dying fire, their swords drawn, peering into the darkness. Their eyes were wide as they watched the monster ripping and slashing at the last remaining men in the camp as they fell to the creature's wrath.

Turning its head slowly, its cold white eyes reflected the silver glow of the moonlight as it stared at the two men. Its left arm hung by ragged threads and swung uselessly at its side. As it turned to face them, the gaping hole in his neck had been torn wider, and deep cuts covered its chest, causing the flaps of skin to expose bone and muscle.

Gregor stood silently behind his guard, holding onto the man's shoulder to use him as a shield against the creature. Raising its sword, the monster dashed forward towards the two, swinging its battered blade. The guard parried the attack and thrust his sword through the creature's chest, pushing it in up the hilt.

The beast pushed forward, dropping its sword as it grabbed the man's face. Sticking its thumb into the man's mouth, it tore open a gash in his cheek as they both fell to the ground. Hacking wildly at the creature with his knife, the man screamed in pain beneath its ripping hands as he stared up at Gregor, waiting for him to come to his aid.

Looking frantically around the camp, Gregor saw the carnage spread across the dark landscape, and fear took over his body. Ignoring the cries of his personal guard, he turned on his heels and began running towards the path leading to Banrielle, hoping to escape unhindered.

Crouching behind a pile of corpses, Skara pulled his poisoned dagger and cut a small gash in Gregor's leg as he ran by. Letting out a sharp gasp, Gregor stopped and looked into the shadows, unsure of what had hit him. Breathing hard, he strained his eyes and leaned in, peering into the night.

Staring back from the darkness was a set of yellow eyes and a set of sharp teeth sneering at him in the dim glow of the dying fires. "I see you, Gregor," Skara said, his voice barely more than a whisper, "And I'm coming for you."

Gregor's face paled as he swung his sword into the shadows around him, hitting nothing but air. Sweat beaded on his forehead as he began to hobble down the trail, his left leg growing stiff as he ran. His breath came out in white puffs, and his lungs ached as he struggled for breath.

"Run, Gregor. Your past is catching up with you. Run, run, run," Skara said, laughing as he ran down the trail behind the man, throwing rocks in his direction.

"What do you want from me, devil? Leave me be!" Gregor said, limping hard as his left arm started to go numb.

"You're almost there, Gregor. The town is just ahead."

Running with everything that he had, Gregor pushed his way through the long grass on the hillside overlooking the town. The buildings were dark, and the shutters were closed tight against the cold night air. Looking for any signs of life, he saw the faint glow of a candle coming from the upper level of the Greencap and quickly began to hobble down the hill towards the single light in the darkness, hoping there would be someone there that could help him.

His left leg and arm felt as heavy as stone as he opened the door to the Greencap, slamming it shut and breathing hard. Latching the bolt, he pulled himself forward, dragging his leg behind him as he hobbled, dripping blood onto the rug. He called out for help, but his words began to slur as his face sagged, and his tongue fell limply out of his mouth.

He could hear the sound of something scraping on the wooden door behind him, trying to claw its way inside.

"Gregor, there's a wolf at the door nipping at your heels. The misdeeds of your past are catching up to you."

Panting, Gregor dropped his sword as his right hand began to tense and twitch. The room around him was dark, and his eyes drifted towards the faint light washing down the stairs in the back of the room. Hobbling to the stairs, he fell onto his stomach and began to pull himself upwards. Each step was harder to climb as he began to lose function in his right leg. Using his last bit of strength, he pulled himself up the final few steps just as he heard the front door unlatch and slam into the wall as it was forcefully pushed open.

Crawling onto the floor of the second level, he lifted his eyes towards the light and saw several candles burning on a small table. Above them were strips of bright yellow fabric braided together and tied into the shape of a circle with bunches of herbs, beads, and trinkets hanging in its center.

Hearing the footsteps coming up the stairs, Gregor closed his eyes against Mary's memorial and rolled over onto his back, his head turned toward the side, facing the stairs. His body was stiff and wracked with pain, and his limbs felt as if they had been nailed to the floor. His breath came out in gasps as he groaned and tried to will himself to move, but his muscles only tightened as he struggled.

Spittle flew from his mouth as he tried to shout, the sound barely escaping his lips as drool ran down his cheek and onto the floor.

"Do you know what I've done to you," Skara said, creeping up the stairwell.

Staring towards the dimly lit door, Gregor could see small, green fingers curl around the wall of the upper floor, the sharp nails scratching the wood.

"I've poisoned you. You won't be able to move, but you'll be able to feel everything I'm about to do to you. In your haste to flee the monster, you came across another one. But the irony is," Skara said, peeking his face around the corner, his sharp teeth glinting the orange glow of the candles, "I may not have become a monster if not for you."

Walking up the last few stairs, Skara stood in the entry-way, his dark clothing wet with blood and his dark hair hanging loosely over his face. Dropping to his knees, he crawled towards Gregor until he only was only inches away, his eyes staring hard at the man's face.

Gregor groaned and tried to move, but his body only trembled.

"Let me tell you a story. Not a happy story like my mother used to tell me, but a dark story about pride and murder—a story about you," Skara said, digging his nail into Gregor's cheek, causing a trickle of blood to drip onto the floor.

Rubbing the blood between his fingers, Skara looked up at the memorial for Mary and moved closer to Gregor's face, putting his sharp teeth directly in front of his eyes. "It was over twenty years ago, now. You were just a keeper then that wanted to show his worth. So, you came looking for trouble in the lower city, where the filth lived. Or so you called us. But you harassed a goblin on her way home and killed anyone that came to help or tried to stop the slaughter. But they couldn't stop it, and you killed them all. You even killed some of the goblins cowering in their houses. Do you remember that?"

Skara sat up and pulled out his dagger and picked up Gregor's hand, sliding the point of the blade under his thumbnail. Gregor groaned in pain as his hand trembled.

"I know, it hurts. But the story isn't over yet. You see, I was under the house, hiding by the river. I had to stay there and listen to the bodies being thrown into the water," Skara said, popping off Gregor's thumbnail before moving to the next finger. "Then, I watched my parent's bodies get sucked under the current as they were swept away in the darkness. That was because of you; because of your call to serve the light. But just because we weren't human, it didn't make us monsters. You were the monster, and now I've let myself become one to fight against them; against you."

Skara pried another nail from Gregor's hand, and then another. "But this is the end of your story, and no one will remember you. Tomorrow when they cut you down, the townsfolk will throw your body in the woods to be eaten by the beasts and rot."

Dropping Gregor's hand, Skara stood and stabbed one of his daggers into the man's leg and stepped over his body. Moving the balcony doors, he took hold of the noose and untied it from the railing. Cutting the length of rope shorter, he tied it back in place and kicked out several of the boards to open a large section beneath the banister. Walking back over to Gregor, he opened the man's cloak and took hold of his shoulders and began to pull. Using all his strength, Skara tugged at the heavy man, barely moving him across the floor. Straining his muscles, he pulled again, only moving him several inches.

"Need some help?" a voice said from the stairwell.

Looking up, Skara saw Faine standing at the top of the stairs. His dark blonde hair was pulled into a messy bun, and splatters of blood stained his face and clothing. His arms were cut and bleeding, and his knuckles were purple and bruised. Stepping forward into the light, Renna and Braig moved up behind him, both covered in bruises and cuts of their own.

Skara looked at the dwarf and wondered who he was but knew there would time to ask questions when this was finished. Looking over at the three of them, Skara nodded his head and reached for an arm. Stepping up beside the man, Faine took hold of one of Gregor's arms as Renna and Braig took hold of his legs. Lifting him off the ground, the four moved him out onto the balcony.

"I've shortened the rope, so it won't break your neck when you fall. That should give you some time to think about how this all started, and how it all ended."

Gregor's eyes were wide with fear as Skara put the noose around his neck. He struggled to move, but it took all he had just to clench his fist. Pulling the knife out of Gregor's leg, Skara and Faine pushed his body over the edge feet first, being careful to let him down gently. As the rope tightened around his neck, his breath stopped in his throat as the noose slowly crushed his windpipe. His eyes darted around the darkened town before he looked up into the heavens and began to pray to the light that he would be spared, but the deep shadows had consumed his flame, and he heard only silence.

A Small Measure

The trail was long and dark as they made their way back up the hill. The moons hung low in the sky, and a golden glow was starting to gently break over the horizon. The forest around them was coming to life with the sound of winter birds singing in the treetops as a light wind rustled the fallen leaves, blowing them into small piles around the tall clumps of brown grass that pushed its way through the underbrush that grew on the hillside. Large lichen-covered stones jutted up near the woodline beside them, rough grey flecked with gold as the rays of light cut across the hills.

Weariness creeping into them, the four trudged up the horse trail and into the encampment. The fires had all burned down to ash and had gone cold, and they stood and looked over the canvas tents that lay empty and stained red with blood. Sauntering towards Gregor's tent, they stepped over the broken body of the guard lying in front of the entrance, his body beaten and mangled.

Looking down at the man as he passed, Skara pulled back the flap, his eyes going wide as he saw the creature that Renna had summoned standing motionless, staring at the canvas wall with blank eyes. A sword was pushed through his chest, dried blood still clinging to the blade. Jumping back,

Skara bumped into Braig and pulled out one of his daggers, cursing under his breath.

"By the stone," Braig said, balling his fists, "what is that monstrosity?"

"Wait," Renna said, stepping in front of the creature. "It's no threat to us."

"What d'ya mean, no threat? It looks pretty dangerous to me," Braig said.

"It's not alive, not really. It's magic. Out of the tent," Renna said, motioning for the creature to move.

Moving to the side to let the creature pass, it shambled out and stood near the guard's body. Renna closed her eyes and held her hands out in front of her, chanting quietly. The creature's body trembled and fell lifeless to the ground as a cloud of black smoke rose from its wounds and dissipated in the gentle breeze.

"Don't worry," Faine said, slapping Braig on the back, "you get used to it."

"I don't know if that's something I want to get used to."

"Before we go in," Renna said, turning to look at Braig, "what are we looking for?"

"Why are ya askin' me?"

"We know they were here for something, and they kept you prisoner for a reason. Banrielle is a small town and not worth coming all this way with a formidable group and a dwarf for no reason."

Braig looked down and shook his head. "You're right, they were after something, and they thought I could find it; but there's nothing here for them to find."

"Then, why were they here?" Faine asked.

"They were here because I told them the stone was here. I knew it wasn't, but I had to get out of that cage," Braig said, his face turning red as he rubbed his forehead.

Renna shifted on her feet and crossed her arms over her chest. "And how did you know you'd get out of the cage here?"

"Because I had a dream about it. I don't know how I knew—it just came to me in a dream. I saw my chains being broken, and I knew I had to get here. Then I saw your wolf in the forest, and I knew this is where I needed to be."

"And they were trying to use you to lead them to a stone?" Faine said.

"They thought they could just keep me locked away and beat the visions out of me, but that's not how they work. I can't control what I dream or see." Braig looked down at his boots, the redness fading from his face. "But I know what they were looking for, and I think I know where it is. But I don't know what it does."

"What is it?" Skara said, moving around to look at Braig.

"It's a black stone that's somewhere in a marsh," Braig said, closing his eyes. "It's dark and dead there. The houses are long abandoned and broken. I hear the vague sound of something banging, and I see the stone falling off a shelf into the mud under some old, broken boards. It looks like a shard of dark glass with the edge of a knife. There's nothing around for miles, just a wasteland."

"The Grey Wastes," Faine said, wrapping one of his arms around his chest and rubbing at his chin with the other. "It has to be. Miles of wastes with marshlands and an abandoned town. There're only so many towns in the wastes and fewer near the marshy shores."

Renna moved inside the tent and began to look through the ornate chest at the foot of Gregor's cot. Pulling out clothing and stacks of paper, she began to read through the letters. Flipping quickly through them, she tossed away anything useless until she reached the last letter and tossed it to the floor after reading it.

"Nothing. But there has to be something here," she said, tapping one of her small tusks with her finger. Pulling out more items from the chest, she reached the bottom and peered inside. In the back-left corner of the bottom panel, she noticed a small hole cut into the wood. Pulling out her knife, she pried the board loose and lifted it out, revealing several letters sealed with wax and a few small coin pouches. Pulling out the bags of coins, she tossed one to Faine, Skara, and Braig and, reached for the letters.

Sitting down on the mattress, she unfolded the letters and began reading.

"What is it?" Faine said, trying to look over Renna's shoulder, breathing into her ear.

"Give me a minute, and I'll let you know," she said, looking up at Faine, moving her head away from his mouth.

Laughing to himself, he moved away and began rummaging through Gregor's bags. Pulling out a long brown tunic, he held it up to Skara. "Hey, I found you a dress," he said, tossing it at the goblin before reaching back into the bag.

The tunic flew through the air, hitting Skara in the chest before falling to the ground. Kicking the tunic away, he moved to the edge of the cot, rubbed his eyes, and laid down on his side.

"I can't go back," Skara said. "It's all over. Mary's gone, the Bramble Thorn is burned, and they think it's my fault. What do I do now?"

"You come with us," Renna said, tapping her finger to one of the letters she was reading. "It doesn't say what it does, but this letter mentions something called a mage stone. It says it's magic but doesn't say how. And not just that stone, others."

"There are others," Braig said, moving closer to Renna. "But I can't see what they look like. It's like they're covered in fog or under flowing water. I can only make out the black shard, but I could see others beside it. There's an aura around each of them, but I don't know what they do."

"Right. This letter is addressed to Gregor and talks about buying a dwarf that can help them locate the stones. It says there's one in Banrielle and for Gregor and his men to meet you at the coast and bring you here. It says that after taking care of some business in Ethilios that they'd be back for answers."

"Who wrote the letter?" Faine said, tossing several more tunics and a white flag with a red lion crest over a black rune surrounded by a yellow circle in Skara's direction.

"It doesn't say a name, but the initials are D.E., and it's sealed with not only a royal seal but the seal of the mage tower in Bright Harbor. Whoever it is wants the stones."

"And that means they're important...and valuable," Faine said. "I bet that flag has something to do with it, too."

Braig lifted the flag and stared at the crest before scowl-ing and throwing it on the ground. "Valuable enough to take me in the dark, lock me in a cage, and torture me for. What-ever it is these stones do, I don't want them falling into their hands. I don't know who the hooded man is that bought me, but I'm willing to bet this is his crest, and he's the one that wrote that letter."

"Don't worry..." Faine said, looking over at Braig with a puzzled look. "I didn't get your name."

"Braig."

"Well, Braig, I'm Faine. This is Renna and Skara. And you don't have to worry, me and Ren will help you look for the stone. And you too, Skara, if you wanna come along," he said, looking down at the goblin.

Braig shook his head. "I can't see why you'd want to get mixed up in all this. Whatever that stone is, it's not just about coin, and it involves me more than it does you. I may not be able to make much sense of my visions, but I get the feeling that something is changing out there. It's as if every-thing started happening at once. It wasn't all good, but it brought me here, and I mean to see it through. But having someone to travel with might help me find it and not be killed along the way. Besides, I don't think you'll have much of a chance without me. So if you're wanting to find out what's going on, it looks like we'll be traveling together."

Skara raised his head and looked over to Braig. Sitting up, he glanced around the tent. "You're right, something is changing. It's like the charge in the air that you feel before a storm. And since I can't stay here anymore, I might as well take my chances with all of you."

"That's the spirit, Skara. Now I don't know about every-one else," Faine said, stretching his arms, "but I don't think anyone is coming into camp in the next few hours, and it's been a long night. I say we stay here and get some sleep."

"And then what?" Braig said.

"Then we take the horses and carts out front, drop some supplies in town, pack our things and head south to Mivara," Renna said, leaning back onto the mattress, her feet resting on the ground. "Then we take a ship to the Grey Wastes in Aerith and find the mage stone. If the mage tower is interest-ed, who knows what kind of magic it holds."

Nodding his head, Faine tossed a sack of clothing to Braig and put one under his head as he stretched out on one of the ornate rugs and covered himself with tunics. "We're heading to see the Sanguine Gulf, Skara. And then away from Uthrea to a new land."

A tingling sensation washed over Skara as he pulled the clothing up over his face. The thought of leaving Banrielle for new places made him excited, but it also filled him with a vague feeling of unease.

SEVERAL HOURS PASSED before Skara awoke to find Renna and Faine gone. Braig was lying on his back with a black cloth draped over his eyes, snoring softly. Pushing the pile of tunics off his chest, he slid off the cot and made his way outside. The sun was at its zenith, and the bright blue of the sky stung his eyes as he emerged from the tent. Squinting as he looked around the camp, he could see Faine and Renna down by the wagons, looking through the supplies.

Picking through the pouches of several of the men lying on the ground, Skara made his way through the camp towards the carts. In the light of the sun, the bodies scattered across the ground looked even more gruesome. Biting flies had begun to hover over several of the dead and flew close to Skara's face as he dug through their pockets. Taking several more coins and small trinkets, he climbed up on the wagon and looked at the goods stacked in the back.

"It's getting bad here with the flies. We should leave soon before the smell draws out something else," Skara said, opening up a crate and looking at the bottles inside.

"Black rum," Faine said, lifting out a bottle and taking a sip. "It's strong but good. You want some?" he said, holding the bottle out to Skara.

Skara shook his head, and Faine shrugged and put the bottle back in the crate. "Save that for later," he said, his voice low. "What else could the smell draw?"

"Spiders, wisps, wolves, the myrrow," Skara said, looking out into the forest.

"What's a myrrow?"

"It's something that eats anything, even the dead. It gorges itself on flesh until it can't hold anymore. Sometimes I could hear it, out there in the dark. Its howls would carry across the hillside as it hunted."

Faine followed Skara's eyes towards the forest, scanning the woodline before looking back at the goblin. "You're just making that up. There's no myrrow out there."

Pulling a piece of jerky out of her mouth, Renna walked up behind Faine and slammed her hand on the wooden planks of the cart, causing Faine to jump slightly. "Oh, they're out there, alright. You better hope that they've already eaten their fill if you ever see one—and that all the extra weight in their stomach slows them down enough so you can get away."

Faine looked around the camp and batted away several of the flies before taking another drink of the black rum. "So, let's get the, uh, wagons hitched up and get moving," he said, tapping the lid of the crate closed and grabbing a piece of dried meat. "You think the townfolk'll be ok if something comes up here?"

"It should be fine," Skara said, jumping off the wagon and looking up at Faine. "It's far enough from town, and whatever comes will move on when it's done."

"Right," Faine said, clearing his throat and adjusting the leather straps holding the supplies in place on the wagon.

Moving off towards the horses, Faine hitched up two of the wagons, each with two horses to pull, the rest tied to a rope attached to the back of the cart. Splitting up and moving around the camp, Skara, Faine, and Renna gathered the blankets and extra clothing from the tents and stacked them on the wagon to take to town. Keeping several blankets and bedrolls for their trip, Renna looked through the clothes to find something warm to wear as they traveled to the coast. Pulling out a thick, grey wool shirt, she slid it over her head and looked over at Faine.

"How does it look?" she asked, holding out her arms.

Looking at the thick shirt hanging over the waist of her dirty brown pants and the spots of mud on her green skin, he turned his head at an angle and frowned. "Here, hold this," he said, picking up a metal cup and sticking it in her hand.

"What's this for?" Renna said, looking down at the cup.

Pulling out a few copper coins, he dropped them into the cup and smiled. "There, the beggar look is complete."

Dumping the coins out into her hand, she threw them at Faine before dropping the cup and glaring at him. "I don't care that you think I look like a vagrant. I'm warm. Maybe you should go wake up Braig and get some clothes and weapons and load them into the cart."

Picking up the coins, he laughed as he turned and made his way back towards Gregor's tent. Walking up the path, he picked up several of the swords and hammers and began stacking them in a pile. Opening the flap, he kicked at Braig's foot, "Are you awake?"

"I am now," he said with a gruff voice. Pulling the black cloth of his eyes, he sat up and looked at Faine, his eyes bleary.

"We have some dried meats fruits if you're hungry, and water in a few skins out here." Moving inside the tent, Faine picked up a large sack and began stuffing it with pants and tunics. "You should grab some before you go, too. It's a long way down to Mivara, and a few changes of clothes can make the trip a little better."

Stretching his back, Braig stood and began looking through the clothing strewn around the tent before shoving a few shirts and pants into a bag. "I know it's a long road. I was in a cage all the way here not far from Mivara."

"Right," Faine said. "Sorry." Looking around for a smaller bag, Faine stuck his head out of the tent flap and yelled for Skara. "Skara, come get some clothes!"

Coming out from behind a tent, Skara struggled to carry a large round wooden shield painted dark blue with a red bear head painted in the center and circled by a blackened metal rim.

"That's a nice shield," Braig said.

Faine let out a small laugh. "Maybe a bit big for you, though."

"It's not for me. I like my daggers. But it looked too nice to leave here."

"If you don't have a use for it, I could find one," Braig said, looking at Faine and Skara.

Handing over the shield, Braig slid his arm through the leather strap and gripped the wooden handle, moving it up and down and punching out, feeling the weight. "This'll do just fine," he said, nodding his head to Skara. "But you found it, and if you want to keep it, it's yours."

"You keep it," Skara said, "I've found enough here to last me while. I'll be fine after I get some clothes."

"Don't forget your dress," Faine said, grabbing his bag and stepping out of the tent. "Braig, can you help me load up a few these weapons on the wagons?"

Grabbing as many weapons as he could carry, he walked with Faine down to the loaded carts. Setting several in the back of their wagon, they loaded the rest onto the cart they were dropping off at Banrielle. Renna watched them as she pulled at the string of a finely carved bow.

"That's nice," Faine said, raising his eyebrows. "Find any arrows?"

Holding up a quiver full of arrows, Renna smiled and set them with the supplies.

"Did you find any more of those bows?" Braig said.

Renna nodded. "I could only find two more. So, we only have three total."

Skara walked down the hill and handed his bag to Faine as he climbed up on the wagon and covered himself with a wool blanket. "Are we leaving now?"

"We have one more thing to do before we go. We know that someone's coming back here at some point, and I don't want them to know what happened. The beasts will take care of the bodies for the most part, but let's stack the tents and burn them. We have what we need, and we're taking the supplies, so there's no need to leave them standing," Renna said as she began tearing down tents and moving them to the center of the clearing.

After taking anything they might need and breaking down the tents, Braig climbed onto one of the wagons and took hold of the reins. Looking back at the line of horses tied to the back, he whipped the reins and steered the cart down the narrow road leading through the forest that would take them to the front gate of Banrielle. Stopping just outside of the encampment, Braig pulled the reins and waited for the other cart. "We should get moving. We need to be miles away by the time we have to make camp."

Climbing into the back of the second wagon, Skara watched Faine climb up onto his horse, with another being led behind him.

"I'll meet you near the field at the top of the hill. I have to go back to the cottage to get our books and gear. Renna, is everything you want ready to go there?" Faine said, turning his horse towards the road.

"Most of it," Renna said, raising her voice as Faine trotted away. "Make sure to grab my bag of herbs and tinctures and get my books!"

Waving his hand in the air, Faine trotted past Braig and moved out of sight around a bend in the trail. Stepping towards the tents, Renna stretched out her hand inches away from the canvas and focused her power down through her fingers. Feeling the heat begin to radiate from her hand, a flame sparked to life on her palm and fell onto the pile of cloth and wood. Walking around the outside of the stack of rubble, she set several fires that began to burn towards the center, growing as it consumed the canvas.

Smiling to herself, Renna could see the white flag with the red lion catching flame as she climbed onto the cart and looked from Skara to the pyre in the center of the camp. "Not too bad for just learning to control fire," she said, making a clicking noise with her mouth to get the horses moving. As the cart rambled forward, Skara climbed onto the front seat next to her and wrapped himself tighter in his wool blanket.

"It's a good fire. There shouldn't be much left here after a few days of scavengers," Skara said, turning around to look at the bonfire behind them.

Thick smoke billowed off the blaze and swirled in the wind as the wagons moved down the road towards town. The brightly colored leaves that remained on the trees around them shivered on their bright white or rough, brown branches, gently rustling as they blew in the breeze. The sunshine filtered through the canopy and dappled the moss-covered ground around them as they rode, glinting against the drops of dew clinging to the foliage.

Leaning back, Skara stared up at the billowy white clouds that floated across the deep blue of the sky, letting himself get lost in the sounds of the hooves clopping against the dirt as the wagon wheels squeaked and groaned over the bumpy path.

Turning the corner, the two wagons meandered down the long road before pulling through the gates of Banrielle. Renna pulled the blanket that rested on her shoulders up over her head and waited outside the gates, keeping the horses steady as Braig pulled the supply cart towards the square.

Reining the horses to a stop, Braig stood and looked at the townsfolk coming out of their houses to see what was happening. Glancing around, he could see that Gregor's body had been cut down, and there were no signs of the noose hanging from the Greencap. "These are all the horses and supplies that are left from the camp of the Brothers of The Flame. I was traveling through the area on my way here to sell my wares and spotted a row of tents through the trees. I took my cart to their camp to see if they were in the market for anything, but they were all dead. It looks like they were attacked in the night by wolves, bandits, or some other manner of foul beasts and were all killed. There was a creature there skirting the forest, but I couldn't get a clear look at what it was. I took this cart of supplies and the horses, packed up the weapons that were scattered, and burned the tents to stop anything else from heading back into the encampment."

The townsfolk poured from their houses at the loud bellow of the dwarf that stood near the square. Their eyes were wide with shock, and Braig could see that several of them nodded their heads to each other as if they felt a small measure of justice had been served. Setting down the reins, Braig pulled the canvas covering off the supplies and gestured to the crates loaded in the back.

"There's food and drink here, along with blankets and weapons. And from the look of things here, the creature or people responsible may have caused trouble here before moving on to the camp, and the supplies here could help fend them off should they attack again. Most likely, someone will come to check on the camp and find it destroyed and come around here to ask questions. I would be sure to let them know about your bandit or creature issue so that they'll be aware of the dangers in the hills around Banrielle. But for now, take these horses and supplies and use them to help farm or keep you safe."

Jumping down from the wagon, Braig walked through the crowd of people gathered around and climbed up onto the seat next to Skara and Renna.

"That was a good spin you put on it," Renna said, her eyes lighting up as she snapped the reins to get the cart moving. "Now, let's get Faine and be on our way. If we make good time, we might be able to make it to Mivara in time to see some Wyldernacht performances."

Meandering slowly up the hill, the wagon stopped next to the field to wait for Faine. Sitting on a rock, Renna watched Braig as he looked through the weapons stacked in the middle of crates. "So, how long were you in that cage before last night?"

Braig stopped digging and looked up at Renna, a scowl forming on his face. "I got caught up on the eastern side of Auren by some slavers. They sold me and stuck me in that cage and put me below decks of a ship. I don't know how long I was there. The days and weeks blurred, and I lost track of time. The only time I could see the sunlight was when someone brought me food and water every few days. I had to sit in that dark hole for weeks before we reached land. The cargo around me shifted and slammed into the cage, keeping me awake. All I could think about was getting out of there. Then we reached the coast, and they put me on the wagon. After that, it was still weeks before you came."

Braig's eyes were dark as he held a sword, rubbing his thumb along the blade. His gaze looked back in the direction of the camp as his hand tightened around the hilt of a short sword, causing the cuts on his knuckles to crack open. A loud call from the woods caught his attention, and he set the sword down and looked towards the woodline beyond the field.

Faine was leading the second horse up to the cart, its back covered with several sacks loaded with their belongings. "I packed everything I could. I had to leave some of your books behind, though. I don't think we could take 'em all on the ship. But I made sure to grab your favorites. I also grabbed this," Faine said, tossing a small bag to Skara. "It looks like your bones and runes. I thought you might want it."

Catching the bag, Skara looked inside and gave a quick nod to Faine before he climbed back onto the cart and settled down on a small bundle of blankets he had made in the corner.

"Thank you for grabbing these," Renna said, looking through the bag of books and herbs. I can sell what I don't need when we get to Mivara."

"Speaking of which," Faine said, pulling out the map he had picked up in Javadi's shop, "here we are, and here's where we're going. Cutting through the forest south will get us to Mivara, and when we find a ship, we can go east across the Sanjal Sea until we hit the Grey Wastes. From what I've heard, there were a few towns along the coast there, but they're empty."

"Not completely empty," Renna said, looking up from the map.

"What do you mean, not completely?" Braig said.

"There are undead there."

"I'd not call that empty then," Braig said as he turned to look at Faine.

Faine scratched the back of his head and rested his hands on the wall of the cart. "So it's not completely empty. It doesn't have people in it. Well, living people. But from what I hear, the dead there are so scattered that you hardly see any. I don't think we'll have any trouble getting in and out."

Skara laid on his bundle of blankets and listened to the three talk about the potential dangers and undead in the Wastes. Picking at a hole in the box beside him, he stuck his finger through and tapped at the bottle inside. "What choice is there?" he said quietly.

"What?" Faine said, leaning over the edge of the wagon.

"I said, what choice do we have?"

"There's always a choice," Faine said, "you just have to choose wisely."

"And the wise choice is to get the stone before someone else does. If Braig was able to see it in his dreams, how long do you think it will be before the person that bought him finds someone else that might help, or at least not hold up under the pressure of being tortured?" Skara said, sitting up and looking at the three.

Renna nodded her head. "He's right. If Braig has seen the stone, there's a good possibility that others have too."

"Then we better get there first," Faine said, moving the bags off the horse and into the wagon.

Tying the packhorse to the back of the cart, Faine moved his horse to the front and began leading the way down the old road. "We all ready to move?" he said, turning the horse in a tight circle on the road to look back at the wagon. "We have a long, dark road ahead of us."

The Broken Temple

The road south out of Banrielle was long and arduous. It had been nearly a week since the wagon had left, and there was still over a week of hard travel before arriving in Mivara. As the cart rattled over the rut-filled road, the cold rain gathered in deep puddles and turned the once hard-packed earth into thick mud that gathered around the wheels, causing them to slide and stick as the horses struggled to pull the weight.

"We can't keep going like this," Renna said, pulling her woolen blanket tighter around her shoulders.

Looking back into the wagon, she could see Skara wrapped up and huddled near a crate in the corner, his face showing a miserable look as the rain ran down his cheeks. His body shook as the water gathered in drops on the wool blanket around him and dripped down to soak into the wooden planks of the wagon.

"We have to stop until this storm lets up before we end up getting stuck or risk the horse throwing an ankle," Braig said, guiding the horses to the side of the road away from the ruts. Faine pulled his hood over his head and kicked his horse into a trot and rode away from the wagon, scouting ahead for a place to rest for the night. Nearly a mile down the road, he reined to a stop at a fork and squinted his eyes as he peered through the trees in both directions. Just around the corner to his right, he thought he could make out what looked like a structure in a small clearing, but the edges of the trees seemed to blend together in the rain, and he couldn't be sure.

Striding forward, he made his way around the bend and saw a lone wooden building standing in the middle of a field surrounded by a broken wooden fence. Guiding his horse through the open gate, he tied it to a post and looked around the field. The grass was overgrown, and vines climbed over the building, snaking their way into the cracks between the boards, prying them loose. The building had two carved statues, one on each side of the double doors, but they were too weatherworn to make out what deity they may have represented. Opening the door, Faine drew his sword and crept inside.

The smell of old, damp wood, mold, and the faint sickly smell of rot filled the room. The roof had a large hole near the back corner, and water poured in, splashing off of a long bench that sat directly underneath, filling the room with a low drumming noise as the water tapped against the wood. The faded grey planks on the walls were warped and covered in patches of dark-colored moss that gathered in uneven clumps along the baseboards. Tattered strips of fabric hung from the bare rafters overhead, and Faine could barely make out the faded symbols of several deities painted on the tattered pieces of bright cloth.

Stained glass from the windows laid in piles on the floor, and a broken wooden podium stood near the front of the room; the sight of which filled him with a fleeting feeling of guilt and sadness, which he quickly shook off, thinking this wasn't the time or place for nostalgia.

Walking between the benches, Faine crept down the middle walkway, looking down the rows of seats for any movement. Reaching the back of the temple, he used his sword to push open a set of doors that led to a small back room. The doors squeaked slightly before stopping on their hinges only partially open. Clenching his left hand into a fist as the sound echoed off the walls, he grimaced and bit lightly at his finger as he pushed the doors open the rest of the way and looked around the room, hoping nothing was around to hear the noise.

The room was bare aside for a single chair and a small chest that sat in the corner of the room near an unbroken window. As he lifted open the lid to the box, several black roaches crawled out from inside and scurried down the chest and under the floorboards. There were several candles in the bottom of the box, along with a stack of paper that had partially dissolved in the moisture. Picking up a sheet of paper, he held it to the light and tried to make out the blurred words. "Something about graves and the forest," he said, dropping the paper and grabbing the candles before he closed the lid.

Setting the candles on the chair, Faine looked out the back window and saw rows of stone tablets surrounded by tall, brown grass sticking out of the ground. Pushing open the back door and stepping out into the rain, he sloshed through the grass and squatted down next to one of the stones and brushed the dead leaves away into a pile. "A gravestone," he said, running his hand over the rough surface. "Lots of gravestones."

Looking around the small plot of land, he could see nearly twenty graves scattered around the grounds. His eyes darted from stone to stone until they reached the woodline just past the clearing. Tilting his head to the side, he strained to look deeper into the forest. The trees were gnarled and broken at their bases and looked as if they had been stacked together to form some kind of structure. Dead cedar boughs covered the top of the wooden posts, and a thick bed of leaves and grass were piled underneath.

Thinking that it must have been a pavilion that had collapsed, Faine sheathed his sword and ran back to his horse. Pulling himself up onto the saddle, he rode back towards the wagon.

"Did you find anything?" Braig said, seeing Faine riding towards them.

"There's an old temple up ahead. It doesn't look like anyone's been there in a long time. It's not perfect, but it's a lot better than being out here. We can put the wagon and horses on the side of the building. There should be enough of an overhang to keep them fairly dry."

Giving the reins a snap, Braig urged the horses on, keeping them on the side of the road as they followed Faine. Pulling the wagon close to the building, they unhitched the horses and tied them to a nearby tree, giving them enough slack to move. Moving their blankets and gear inside, they set them in a pile and pulled a long pew in front of the double doors in the front and back of the room. Spreading out their bedrolls near the fireplace, they broke off pieces of the benches, tossing several into the hearth and throwing the rest into another pile that could be added through the night.

Using her magic, Renna started a fire and began digging through her pack for some dry clothes. "I hate being in wet clothes," she said, facing away from the others as she pulled off her shirt and tossed it to the floor beside her. Her shoulders and back were firm and taut, her muscles flexing as she slid her arms through the sleeves. Her pale green skin was covered in scars running in different directions across her back and down to her waistline. Pulling the shirt over her head, she picked up her wet clothing and set it near the fire to dry.

Noticing the scars, Braig glanced over at Faine, who only looked back before slightly shrugging. Thinking that this wasn't the time ask about how she got them, he pulled a piece of dried meat from his pack and began to chew absently, closing his eyes and leaning back onto his bedroll. Listening to the sounds of the crackling fire, he let his limbs fall to his side, feeling the stiffness ease from his aching muscles as he quickly fell asleep.

THE SKY WAS DARK, AND lightning split the clouds as Braig walked onto the desolate field. The dry, blackened soil beneath his feet crumbled under his boots, and his throat felt dusty and raw. Filtered light illuminated the landscape around him, and he could see rolling hills that seemed to stretch out to meet the horizon. Large black stones were scattered across the field and stabbed upwards towards the sky. The sparse trees that dotted the hills were short and twisted, their grey branches covered in long, sharp thorns with deep red tips. In the distance, he could see a tall, spiraling tower, reaching high into the darkened sky, its walls surrounded in a faint aura of blue flame.

Covering his face to shield his eyes from the blowing dust, Braig gritted his teeth and made his way towards the dark tower. A slight hum filled his ears as he grew closer, and he could see the faint silhouette of several dark masses gliding between the jutting stones as he pushed forward. Pulling his shirt over his mouth, he coughed as the black dust swirled around him, coating his lips and beard with a thick black powder. Catching movement out of the corner of his eye, he turned his head and saw a naked, pale man limping towards him from behind one of the stones in the distance. His arms were outstretched, and his head flicked back and forth in the air as if he was following Braig's scent.

Reaching to his belt for his dagger, he felt the empty scabbard and glanced on the ground around him, hoping that it may have fallen out as he walked. Seeing no signs of it, he picked up a handful of black dust and held it tightly in his hands, ready to throw it at the man's face if it came to a fight. Brushing the dust out of his beard, he strode forward, reaching out his left arm, ready to fend off an attack.

The pale man shambled forward, his thin body covered with loose flesh that hung like a rumpled sheet hanging on a line to dry. Folds of skin hung off his narrow frame and trembled as he walked faster, his face darting from side to side. Readying his hand to throw, Braig planted his feet and watched the creature stumble forward, his eyes growing wide. The man had a large nose that sniffed furiously as he moved closer, but his eyes and mouth were shut tight, the upper eyelids and lip pulled over the lower and sewn closed with thick thread.

Breath catching in his throat, Braig dropped the handful of soil and covered his mouth, coughing harshly as the wind whipped the dust up around him. Looking towards the glowing tower in the distance, he took off in a sprint around the man, keeping distance between them as he ran. The pale man's hand reached for him, his long bony fingers wriggling and clenching as he pulled empty air towards his sewn mouth.

Passing well beyond the man's reach, Braig could feel an intense hunger fill his body. Visions of large plates of food filled his head, and he could see plump arms and thick fingers digging utensils into rich desserts before shoveling them into a waiting mouth. He could see fattened legs struggling to climb a set of stairs before falling to the basement to hit with a thud as the stairs gave way beneath him. He felt the fear and uncertainty of waking up blind and unable to speak, a sense of insatiable emptiness growing inside as fingers ripped at the unyielding threads binding eyelids and lips tightly shut.

Shaking his head, Braig cleared the visions from his mind and pushed closer to the tower. His legs burned as he sprinted past grotesque figures emerging from behind rocks or drifting through the shadows. As the lightning flashed, he could see the distorted bodies of men and women lurking in the shadows, forming a loose circle around him.

"You shouldn't be here."

Turning around, Braig could see a cloaked figure standing only several yards away. His long, black hair hung loosely over his shoulders and blew in wisps around his pale, sharp features, his pointed ears pushing through several knots. His deep blue eyes cut like a knife into Braig as he scowled and stepped closer, teeth flashing under his cracked lips.

"You're not the one I've been waiting for," the elf said as he took another step towards Braig. "You don't belong here. Not yet, anyway."

"Who are you?" Braig said, looking at the distorted and bloated bodies around him.

"You know who I am..."

A bright light flashed in front of Braig's eyes, his head rolling back as visions pierced his mind. He could see the elf standing at the top of a tower, looking down at men, elves, dwarves, and orcs working in chains below him. The light flashed again. He could see the enslaved workers revolting, breaking their bonds and fighting their way free as arrows flew around them. Flash. He watched as a hammer struck blow after blow on white-hot metal, forging the long blade of a sword before being quenched. Flash. He saw the sword placed in a circle of runes, surrounded by high elves strengthening it with magic. Flash. The elf placed his hands on the sword and called down a golden dragon out of the sky and held it in place with spells and enchanted chains. As it was held in place, the elf used the sword to slay the dragon, catching its blood in his hands and consuming it.

The light flashed again in Braig's eyes, and heat surged through his body. He watched as the elf stood in the tower, blood pouring from his hands and mouth as the tower began to shake. A great chasm split across the land, sending sections of the town of Ruwen down the deep fissure and releasing dark magic upon the face of Hiraeth. Flash. He watched as the elf led his Fallen armies against the forces of the Reverent in a great battle. After stabbing Tuvak with Uvereth, the defiled blade, light exploded from the slain man and engulfed the elf, destroying his body and sending the Fallen armies fleeing the battlefield.

The visions faded from Braig's mind as he stared at the elf. "You're Emin, the Defiler. The high elf that released dark magic and broke the world with his hubris. It was you, and all of the Thiarri caught up in your lies that brought darkness into the world. You thought you had the right to control anything you laid your eyes on!" Braig clenched his fists as he took a step towards Emin. "You kept us as slaves and tormented my people."

"The darkness was already there, hiding behind every good intention or white lie. And let's not forget, I also created your people," Emin said as he leaned against a nearby rock. "If not for me, your kind wouldn't exist."

"That doesn't give you the right to keep us in chains and use us as you see fit!" Braig's face was distorted in anger and fear as he noticed the circle of looming bodies growing steadily closer.

"This isn't the time or place for this. You're not the one that I'm waiting for, and it looks as though we both have more pressing matters to deal with. Now, wake up!"

"Wake up!" Braig heard again, his body shaking. "Wake up, damn you!"

Braig's eyes opened to the dim light of the temple, Faine standing over him, shoving him with his foot and shouting down at him.

"On your feet!" Faine said, shoving his boot into Braig's side. The silver blade of his sword reflected the fire burning in the fireplace as he held the sword close to his body, ready to strike.

A loud thud echoed through the room as something heavy slammed against the front doors, rocking the bench that had been pushed in front of it. Scrambling to his feet, Braig grabbed his sword and shield and stood next to Faine and Renna, ready to fight whatever was about to break into the room.

Crouching in the corner near the doors, Skara pushed himself against the wall and gripped his daggers, ready to lash out at the creature from behind as it burst through. Looking over, he watched as Faine and Braig moved in front of Renna, providing cover while she readied her bow and stacked her arrows against the wall. Keeping his daggers tightly in his hands, he leaned against the wall and covered his head as another hard thump knocked several boards loose and sent them falling just feet away.

"It's going to bring the building down if we don't do something!" Faine said, looking over at Renna.

"Then I say we let it inside," Braig said, growling and hitting his sword against his shield.

Faine turned his eyes towards Braig and gave him a confused look. "Are you crazy?"

"We have to do something. It's either die getting crushed or die fighting," Braig said as the banging on the door stopped.

"Wait," Renna said, looking out of the windows. "It's moving."

Stepping up to the side window, they looked out into the darkness and strained their eyes as they looked for any movement. Through the breaks in the clouds, the light of the two moons shined brightly down from the star-flecked black sky, illuminating the wet field and trees around them. Seeing a flash of white darting behind the trees a short distance away, Skara leaned his head out the window and listened.

"There it is," Skara said, pointing. "It's going for the horses."

"By the stone, what is it?"

Skara looked up at Braig. "It's a myrrow."

A loud whinny broke out as the horses stamped and pulled at the ropes that held them in place. A hard thud shook the building as the bloody carcass of a horse was thrown against the wooden planks. Swallowing hard, Faine pushed his head out of the window and looked at the crumpled body just outside. The horse's legs were broken and twisted, and large gashes tore through its neck and side, spilling its innards into a steaming pile on the ground next to it.

Pulling his head back inside, Faine leaned against the wall, closed his eyes, and took a deep breath. "What are we gonna do?"

Skara looked around the room and up at the hole in the ceiling. "We can get on the roof. Me and Renna. Then you two could circle around outside and draw its attention. When it turns to follow you, I can cut it from behind, and she can hit it with arrows."

"Attack it from both sides. That might just keep us all alive," Braig said, looking up at Faine. "And it's better than waiting for that thing to bring the building down around us."

"It could work," Renna said as she looked up at the hole. "Quickly, help me move a bench."

Faine and Braig grabbed the ends of one of the long benches and propped it against the wall under the hole, setting the podium next to the upturned pew.

"You be careful," Faine said, clenching his jaw.

Smiling slightly, Renna climbed up onto the podium, pulling herself onto the bench and into the rafters above. Nodding to Faine and Brain, Skara quickly scampered up behind her, following her out of the hole onto the roof.

"Are you ready?" Braig said, adjusting his shield.

Faine glanced up at the tattered strips of cloth hanging from the rafters, the words and images of the deities nearly faded away, leaving only blotches and stains where their hallowed words once rested. Shaking off a chill running up his spine, he let his heart harden against the lost words and turned his eyes away from the gently blowing fabric. "I am."

Pulling the heavy bench away from the back doors, the two hurried through the small room and into the waiting shadows of the forest. Keeping low and watching their footing to avoid stepping on anything that would make too much noise, the two positioned themselves in the woodline, glancing at the roof to see Skara and Renna crouching on the wooden shingles at the highest point.

Peering around the trunk of a tree, Braig and Faine could see the hideous creature hunched over the dead horse, its long fingers digging into its torso, ripping off chunks of flesh and pushing them greedily into its mouth. Its spine and ribs pushed out against its grey skin that looked thin and tightly stretched over the protruding bones. The myrrow's limbs were long and spindly and pulled close to its body as it ate.

Shifting on his feet to get a better look, Braig stepped on a small twig, snapping it loudly beneath his heavy boot. Stopping dead in his tracks, he looked over at the creature as its head turned sharply in their direction, the small holes on the side of its head listening for any sounds. Its blood-drenched mouth quivered into a snarl as sharp teeth gnashed at the flesh inside its quivering maw.

The myrrow slowly turned, standing nearly eight feet tall as it stretched out its long limbs and looked towards the forest. Faine could see the fresh blood dripping from its sharp teeth and claws as he shrunk back against a tree, trying to stay out of sight as the bony creature stepped forward. The horse had been almost picked clean and eaten, and the creature's stomach was distended and bulging, shaking as it moved. Its long limbs bent and twisted as it turned its head from side to side, sniffing the air with two dark holes where a nose should have been.

Startled by a loud yell beside him, Faine quickly turned his gaze towards Braig as the dwarf darted from the bushes, running wildly with his sword raised and shield held close to his body. Gripping his sword, Faine dashed out behind him, pulling a dagger from his belt.

The myrrow crouched defensively as it swung a long arm, knocking forcefully into Braig's shield, sending him flying back to land hard in the mud. Dodging a swing of the myrrow's clawed hand, Faine slashed with his sword and dagger, drawing a cut down the creature's arm.

"Put an arrow its shoulder on the left," Skara said, running down the slanted roof.

Nocking an arrow, Renna pulled back on the string and let loose. The cord thrummed as the arrow flew past Skara and struck the myrrow in the shoulder just as he jumped off the edge of the temple roof, his dagger in his right hand. Landing hard against the myrrow's back, Skara grabbed the protruding arrow shaft and held on as he stabbed his blade into the creature's side.

Shrieking in pain, the creature reached its spindly arms over its shoulders and tried to pull the goblin off its back. Skara twisted and moved, dodging its clawed fingers as he clung to the arrow shaft, stabbing and cutting wildly. The myrrow writhed and fell back, slamming its shoulder against the wall, its hard bones digging into Skara as it tried to shake him loose.

Seeing the small opening of a broken window behind him, Skara let go of the arrow just as the creature crushed against the wall, sending him flying towards the temple floor, knocking the wind from his lungs as he landed on his back.

Outside, Braig climbed back to his feet and charged at the myrrow, planting his feet and blocking the powerful swings as its claws scraped down his shield, leaving deep scratches across the paint. Moving in to strike, his sword swung down hard against the myrrow's knee, bouncing off of solid bone just beneath its thin skin. Leaping back as its long arm swung in a wide arc, Braig and Faine circled the creature.

As the myrrow reached out its hand to try to pull out the shaft in its back, Renna nocked another arrow and pulled the string back as far as she could. Just as its fingers began to grip the shaft, she fired, pinning its bony hand to its left shoulder, the arrow emerging through the front of its torso. Loosing another arrow into its spine, it dropped to its knees and thrashed wildly, dark blood oozing from its wounds.

Running forward, Braig spun on his feet, turning to block the myrrow's left arm with his shield as it swung. Pivoting and stepping in closer, he continued his spin and swung his sword horizontally in a backhand slash and sliced open the beast's stomach. Coming in behind him, Faine slashed downwards, crossing over Braig's cut, opening the creature's belly in a cross pattern.

The myrrow screamed in pain and clutched at its bulging stomach as the weight of the horse it had eaten pulled its innards through its long fingers, sliding out into a thick pile on the ground. The creature fell forward onto its torso, half-chewed meat and blood spilling around its body as it gasped for breath.

Leaping from the window behind them, Skara landed on the myrrow's back, stabbing his daggers into its neck, severing the arteries. Breathing hard, he looked up at Faine and Braig. "You can't be too sure with these things. Better to be safe."

Running his hands through his tangled hair, Faine looked at the myrrow lying on the ground. "I should have known there'd be something here. I saw something about the graves and the woods on an old note, but I couldn't make out anything else. I guess that's why no one's been here in a while." His face contorted in disgust as thick blood poured across the ground, giving off a smell of rotting flesh. Covering his nose with his arm, he looked down at Skara. "Do you think we have to worry about any more of these things?"

"No," Skara said, wiping off his daggers and sheathing them, "They're territorial, and they'll kill each other if there's another one within a few miles."

Looking over at Braig, Faine sheathed his weapons. "You alright? You took a pretty good hit there."

"Aye, I'm fine. It'll take more than a bump to take me down. But I don't know how you didn't get crushed though," Braig glanced over at Skara and then at the window. "If it hadn't been for that window..."

"Sometimes I get lucky," Skara said, rubbing his fingers lightly over the upper left side of his chest, tracing something under his shirt with his fingertips.

Faine took several steps back and looked up at the roof. "Everything good up there, Ren?"

"I'm fine. I wasn't sure if we were going to make it out of that one, though." Renna said, peering down from the broken roof.

Skara pulled the arrows out the myrrow's back, rolling one of the shafts between his fingers as he glanced up. "We may not have if you missed your mark with any of those arrows. If you would have missed-"

"You would have bounced off this thing's back like a little pebble hitting a stone." Faine laughed and nudged the creature with his foot. "Gods, this thing stinks. Let's get back inside."

Walking back into the broken temple, they closed the back door and moved into the main room, barring the way with a heavy bench as Renna climbed down onto the rafters and dropped to the floor.

Taking her arrows from Skara, she placed them back into her quiver. "So, what should we do now?"

"We should get some rest," Faine said, sitting down on one of the water-stained benches. "You three get some sleep, and I'll take the first watch."

Shaking his head, Braig stepped up to the fireplace and threw a few more pieces of wood on the glowing coals. "No, I'll take the watch. I almost slept through this whole mess because of some damned dream, and I'm not ready to sleep again yet. I can always nod off in the wagon if I need to. Can't be any more than a few hours before sunup anyway."

Faine stepped towards his bedroll and pulled out his sword and dagger and laid them down on the floor. "If you insist, I could use some sleep. I'd rather not fall off my horse tomorrow."

Skara moved his bedroll closer to the fire and pulled the blanket over his head as Renna walked over and sat next to Braig on the bench.

"What was the dream about?"

Braig looked down at his hands and pulled at his fingers, cracking his knuckles. "It wasn't anything. It was just a dream."

"I'd really like to hear it if you don't mind telling me," Renna said, placing her hand on Braig's shoulder. "I don't think I'm ready to sleep yet, either."

Braig stiffened briefly as her hand touched his shoulder. He glanced up into her eyes, one light, one dark, and relaxed slightly. "It's like I was somewhere else. It's hard to tell sometimes if things are visions or just dreams. Most of the time they're as unclear as muddy water, but this time was different; I knew what I was saying and doing. I've never had that happen before."

Braig went on and told Renna about what he had seen, keeping his voice low as he talked about what had happened with Emin, occasionally glancing over at Faine and Skara lying next to the fire, unsure if they were listening. Wringing his hands together, he looked up at Renna. "I don't know why I'm telling you all this, and I don't know what to make of it. What do you think?"

Leaning back against the bench, she crossed one of her arms over her chest and tapped on one of her tusks with her finger. "Well, if it was a vision, why were you there? And what did Emin mean when he said you weren't the one he was waiting for? It's been thousands of years since he was killed, maybe his spirit has been waiting in Thodun all this time."

"Thodun?"

Renna pursed her lips, thinking about what she had read about the land of the dead. "It's the place between life and death. If someone dies and they aren't accepted by their deity, they can be sent there to pay their debt. And sometimes, for whatever reason, souls can get trapped there."

"Trapped there, or held there to wait for someone? Is it possible for someone to stay by choice?"

"I can't answer that. I've read stories about people traveling to Thodun and returning to tell the tale, but I thought those were just stories. But if Emin said he was waiting for someone, there's a good chance that he could be waiting for another thousand years. Time is different there."

Braig's head was flooded with thoughts about Emin as he looked over at his shield against the wall. But as Renna had said, if time was different there, it could be another thousand years before anything happens. "Then, only time will tell."

Renna nodded and stood, stretching her arms as she walked over to her bedroll. "Speaking of which, we don't have much time left before morning, so I'm going to try to get some rest. Just shout if another myrrow shows up."

"Don't say that," Faine said, turning over in his blankets, wiping a bit of drool off of his cheek. "No more myrrows."

Braig stroked his beard as he watched the doors and waited for the sun to rise. As the hours passed, he thought about what he had seen in his dream and what Renna had said. But why was he there, and why did it feel so real? Was something or someone sending him a warning that Emin was trying to break out of Thodun and pick up where he had left off. Even if there was a way to escape, he had been killed a long time ago, and things were different now. And if he did somehow break free, would there be any way to stop him? Shaking the thoughts out of his head, he watched out the window, trying to keep his mind clear until he could see the sun breaking over the horizon.

"Time to wake up," he said, nudging each of the three awake.

Faine groaned and rolled over off his bedroll, watching Skara as he stretched his arms and rotated his upper body to pop his back.

"I hate sleeping on wood," Faine said, face down on the floor. "It's so hard."

Rolling up her blankets, Renna picked up her bedroll and began kicking Faine lightly in the side. "Then get up off the floor. Let's get packed and get out of here."

Pushing himself up, Faine grabbed his blankets and pack and slid the bench away from the door. Heading to the cart outside, he looked down at the half-eaten horse and sighed. "Why did it have to eat my horse? I liked that horse."

Hitching two horses to the wagon and saddling up the third, he pulled the cart away from the side of the building and stopped out front. Putting a large stone in front of the wheel, he pulled out several pieces of fruit and bread and set them out on a piece of cloth, eating absently as he stared at the temple and waited for the others.

After packing their items in the cart and taking the necessary morning breaks before leaving, Faine moved the stone away from the wheel and mounted his horse as Renna, Skara, and Braig climbed onto the wagon. Eating their breakfast as they pulled away from the temple, they were glad to have made it through the night and to be back on the road.

The White Tower

Drasa strode down the long stone corridor, his white cloak gently flowing behind him. Rows of windows lined the walls, looking out over the sprawling city below. Straightening his burgundy tunic, he stared at the ornate wooden door at the end of the hall. Taking a moment to collect his thoughts, he walked to an open window and leaned against the cold stone frame, looking out over the city below.

Ethilios, the city of light, radiated out in large circles with a tall white structure— Unaeyl, the mage tower of Bright Harbor—standing at its center, with the castle of House Egara on a hill overlooking the port and merchant district of the city just a short distance away.

Below, the city was alive with trade and the production of goods: fisheries built on the water to the east; fertile farmland and lumber mills to the west; and stonemasons to the south, all able to sell locally, or ship their goods far across the land or sea on one of the many established trade routes.

Merchants, farmers, townsfolk, and performers crowded the streets, selling their wares from shops or wagons, performing for onlookers, or visiting one of the many inns or pubs; all under the protection of the crown as long as they abided by the king's laws.

Various temples stood throughout the city, each with shrines to the deities of the Reverent and the Unbroken, allowing free worship of one or several gods. Any worship of the Fallen deities was outlawed and punishable by fine, imprisonment, or in some cases, death. Guildhalls representing healers, fighters, scribes, mages, and many others dotted the city, but none had been able to help their king.

For hundreds of years, House Egara had ruled over Ethilios, building it and watching it grow; and now, Drasa thought, it could all topple if things were left as they were. Taking a deep breath, he walked to the heavy door, knocking softly before entering the dimly lit room.

The single large window was open, the sheer drapes blowing in the ocean breeze, letting in fresh air to the slightly stagnant chamber. The room was decorated with crests and flags from the surrounding lands that House Egara kept as allies, and books lined the shelves around a four-poster bed near the back wall. Setting down her book, Drasa's mother looked towards the door.

"How is he today?" Drasa said, standing next to the edge of the bed, watching his father's chest rise and fall with slow, steady breaths.

The king's face was pale and gaunt, his beard and hair long but neatly trimmed. A thick blanket covered his body from the waist down, and his arms were folded over his stomach. The soft sheets were deep red, making his skin look even paler as he laid nearly motionless on the bed.

"The same as yesterday. Still no change, I'm afraid," Samari said, motioning to the chair next to her.

"Have the healers been here today?"

"They have. But you know there's nothing they can do. They've all tried."

"I know," Drasa said, looking over at his mother. "But I feel like we're missing something. I have the acolytes and scribes scouring the library for something that can help, but there's just not much written about the sleeping death. I don't understand why no one has been able to find a cure yet." Drasa gripped his mother's hand and looked over at his father. "I'll find something. There's a way, we're just not seeing it."

"I know you will, dear. It just takes time."

"And time is something we're running out of. Every day it seems like things are getting worse. On the surface, the water is still; but underneath, there's a strong current dragging down anything in its grasp."

Samari looked at her son, her mouth tightening into a thin line. "You know that's not true. Your father has kept the city safe and prosperous. And you'll do the same when the time comes. You're strong and can continue to lead our people down the right path."

Drasa reached his hand towards the small table sitting next to the bed and carefully picked up his father's crown. Running his hand over the silver filigree, he let his finger rest over a small amber stone inlaid into the metal. The crown had been passed down from king to king for generations. Its steel bent and reshaped, its beautiful metal shined and reworked, the worn stones removed and replaced — every stone but one.

"And what if the path is no longer clear?" he said, letting his mind drift as he rubbed the smooth surface of the stone.

"Sometimes we have to let our hearts guide us, not just our minds or some council of old fools who think they know what's best. You're an Egara, and you'll do what's right."

A sharp knock on the door pulled Drasa from his thoughts as he laid the crown back on the table. "Enter."

The door opened slowly, letting in a cross breeze that blew out a lone candle burning on a nearby desk. Two guards entered the room, partially closing the door behind them. "Begging your pardon, lord. There's an urgent message for you from Senna. She's waiting downstairs for you."

"Tell her I'm on my way."

"Yes, lord," the guards said, both placing their fists over their heart before leaving, closing the door behind them.

"Duty calls, mother," Drasa said, pushing himself up from his chair and kissing his mother on the forehead. "Keep an eye on him, won't you?"

"I always do," she said, watching him walk towards the door. "Son,"

"Yes, mother?"

"Your father knows what you're doing for him and the kingdom."

Drasa smiled weakly and nodded, stepping through the door. "If only he did."

Walking down the long corridor, Drasa hurried down the stairs, turning into a small antechamber that led into a large study. Running his hand along the wall, he felt a cool draft escaping between several of the bricks and leaned forward, pushing open the hidden doorway in the small room. Pushing the door closed behind him, he stood quietly in the darkness.

Feeling a tingle in the air, the hair on his arms stood on end as the torches leading down the stairwell sprang to life, sputtering bits of spark onto the stone stairs below them. As he descended the stairs, he could hear the faint sound of the torches being extinguished behind him, leaving the pathway up shrouded in darkness.

Reaching the bottom of the stairs, a dark-haired woman in a long, black surcoat and pants greeted him with a slight bow.

"My lord."

Nodding his head in response, Drasa held out his hand towards the tunnel ahead of him that connected the castle to the lower level of the white tower. The passageway was long and dark with moisture dripping from the ceiling, landing in small puddles on the cobbled stone floor. The rounded walls were reasonably stable, with only several small cracks letting in bits of dirt that pushed its way through the holes. Above them, they could hear the rumbling of cartwheels rolling down the street and the muffled conversations of the crowds of people talking above them, unaware that the prince and the archmage were passing right under their feet.

Aside from a small number of mages or castle staff, knowledge of the tunnels was kept hidden from nearly everyone. If word of the underground tunnels were to reach the wrong ears, it could put the tower and the castle in danger; and in the coming times, it was a risk they couldn't afford.

"So, what's the urgent message?" Drasa said, following closely behind the woman.

"I've received word from the tower in Sonosa. It looks as if the brothers that were hired to keep the dwarf safe are all dead."

Drasa stopped and waited for Vaeloryn to unlock the door leading into the lower chambers of the tower. "I can't say I didn't see something like this coming. Plans rarely work the way they should. What happened?"

"Not here. You never know who could be listening. Let's speak in my chambers, and we can discuss the issue in more detail."

Locking the door behind her, the pair climbed the stairs to the ground floor of the tower. Opening the door slightly, Vaeloryn peered out around the hidden door behind the bookcase before stepping out between long rows of books and scrolls in the back corner of the general library. Walking quickly through the main hall, she pulled open a thin, decorative gate that led into a small metal-framed box.

"After you, my lord," she said.

Pursing his lips, Drasa looked from the opening to the numerous flights of stairs before stepping inside. "I don't like this device. I don't trust it."

Smiling to herself, Vaeloryn stepped in and closed the gate. "It's about trusting me. Or would you rather walk up all the stairs to my rooms at the top of the tower?"

Drasa held on to the front of the gate as the lift began to rise. "I'd rather not."

"Good. It's quite simple, really. The box is attached to a counterweight above us. By controlling the flow of magic, I can make the box, and us, slightly lighter. This lets the box be raised slowly to the floor we need. And it's enchanted to lower itself slowly back to the first floor when we step out. It's about using slight amounts of energy to allow something to work naturally, that's all."

"I would feel more comfortable if people hadn't died in it."

"People died," Vaeloryn said as she opened the gate to her study, "because they didn't possess the skills to make it work properly. It keeps them in check. If they can't harness the slight amounts of magic to make something simple work, how they expect to do greater spells. And," she smirked, "it makes them study harder, so they don't have to keep walking up countless stairs."

"How very diabolical," Drasa said, sitting in a chair near the fireplace and glancing down at the stack of unburned logs. "Would you mind?"

"Fyrana," Vaeloryn said, waving her hand towards the hearth as she sat across from Drasa. A sharp crackle sounded from the fireplace as a flash of blue flames engulfed the logs before softening to a glowing orange.

"So, tell me what happened."

"I received word from a messenger in Sonosa. He said that the dwarf had escaped with a goblin, half-orc, and an elf. The brothers and their mercenary band were all killed. There are rumors that necromancy was used."

"And what of the stone? Was it found before the dwarf escaped?"

Vaeloryn shook her head. "No. I don't think the stone was ever there to begin with."

"And you don't think the necromancy had anything to do with the stone?"

"I don't. I believe there was a mage there. Possibly aberrant, but strong for being untrained," she said.

"And which way were they heading when they left Banrielle?"

"Our scout says they were on the road heading south. Unless they cross the mountains and manage to survive the Corsaro desert, they'll be heading to Mivara."

Drasa clenched his teeth as he gripped the arm of the chair. "So, not only did we lose that lying, thieving dwarf, but we've lost several good warriors! And now he's traveling with a mage, and the gods only know who else. And to make it worse, we're still no closer to finding the stone."

"We're still working on the others, but no one has told us anything useful. Any of the oracles or mystics we've spoken to so far have yet to have a vision of the stones."

"And have you tried forcing them?"

"Yes. Any attempts, whether through pleasantries or torture, have yielded nothing substantial. It seems like the visions are either random or meant for a certain few."

"And which do you think it is?"

"I believe it's random. There are so many streams of magic and energy that one single person wouldn't be able to see them all. It's like a mirror reflecting an image too large for one person to see or comprehend, so it's broken into smaller pieces. Or shattered visions, if you will. The vision is there, but scattered and broken like a puzzle."

Drasa rose from his chair and stood in front of the fire, warming his hands. "We'll get our answers one way or another. The stones are out there; we just have to find them. Or, more accurately, we have to find someone to lead us to them.

I want you to instruct the mages to look for anyone with any signs of clairvoyant abilities. Have them sent to you and report your findings to me after you test them. We want to encourage their visions naturally before we move on to harsher methods. We can't have word getting out about any experiments gone awry in our tower."

"And what of the dwarf and his companions. It's not too late to catch them."

"I want you to take word back to the mage tower in Sonosa. Tell them to send a raven south to Mivara with the message to be on the lookout for any of the four. Let them know I want word of the bounty to fall on the right ears and that I'll pay three gold for each, provided they're alive. And if we find one, the others won't be far away. When they're captured, have them send word immediately to the Sun Spear docked in Braval. Tell them my ship can be there within a day for them."

Vaeloryn nodded her head and walked over to a large table covered in scrolls and small bottles of colored liquids. Clearing a section to work, she unrolled a piece of leather and placed several small stones on its surface. Uncorking one of the bottles, she let several drops of dark green liquid fall onto each of the smooth rocks before placing them in a pouch at her waist.

"And what should I tell the temple about their lost brothers? They're going to want retribution?" she said, strapping a sword and dagger onto her belt.

"Assure the brothers that those responsible will be punished for all to see. I'll make them wish they never interfered. But foul creatures do foul things; it's in their nature."

"Yes, my lord," Vaeloryn said, stepping into an intricately painted runic circle in the center of the room. Taking the dagger from its sheath, she removed one of the stones from her pouch and placed it on the ground in front of her as she kneeled. Cutting a shallow line across her forearm, she let her blood drip down onto the stone and mix with the green tincture, causing a small puff of acrid smoke to rise from its surface as it bubbled and hissed.

"Ental ama duin falza zen," she said, grabbing the stone off the floor.

The heat burned her palm as she held the stone out in front of her. The air around her hand bent and rippled like disturbed water before being sucked inwards like a whirlpool. Before her stood a swirling portal that opened into a vast field of dark stalks of weather-rotted wheat. The trees in the distance were bent and twisted against the fierce wind rushing over the hills. Lightning flashed, and she could feel the rumble of thunder reverberating in the air around her.

She had always hated going into the Somber Vale, and this time was no different. There were creatures here that could tear you apart physically, mentally, or both. Some were even creations of your own nightmares brought to life. And once she stepped through the gate and released her spell, the portal would vanish, and she would have to brave the dangerous middle-realm, relying only on the subtle traces of magic that flowed like spider-silk on the wind to guide her to the closest keystone. And although hours or days could pass for her, only minutes would pass before she stepped through the portal at Sonosa; assuming she could find a gate to per-form the spell on to open a portal.

Rising to her feet, she sheathed her dagger and reached her hand into her pouch to make sure she had multiple stones. Unsure of what might be waiting on the other side of the portal, Vaeloryn pulled out a single stone and placed it in her tall boot for safekeeping. If she had to run or somehow lost her pouch, she wanted to make sure she had a way out, even if that meant having to make the long journey back to Sonosa on foot.

"Be careful in the Vale," Drasa said, moving over to peer into the portal. "Take some time to rest after you arrive. Things should run smoothly here for a couple days without you. But come back to me as soon as you hear word of their capture. With the reward I'm offering, it shouldn't take long for someone to find them."

"And what about your father? Do you have everything you need for him while I'm away?"

Drasa shook his head. "The priests and healers have all been to see him already, and no one can figure out how to stop the sleeping death. And I doubt anything will happen while your away. But don't worry, he's out of the way, and I don't plan on waking him up anytime soon. I have him where he needs to be."

Placing her hand over her heart, Vaeloryn bowed and stepped into the portal. "I'll be back as soon as I can," she said, her voice distorted through the rippling vortex.

"I hope your journey through the Vale is fast," Drasa said, stepping clear as the portal closed, leaving a slight buzzing in his ears.

Uncorking several of the bottles on the table to sniff at their contents, Drasa looked around the empty room, the air still tingling with energy. Feeling slightly uneasy, he reached inside a trunk near the wall and pulled out a long, tattered cloak, throwing it over his shoulders as he raised the hood and walked to the double wooden doors of Vaeloryn's chambers. Stepping out into the hallway, he looked over the balcony and down row after row of stairs leading down the ground floor. "Should have had her take me down first," he said, mumbling to himself as he started down the stairwell.

After descending to the bottom of the tower, Drasa leaned against an expertly crafted marble statue of Falinxa, letting the cold stone press briefly against his hot cheek before dabbing the sweat from his forehead and tying a thin piece of material over his face, obscuring his identity. Glancing around the room, he scampered towards the door, pulling his left leg behind him as if he had been injured.

Pulling the hood tighter around his head, he made his way down the city streets, avoiding contact with as many people as possible. There were plenty of cutpurses here, and he didn't have the time or patience to deal with any of the scum that flooded into the city. Turning onto the wharf, he headed for a small pub at the edge of the docks.

Hobbling through the door, he made his way to the back and fell hard onto a chair, stretching his leg out straight in front of him as he rubbed his knee.

"What'll it be?" a loud voice said, coming from across the room.

"Whatever's strong and cheap," Drasa said in a rough voice.

"Yeah, well, I ain't on the menu," the barmaid said, getting a laugh out of several of the people in the bar.

Drasa nodded his head and waved his hand, motioning for the whiskey on the back wall. "A double whiskey, then."

The barmaid raised her eyebrows and poured a double whiskey, spilling more than a few drops as she carried it to the table. "You got coin for this? You'll find no charity here."

Drasa pulled out a few coppers and set them on the table. "I need something else too."

"I already told you I ain't on the menu," she said, reaching out to take the coins.

"I'm not interested in that. If I wanted to feel dirty, I'd go roll around with pigs. No, there's another few coppers in it for you if you go tell Rogden I'm here."

"You want me to tell Rogden that you're here? If you know anything about 'im, you know he'll break you in half if you waste his time."

"You want the coppers or not?" Drasa said as he pulled out three coppers and held them in his hand.

"A'right, I'll take 'em."

Drasa closed his hand. "After you tell him I'm here."

"And who should I say is here, then?" the woman said, putting her hands on her hips.

"Tell him Leshok is here to see him."

"Very well, Leshok," the barmaid said, rolling her eyes. "You sit tight, he's out back. But if you're anyone he knows, he'll be right in. And I hope for both our sakes that you are. I really don't feel like cleanin' up your blood today."

Taking a sip of his whiskey, he watched the barmaid open the back door and head outside. Sticking his tongue out slightly, he looked down into his cup. The whiskey tasted like it had been mixed with saltwater. Or maybe the glass had been rinsed in the ocean. Pushing his drink to the side, he saw the back door swing open and the barmaid pointing to his table.

Ducking through the doorway was a muscular, shirtless man. His upper body was covered in tattoos, and a small gold ring hung from each nipple. Nodding to the man, Drasa kicked the empty seat across from out from the table and motioned for him to sit. As Rogden walked across the room, he reached behind his back and pulled out a darkly stained canvas bag and dropped it onto the table.

"You bring the coin?" Rogden said, leaning over the table.

"Don't you be forgetting me, now," the barmaid said, pushing in closer.

Drasa scowled under his face-wrap as he pulled out a small pouch. "Here's your coins, as promised," he said, handing the barmaid three coppers. "Now, off with you. I have business."

Feigning a curtsy, the woman grabbed the coins out of his hand and walked back over the bar.

"How many are in there?" Drasa said, eyeing the blood-stained bag.

Rogden leaned closer to the table. "There are seven."

"Seven? These are supposed to be pairs. What happened to the eighth?"

"The eighth managed to wiggle free before I could get it. And if I find it, it'll be in the next batch."

Pulling out seven silver coins and five coppers, he handed them to Rogden.

Shuffling through the coins, Rogden glowered down at Drasa. "Where's the rest?"

"It got away. But if I find it, it'll be in the next batch."

Laughing to himself, Rogden slapped the table as he put the coins in his pouch and looked down at the cloaked man. "Fair enough. Give me a month, and I'll get you some more."

"I'll be back when I see your ship come to port. And don't be afraid to get me something local if you can. I'll pay you for each pair, as per our arrangement."

Picking up the bag, Drasa hobbled out the door and onto the street. Cutting down an alley, he stopped behind a building and opened the bag and looked inside. Several pairs of fangs and green, black, or red ears filled his bag—trophies from the vile creatures he believed were a plague on this world.

The Roads of Mivara

The days passed quickly as the wagon rattled south towards Mivara. The rolling hills and forest around them had begun to flatten and stretch out in large fields filled with tall green grass and bright red flowers. The dark grey rain clouds that had followed them for most of the journey had broken and given way to clear a clear blue sky. Becoming increasingly warmer the farther they traveled, they had shed their woolen clothing for lighter pants and tunics and had to occasionally wipe beads of sweat from their foreheads.

Rounding a bend in the road just over a small hill, Renna pulled the wagon to a stop as the Sanguine Gulf came into full view. The smell of the ocean was heavy in the wind, blowing the last remnants of the cold forest out her bones. In the distance, she could see large ships dotting the coastline and rows of blue and green buildings lining the intersecting streets leading to the docks.

On the east side of the city were several fisheries with lines of ships waiting to sell the day's catch. A long string of buildings led off of the wharf and sailors walked the wooden dock between the rows of inns, shops, and pubs, shouting to one another as they went about their work. The center of the city stretched from the north entrance to the southern section and shoreline.

The heart of Mivara was made of long cobbled streets that crossed between bright, beautifully painted shops that bustled with activity as merchant wagons delivered goods and performers drew crowds in the square. The southern district of the city was full of taverns, inns, theatres, and entertainment halls; while the western portion held many of the homes in the area—although living spaces, both large and small, were scattered throughout every section of the city.

A broad smile crossed Renna's face as she shook Skara awake and looked over at Faine. "I can't believe we finally made it. It feels so nice to see something besides rain and trees."

Sitting up from the back of the wagon, Skara looked out between Renna and Braig's shoulders, his eyes going wide as he looked towards the blue water flecked with burgundy kelp.

Wheeling his horse around to face the wagon, Faine glanced over at Skara. "So, what do you think? A big change from living in the woods all those years."

Skara sat up with his hands tight on the back of the wooden bench in front of him. His eyes were wide as he looked out over the bustling city filled with colorful buildings of teal, green, blue, yellow, and red that stretched up to the shoreline. Closing his eyes, he could hear the faint sound of the waves crashing on the shore and the sound of laughter and music drifting up from the many inns and theatres. He thought about how dark Sonosa and Banrielle seemed to compared to the lively buildings and atmosphere here, but he also knew that just because it was bright on the outside, it didn't mean that it didn't have a dark side. And in his experience, the more people there were, the better the chances of it finding him.

Trying not to let his thoughts get the best of him, Skara looked over at Faine, his eyes still wide. "There're so many colors here. So many people."

"There are. But we'll only be here for several days at most, so we better make the best of it. And if you think it looks interesting from here, just wait 'til we get closer," Faine said, clicking his tongue as he gently nudged the horse forward.

Crossing through the gate, Faine stopped his horse at one of the crossroads. "It looks like there are quite a few inns around here. Anything catching your eye?"

"Something with soft beds and hard drinks," Braig said as he looked up and down the streets.

Renna gave the reins a light snap, keeping the horses at a steady pace. "Let's move a bit deeper into the city. We'll be closer to the theatres there."

Keeping his horse alongside the wagon, Faine looked up and down the lines of buildings as they made their way deeper into the city. Merchant stalls lined the side streets as vendors called out or carried their goods to the side of the wagon, holding them up for Braig and Renna to see.

"Move away from the cart!" Braig said, waving his hands towards the merchants, trying to shoo them away. "Unless you sell ale or weapons, you'll not get any coin of mine."

Skara leaned back into the cart and crossed his arms over his chest as groups of people passed hurriedly beside the wagon in every direction. Keeping his head low, he peered through the gaps in the sides of the cart and watched the people rush by, busy with their daily lives.

"There's one," Faine said, pointing his finger. "The Maiden's Locket."

Pulling the horses and wagon into the covered stable, Faine handed the reins to the stable boy and pulled out a silver coin. "Can you give the horses some food and water, and a good brushing?" The boy eyed the coin and looked up at Faine. "I can, indeed, sir."

Turning to walk away, Faine looked back and pulled out another silver coin, holding it between his fingers for the boy to see. "You don't know of anyone looking to buy any goods or horses, do you?"

"I do, sir. There's a merchant a few streets down that trades in horses."

Braig grabbed his pack off the wagon and set it down near the back wheel. "Then I guess that's where I'm headed. Who am I looking for?"

"Her name is Ferhani, sir. She has black hair and a small tattoo over her left eye."

Faine flipped the coin to the boy and looked over at Braig and raised his eyebrow. "I can go talk to her if you'd rather get us a few rooms."

"I was a merchant before all this. I think I can handle selling some supplies and horses. Besides, I need to stretch my legs. All that time in the wagon made me feel cramped."

Faine raised his hands and smiled. "I bet. Not much room up there...tight on the legs," he said, gesturing down. "But that's good with me. I'll get us some rooms."

"Aye, my legs might be shorter than yours, but they're still long enough to kick your ass!" Braig said, mumbling something about pointed ears under his breath as he turned away and stepped out into the busy streets to find Ferhani.

Grabbing their gear off the cart, Faine smiled to himself as he walked with Skara towards the inn.

"You coming, Ren?" Faine said, turning back to watch Renna dig through her supplies.

"I'll be there soon. I need to grab some of my books before Braig sells them all."

"Hmm. Good idea." Faine walked back over to the cart and pulled the lid off one of the crates and shoved several bottles of black rum into his bag. Motioning to Skara, he held out another bottle as he walked. "Better to have more than not enough."

"You can keep it," Skara said, following behind Faine into the inn.

The main room was broad, with several tables in the center and a small stage in the back corner. A bar ran along one wall, and two sets of stairs, one on each side of the room, led to the second floor. Large oval windows stood open, letting in the cool breeze that fluttered several tapestries hanging on the wall, each depicting stories of life on the ocean.

One showed a ship on bright blue water being pulled under by massive tentacles wrapped around its hull. In another, mermaids rested on the rocks near the shoreline, looking out at the moons shining over the water as they combed the blonde hair that hung over their bare chests. Quickly turning his eyes away, Skara looked back to Faine as they walked up to the innkeeper.

"I need four rooms."

The man looked down at Skara and scowled. "I ain't got no room for trouble-makers here."

Faine laughed as he leaned against the counter. "We're hardly here to make trouble, good sir. We're just here passing through on orders of the temple."

"What d'you mean, orders of the temple?" the innkeeper said, eyeing Skara.

"You see, brother Mordhir and I are priests. We're on our way to Aerith for a pilgrimage up Caidan's Pass. There's a temple at the top, and we mean to study there."

The door to the inn swung open as Renna hurried inside, her bags slung over her shoulder and several books in her hands. The barkeep's face turned into a frown as he looked over the orcish woman.

"Ahh, there you are sister Onthera. I was just telling this man about our pilgrimage to Caidan's Pass. He seems rather interested. And as always, you have your holy books in hand. It's hard to tear our sister away from her studies. Perhaps you would like to hear a short sermon? I'm sure sister Onthera would be more than happy to enlighten you."

The barkeep quickly shook his head as he glanced over at Renna.

"Some other time then," Faine said, smiling. "But, as I said before, we're just passing through and only need a place to stay until we can catch a ship." Pulling out two gold coins and a small red gem, Faine slid them over to the innkeeper. "I trust this will pay for our four rooms and meals for our stay."

The man picked up the coins and looked over at Renna and Skara. "Priests or no, I don't want no trouble while you're here."

Faine raised his hand and held it over his heart. "By the light of Falinxa, you'll get no trouble from us. We're just here to have a drink or two, see some acts, and enjoy a respite before setting sail." Grabbing his bags, Faine took hold of the room keys and handed one to Skara and Renna.

"Wait. Who's the fourth room for?"

Faine lightly sighed and turned back towards the innkeeper. "Our fourth companion is our guard. He's a stout dwarf that was sent with us by the Temple of Divine Light to escort us to the top of the pass. Now I know what you must be thinking, hearing talk of a guard, but we mean no harm and want no trouble; these weapons we carry are purely for protection. For I fear," Faine said as he glanced around the room and leaned in, "we don't know how to use them."

Smiling and leaning back from the bar, Faine nodded his head at the innkeeper. "May the light guide your path."

Following Faine, Renna and Skara mumbled a blessing of the light under their breath and walked upstairs into their rooms.

WEAVING BETWEEN GROUPS of people gathered around the shops and stalls, Braig scanned the streets for the woman with a tattoo over her left eye. Ahead of him, a short man with a thick, brown mustache that curled up at the corners had gathered a crowd in front of his stall. Standing on a sturdy wooden table, his bright red shirt flashed in the sun as he pointed into the crowd.

"You sir, what is that ails you?" the merchant said as he stepped over several of the bottles laid out across his table.

The man looked around at the men and women next to him to see if he was the one the merchant had spoken to. "It's my shoulder. It's been giving me fits, and I can't lift a thing anymore."

The merchant swung his hand and pointed his finger at a woman near the back of the crowd. "And you?"

The crowd of people turned around to look at a thin, olive-skinned woman with long black hair pulled into a tight bun. Pulling the frayed green shawl over her shoulder, she stood, using a set of crutches to help her keep her balance. "It's me leg, sir. I fell off the mast on me ship and broke it. I ain't been able to set foot on a boat again," the woman said, smoothing out her white top and long brown skirt.

The merchant nodded his head and motioned for the woman to come to the front of the crowd. As she turned and hobbled her way to the front, Braig could see part of a small tattoo over the woman's left eye that had been partially hidden by a loose-fitting headwrap tied around her forehead.

Stepping closer to get a better look, Braig climbed onto a nearby crate and watched the woman make her way to the front of the crowd. Crossing his arms, he leaned back against the building, a knowing smile crossing his face.

As the woman stood in front of the crowd, the merchant put his hand on her shoulder and gestured out towards the onlookers. "If you don't mind, could you tell us how long it's been since you had your dreadful fall?"

"Nearly seven months now," the woman said, steadying herself with her crutches.

"And what if I told you that I could fix your broken leg and that you could be back out on the waters as quick as you please?"

Looking towards the merchant, the woman's eyes sparkled with moisture. "If only I could, sir. But I ain't been able to afford a healer. I 'ave to beg just to scrape by and put food in me belly."

The merchant looked down at the woman, pity in his eyes. "Oh, precious girl. I know the healers can ask for a hefty price, and their visits can sometimes be few and far between. But alas, with my potions, you won't have a need for a healer for breaks and sprains." The merchant picked up a vial of red liquid and held it out in front of the crowd. "Made from the finest healing herbs. Drip several drops in your food or drink once and day feel yourself begin to heal. By the time you've finished the bottle, you'll be as strong an Ineren horse, and just as healthy."

"The does sound good, sir. But I'm afraid I can't afford it," the woman said, pulling out a single copper coin.

"My dear, I will make an exception for you today. To get you back on your feet and demonstrate the healing power of Wendall's potions, I give you this." Reaching into a pouch on his side, the merchant handed the woman a small vial and twirled the ends of his mustache as she turned it over in her hands.

"Thank you, sir. I'll put it in me drink straight away. I don't know how I can e'er repay your kindness," the woman said as she looked over the crowd and back to the merchant.

"There's no need for repayment. For as you said, this an act of kindness. What you hold in your hand is a concentrated solution of the potion you see on the table before you. It is my only strong potion in my current stock, and I have been saving it for a special day. I feel it is only right that you have it." The merchant bowed and nodded as applause and murmurs broke out in the crowd. "Now, my dear, if you would be so kind as to open the bottle and drink the contents. Your leg will be healed, and you will be free to sail the seas once more."

Pulling the cork off the top of the bottle, the woman held it to her nose and sniffed the contents. "It smells sweet." Pressing the bottle to her lips, she tilted it backwards, draining the red liquid into her mouth. Setting the empty bottle back on the counter, the woman raised her eyebrows and looked up at the merchant standing on the table. "It feels warm. I can feel something happening." Leaning her crutches against the stall, the woman took an unsteady step, gently putting weight on her injured leg.

"Please," the merchant said, looking out over the crowd, "tell us how you feel."

Putting her hands over her mouth, tears streamed down the woman's face. "Gods, I can't believe it. I can walk again." Raising her hands over her head, she reached out and hugged the merchant and jumped up and down on her leg. "It's healed. I don't feel any pain. Thank you, sir. I'll always be in your debt."

The crowd broke out into cheers and applause as the woman jumped and spun in front of them. Her long brown skirt twirled as she danced, raising her hands in joy. Smiling one last time at the merchant, the woman wiped the tears from her eyes and strolled quickly down the street, cutting down an alley and out of sight.

Braig could hear the merchant telling the customers to form a line as he jumped off the crate and ambled down the street towards the alley. Walking past a small group of men playing dice against the wall, he could see the now crutch-free woman pulling off her skirt to reveal a tight-fitting pair of brown pants with several pockets sewn up the sides. As she reached down to tie the laces on her calf-high boots, he saw the hilts of the daggers that she kept tucked securely in each.

Keeping his hands in clear view, he sauntered through the alley towards the woman, stopping in his tracks as two large men stepped out from behind a nearby wall and blocked the way. Turning his head to look back, he saw that the men that had been playing dice were now on their feet and blocking any retreat they thought he might try to make.

Braig looked past the men and held up his empty hands. "I'm just here to talk. I was told that you might be in the market for some horses and goods."

The woman dabbed her face with her tattered shawl and tossed it to the ground as she walked up behind the two men. "And who told you that?"

"The stable boy at The Maiden's Locket mentioned your name and tattoo," Braig said, pointing towards the cloth tied around the woman's head.

Smirking, the woman pulled off the headband and shoved it into one of the many pockets on the sides of her pants. Pulling out a small metal pin from her hair, it fell in thick black waves over the soft, white shirt that clung tightly around her chest. "You have good eyes, dwarf, but they need to be looking up here," the woman said, letting out a laugh as she watched Braig's face redden slightly. Taking a leather cord off of her wrist, she tied her hair back into a ponytail, causing her shirt even to pull even tighter. "Now, what is it you're trying to sell me?"

Standing up straighter, Braig crossed his arms over his chest and stroked his beard. "Well, I have several books, a few horses, rum, weapons, and some other supplies I picked up along the way. Unfortunately, I'm all out of red potions."

The woman eyed the dwarf she shifted on her feet. "Liked the show, did you?"

"It was entertaining. You played your part right. But do those potions even work?"

"They do work, dwarf. Otherwise, I wouldn't sell them. The act helps drum up business, and I give the merchant a small cut of the profits for selling them for me. I don't have to waste a real potion for a demonstration, and people feel more comfortable buying from a generous person that helps the needy. Now, back to business. First off, what do I call you? Second, why are you looking to sell all the goods you've picked up on your way here?"

"You can call me Braig. And what is it I should call you?"

"Ferhani."

Braig rolled the name over in his head. Ferhani. A beautiful name for a beautiful woman. "To answer your second question, that's what merchants do with goods they don't need before they sail out of a port town."

Ferhani looked up at the men standing behind Braig and motioned for them to go back to their game. "You're a merchant?"

"Used to be. Still sell things from time to time. So," Braig said, motioning down the alley, "are you interested, or do I need to go somewhere else?"

Ferhani looked at the two men standing beside her and motioned for them to follow. "Let's go take a look at what you've got. Right this way, Braig," Ferhani said, extending her arm and gesturing for the dwarf to follow her behind the back of a nearby building.

Cutting down several smaller streets, Ferhani led them to the backside of the inn and walked around to the stables.

"Is this your cart," she said, waving her hand towards the dusty wagon.

Braig rolled down the dirty canvas covering the supplies and dropped it on the ground beside the wagon, sending a cloud of dust into the air. "It is. Everything but my gear is for sale. That includes the cart and the horses."

Moving around the wagon, Ferhani pried open several of the crates and dug through the supplies. "A few bottles of black rum, some old bread and fruit, some weapons, and," pulling a dirt-crusted woolen sweater up from the back of the wagon, Ferhani made a disgusted face as she dropped the shirt and glanced at Braig, "some old pieces of clothing."

"Don't forget about the horses," Braig said, pointing to three of the horses in the stalls nearby.

"And the horses." Ferhani looked over the crates and sent her two guards over to check the condition of the horses. "What are you hoping to get from all this...road-weary gear?"

"I'd say that six gold sounds about right to me."

Ferhani looked at the dwarf and raised her eyebrows. "Six gold, are you daft?"

Braig tightened his arms across his chest, a stern look crossing his face. "That's a fair price. What you'll get from the horses, weapons, and rum should more than cover your costs here and put some coin in your pocket. Now, I'm not looking to run all around the city to sell all this, but I will if I have to."

"I'll give you four," Ferhani said.

"I'll take seven."

Ferhani shook her head and looked over the goods. She knew that six gold was a fair price, and she could make that back within the day off the weapons and the cart. But if she could pay less, she would. Looking towards the men inspecting the horses, they gave her a nod as they patted the horses and shut the stall doors.

Ferhani looked over at the crates and back over to Braig. "Where is it that you need to take a ship to?"

"Not that it's much of your concern, but I need to get to Aerith, just north of Yonkai."

"Here's what I'll do," Ferhani said, reaching into her pouch. "I'll give you four gold-"

"I'll not take it."

Eyeing Braig, she pulled out four gold coins. "Like I was saying, I'll give you four gold and passage for you and your companions on one of my ships."

Braig ran his hand through his beard and studied Fer-hani. "How do you know I'm not alone? And how do I know you're not just trying to sell me the red potion?"

Leaning closer, Ferhani put her face a few inches from Braig. "Aside from the different sized footprints all over the wagon, I have eyes across the city and know when an inter-esting group of travelers comes into town. And you don't, dwarf. I suppose you'll just have to take my word." Standing up straight, Ferhani sighed and handed Braig the coins. "Here's your gold. My men will take the wagon and the hors-es. Meet me down at the dock tomorrow morning on the south side. Look for a dark brown boat with white and yel-low sails. The Wind Cutter doesn't leave for a few days, but I'll introduce you to the crew and make all the arrangements. I'll see you bright and early."

Running her fingers through Braig's beard as she walked by, Ferhani strode onto the busy street and disappeared into the crowds. Pulling at his beard, he grabbed what was left of his gear off the cart and walked towards the door of the inn. Smiling to himself, Braig opened the door and stepped in-side.

The barkeep looked down at Braig as he strode into the room, eyeing him suspiciously. "I was told there'd be a dwarf coming along soon. I suppose you're with the elf and those other two?"

Braig stiffened as he set down his gear. "What's that sup-posed to mean, those other two?"

The barkeep tensed visibly but stood taller, lifting his chin higher into the air. "I'll tell you the same thing I told them. I ain't gonna be having no trouble here. The elf told me you was here to keep 'em safe, and you can do that. But you stir up anything, and you're all out."

Braig adjusted his shoulders, popping the bones in his spine. "Just tell me where my room is."

"Up the stairs, and down the hall on the left. It's the last room near the end. But you'll need this to get in," the barkeep said, tossing a key to Braig and giving him a dirty look.

Taking a deep breath, Braig grabbed his bags off the floor and stared at the man as he walked away. Climbing the stairs to the second floor, he plodded down the hall, unlocked his door, set his gear on the floor, and fell face-first onto the bed. Closing his eyes, he sank down into the mattress. Just as he was about to drift off, a loud knock hammered at his door.

Groaning, Braig opened his eyes, his face still buried in a pillow. "What do you want?"

Faine opened the door and stuck his head inside the room. "I heard you coming down the hall, and it woke me up. Did you have any luck selling the horses and cart?"

"It's gone. I hope you had everything you wanted because I sold everything with it," Braig said, sitting up and looking at Faine.

"Get a good price?"

Braig pulled four gold coins out of his pouch and tossed them onto the bed. Faine looked down and frowned slightly. "I also have this," Braig said, pulling the gold coin out of his boot. "I took it off one of the brothers back in Banrielle."

Faine looked down at the coin and wondered about the piece of gold he had lost in there in the inn. "I hope that's enough to get to Aerith. We all have some coin on us, but I don't know how much passage is or what we might need on the road."

Braig put the coins back into a pouch and shoved them under his mattress. "We don't have to worry about spending the gold on a ship. Part of the deal was our passage."

Faine nodded his head and rubbed his hand over his slight beard. "That's a good deal. You must have a way with words. When do we leave?"

Stretching back out on the bed, Braig covered his eyes with a pillow and waved his hand towards the door. "I have to go down to the docks in the morning and to meet Ferhani and see the ship. Not quite sure of the details yet."

"We could all use a good night or two of rest anyway. I know Renna's most likely going out tonight, not sure what I'll do yet. But I'll be in the tavern for a while. If I don't see you later tonight, I'll meet you in the morning and go with you to the docks."

"Don't forget to shut the door on your way out," Braig said, pulling the outer edge of the blanket over his stomach and rolling to his side.

Closing the door quietly as he left, Faine padded down the hall and knocked on both Renna's and Skara's doors, telling them to meet him downstairs when they were ready. Walking down the stairs, Faine took a seat at a table near the stage and waved over a barmaid.

After setting down a tray full of drinks at a full table, she strode over to Faine and smiled. Her cream-colored shirt hung loosely over her chest and was tied into a knot near her hip, showing a sliver of her stomach as she moved. "What'll it be?"

Faine looked up at the barmaid, giving her a smile as he leaned back in his chair. "Anything unique here that a lonely traveler like myself should try?"

The barmaid tilted her head to the side and put a hand on her hip. "Oh, indeed. We have a nice ale made with cinnamon and ginger, brewed right here in town."

Faine tapped his fingers on the table as a slight smile spread across his face. "Hmm. Is it spicy?"

The barmaid leaned down closer to Faine, resting her arms on the table as the neckline of her shirt draped lower on her chest. "It has a bit of spice. Maybe a bit more than you can handle. But the honey gives it a nice, sweet finish."

Faine smirked as his eyes studied the barmaid. "I think I can handle a little spice. I'll take one."

"Coming right up." Giving Faine a quick wink, the barmaid turned and walked back towards the bar, her brown skirt flowing out behind her.

Looking up at the second floor, Faine saw Skara and Renna walking down the stairs. Renna was wearing a light blue dress with a pale green bodice with black lacing on each side. Her hair was pulled up into a loose bun with a small red flower tucked into it. Waving them over, he pointed to the chairs next to him. "Well, don't you look nice. Spending the evening out, are we?"

Renna looked down and smoothed her dress. "I didn't feel like sleeping, so I went out and picked this up after I got settled in. I thought I'd go see something at the theatre and wanted something nice to wear. I don't think showing up in dusty clothing is very becoming."

"Well, you look magnificent. In fact, I'd say you're hoping to catch someone's eye tonight. Maybe even a bit more." Faine said, raising his eyebrows.

Renna blushed and looked up at the barmaid as she brought Faine's drink. "I'll have what he's having. What about you, Skara?"

Skara looked up at the barmaid and shook his head.

"I think we could all use something to eat. Not sure what's on the menu here, though."

"I have just the thing," the barmaid said, strutting back to the bar. Keeping her eyes on Faine, she poured another mug of ale and walked it gently back to the table, carefully setting it down in front of Renna. "I'm sorry. I may have filled it a bit full. Let me run to the kitchen, and I'll be right back with your food."

"It's fine," Renna said, picking it up slowly to take a sip.

Faine took a long drink of his ale and let out a small burp. "What about you, Skara? Heading down to the water tonight?"

Skara glanced around the room and felt an uneasiness creep up his spine. He was already getting several glares from the other patrons, and he knew that it would only be worse if he went out onto the crowded streets. "I think I might just stay in. I haven't done much carving since we left."

"There'll be plenty of time for that on the ship. Who knows, maybe the sailors can show you a trick or two. I hear some of them are pretty good at scrimshaw. While you're here, you should go out and see the town or the ocean. Or, you can always come out with me. You didn't come all this way just to do nothing, did you?" Faine said, scratching at his unshaven face.

"And where are you going?"

Faine took another long drink of ale and twirled his finger in a circle. "I'm going to the pubs. There's quite a few in the general area, and I'm planning to see them all. Well, most of 'em anyway. After that, who knows where I'll end up."

Renna shook her head and took another sip of her ale. "Most likely in a ditch somewhere. You keep drinking like that, and you'll be feeling it in the morning."

"Speaking of the morning, Braig sold the horses and supplies. He's arranged for us to check out a ship a little after first light. I don't know much about it, but that's the plan. So I say we see what the town has to offer tonight and meet up in the morning to head down to the docks to check it out."

"I'll try to meet you before you leave, but I may just head to the archives and see what I can learn about the stones. If I don't make it, I'm sure you can fill me in on the details." Standing up and looking towards the door, Renna took one last drink and set her mug down next to Faine. "Here, you can finish this. I need to get going before it gets too dark. Maybe I'll catch up with you in a pub later."

Faine leaned forward and knocked on the table. "Are you good to go out alone?"

Renna put her boot up on her chair and patted the dagger there. "I'm good. You just watch out for yourself and try to stay out of trouble."

"What fun would that be?" Faine said, smiling at Renna as she turned and walked out onto the busy street. "Well, it looks like it's just you and me, Skara, me boy."

Skara turned his head and looked at the tapestries hanging on the walls as the barmaid brought out a plate of hot dates wrapped in thinly sliced ham coated in a thick syrup.

Setting the dish on the table in front of Skara, the barmaid smiled. "Made fresh this evening. The dates are stuffed with sharp cheese and pine nuts, and the sweet glaze has a hint of peppers to give it some heat."

Skara looked down at the dates and stabbed one with a knife, the thick sugar glaze clinging onto the thinly sliced meat as melted cheese pressed out of a slit in the side. The warm syrup dripped down the blade as he pushed the whole date into his mouth. Looking over at Faine and the barmaid, his eyes were wide as he nodded and chewed.

"I'm glad you like it," the barmaid said, smiling at Skara and lightly touching Faine's arm. "Let me know if you need anything else."

Faine winked at the barmaid and watched her walk away before turning back towards Skara. "First time having a date?"

Skara nodded and took another bite. "It's good. It makes my mouth burn, though."

Faine slid the mug of ale that Renna had set down over to Skara. "It's the peppers. You know, we're only going to be in town for a few nights. I know you're hesitant to get out, but it was a long road here, and you should see what it's like before we leave. Maybe we'll even make it all the way to the beach. Dark waters can still hold beauty."

Skara glanced out towards the busy street and back towards the dates, stabbing another with his knife. He thought about the longing for adventure he had felt back in Banrielle when Faine was describing the red waters of the Sanguine Gulf, and he didn't want to miss out on seeing something new because of fear. It had stopped him too many times in the past, and there were too many things he wanted to see here. "You're right. I didn't come all this way to stay inside."

Finishing the ale in his mug, Faine set it down with a hard thud on the table. Looking over towards the bar, he watched as the barmaid poured several drinks, glancing his way and smiling as she moved towards the end of the bar. Setting down one last drink, she looked over at Faine and tilted her head, motioning to the door leading out of the bar into a back room.

"Good, that's what I wanted to hear. Just give me a few minutes and we'll get moving. I, uh, just need to make a quick run before we leave," Faine said, nodding towards the back room as he took a quick drink out of Renna's mug. "And as you can see, things are a lot different here. We're not in Banrielle anymore."

Setting the mug down, he gave Skara a quick smile as he turned and strolled towards the back room, tying his hair back with a leather cord as he went.

A Heart in the Darkness

Renna opened the front door of the inn and stepped out onto the crowded streets. The temperature had dropped slightly since they had arrived, but it was still warm compared to Banrielle. The sky was a crisp, deep blue as the sun sank slowly towards the horizon, casting an orange glow across the thin white clouds that drifted across the sky. A warm breeze twisted down the wide streets, pulling at the red flower in her hair and fluttering the flags and signs that hung outside of the shops. Reaching up, she pressed the stem back into her bun and walked deeper into the city, checking the signs on several theatres as she went.

Walking up to the front booth outside of the Silver Penny Theatre, she knocked lightly on the wooden counter just outside of the main entrance. A man with short dark hair and an elegant white shirt sat on a stool behind the counter, reading from a thin, leather-bound book. Hearing the knock, he closed it slightly and looked up at Renna, his smile fading as he saw her small tusks and pale green skin.

"Can I help you?" the man said, looking as though he had been disturbed.

Renna ran her hands over her skirt to straighten it and stared into the man in the eyes. "Yes. I was hoping to find a showing of The Black Dragon or any Wyldernacht readings. Are there any in town?"

The man sighed lightly as he closed his book, holding the page with his finger. "There aren't any showings in theatres, but there's a good reading down at the Last Chance pub. I hear that Bodhran the Beardless will be performing. No doubt it'll be something to see. But that doesn't start for another couple of hours."

As the large red door to the theatre swung open, Renna turned her head and peered into the lobby as a man dressed in fine clothing made his way inside. She caught a brief flicker of candlelight pouring from inside and looked back towards the man in the booth. "And what's playing here?"

The man's eyes glanced down to a small piece of paper, looking over the days and times. "Starting soon...will be the Witches of Wren."

Pulling a small wisp of hair behind her ear, Renna glanced down at the piece of paper the man was reading from. "I'm not familiar with them. What do they do?"

The man marked his book with a slip of ribbon and set it down on the counter and rubbed his forehead. "I'm not sure if it's something you'd be interested in. The performers dance and use a bit of magic. They don't brawl or tell bawdy jokes." Noticing the scars on Renna's arms, he pointed down the lane and nodded his head towards a row of shops and inns. "There's a pub right down the street that might be more to your liking if you're just looking to pass the time."

Renna's eyes were hard as she stared at the man, and she briefly considered pulling out her dagger to teach him some manners but quickly thought better of it. If this had been a smaller town without so many people milling about, or she hadn't been waiting for months to see a show, she may have had more to say to the man. "I'm here to see someone perform, not just sit at a pub swilling ale to pass the time."

The man looked out behind Renna, shaking his head as he reached for a ticket. "As you say, miss. Now, if you'd like a ticket, that will be one silver. If not, there are people waiting behind you, and I have to ask you to move along."

Glancing over her shoulder, Renna saw several people waiting in a line behind her, each glaring at her. She wasn't sure if it was because of her skin, or because they were growing impatient, but she didn't like the feeling of so many eyes watching her. "Yes, I think I'll go inside and see the show." Setting a silver coin down on the counter, she snatched her ticket out of the man's hand and flashed him a quick, fake smile. Hurrying away from the booth, she pulled open the heavy door and stepped inside.

The floors were covered in soft, red rugs accented with gold filigree, and the smell of spice packets burning on hot coals wafted through the room. Paintings hung along the walls, each showing past performers or shows, some of which were signed or marked with a handprint from the performers themselves near the bottom corner. White tiles flecked with silver lined the ceiling, sparkling in the dim glow from the ornately carved candles that hung in the chandelier above her.

Lifting up her long skirt just above her boots, she walked up several stairs to a set of double doors and handed her ticket to the doorkeeper. Placing the stub in a blue velvet bag, the man smiled and bowed his head slightly as he pulled open the door and motioned for her to step inside.

Strolling down the aisle, she let her eyes adjust to the light as she studied the room. Sets of flickering candles in hammered metal sconces with red glass shades lined the walls, causing the shadows around it to dance to the low thrum of music coming from the large stage in the front of the room. Rows of seats with soft cushions sat in the center with aisles running down each side, gradually sloping towards the stage. Above the edges of the platform on the left and right were two small balconies, each with several seats, filled with men and women looking down excitedly at the musicians.

Taking a seat near the aisle several rows back from the stage, Renna gazed around the theatre, watching people as they poured in and filled the empty spaces around her. Just as the last seats were filled, the low, rhythmic tap of the drums grew louder as nearly a dozen small blue and orange orbs of arcane flames floated from the sides of the stage and circled above, casting a bright light on the men and women that sat in a semi-circle with their instruments.

Striking up a steady beat, the music echoed off the flickering red walls, and the heavy pounding of the drums sounded like a beating heart as five women made their way to the center of the stage, their faces and bodies obscured by thin black cloaks.

The crowd fell silent as the women stood motionless, waiting as a tall, thin man walked onto the center of the stage, his black robes swaying behind him. Pulling back the hood of his cloak, his long hair fell over his shoulders as he lowered his head and tugged the cuffs of his shirtsleeves back over his wrists.

Turning his head towards the crowd, bright blue eyes stared out over his pointed nose and sharp features, darting from one person to the next, like a falcon observing its prey. Throwing the cloak back with a flourish over his shoulders, he raised his hands slowly into the air, and the beat of the drums grew softer. Clearing his throat, the man's melodic voice drifted out across the room.

"Ladies and gentlemen, I ask you to hear my words and take them to heart. For what you are about to witness is a show unlike any other you have seen. Hailing from a small village far to the east, the women you see before you have forged their bodies and arcane skill against man and beast alike."

The man paused as he gazed out over the captivated crowd, letting a deep silence settle over the room as the slow beat of the drums gently faded away. Leaning forward, Renna held her breath as she watched the man standing on the stage and waited for him to continue. Wiping her palms on her skirt, she listened to the soft breathing of the men and women seated around her, keeping her eyes focused on the thin man standing on the stage. With a wild gesture of his hands, the drums began to beat hard and fast like a frightened heart in the darkness, and the man's voice rang out like a bell over the crowd.

"From hunting foul beasts in the cold dark of the dead of winter, to dancing with the Fae near the warmth of a glowing fire under the light of the moons in a summer field; the women you see before you have become as sisters, and have honed their craft and learned to bend the elements to their wills. Traveling deep in the forsaken desert across the mountains to the west, they have seen the luminous waters of the oasis and bathed in its crystalline pools. They have touched the sun-charged sands that illuminate the darkness with their glow, and have held council with the wise elders of the Dah'shi. And all that they have learned, they bring to you here and now."

Moving slowly across the stage, the man stood behind the five women, pulling their black cloaks away one by one before stepping to the side, arms outstretched as he swept into a low bow. "Lords and ladies, without any further ado, I present to you, the Witches of Wren."

As the man scurried away, the beat of drums grew louder, and the women began to slowly sway. Their arms hung loosely at their sides as they looked down at the stage, long hair covering their faces, their skin ranging in tone from pale pink to dark brown.

Sitting up straighter in her seat, Renna watched as the balls of light swirled in tight circles above the women. Their hips moved and swayed as flames licked up one arm and down the other, illuminating the bare skin that showed clearly beneath the sheer material that was wrapped over their chest. Their loose black pants were tight around their ankles, and their bare feet slammed against the wooden planks in unison with the pulsing beat of the drums.

Dancing in circles around the stage, they danced and swayed as the music changed from intense drumming that vibrated inside Renna's chest, to the soft plucking of strings that carried as lightly as a bird's song through a spring meadow. Sweat glistened on their bodies as they moved and jumped, singing loudly as they cast fountains of ice and fire from outstretched hands. Flurries of sparks blew across the stage as their bodies twisted and writhed against one another, letting soft blue flames flow like a wave from one body to another.

Sitting on the edge of her seat, Renna gripped the fabric of her skirt, gazing wide-eyed as the women flipped and tumbled across the stage. Orbs of electric energy and flame flew from one woman to another, gliding gently through the air only be caught and transformed before being thrown once more. Their bodies moved and shook as they balanced and twirled on the tips of their toes or the balls of their feet, arms and legs swinging gracefully as their toned muscles bent and flexed as they jumped and rolled. Their delicate voices rose in harmony above the pulsing drums, flutes, and strings, floating out like a light breeze over the crowd.

Renna watched in awe as the dancers glided across the stage, moving in organized chaos as one dance faded into the next, and the minutes turned into an hour. Their movements were as soft and smooth as flowing water, yet powerful enough to move even the heaviest heart of stone.

Flashes of light burst across the room, brilliant blues and purples lighting even the darkest corners of the theatre as streaks of lightning ripped across the stage from one witch to another. Thunder rumbled and echoed off the walls as they stomped their feet, chanting in a language that Renna had never heard before.

Exhaustion clear on their faces, the witches moved to the front of the stage and looked out over the crowd, their hair wet and matted with sweat. Joining their hands together to form a circle, they twisted and swayed to the beat of the drums, chanting quietly as bolts of lightning arced between them, splitting the air with sharp crackles and flashes of light. Inside their circle, the swirling wind became more intense as the lightning sparked and flared, becoming a single ball of brilliant white light. Flames danced on the tips of their fingers, leaping out to ignite the ball of energy as it whirled across the stage, popping and hissing as colored smoke drifted upwards towards the ceiling.

Standing behind the blazing orb, the witches traced their fingers over the floating, spinning ball, causing deep blue cracks to form on its surface. Clapping their hands loudly in unison, the orb collapsed in on itself before exploding outwards, sending a wave of bright, colorful lights that flamed and sparkled, fluttering like butterflies above the crowd. Stretching out their hands, thin strands of white light shot out from their fingertips, striking each of the floating wisps, splitting them into hundreds of shimmering pieces that drifted down like falling snow onto the onlookers below.

The colors fell gently, flecks of light cutting through the shadow-strewn, silent room, and Renna opened her hand, letting the pieces land on her palm. Warmth spread up her arm as the speckles of light burst in flashes of warm and cool colors before melting away like a snowflake on her skin. As the colors faded, the crowd erupted in cheers, standing and applauding the women and the musicians on stage as they bowed deeply until thick, dark blue curtains swung closed, blocking them from view.

Renna sat in her seat, amazed by what she had just seen. The way they controlled magic was incredible. How could they flip and roll and still keep their focus? How were they able to use their magic together without it burning or ripping each other apart? Although she had seen powerful spells, she had never seen them used like this before. Giving her small tusks a couple taps with her nail, she thought about their clothing, or lack of thereof, and felt her heart skip a beat and a blush rise to her face. Smiling to herself, she stood and straightened her skirt as she waited for the aisle to clear before stepping out and moving towards the door.

As she walked down the aisle, Renna noticed a plain-faced woman with red hair watching her from the back of the theatre, her foot propped up on the seat in front of her. Her dark brown boot was scuffed and worn with small bones tied onto the straps. Dagger sheathes ran up the length of her tight, brown pants and up onto the thin black leather bodice covering her white blouse. Freckles dotted her nose and upper cheeks, and as she pulled her hair behind her ears, Renna could see a long, thin, crooked scar running across the right side of her face.

Smiling, the woman nodded as Renna walked by, her green eyes reflecting the dim glow of the candles on the walls. Sinker deeper into her chair, the red-haired woman looked back towards the stage as Renna opened the door to the lobby and made her way out onto the street. Stopping at the booth once more, she knocked loudly on the counter, not waiting for the man to look at her before speaking.

"Where did you say that the Last Chance was at?"

Not bothering to look up, the man pointed his finger down the street. "Down the street a ways, take a left at the crossroads, and it'll be on your right. It has a faded yellow sign hanging out front. You can't miss it."

Giving the counter one last hard knock, Renna meandered down the dimly lit street, looking into the shops and pubs as she passed by, listening to the music and laughter that poured from the buildings as she made her way to the crossroads. Down each lane, lanterns hung on thick wooden poles that lined the side of the cobbled streets. Turning her head to the left, she caught a glimpse of yellow out of the corner of her eye and saw a deep blue two-story building resting between two small, dingy shops a short distance away. Hanging on the front of the building just under the overhang of the balcony, a large yellow sign with the words Last Chance Pub painted in ornate letters swung gently in the cool night breeze.

Turning the corner, she made her way through the crowds of people and pushed open the front door. The room was well lit, and a wooden stage was positioned near the back of the tavern. A long bar ran along the left side wall, and round tables were scattered around the room, leaving enough space to comfortably walk between them. To the right, a fire crackled quietly in the stone hearth, gently lighting the room with a soft orange glow.

Along the walls, lengths of rope tied in ornate sailing knots were fastened on wooden plaques between the decorative lanterns that hung on blackened iron hooks. Covering the banister and balusters around the balcony, gold fishing nets twisted around the lightly stained wood, spiraling up the handrail that led up to the second story. On the wall be-hind the stage, several small porthole windows swung open into the night, letting in the salty ocean breeze.

Moving to an empty table near the front of the room, several men at a nearby table whispered to one another, pointing their fingers in her direction as she sat down. Look-ing around the room, she noticed that aside from a few elves near the bar, everyone else was human. Shifting nervously in her seat, she reached down to check the dagger in her boot and crossed her arms over her chest. Seeing several more glares from people seated at the tables around her, she con-sidered leaving and glanced back towards the front door and saw the red-haired woman from the theatre sitting at a table near the entrance.

Turning back towards the stage, Renna tapped the back of her thumb on her tusks as a barmaid set a mug in front of her.

"Wait. I didn't order this."

The barmaid gestured back towards the red-haired woman near the door. "From the woman in the back."

Picking up the mug, Renna swirled the liquid around be-fore smelling it. "What is it?"

"Honey-thorn mead. Quite popular 'round here," the barmaid said, glancing over at several customers seated at a nearby table. "Anything else I can get ya?"

"No. Thank you," Renna said, taking another sniff of the mead as the barmaid hurried off to another table, taking or-ders and setting drinks down as she went.

Turning to look at the woman, Renna raised the mug to her and smiled. The red-haired woman leaned forward, put

her arm on her table, and hoisted her tankard before taking a long drink. Setting her cup back on the table, Renna
pulled a small vial out of her pouch and poured it into the
mead, hoping to dilute any poison that might have been in
the mug. She wondered if the woman was following her, and
why she would buy her a drink. There had been more than a
few pointed fingers and whispers in her direction, and it put
her on edge. If anything had been put into her drink that the
antidote couldn't counteract, she would be able to tell. And
if not, she would at least try to take the woman with her if
nothing else.

Taking a sip of the mead, she let the liquid rest on her
tongue, waiting for anything that tasted bitter or stung the
inside of her mouth, but nothing came. Picking up only the
sweet notes of the honey and a slightly herbal taste, similar
to sage, she felt reasonably sure the mead was safe to drink.

Swirling the mead around in her mug, she took a long
drink and looked back up towards the stage, catching another sneer from a man seated at a table a short distance away to
her left. Shaking her head, she clenched her teeth and turned
her eyes back towards the empty stage, waiting for someone
to make a rude comment or pull a knife. She wondered why
she was getting so many dirty looks here. This was a port
town and had to see quite a few travelers passing through.
Although most of the people here at the Last Chance were
human, they were acting like they had never seen anyone
with orc blood before.

Setting her mug down hard onto the table, mead spilled
over the rim, splashing down onto the polished wood.
Pulling back several fallen strands of hair, she flexed her mus-

cles as she tightened the loose bun and adjusted the red flower tucked into her dark hair, giving the men a menacing look as she bared her teeth and small tusks. The men scowled and looked as if they were about to stand when a short, plump man in a light purple tunic and black pants walked onto the stage.

"Good evenin', and welcome to the Last Chance Pub. We 'ave a fine show for you tonight, and a tale of which I'm sure you're familiar. But I know that you've been waitin' long enough for the readin' and that you most likely didn't come down here to listen to me ramble on like I tend to do. And if ya did, you can come find me at the bar." The man on stage let out a laugh as the crowd smiled and nodded to each other as if they had heard the man tell one too many long-winded stories. "So, grab a drink, sit back, and enjoy the telling of the story of Wyldernacht by our special guest. For your listenin' pleasure, I present to you Bodhran, the Beardless."

The short man clapped his hands and stepped towards the bar as a broad, beardless dwarf walked onto the stage, emerging from behind a curtain that covered the doorway to a side room for performers. The dwarf was dressed in brown woolen pants, leather boots, and a long-sleeved beige shirt. Rolling up his sleeves to his forearms, he cracked his knuckles and ran his hand through his disheveled brown hair, trying in vain to pull back the pieces that hung slightly over his ears. Dark, bushy eyebrows rested above his deep brown eyes, broad nose, cleanly shaven face, and wide grin.

Sitting up higher in her seat, Renna watched the dwarf set down several scrolls on a narrow table and begin to untie the leather cord that held one of them closed. She had only seen a handful of dwarves in her travels, including Braig, but she had never come across one without a beard. Glancing back, she looked at the red-haired woman near the door and smiled, taking another drink of her mead. Although she was still unsure of the woman, she had the feeling that it wasn't her that would give her trouble. The woman returned the smile and made a motion that looked like she was stroking a long beard before raising her cup and looking back towards the stage, waiting for the dwarf to speak.

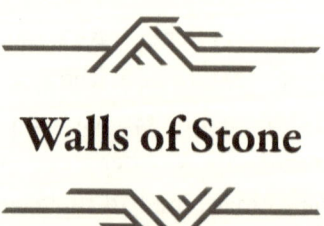

Walls of Stone

Skara watched as Faine closed the door to the back room, leaving him sitting alone at the table. Using a knife, he stabbed another date and popped it into his mouth, grinding the soft fruit between his teeth as he surveyed the room. Several men at a table near the back of the inn eyed him, murmuring to one another as they glanced towards the door Faine had gone through.

Hearing a sharp laugh from the front of the room, Skara turned his attention towards the barkeep, watching as he poured several drinks for the patrons at the bar, occasionally looking in his direction as he spoke. Feeling the thud of boots vibrating across the wooden floor, he glanced back towards the whispering men, his muscles growing tense as he fixed his eyes on the pair approaching him.

"I hear that someone's been asking around town about a little goblin and his thieving friends. They say there's a good price for anyone that brings 'em in. And bad luck for you, but it looks like your elf friend left you out here all alone," the man said, reaching down and taking a date, smirking as he stuck it in his mouth. "You wouldn't happen to know anything about that, would ya?"

Skara drummed his nails on the table and kept his eyes on the platter of dates. "I can't say that I do. Now, if you don't mind pissing off, I'm not looking for any company."

The man laughed as he leaned in, putting his palms on the table. "Ya see, I would do that if I didn't think you were the little bastard they were looking for. And even if you're not and we turn you over to the guards, it's one less monster on the streets that we have to worry about. Can't have something like you goin' 'round spreading your filth all over town."

A flash of anxiety washed over Skara as he turned his gaze towards the front door. He knew that if he ran, he could lose them on the busy streets, but that would also mean that Faine would most likely be their next target. And if he were to get lost, he might end up getting caught by someone else. He didn't know how there could be a bounty for them, or how anyone knew that they would be here—but he knew that there was going to be a fight, and he would have to strike first.

The man looked down at Skara, eyeing him as he turned his head towards the door. Slapping his hand on the table to get the goblin's attention, the man glanced over at his friend. "Haldon, why don't you go and get the guards before our little friend decides to try and make a run for it. I think they'll wanna know we found 'em. And I wanna collect the reward."

Haldon smiled, his nearly toothless sneer revealing several black, rotted teeth. "I'll let 'em know. Keep an eye on 'em 'til I get back, Pogrel. Word is they want 'em alive." Turning towards the door, Haldon scurried out of the inn, trying not to draw too much attention to himself. Pushing open the front door, he stepped out onto the busy streets and darted towards the guardhouse as soon as he reached the darkening lane.

Smiling, Pogrel reached down and picked up another date, shoving it into his mouth, letting bits of cheese fall onto the table as he chewed.

Skara scowled at the man as looked up from the table, his grip tightening on the handle of the knife. "Don't do that again."

"And what are you gonna do if I do?"

"Do you really want to find out?"

Pogrel let out a slight chuckle as he peered down at Skara. Reaching his fingers out, he moved his hand towards the tray, slowly walking his fingers along the table, taunting Skara.

"I don't want any trouble, but this is your last warning. Leave me alone and let me eat in peace."

The man leaned in, leveling his gaze with Skara. "You already got trouble, you little shit!" Laughing as he glimpsed back at his lanky friend still sitting at the table, he reached his hand forward and grabbed another piece of food.

Dashing forward, Skara caught the man's hand, pulling it closer to his face. Clamping his teeth down hard, he bit off two of Pogrel's fingers and spit them out onto the floor. Screaming in pain, the man jerked his arm back as blood poured down his hand and onto the floor. Drawing a dagger, the lanky man jumped up from his table and charged towards Skara, sending a flurry of people rushing out onto the streets, screaming, and calling for the guards.

Ducking under the table, Skara stabbed his knife through the Pogrel's boot before tipping the table forward, knocking him off balance. The table and tray clattered to the floor as the bleeding man fell hard, holding his injured hand close to his chest as he pulled at the knife that pierced his foot with the other. Stepping over his injured friend, the lanky man bolted around the side of the table and slashed down with his dagger.

Putting a chair in between them, Skara kicked it forward, smashing it into the man's shins. Turning to run, Skara's back erupted in pain as the chair crashed into him, knocking him to the ground. Falling to his knees, he felt the man wrapped his long arms around his torso, squeezing hard as he was lifted off the ground.

Kicking his legs, Skara tried to wriggle free but was held in place as Pogrel hobbled up in front of him, his lips pulled into an angry sneer. Dark blots of blood covered his shirt, oozing out from the two jagged stumps where his fingers had been. Drawing back his uninjured hand, he slammed his fist hard into Skara's face, sending a stream of blood pouring out of his nose and mouth.

"Don't kill him. They need 'im alive, or we don't get no pay," the lanky man holding Skara said, keeping a tight grip on him.

"I know they need 'im alive! But that doesn't mean he has to be in one piece. Look what he did to my fingers. Maybe I should just take his whole hand. That'll teach 'em a lesson," Pogrel said, pulling back his fist and punching Skara one more time.

A wave of darkness fell over Skara like a thick blanket, briefly blotting out the lights and sounds around him. Stars floated in front of his eyes as his head sagged, and his body went limp. Raising his head slightly, he looked past Pogrel and saw the door to the back room slam open as Faine glared across the room, his shirt wrapped tightly around his hand. His muscled torso was covered with several tattoos and scars, and his chest heaved as heavy breaths escaped his lips. Clenching his fists, he charged from the room, picking up a wooden chair as he ran. Raising the chair above his head, he smashed it down onto Pogrel's back, breaking it into several large pieces. Kicking the man over, Faine picked up one of the heavy chair legs, holding it like a club as he took a step towards the other man.

Holding the dagger to Skara's throat, the lanky man glanced around the room, looking for an easy escape route as he backed up closer to the front door. "Come any closer, and I'll kill the wretch."

Faine held up his hand and took a step back. "You know that's not how this is going to go. If you kill him, your injured friend down here dies. Then, I'll break as many bones in your body as I can before killing you. I'll put through as much pain as possible before I decide how you should die."

Skara struggled weakly as the man eyed Faine, glancing down at his friend as he rolled on the floor, blood oozing from his hand and out of his boot. "What, you think I'm just gonna let 'im go? The way I see it, I only have to wait for the guards to show up and take you both away. Then I go about my business and collect my reward."

Faine shook his head as he knelt next to Pogrel, grabbing him by the hair and lifting his head up off the floor. "You think it'd be that easy? The cell wouldn't hold me for long. And even if it did, I'd send one of my contacts in the city to take care of you. Now," Pogrel moaned in pain as Faine stuck the jagged end of the chair leg into his mouth and began to pry it open, "put the goblin down, or I ram this piece of wood through the back of your friend's neck."

The lanky man gave Skara a hard squeeze and held the dagger up to his throat, pushing the sharp tip into his skin, drawing a trickle of blood. Gasping for breath, Skara kicked his legs and tried to break free of the man's tight hold.

"This is your last chance," Faine said, pushing the wooden leg deeper into Pogrel's mouth, choking him as he tightened his grip on Pogrel's hair.

Growling, the man shoved Skara to the side, smashing him hard into a nearby chair as he rushed towards Faine, slashing down towards the kneeling elf with his dagger.

Pulling the club free, Faine stood and raised his arm, blocking the man's swing as he kicked out with his foot, catching the man hard in the gut. Letting out a quick cough, the man thrust at Faine, swinging the dagger wildly as he held his torso and tried to catch his breath. Sidestepping the attack, Faine brought the club down, striking the man hard in the hand, knocking the dagger to the ground. Grunting in pain, the man lunged at Faine, trying to drive him backwards and knock him off balance.

Heavy blows hammered Faine's arms and sides as he moved backwards, arms tucked tightly to his torso as he tried to block the man's powerful attacks. Tossing down his club, he unwrapped the shirt from his arm and pulled it tight between his hands, using it to parry the man's attacks. Dodging several more quick punches, Faine caught the man's wrist in the fabric, wrapping the material tightly around his arm. Darting around to the man's back, Faine pulled hard on the line, binding the man's wrist to his chest as he twisted the fabric around his neck like a noose.

Gritting his teeth, Faine pulled the knot tighter, choking the man as he pressed his elbows hard into his back. "You see what happens when you don't listen. You should have just walked away."

Turning around, Faine ducked under the shirt, pulling it over his shoulder. Leaning forward, he lifted the man off the ground like a sack, holding him in the air as he flailed his legs, trying to get his feet back on the floor.

Breathing hard, Faine held the struggling man until he fell still, letting his body fall limply to the floor. Touching the bruises forming on his ribs, he grimaced as he walked over to Skara, stepping over Pogrel as he crawled towards the door, a thin line of blood trailing behind him.

Sitting down on the floor next to Skara, Faine slipped rumpled shirt back on and leaned his head back against the top of an overturned table. "You doing alright?"

Skara wiped the blood off of his mouth as he watched Pogrel. "I'm fine. But we need to find Renna and get out of here. Someone knows we're here and what happened in Banrielle. There's a bounty out for us."

Faine lifted his head and looked over at Skara, shaking his head. "That doesn't make any sense. How could anyone know where we are? How does anyone even know who we are?" Faine rubbed his eyes and stared at the floor as a loud voice cut across the room.

"There they are! Seize them!"

Five armed guards rushed at them from the door, heavy chainmail showing beneath their blue and green tabards.

Glancing over, Faine spoke quickly, keeping his voice low. "Do what they say, Skara. Don't fight them, or they'll kill you. No bounty will stop that if you give them any reason to hurt you." Putting his hands above his head, he leaned forward, showing that he was unarmed.

The guards lifted Faine off the ground and bound his hands. Pointing their swords at Skara, they pulled the daggers out of his belt and dropped them on the floor. Wrapping a rope around his torso, they yanked him to his feet, keeping a tight hold on the line.

As the guards looked at the destruction around the room, Haldon burst through the door and ran over to Pogrel. Checking his wounds, he glanced up at the nearest guard. "He needs a healer. Look at his hand. Look at what that monster did to 'im."

Pulling Skara and Faine over towards Pogrel, one of the guards gestured towards the dead body, then down to the injured man. "What do you have to say about this?"

Faine turned his eyes towards the men before looking back at the guards. "We were defending ourselves. We just wanted to sit in peace, but these men wouldn't leave us alone."

Haldon opened his mouth, anger crossing his face. "They're criminals. We heard that someone wanted 'em caught and we saw 'em. I didn't think it would turn out this way."

Skara clenched his fists, tugging at the rope as he scowled at the man. "It wouldn't have had to if you had left me alone. I told you to go away, but you didn't listen. Looks like your friends got what they deserved."

In a quick back-handed swing, the guard slapped Skara across the face. "You shut your mouth, filth. You're lucky we don't kill you right here for this. Take 'em away. We'll deal with them later after we clean up this mess. And will someone fetch us a damn healer!"

Spitting a trickle of blood onto the floor, Skara followed the guards out of the inn, his arms held fast to his sides by the rope. Turning out onto the street, crowds of people stood on the side of the lane, watching as Skara and Faine were escorted out of the inn. Two armed guards led the way, shouting for the onlookers to clear a path, while two followed behind, keeping their captives in the middle. Whispers and shouts spread through the crowd about the destruction the two murderers had left at the inn, and how they needed to be locked away for the safety of the town.

After walking for nearly a mile through the winding streets towards the dock district, a vast expanse opened into a barren yard surrounded by the backs of buildings and a small strip of dense forest to one side. In the center was a large stone building, its pale stone glowing orange in the lantern light. A tall watchtower stood at the entrance to the prison and was surrounded by four smaller towers standing at every corner of the square structure, all connected by long walkways that ran along the top of the stone fortress.

Black iron bars covered the small windows and a heavy gate barred the main entrance. Shouting to the gate guards keeping watch on the wall, the gates creaked open, raising into a slot that led up into the central tower.

"I don't remember seeing this when we were pulling into town. But it looks cozy," Faine said, looking up at the massive gate being pulled upwards into the gatehouse.

"You keep your mouth shut, scum," one of the guards said, pushing the two through the open gate. "From this point on, you only speak when spoken to."

Passing through the door, the thick walls of the fortress rose up in an archway around them. Reinforced wooden doors stood on each side of the wall, leading up a stairwell into several small rooms and sleeping quarters in the towers. The inside of the prison stretched out in five cell blocks leading off like fingers from the central corridor with three on the left and two on the right. Each cell block held ten cells, five on each side divided by a smooth walkway patrolled by guards, with the back half of the fortress leading to an open yard for prisoners to be occasionally let out into the fresh air. Continuing past the cells, Skara and Faine were led to a small holding cell in the back righthand corner of the building.

"Welcome to Stonekeep. Better make yourselves comfortable. You may be here a while," one of the guards said as she removed their bindings. "Got any questions?"

The small cell sat in the corner of a larger room and was surrounded by walls on each side. Two of the walls were made of the thick stone of the fortress with only a single, barred window looking out towards the backs of several shops that stood outside of the clearing, while the other two were made of black pitted metal bars. The floor was made of smooth stone that had buckled and split with dirt rising through the gaps. A worn hay mattress was tossed into the back corner, stained and damp from any number of liquids that could have soaked into the fabric.

Rubbing the rope burns on his wrists, Faine looked up at the guard and smiled. "If it's not too much trouble, would it be possible to get a few pillows and some mugs of ale? Or maybe a few bits of cloth to hang up around the cell for a bit of privacy?"

The guard smirked at Faine and slammed the door shut, rattling the cage as she locked the door. "Let's see how long you keep that sense of humor in here. You got it easy tonight. Come tomorrow morning, the commander'll be in and sort you out. But don't worry, I'm sure he'll fix you both up real nice." Laughing to herself, the guard slid the keys into a drawer in a nearby desk and motioned for one of the guards to stay and watch the prisoners as she walked off down the main corridor.

Sighing, Faine sat down on the uneven floor and rubbed his sore ribs as he glanced around the dimly lit room. Lanterns hung on the walls outside of the cell, casting flickering shadows of the bars along the back wall. The faint smell of the ocean blew in through the small window, helping to drown out some of the foul odors that wafted inside the dense stone walls. Touching his fingers to a small cut on his left bicep, he looked over at Skara sitting in the corner. "Don't look so worried. We'll find a way out of this."

Skara pulled his legs up to his chest and rubbed his hands roughly through his hair. "What do you mean, don't worry? I don't know if you've noticed, but we're sitting in what looks like a pretty heavily guarded prison."

"I've been in worse."

Skara shook his head and pulled out a small antler tip necklace from under his shirt and rubbed his fingers slowly over the rune carved into its surface. "If I knew I'd just end up rotting in a cell, I would have stayed back in Banrielle. And that's if I even live long enough to rot."

Faine glanced over at Skara and smiled. "Well, you're gonna rot one way or another. If it's not here, it'll just be somewhere else."

Skara scowled as he threw a clump of dirt at Faine. "This is your fault. If you hadn't scampered off for a tryst with that barmaid, we might not be in here right now."

"I can't help it if the women find me irresistible. Besides, I had just spent weeks on the road with all of you and needed someone that smelled pleasant to get the stink of the road out of my nose." Faine looked down and pulled at a small patch of grass growing between several of the cracked stones on the floor. "But don't worry about this. This is just a minor setback. We'll be outta here in no time."

Skara sighed as he leaned his head back against the wall. "I hope so. Otherwise, I might just have to take one of your ears and offer it to the guards as payment for my release."

Faine smiled to himself as he looked up through the bars in their cell. He had a feeling that Skara was making a joke, but he didn't want to be stuck in jail long enough to find out.

BRAIG'S EYES DARTED open as a loud knock rattled the wooden door to his room. "I told you to leave me alone."

"And I told you if there was any trouble that you'd be out. Your time here is over."

Slamming his feet to the floor, Braig ran his hand through his beard and stomped over to the door, jerking it open. "By the stone, boy! I told you I didn't want to be bothered."

The innkeeper and two armed men stood outside in the hallway, their faces stern as they looked down at the dwarf. "Get your bags and get out."

"What's this all about? What reason do you have to be here banging at the door? I've been in my room all evening."

One of the men stepped forward and squared his shoulders as he rested his hand on his sword hilt. "Your friends caused a bit of a tussle and are in jail where they belong. And if you don't want to join them, you need to shut your mouth and do as your told. The innkeeper said he wants you out, so that's what you're gonna do." The man looked at the bags thrown around the room before turning his eyes back to Braig. "And we'll be taking any coin you have to help pay for the damages."

Thinking about the coins hidden under his mattress, Braig glanced at the bags lying on the floor near his bed, anger rising up inside of him as he glared at the innkeeper. "We don't have any coin. All we have left is our road-stained clothing that stinks of sweat and horse. It took all we had just to get here and pay for our rooms. And since we haven't even stayed a night, I'm sure the amount we paid will more than cover the cost of any damages." Looking up at the two men,

Braig stretched his shoulders and clenched his fists. "Now tell me what happened down there. Where are my companions?"

The two men glanced at each other and stood up straight, bracing themselves in case the dwarf decided to charge them. "Your friends are murderers. They've been taken to The Fist where they belong."

"Murder! What proof do you have?"

The innkeeper waved his arms towards the main room below. "The bloody elf the guards have in custody, and the dead body down there on the floor is proof enough. The elf said you was priests that wouldn't cause any trouble, but I should have known better when I saw two green-skins with 'im. Now I have to spend hours scrubbing blood off the floor. That's what I get for trying to be gracious and give travelers a place to stay. I should've trusted my gut. But that's enough chatter. Get your bags and get out. I have more problems to deal with and don't have time to waste on the likes of you."

Braig let out a grunt and ran his hand over the back of his neck. He knew that trouble would eventually find them, he just didn't think it would be this soon. Glancing at the bags on the floor behind him, he leaned his head out of the door and peered down the hallway. "You'll have to give me some time. I have to get all our gear. It's not just me that had things here."

One of the men stepped forward, pushing his head into the open door as he scanned Braig's room. "You better make it quick. And we'll be here watching to make sure you don't steal anything."

Braig clenched his teeth as he made his way around the room, grabbing his clothing and keeping his distance from the coins hidden under his mattress. If the men knew he had any gold, they would likely take it for themselves, not caring whether or not the money they had already paid covered the damages. With his bag flung over his shoulder and his arms full, he moved from room to room, gathering all of their supplies and stacking them in a single pile in the hallway.

Glancing down at the mound of sacks, Braig stared up at the two armed men keeping an eye on him. "And how am I supposed to carry all this? I don't suppose you're gonna offer me a horse and cart since you're throwing me out of here, are ya?"

"That's not our problem. Now pick up this trash and get moving. Make a few trips if you have to but get it out of here."

Braig clenched his fists and began to load bags onto his back and walk down the stairs. The room below him was covered in bits of smashed wood and fresh blood on the floor. Noticing several guards inspecting the body near the corner of the room, he kept his head down, trying not to draw too much attention to himself. Stopping to pick up Skara's daggers, Braig pushed his way through the small crowds of onlookers and strode towards the door.

Calling over the stable boy, he told him to keep an eye on his bags while he made several more trips into the inn to gather the rest of their gear. Piling their supplies in a nearby alley, he made his way back inside, keeping his head low as he made several trips back and forth for the rest of their belongings.

After grabbing the last of his bags, Braig turned to look at the broken tables and blood strewn across the room one last time. He wasn't sure what happened, but he knew that a place with a name like The Fist wasn't anywhere he'd want to be.

Noticing the scowl on the innkeeper's face, Braig glanced over his shoulder at the two armed men behind him.

"You see what your friends did down here? Now keep moving before we make you look like that body over there on the floor."

Shaking his head, Braig gave the innkeeper one last glare before he stepped out of the front door and trudged over to his bags stacked in the alleyway next to the inn. Leaning heavily against the wall, he slid down to the dirty cobblestones and rubbed his hands roughly over his face. Not sure of what he should do next, he looked up at the stable boy standing in the shadows next to him.

"I need you to do one more thing for me," Braig said, looking around to make sure no one was nearby.

"What'll that be, sir?"

"I need you to run and fetch Ferhani for me. There's some coin in it for ya if you hurry. Otherwise, there may not be anything left I can give you."

The boy looked up and down the road and nodded to Braig. "I'll be back as soon as I can, sir. But I can't guarantee that she'll come."

Braig sighed as the boy took off running down the road, leaving small clouds of dust behind his heels as he ran. Pulling his shield closer to his chest, he watched crowds of people as they sauntered by, eyeing all the bags sitting next to him in the dark alley. Clenching his sword in his hand, he gazed down the road, hoping to see a familiar face sooner than later. "She'll come, boy. She has to come."

A Tale of Sigurn and Ingrid

B odhran stood as silent as stone on the stage, his thick fingers holding the long scroll open in front of him, letting its length rest neatly on the floor in front of his feet. The low hum of chatter fell silent as Bodhran turned his eyes from one table to the next, studying the crowd. His voice boomed across the room as he spoke, reading aloud from the scroll.

"The tale of Sigurn Follan and Ingrid of Drell is a story of bravery, love, victory, and also of tragedy. Our tale begins in the northern reaches of Svegard over a thousand years ago, on a morning not unlike any other for our heroines. For our heroines, you see, were hunters of great renown. Not simple hunters like you or I, but hunters of great beasts and abominations of dark magic. They were called from town to town, land to land, to vanquish the loathsome creatures that brought havoc or left death in their wake. But it was in Wolden that they began what would be their greatest triumph and last great hunt. For it was on this morning that they were called eastward to hunt a foul and terrible evil that had befallen the city of Hammerhold.

"For you see, the great keep of Hammerhold held many riches of both gold and magic. The dwarves and men inhabiting the city had been burrowing deep into the heart of Hi-

raeth to find the treasures that ran through its veins while es-
tablishing trade routes on the surface to sell their beautifully
crafted wares. But tales of the precious gems and metals soon
spread and began to attract unwanted attention. For greed,
you see, is a powerful thing that can corrupt even the purest
of intentions. It began with creatures pouring from the dark
tunnels deep beneath the ground, claiming lives as they filled
their bellies on the flesh of their victims and stuffing their
pouches full before scurrying back into the darkness. But the
worst was yet to come."

Pausing to give a quick glance over the crowd, Bodhran
adjusted the scroll and took a small sip out of a cup sitting
on the small table next to him. As a brief silence filled the
room, he let his intense stare fall onto several of the men and
women in the crowd before lowering his eyes back to the
scroll.

Renna could hear low whispers from nearby tables as
several mugs clinked against the wooden tabletops as people
took long drinks of their ale, their eyes wide as they waited
for the story to continue. Raising one of his arms high into
the air, Bodhran's loud voice bellowed across the open room,
bringing an end to the low murmur of whispers as he continued to read from the long scroll.

"Soon, over the hills to the east, a shadow emerged,
blocking the light of the sun as it flew, casting a deep shadow
across the walls of the keep. It was a large winged creature,
the likes of which had not been seen for over a hundred
years. But this was not the first time this creature had been
seen, for it was known throughout the land as a scourge, a
desecrator of temples, and a destroyer of fields. It had been

dormant for so long that most believed the creature was nothing more than a fable told to scare small children into doing what they were told. But alas, it had returned once more to cause chaos and leave destruction in its wake. It was, you see, the Black Dragon of Edinmoore."

Renna shifted in her seat as she took a long drink of her mead, draining the mug and holding it up in the air, motioning for another. As the barmaid refilled her cup, Renna set down several copper coins on the table, never turning her attention from Bodhran as he continued to speak, his voice steady and deep.

"And so, word had been sent westward on the wings of a raven to call for the aid of Sigurn and Ingrid, the great slayers of beasts. For those inhabiting Hammerhold knew not what to do against a creature such as this and were hard-pressed to keep the dragon at bay. But the distance was great, and no one knew if word of the beast would reach them in time. And as the days passed, hope began to fade for those in the keep as they saw no signs of Sigurn and Ingrid on the horizon.

"But, unbeknownst to them, Sigurn and Ingrid were within two days of the keep, pushing ever onwards, stopping to rest only when exhaustion nearly pulled them from their saddles. For it was a long ride, and the blowing snow slowed their horses and caused delay, and two days was far too long for those at the keep to withstand the might of their fierce tormentor."

Bodhran set down the scroll and lowered his voice, looking out across the crowd as he spoke, a slight waver in his voice. "The burden of the attacks was too much to bear, and the foundation of the keep had been shaken and left to crumble. The city of Hammerhold was brought to ruin, and the keep collapsed, burying most of the inhabitants and treasure beneath its great walls. But despite all the death and destruction, the dragon was not yet satisfied, and its bloodlust not yet sated. Turning its gaze south, the beast began its journey across the Usarq to the land of Breoce in Auren."

The crowd sat in silence as the weight of his words sank in. Although the destruction was far to the west, stories of the loss of life had traveled across the ocean with merchants, bards, and those that had seen the death firsthand. It could have just as easily been Uthrea that had felt the wicked bite of the dragon, and the fear that it could happen again was always waiting, pushed deep into their souls, hidden away out of sight.

Straightening his shoulders, Bodhran took a deep breath, bowing his head slightly as he picked up the scroll and continued. "And as Sigurn and Ingrid looked upon the ruin of Hammerhold, they were shocked to see so few survivors. Cold, starving and afraid, those that had lived were huddled close to the crumbled walls of the once great keep and were warming their bloodied, cracked hands near the small fires that were littered across the wreckage. After hearing the story of the downfall, Sigurn and Ingrid gathered a small crew of willing and able sailors and set off across the Usarq Ocean to track the beast, hoping to finally end its tyranny and spare other towns from suffering the same fate as Hammerhold.

"But again, they were too late. As the pair set foot on land and made their way to the town of Blackbriar, they were told by travelers and townsfolk that the dragon had been seen flying southward, heading towards the village of Siegen. Again, the two huntresses were too late. As Sigurn and Ingrid arrived in Siegen, it was in ruins, smashed like a pebble under a hammer. The buildings and homes were broken and destroyed. The stones of the once tall towers were crumbled, feeble, and hunched like an old man that had seen too many winters. The bare bones of the town were scattered across the landscape, and the weeping could be heard from every direction. Although they couldn't match the speed of the dragon, they pushed onwards, determined to follow the beast to the ends of the world if they had to. Immediately, the pair set off and continued their hunt for the Black Dragon of Edinmoore."

Bodhran stretched out his arms, pointing off towards the distance, motioning with his hands as his voice became louder and faster with the twists of the tale. "Continuing forward, their hunt led them over hills and forests, across plains and valleys, only to arrive in Norgrath, which had been decimated. The shops were torn apart like paper in the rain. The thatched roofs and stables were covered in mud and littered with bloody bones. The great beast, it would seem, had grown hungry and had eaten the livestock and several of the inhabitants of the town. But there was a glimmer of hope amidst the destruction, and the townsfolk weren't as unprepared as the other unfortunate towns.

"Norgrath, being so close to Smuggler's Pass, had its fair share of trouble and had made preparations to protect themselves as best they could. And because of earlier attacks on the city, large harpoons had been crafted that were capable of piercing the hulls of attacking vessels. These bolts helped to keep bandits or raiders at bay that might be looking for what they believed to be easy treasure from the town or to stop those trying to escape into the rocky crags of the pass. And it was with one of these bolts that the dragon was injured. The shot, while missing its mark, was able to pierce one of the thin membranes on the wing of the beast, tearing a large hole that slowed the dragon's flight. Knowing this could be their only chance, Sigurn and Ingrid set out to try to head off the beast before it reached the next town to the west.

"The pair, bolstered by hope, boarded a small vessel and began to navigate through the treacherous rocks that littered Smuggler's pass. Time seemed to slow as they spent the day-light hours scanning the horizon for any signs of movement, and it was on their second day in the pass when they noticed something dark flitting in the sky several miles ahead of them. It was the black dragon, darting from massive stone to massive stone above the still, deep waters below. It would seem that the damage to its wing had worsened when it tried to fly, and it now had a jagged tear running the length of a single membrane of its tri-sectioned wing. And although injured, its wings weren't completely useless, and it was still able to carry itself nearly a mile before it needed to rest.

"But as the pair grew closer, the dragon became aware of their presence and flew towards the mountain range that fol-lowed the river on its southern side. Using its sheer strength, it flew high into the sky, landing on a jagged outcropping of rocks near the peak of the mountain, clawing its way up-wards and over until it was out sight. Knowing there would be no way to follow its route over the steep mountain, Sigurn and Ingrid sailed onwards, desperately looking for any pathway that cut through the towering stones of the mountains. Had it not been for the Thiarri in their high elven city of Lunorin, Sigurn and Ingrid could have passed through the mountain range on the heels of the dragon, possibly overtaking it before it could make its escape. But alas, nearly half a day had passed when they finally reached a point beyond the mountain range that would allow them to head south without passing through the hostile land of the Thiarri."

Several hisses and boos came from the crowd at the mention of the high elves. Mugs and fists pounded steadily on the tables, and Renna saw several dirty looks pointed in her direction as Bodhran raised his hands in the air to silence the crowd. She had no idea why she would be getting dirty looks at the mention of high elves. Although she had elvish blood, it was clear that she also had orcish blood flowing through her veins. Thinking that it was most likely just ignorance or general dislike for anyone different, she shook her head and took another drink of her mead and turned her attention back to the dwarf as his voice drifted across the room.

"It was a grueling ride towards the town of Asheborn, but by luck or sheer force of will, Sigurn and Ingrid managed to arrive before the dragon and made haste in their preparations, for the dragon could arrive at any moment. As Sigurn rallied the warriors and all able-bodied peasants in the town, Ingrid prepared spells and rituals to aid her in the upcoming battle. Defenses were set as best as could be managed, and those that couldn't fight were evacuated south to cross the ferry and make their way to the port city of Marillia."

Moving to the edge of the stage, Bodhran's eyes flickered from one person to the next as he continued, his voice low and soft. "As the sun began to set and the torches were lit throughout the town, Sigurn and Ingrid rested on the battlements. Their journey thus far had been long and full of peril, and their bodies were weary from the hard road. But alas, there could be little rest when facing such a beast as the Black Dragon."

The entranced crowd leaned forward in their seats, hanging on every softly spoken word. A heavy silence fell over the room as all eyes stared towards the stage. Suddenly, Bodhran clapped his hands loudly, the sharp noise echoing off the walls. Renna, along with several others in the pub jumped at the sound of the thundering clap. Letting out a slight laugh, she leaned back in her chair and checked the flower in her hair before looking around the room at the other patrons that were smiling at the brief fright.

Raising his voice, Bodhran waved his arms and shook his hands furiously as his pace quickened. "But unfortunately, their rest was short-lived, as all heard the crashing sound, growing louder as it crashed in closer and closer. To the east of town in the darkly dense forest, the trees bent and snapped as the monstrous creature pushed its way through, roaring and hissing in its blood craze. Its great, black body slithered like a snake through the trees, and its long, sharp, piercing tail waved above the tops of the cedars, like a great spear being carried into battle.

"The time had arrived. All of their hardships and joys had led them to this point, at this time—the following of the flowing threads of fate that would either continue to weave the story of their lives…or be snipped from the very tapestry of mortal life. It had all led to this.

"The dragon stepped into the clearing to stare into the faces of the frightened onlookers. Its heavy steps shaking the very ground, causing even the land to tremble at the might. Opening wide its fearsome maw, its heaving chest expanded with a deep breath that exhaled into a mind-piercing screech, causing all to cower and cover their ears against the shrill cry. And with a mighty flap of its wings, the dragon ascended and move forward towards the meager defenses that had been made.

"Sigurn steadied herself and called for a volley of arrows, which did little, if anything, to slow the beast. As it flew forward on broken and unsteady wings, its razor-sharp talons tore through the defensive walls before landing roughly in the heart of the town. Its tail swung from side to side, smashing person and building alike, with regard for nothing but its own bloodlust. As Ingrid looked on, she couldn't help but think that the dragon was terrible, yet beautiful to behold. Its scales were smooth with sharp, thorn-like points that shown with a bluish hue as the light of the torches cast faint light onto its writhing body. Its four legs were powerful and taloned, and its pointed yellow teeth glinted with flecks of red as it tore apart any living creature that got too close. Beautiful, she thought, yet terrible.

"But one by one, all that challenged the dragon were struck down. Yet in its wild thrashing, it had destroyed several of the storage buildings containing food and supplies. In the destruction, numerous barrels of potent alcohol had burst and now covered the walls and ground beneath the dragon. As the fumes rose around the great beast, the flammable liquid spread across the ground to reach a fallen torch, causing a bright flash of blue flame that quickly engulfed the dragon, causing it to reel backwards. The ground beneath its feet lit up in flames, and the fire licked at its belly. And while its scales were hard like shields, its eyes had been seared the blast.

"The great dragon began to swing its head from side to side, crashing into the crumbling structures of stone buildings, wildly trying to escape the flames and regain its vision. The dragon, feeling a sudden sense of fear, began to flap its wings to try to clear itself from any danger; but its wings were now greatly torn, and the flames had singed them, burning their edges like a piece of parchment. As soon as the dragon tried to fly, its wings would give out, and it would fall the short distance back to the ground.

"Agitated, it tried again, getting a bit farther and higher, only to fall once more. And in its blind escape, as its massive body dropped down above the rubble, the right side of its neck caught on a thick, sharp piece of timber that had once been part of the foundation of a building. The broken shard of shattered wood caught under one of the scales of the dragon's neck, tearing it loose. As the blood fell from the open wound, the dragon screeched in pain, digging its talons into the rubble as it propelled itself forward and up, using all its strength to fly away. And with tattered wings and sheer force, it was able to fly unsteadily through the forest to the east and back towards the mountains. Sigurn, Ingrid, and a handful of warriors from Asheborn gave pursuit.

"For what seemed like countless hours the party gave chase, hoping to gain ground on the injured dragon. And although the broken trees cut a clear path through the forest, food and rest were scarce as they moved towards the base of the mountains. Weary and unsure of the upcoming battle, the warriors sought shelter in the fallen trees and huddled next to small fires as they honed their blades and wondered if they would finish the hunt in victory, or take their place among the heroic dead. All the while, they could hear the screeches of the great beast in the distance, waiting for them somewhere in the darkness."

Renna felt a shiver roll down her spine as she imagined being huddled in a broken forest, hearing the screeches of a great beast lurking somewhere in the shadows beyond, wondering if it was watching you from the darkness. The loud thud of a mug being set on a nearby table pulled her out of her thoughts, but the feeling of being watched still prickled at her mind. Taking a quick glance around the room, she saw several men at a table in the back corner laughing to themselves, staring in her direction and making obscene gestures with their hands and mouths. Not wanting to interrupt the reading, Renna shot them a quick scowl and stretched out her middle finger in their direction before turning her attention back to Bodhran. The men at the table laughed and nodded to each other as the dwarf cleared his throat and continued to speak.

"The dawn broke early the next morning, and the frost glinted faintly in the dim light that filtered down through the trees. But there were no sounds to be heard, no life rustling through the branches. Gone was the winter bird, and with it, its song. The forest was empty and silent as they made their way out of the trees and into the vast clearing before the base of the mountain. And as they set foot into the barren field, there sat the Black Dragon of Edinmoore, its forked tongue flicking from its mouth, warning them to stay away.

"But the group of eight advanced forward, despite the warning, with Sigurn and Ingrid leading the way. And as they pressed onward with swords and shields at the ready, the dragon let out a roar that shook the ground and charged at the companions. Calling on the magic inside of her, Ingrid quickly loosed a ball of fire from her hands that struck the dragon square between the eyes, causing it to stagger. Using the fleeting moment to her advantage, she quickly followed with a tangle of roots and vines that erupted from the ground to wind around the dragon's legs, slowing its advance to a crawl as the thorned branches twisted and tightened over its body. But the dragon was all muscle, sharp teeth and claws, and the vines that held it began to strain and snap under its writhing.

"Seizing what could be their only opportunity, the group began to spread out around the dragon in hopes of surrounding it. But the dragon had become enraged, and its wings strained against its bonds as it whipped its large head from side to side, eyeing the hunters with blurry vision before turning to focus its gaze on Ingrid. And as their eyes connected – deep brown to seared black and red - the beast hissed sharply, letting out a piercing screech that forced Ingrid to drop to one knee and summon an arcane shield, dulling the sharp blast that threatened to cut through her like a knife. Straining to withstand the blast, she held the magical barrier until the fearsome noise abated, leaving her disoriented in its wake. Ears still ringing from the cries, she rose unsteadily to her feet and outstretched her hands, sending a stream of snow and ice towards the beast; but the dragon's hardened scales only glazed over before the ice cracked and fell in a heap to shatter at its feet."

Renna could feel her heart beating faster and noticed that she was gripping the edge of the table with one hand and her mug with the other. Leaning back in her chair, she drained the last bit of mead from her cup before crossing her arms over her chest, tapping on one of her tusks with her thumb. Glancing towards the table in the back of the room, she saw that all but one of the men that had been making gestures towards her had their eyes fixed on the stage, enthralled by the story; the last sat stone-faced, staring in her direction. The muscles in his jaw were clenched, and his eyes were wide as he stared out of the dark corner, a slight smirk turning up the edges of his lips.

Feeling a tightness growing in her stomach, Renna reached down and felt for the dagger in her boot before looking back towards the door. If she decided to leave now, the crowds outside on the streets might be thinner, but she wasn't sure if that would be better or worse for her. She knew if it came to a fight, she could take care of herself, but the unfamiliar streets and an unknown number of attackers that could come from any direction would put her at a disadvantage. Hearing Bodhran's loud voice echo through the room, Renna gave one last glance behind her and noticed that the red-haired woman was still watching the show; and that at least brought her a small measure of comfort, even if she didn't know why.

"Seeing the ice spell fail, Sigurn knew that the only chance they had was to go for the wound below the missing scale in the dragon's neck; the single opening on its armored body. And while Ingrid held its attention with spells of fire, ice, and shards of stone, Sigurn gave the order for all to release a volley of arrows and aim for the dragon's bleary eyes or torn neck. But alas, the arrows bounced and shattered off the blackened scales with not one reaching its mark. Hope was losing its hold in the hearts of the men and women, and desperation was rushing in to take its place.

"And it was in this desperate moment, while the dragon's head was raised in a loud roar, that several of the warriors bolted passed Sigurn towards the neck of the dragon, hoping to pierce its wounded flesh with sword and spear. Sigurn shouted for them to halt, but they didn't listen, or couldn't hear over the sound of snapping vines and the bowel-shaking, thunderous cries of the great beast. Without thinking, she sprinted behind them—though there was no chance to catch them in their mad dash. But the vines that had twisted and tangled around the beast could no longer hold the thrashing might beneath them, and the dragon's wing burst free, smashing hard into the three charging men. Their bodies bent and flailed as the force of the blow sent them flying through the air, crashing like a wave of crumbled bone and broken armor directly onto Sigurn.

"The force of the men hitting her body twisted her around and brought her to her knees. Disoriented, Sigurn's head spun as she struggled to catch her breath as the ground moved and shifted beneath her. But just as she began to rise, another wave crashed hard into her back, forcing the air from her lungs in a loud gasp. There, protruding from her chest was the tip of the long, spear-like tail of the dragon, dripping red with Sigurn's blood. Gripping the tip of the tail tightly in her hands, the intensity of the pain shot through her body, filling her with an icy cold that sank deep into her bones. She could hear the hiss of the great beast behind her, mocking her vain efforts to bring its reign of terror to end. Then, everything fell silent. The sounds of crackling spells, snapping vines, the clattering of sword against shield, and the sound of Ingrid's cries all fell away to nothing. And as her vision faded to the encroaching darkness, she turned her head to see Ingrid, the women she had loved for so many years, falling to her knees, her mouth opened in a silent scream. And as the tears fell from her eyes, Sigurn smiled, and all faded to black."

A small gasp escaped Renna's lips as her hand rested over her mouth. Her eyes were wide and damp, and her mouth felt hot and dry as her breath caught in her throat. She couldn't imagine what it must have been like to watch the person you loved be killed right in front of your eyes, and not being able to do anything to stop it. Wiping a single tear off of her cheek, she pushed down the ache and longing she felt growing in her chest and took a quick drink of mead to help steady her nerves. Setting the cup down quietly, she leaned forward, resting her arm on the table as she scratched at the hard surface with her fingernails, staring at the stage and letting herself get lost in Bodhran's words.

"Ingrid, her heart now heavy with grief and anger, had watched as the men charged the dragon while Sigurn yelled at them to stop. But they wouldn't listen. She had watched as they flew into Sigurn, knocking her backwards. And she watched as the dragon looked directly at her and sneered, exposing its teeth in a grotesque smile as it plunged its tail right into Sigurn's heart; and it was in that moment that Ingrid knew, even if she somehow lived, that the dragon had just killed them both.

"Feeling the burden of the death of her beloved dragging her down, Ingrid fell to her knees, all her hope lost, blowing away like a leaf on the cold wind. She had seen Sigurn smile at her one last time before her glowing light was snuffed from the world. Then, still in shock, she looked on in horror as the creature lifted Sigurn's body into the air and tossed it aside like a crumpled rag doll with a quick flick of its tail.

"The remaining warriors let out war cries as they charged, swords and axes glinting in the morning sun. And although they struck with all their might, their blows did little against the hard, shield-like scales of the beast. But the dragon paid no attention to the warriors at its legs. Instead, it only snarled and flicked its tail toward Ingrid, spattering her face with the still-warm blood of Sigurn; and deep inside, Ingrid felt her heart break. But it was in this moment that something else inside her broke; like a dam unleashing its torrent after heavy rain. There was a power there. Something she had never felt before welled up inside her. Drawing her sword, she heard the great dragon hiss in what could only be laughter as she sprinted forward, quickly closing the gap between them.

"Just as she was nearing its great maw, its taloned hand reached out, catching her in its grasp. Its sharp claws tore into her, burying themselves in her flesh as its grip tightened around her body, nearly squeezing the breath out of her...nearly. And as the dragon drew her closer to its jagged teeth, a great burst of energy exploded from Ingrid. It was like a roaring clap of thunder that shook the ground, bursting outwards in all directions in a brilliant sphere of white light that extended farther than her vision. The warriors fighting below her were knocked aside, and a great and heavy silence fell over them.

"Stunned by the blast, the terrible beast tilted its head backwards, the taloned hand gripping Ingrid swaying closer to its body, bringing her within striking distance of its open wound. Drawing on the immense power she felt welling up inside her, she channeled one last spell into her sword and plunged it deep into the gash in the dragon's neck. The sharp blade cut effortlessly through the muscle and sinew, unleashing the full force of Ingrid's power into the very blood of the beast.

"Screeching in pain, the black dragon whipped and writhed against the fury that burrowed its way deeper into its body, but it was too late. The sword, held tightly in Ingrid's grasp, had seared itself to the muscle, halting the dragon's movement as it began to turn its body to stone, spreading from the wound outwards. Ingrid gritted her teeth as the dragon's head turned to look at her, snarling, hate filling its hazy eyes.

"But there was no stopping the spell that coursed through its veins, moving swiftly down its body into its tail,

and finally into its claws, which pierced Ingrid's flesh, allowing the untamed magic to flow back into her. She could feel
the tightness growing in her chest, stiffening her limbs, binding her together in hatred with the monster that had killed
Sigurn. And as her body turned to stone, she glared defiant-
ly into the eyes of the beast and took satisfaction in knowing that its reign of terror was finally over, and she had her
vengeance for the death of Sigurn.

"And from that day forward, the mountain to the west
of Lunorin had become known as The Sleeping Mountain.
For you see, the spell was so great, its magic so powerful and
enduring, that no sounds are heard on that section of the
mountain. It's as if no wind rustles the leaves, and no birds
sing in its branches. And if you make the journey to the base
of the mountain, you will see the great dragon and be able
to pay your respects to Ingrid, for their bodies remain there,
locked in stone to this very day."

The room was silent as Bodhran rolled up the scroll and
held it under his arm while he took a long drink. Renna
wiped away the tears on her cheek and looked around the
room, watching as others dabbed their eyes or whispered
to each other, nodding their heads as they pointed towards
the stage. From the back of the room, the sound of clapping
echoed off the walls of the pub, pulling people back into the
present moment. Applause erupted across the room as chairs
and tables skidded against the hardwood floor as Bodhran
received a standing ovation. Renna quickly stood and began
clapping and shouting, watching as the beardless dwarf
bowed several times before picking up his scrolls and saun-

tering off the stage into the back room, nodding his head to the audience as he walked.

Exhausted from the tale, Renna collapsed back into her chair and motioned for the barmaid to bring her another mug of mead. Putting her head into her hands, she closed her eyes, rubbing them as she waited for her drink. Hearing the sound of footsteps coming up to her table, she opened her eyes and reached for her mug, thinking the barmaid had come to refill it. Feeling that it was still empty, she looked up to see two of the men that were making rude gestures at her standing at the edge of the table, half-smiling as they stared down at her.

"So, what'd ya think of the show, love? Get ya thinkin' about things, did it?" The man winked and took a drink from his mug, smiling as he wiped some ale froth out of his thick mustache with his fingers.

The man that had been smirking and staring at her through the show laughed and nudged the other man with his elbow. "Course it did. All these whores are the same. Always thinking 'bout love. But more than that, they're always thinkin' 'bout coin. Isn't that right, sweetheart? Cause sometimes, they go together, love and coin."

Renna gripped her mug and scowled at the two men standing at the edge of her table, ready to lash out if someone put a hand on her. "Don't mistake me for my mother. I'm not for sale. So why don't you bastards stumble back to your table and leave me alone before you regret coming over here."

"Don't be like that. You know just as well as I do that you're looking for some coin. And I have some for ya if you do what we want. How else are you gonna afford to buy pretty dresses like the one you're wearin'?" The smirking man took out several copper coins and one silver and slapped them down on the table. "Now, this should be more than enough for me and my friend here. We ain't never been with an orc whore before, but I bet you'll have no trouble taking care of the two of us."

The second man laughed as he smoothed his mustache and stared down at Renna. "That's right. I hear that orcs are tough. But you got the look of an elf, though. You look like a good half-breed that knows how to take care of herself. So how about it, love?"

Renna stared at the men as she pushed the coins off the table onto the floor. "I warned you once. Now pick up those coins and move away. If you're looking for some action, it won't be from me. So why don't you just take each other out into a dark alley and be done with it? You don't need some half-breed to do it for you."

The smirking man slammed his hand down on the table and leaned closer to Renna. "If you ain't gonna play nice, we don't have to either. You know how many people go missing 'round here? I could drag you away and kill you in an alley. I could just tell everyone that you tried to rob me. No reason they wouldn't believe me, you bein' a beggar orc-whore and all."

Renna thought about those words and how many times she'd heard them in her youth —orc whore. It was like a stain on her mind that she didn't think would ever be washed away. She thought about all the whippings she'd gotten when she would try to hide or act out of line. Or all the nights she spent alone with her books. But most of all, she thought about how her mother never protected her and how her life could have been so different if she had stayed with her. If she hadn't fled, she very well could have become those two words that were being thrown at her now.

Anger seized her, and her jaw clenched as her hands balled up into fists. Sliding her chair backwards, she started to stand when a woman's voice spoke up from behind her.

"I believe the lady said no."

The two men looked over Renna's shoulder and laughed at the woman standing behind her with her hands resting on her hips. "Oh, is that right? And are you plannin' to take her place, then?"

Renna turned her eyes towards the two men as the red-haired woman stepped around the side of the table and kicked the coins on the floor, scattering them under the near-by tables and drawing the attention of several of the people seated nearby. "No. As far as I'm concerned, you can take those coins there and shove 'em right up your ass."

"Looks like we got us a feisty one," the man with the mustache said, stepping up beside his friend.

The smirking man stepped up closer to the woman, his face nearly touching hers. "Looks that way, don't it? And we know just what to do with feis-"

The red-haired woman slammed her forehead into the man's nose, breaking it with a loud snap. The man stumbled backwards, tripping over his friend as blood poured from his nose. The mustached man stepped forward, his fists balled and ready to fight. Behind him, two more men from the back table stood and stomped towards their downed friend, pre-pared to jump into the brawl if one broke out.

Renna stood and pushed the table over on its side, creating a barrier as she reached for the dagger in her boot.

The red-haired woman looked over at Renna and winked, putting her hand on her arm before she could unsheathe her weapon. "Don't worry, I'll take care of it."

Stepping forward, the red-haired woman held her hands out to her side, palms facing the men. Blue-green flames erupted on the tips of her fingers and spread up her arms. "The first one to step up is gonna be the first one to get burned. You ever see what happens to a sausage that gets cooked too long over a fire? Because you're about to see it firsthand." The woman looked at the four men in front of her, their eyes wide and glaring. "What about it mustache, you want a go with me? I didn't think so. Now, if you don't mind, I'll be walking the lady home. And thanks for taking care of our tab."

The woman started backing towards the door, glancing over at Renna as she moved back. "You ready to go?"

Renna gave the men one last look before she turned her back to them and strolled out the door, holding it open for the woman behind her.

"Thanks for the exciting evening, gentlemen. And if any of you decide to follow us, I'll torch the prick off your body so fast you'll have to squat the next time you need to take a piss. Now I suggest you clean up this mess and sit back down. Understand?"

The men nodded as they looked around the room, not saying a word. The red-haired woman nodded in return as she backed out the door, letting it slam closed as she stepped out into the black night.

A Reason for all Things

B raig leaned his back against the cold stone wall as he looked up and down the dark alley. The orange glow of the flickering lanterns lining the city street cast dancing shadows on the walls around him, setting him on edge. Most of the shops had closed for the night, and aside from a few stragglers stumbling out of the pubs, the lane was nearly empty. But being alone in an alley with gear that could be sold for a good bit of coin made him a target for any thief or cutthroat looking for a mark, and he had noticed more than one suspicious look in his direction as he sat outside the inn. He had no idea what dangers might be lurking in the quiet darkness that loomed around him.

It had already been several hours since he had sent the stable boy to find Ferhani, and he wondered if she would bother to show up or had even gotten the message. What reason did she have to help him now? After all, their business was almost done. All he had to do was show up in the morning, find out when and where to board the ship, and be on his way to the Grey Wastes to find the stone; although he didn't know what good it might be to him. But if it was important enough for the brothers to keep him caged and torture him to try to find it, he'd rather have it be in his hands than in theirs. But leave it up to the drunk elf and the goblin to get into trouble on their first night in town. And where in the hell was Renna when you needed her? At least she could have kept an eye on things.

"Or maybe if ya had stayed down there with 'em this wouldn't have happened," Braig mumbled, giving his beard a slight tug. Glancing down at the supplies thrown into a pile beside him, Braig kicked at Faine's bag of clothes, cursing under his breath. "And what am I supposed to do with all this junk?"

"Why don't you just leave it there, old man. I'll take it off your hands."

Grabbing his sword and shield, Braig looked down the alley and squinted his eyes, trying to see where the voice came from. "It's not yours to take. And if ya think you can shake me, you should think again."

"We're giving you a choice, dwarf. We could have easily killed you where you sat," a low voice said from behind him.

Turning his back to the wall and pulling his shield closer, Braig crouched and looked at the cloaked figures approaching from each end of the alley. "You could have tried. Now, why don't you turn and head back where you came from before you get into something you can't handle."

Pulling back her hood, a tall, broad woman stepped forward, eyeing Braig as she cracked her knuckles. Her blonde hair was short and disheveled, and her face was covered with small scars and smudges of dirt and oil. Undoing the clasp on her cloak, she wrapped the thick material around her left arm, keeping a tight grip on the remaining fabric that hung loosely from her hand. Unsheathing a dagger from her belt, she looked over at her companion and motioned for him to advance and flank the dwarf.

Removing his cloak, the man wrapped it over his arm and pulled a small, curved dagger as he crept forward, keeping his eyes on Braig. His footsteps were quiet, and his clothes were dark and loose, blending smoothly into the darkness around him. If it weren't for the glow of the lanterns on his blade and the buckles on his vest, he would have looked like nothing more than another shadow. "You hear that rattling coming down the street? That's the sound of our wagon comin' for us...and to carry your corpse away to the docks if you don't step aside."

Braig gripped his sword and stepped closer to the pile of gear, putting his foot behind Faine's bag of clothing, a low growl rising from his throat. "I'm giving ya one last chance to walk away from this. There doesn't have to be any bloodshed tonight. I have enough on my mind. I don't want to have to worry about drawing any more attention when I'm riding down the road in your wagon with bits of the two of you all over me and my sword."

The man looked over at his companion, a brief look of doubt crossing his face.

"Enough talking," the woman said, inching closer to Braig. "If you won't give us what we came for, then we've no choice but to take it."

Kicking his foot forward, Braig launched Faine's bag of clothing towards the woman, throwing her off balance as she held her arms up to stop the bag from hitting her in the face. As the woman stumbled backwards, Braig pushed himself off the wall and charged at the woman, smashing into her stomach with his shield, knocking her hard onto her back. Taking advantage of the situation, Braig raised his sword above his head, ready to strike the woman's neck when he felt something heavy slap into his arm and tangle around his sword, nearly pulling the weapon from his hand.

Turning quickly, Braig shook his sword, freeing it from the cloak as the man circled around, blocking his path to the woman. The man swung his cloak again, trying to catch Braig off guard as he lunged forward. Stepping backwards out of the reach of the dagger, the heavy material smacked into the shield, getting hung on its pointed edges. As the man pulled hard on his cloak trying to rip it away, the woman slashed at Braig, nearly striking him several times with her thrusts.

Holding tightly onto his shield, Braig thrust his sword upward, stabbing through the cloak, cutting a long slash in the fabric as he stepped backwards, pulling himself free. The daggers thrust and slashed as Braig moved and parried, being pushed closer to the street. Behind him, he could hear the rumble of the wagon as it rolled down the lane, stopping at the head of the alleyway behind him. Glancing quickly over his shoulder, he saw two large men jump from the wagon, each with large clubs in their hands.

"By the stone! Where's that damned woman when you need her?" Braig said, pushing forward, swinging his sword wildly and catching the cloak-wielding man hard in the arm, severing his hand with the blow.

The man screamed in pain and wrapped the fabric of his cloak over the muscle and bits of bone protruding from his arm, trying to stop the flow of blood pooling out onto the ground below him. Trembling, he stepped back, moving deeper into the shadows as he stared at his severed hand lying on the ground near Braig's feet.

"The damned woman is right here!" Ferhani said, sauntering up behind him, her two companions running past her towards the dagger-wielding attackers, clubs raised.

Wounded and seeing that they were outnumbered, the two thieves retreated farther down the alley, leaving the man's hand behind in a puddle of dark red. "This isn't over. There are more of us on the way right now. They'll be here any second."

Ferhani laughed as she stepped past Braig. "Will they, now? I wouldn't be so sure about that. We passed them back on the road where they tried to rob us. You like the cart?"

The man and the woman glanced at each other before turning and running down the alley, the man leaving a trail of blood as he went.

"Gilly, Lutnar, follow them and finish the job," Ferhani said, waving down the alley. "Make it quick."

The two men nodded and ran off down the alley, following the trail of blood into the darkness.

Braig leaned over onto his shield, trying to catch his breath. "I didn't think you'd come. I sent the boy after you hours ago."

"I know. But I wanted more information before I came traipsing down here with no answers."

Standing up straight, Braig sheathed his sword and rested his arm on his shield. Taking a deep breath, he looked up at Ferhani. "Well, out with it. What'd ya find out?"

"Your friends have been arrested for murder."

"I could've told you that. Did you hear where they're at, or why they got into trouble in the first place? They wouldn't just start a fight for nothing. They knew we had plans to leave soon."

Ferhani shook her head. "I don't know everything, but it looks like there's a warrant out for all of you. Something about an issue with someone with some power back in Banrielle."

Braig scowled and clenched his fists. "It's those damn Brothers of the Flame. I didn't think there were any left that could have seen us—or any that were left alive that could have made it anywhere to tell anyone."

Ferhani raised her eyebrows. "Sounds like you can handle yourself pretty well in a fight. And from what I've seen here, it's no wonder you made it out of Banrielle alive. But I feel like it's more than just the Brothers. I've seen their temples in a few towns, but it's someone else. Someone with a bit more sway. I don't know who yet, but your bounty is fairly high and being paid out by someone with the initials D.E."

Braig rubbed his beard and looked over at the pile of gear near the wall. "Well, I'm hoping it's not something you want to collect on. But if there's a bounty, why didn't the barkeep turn me in? He had plenty of reason after what happened there."

Ferhani laughed and looked over at the wagon. "The barkeep has secrets of his own. Too much attention might get people talking, which might lead the guards to the casks of illegal spirits I sold him that are hidden in his basement. Better to just get you out than risk himself. And you don't have to worry about me. I have no interest in collecting on it. I've been in similar situations a time or two and had to find a way out. It's not easy, but there's always a way."

"And what about the elf and the goblin? Where are they being kept? I can't just leave here and forget about them."

Looking down the alley, Ferhani waved and gestured towards the wagon. "Everything finished, Gilly?"

Gilly and Lutnar walked up beside Ferhani, their brown, sleeveless tunics covered in small spatters of blood. "It's all taken care of."

"Perfect. Now let's get this loaded and get out of here."

"Wait," Braig said as he stepped towards the pile of gear. "I asked a question, and I need an answer."

Ferhani sighed as she held up her hand to Gilly and Lutnar. "Your friends are fine for now, but they only have a couple days before a ship comes for them. Unfortunately, they're being held in Stonekeep—or as people around here call it, The Fist. And before you ask, it has high stone walls and only a few doors, making it a bit tricky to get into. But now's not the time or place to talk about it. Let's load the gear and get out of here before it gets light."

Braig looked over at Ferhani as Gilly and Lutnar loaded the cart. He wasn't sure if he could trust her, but at this point, he had no choice. If he stayed out on the streets, he could be killed, or picked up by the guards and thrown into a cell alongside Faine. "I know you've done more than enough already, and I don't know how to repay you, but there's one more thing in my room, and I can't get back in to get it."

"And what's that?"

Braig pulled at his beard and looked around the alley. "I have the pouch of coins from our business earlier. It's under the mattress. Upper level, last room on the left."

Sighing, Ferhani ran her hands through her hair and walked past the cart and onto the street. Braig rubbed his eyes and began loading the wagon, tossing his sword and shield into the back when heard footsteps thumping against the cobbled street behind him.

"Braig? What's going on? Is everything alright?" Renna said, running up to stop at the wagon, the red-haired woman following close behind her.

Braig held up his hands and looked up at Renna. "There's a problem we need to deal with."

"What kind of problem? Where's Faine and Skara?" Renna said, breathing heavily as she ran around the cart towards the street looking for the other two. "Where are they, Braig?"

"Now hold on. They've been arrested for murder. There's a bounty on our heads, and they got into some trouble. They're at Stonekeep for now. And someone's bound to be coming when they get word they have 'em."

Renna put her head into her hands and leaned against the wagon. "That's it, I have to go. We have to go there now. We can't leave them there."

The red-haired woman stepped up to the edge of the wagon and looked over at Renna. "It's a fortress. If you tried to barge in, you'd barely make it ten feet before you were filled with swords or arrows. I'm sure there's a way in, but it won't do any good if you die trying."

Braig looked over at the woman before looking back at Renna. "And who the hell are you? Renna, you know this woman?"

The red-haired woman looked down at Braig and put her thumbs under her belt, letting her arms relax. "The name's Aenwyn. I was just walking the lady home from the pub. You can never be too careful out here...and I'm only trying to help."

Braig stared up at Renna as she vaguely nodded and looked over at Aenwyn.

"You're right. But leaving them there isn't an option. They wouldn't think twice about coming in for us," Renna said, looking over at Braig. "You know what it's like to be in a cage. We have to do something. We can't just leave them there to rot."

"And you won't," Ferhani said, handing Braig his pouch of coins. "Here's your coins back, less one for my troubles. Now, everyone on the wagon. We can discuss this in a safer place. I have a proposition for you that can work out for all of us."

THE NIGHT AIR WAS COLD and calm as Skara stared out the barred window in his cell. The two moons hung bright in the sky, one large, one small, blotting out the nearest stars with their light. Thinking about what led him here in the first place, he wondered if leaving Banrielle was the right decision. If he hadn't gone to the cave or into town, the inn wouldn't have been burned, and Mary would still be alive. But then again, so would Gregor. Maybe if he had gone back home and waited after killing the brothers, he may have been able to go back to the way things were—or at least something similar. But those weren't the choices he had made, and now he was stuck here with no idea what was going to happen come morning.

Rubbing his hand over his tunic, he loosely traced a symbol on his chest as he mumbled to himself. "You're supposed to help me find my way and keep me from getting lost. Some good you've been."

"Talking to yourself over there?" Faine said, not moving or opening his eyes. "I hope it's a good conversation."

Skara leaned his head against the stone wall and looked over at Faine. "Do you ever think about what got you here?"

"What do you mean?"

"The choices that got you here. Don't you ever wonder what would've happened if you stayed in Murwood?"

"I think about it from time to time. But I think this is where I'm supposed to be," Faine said as he sat up, leaned his back against the wall, and looked around the barren cell. "Well, maybe not here exactly. But you get the idea."

Skara turned his head and looked back out the window. "I just wonder if things would have been different if I had stayed at home instead of going out that morning."

"Of course, things would be different. I most likely wouldn't be here. If it weren't for you, I would have died in that cave and been shat out by a spider."

"And if it weren't for me, Mary would still be alive."

Faine rubbed his hand on his knee and looked over at Skara. "That's not on you. You can't blame yourself for what happened. The brothers abused their authority and used it to manipulate and torment others. I don't have to tell you about that, though. You lived it."

"I know, but-"

"But those things happened, and you can't change it. But you did change what could happen in the future. How many more lives could you have saved by killing Gregor? How many other families had he broken before your paths crossed again? I'm not a big believer in all that fate bullshit, but every now and then, for whatever reason, I think we're in the right place at the right time."

Skara turned to face Faine, crossing his legs and resting his elbows on his knees. "What do you mean?"

Faine let out a soft laugh. "I don't know if you're going to believe me, but I was on my way to becoming a priest before I left home."

"And what changed your mind."

"Corruption and greed. Not my greed, though. I know I have a streak of that in me. No, it was the greed of the priests in the order. It was the comforting of the weak and sick with one hand, and the cutting of their coin pouch with the other. It seemed like no matter what I did, it never really made a difference. It was all just about lying and scheming to move up in the ranks. So really, just another part of life. But it was after a heavy night of drinking and thinking that I decided to let it go and forge my own way—to not be another pawn in the games of men and gods."

"What happened?"

"I had a dream that I came to a fork in the road, one to the left, one to the right. Not sure of which path to choose, I closed my eyes and let my instincts guide me. As I began to walk the shadow-strewn path, the moonlight glimmered through the trees, helping to light my way in the darkness. I could hear strange whispers blowing in the wind, almost like they were inside my head, but too faint to really make out any words.

"As I came to a small clearing, I saw a large stone covered in carvings and inscriptions. At the base of the stone was a massive wolf that just sat there and watched me, like it was curious why I was there, or that it knew I was coming. So I stepped into the clearing, walked up the stone dais, and saw something sitting there, just visible in the moonlight."

"What was it?"

"It was a dagger. And as I reached my hand towards the hilt, the whispers in the breeze began to get louder and louder until they were screams burrowing into my head. I had no idea how to make it stop, so I reached my hand out and took hold of the dagger, and suddenly, all went silent. I felt something shift and change inside me like something had finally woken up. And I knew then what it meant. It was something that I had known all along and never accepted."

Skara moved closer to Faine, strands of black hair hanging loosely over his wide eyes. "And what's that?"

"That I belong on the shadowed path. My place wasn't in some church kneeling and doing nothing. My place was out in the darkness, in the world, with a dagger in my hand. I realized I could do more of what I think is right by being the wolf that devours rather than the sheep led to the slaughter. Life is what you make it. Sometimes it feels horrible, and sometimes it's beautiful. You never really know where your place is until you go out and find it. So, I packed a bag, said my goodbyes, and left." Faine glanced over at Skara as he sat cross-legged and staring. "At least that's what I got out of it. But who knows, maybe I'm wrong and it was just a dream. Or maybe it was all the ale and ember-bloom I had. Who really knows, right?"

Skara moved slowly back against the wall, pulling his loose hair back and tying it into a ponytail. Maybe Faine was right about getting out and finding your place in the world. Although his life wasn't bad in Banrielle, there was always the feeling that it wasn't the way it should be. Killing the brothers had come so easily to him; almost second nature. But what did it mean? Did it mean that his place was on the shadowed path, too? It could be possible that things happened the way they were meant to. He found Faine in the cave, was poisoned and cured, and was finally able to fulfill his promise to his family about killing Gregor. And who knows how many others rest peacefully now that he's dead. Maybe a dagger really can make a difference.

Skara looked back over at Faine, who had moved back onto the floor, his eyes closed, and his arms pulled close to his chest. "And what about Renna? How does she fit into all this?"

"That's not really for me to tell you. She's had some hard times, and we share a lot of the same ideas. We can take care of ourselves, but we also take care of each other. But she wants to run towards adventure—sometimes even if it takes her somewhere she shouldn't be—and I'll be right there with her. She might tell you more about it someday. But that's enough for now. We have an early date with the commander, after all.

Nodding his head, Skara pushed himself into the corner and closed his eyes, letting his mind wander as he drifted into an uneasy sleep, only to be awakened just after dawn by a guard banging his club against the bars of the cell.

"Time to get up, you filthy arda," the guard said, setting down a chunk of bread and a bowl of broth. "Pull yourselves up and crawl over here and eat. The commander will be in shortly, and you're to be up and ready. You answer his questions and show some respect—or me and the boys'll take you out in the yard and teach you some manners." The guard laughed as he banged his club against the bars and walked back up the corridor out of sight.

Skara rubbed his eyes and looked over at Faine. "What does arda mean?"

Brushing the dust of his clothing, Faine walked over to the loaf of bread and tore it in half, tossing a hefty piece to Skara. "An arda is a bug that lives over in the desert. They push around big balls of shit. I think they eat it or build with it or something. I don't really know."

Skara shrugged his shoulders and took a bite out of the bread, pulling hard as he tore off a small piece and began to chew. "This bread is tough."

"Yeah, it's hard. Probably leftovers from the inns and bakeries. Or made somewhere a week ago. I guess that's why they gave us the broth," Faine said, looking down at the bowl of brown liquid. Thin white specks floated on the surface, and he could see bits of something thick and dark sitting on the bottom. Lifting the bowl to his nose, he briefly smelled the broth before making a gagging sound and setting it back on the floor. "But it's rancid, so I'd stay away from it."

Skara took another bite of his bread and went to stand next to Faine, resting his arms on the bars. "What do you think they're going to do with us?"

Looking down the corridor, Faine could hear heavy boots slapping against the stone floor, heading in their direction. "I'm not sure, but I think we're about to find out. Get your arms out of the bars and move back. We don't want to be near their clubs."

Pulling his arms out of the bars, Skara stepped back towards the middle of the room, still clutching his bread. Turning his head towards the sound of the footsteps, he watched as a tall man with heavy brown brigandine armor strolled down the hall. His thick arms were covered by a dark green gambeson, and he held a slightly rusted helmet under his arms. As he moved closer to the cell, Skara could see that his hands were worn and callused, and he seemed more than capable of wielding the long sword that hung from the belt at his hip.

The large man handed his helmet to one of the guards and stepped towards the bars. "I'm gonna make myself clear here. The two of you are murderers and deserve to be locked up in this cell. If I had my way, you'd be hanging from a rope right about now in full view of the town. But my orders say to hold you until someone comes for you, so you'll be spared the noose for now. But orders or no, you cause any trouble, and you won't be boarding that boat alive, you get me?"

Stepping forward, Faine rubbed his hands over his face and eyed the man. "I understand why we're here, but what orders do you have to keep us here? Who's coming for us?"

The commander shook his head and laughed. "You people are all the same. You get taken in, and you forget about all the shit that you've pulled. Banrielle, that ring any bells in that soft head of yours?"

Skara clenched his fist, crushing his loaf of bread as he inched closer to the bars. "For what they did, they got what they deserved."

Seeing the two guards reach for their clubs, Faine reached out and put his hand on Skara's shoulder before he could move any closer.

The commander leaned forward and looked down, locking his eyes with Skara's. His hand gripped the hilt of his sword as he squared his shoulders and gritted his teeth. "You got some balls sayin' that. You think you can attack the priests and soldiers of the temple and just run away, not giving a damn about anyone but yourselves? You Fallen are all alike. You think you can kill whoever you want and send the world back into chaos, but I won't have it."

Skara scowled as he pulled against Faine's hand, trying to move closer to the bars. "I'm not Fallen."

"Unbroken, maybe. But I know an enemy of the Reverent when I see one."

"So, what's going to happen to us, then?" Faine said, keeping his hand on Skara's shoulder.

"Right now, you're going to stay in this cell and keep your mouths shut until the ship comes to take you back to Ethilios."

"What do you mean back to Ethilios? We've never been there before," Faine said, glancing down at Skara, a confused look on his face.

"Maybe, but you killed the brothers of the temple in Banrielle, and they were under orders," the commander said, scowling at the pair. "And you murdered them for it."

"Orders from where?" Skara said, pulling his shoulder out of Faine's grip.

The commander smiled as he took back his helmet and started walking back down the corridor. "For your crimes against Mivara and the brothers, you're on your way to Bright Harbor to be tried by the king.

The Will and the Word

Renna paced the room, tapping the back of her thumb to one of her tusks as Braig sat at a nearby table with Aenwyn, rolling a coin between his fingers. After leaving the alley near the inn, the group took the cart to a small warehouse near the docks, unhitched the horse and pushed the wagon through two tall doors into an open section inside the building. Numerous crates were stacked around the room, making a tight maze that led to a back stairwell leading to a room with several beds, nightstands, and two round tables.

A woodstove sat in the back corner with a dying fire burning inside the blackened iron frame, gently warming the room against the cool breeze coming from the ocean. The sun was just beginning to rise, and sharp rays of orange cut through the smudged glass window, casting slivers of light onto the tops of the faded brown tables. Pouring four cups of hot tea, Ferhani set them on the table and sat down in the chair next to Braig. Taking a sip, she gestured to an open seat at the table and slid a plain white cup towards Renna.

Walking quickly to the table, Renna sat down, slid the cup to the side, and looked over at Ferhani. "We've wasted enough time getting somewhere safe to talk, so let's talk. What's your plan to get Faine and Skara out of Stonekeep?"

Ferhani ran her hands through her hair and took another drink of her tea. "I have a plan that could work, but it won't be easy. And it's an arrangement that helps us both. You need something from me, and I want something from you in return."

"Anything you want," Renna said, leaning forward. "We can't leave them there. We don't even know what they're planning to do with them."

"Renna," Braig said, louder than he had intended. "Hear her out before you agree to anything. The price might be higher than you think."

"Smart and handsome," Ferhani said, winking at Braig. "But he's right. Getting in and out of Stonekeep takes some connections and effort on everyone's part. But I have to ask," Ferhani said, looking over at Aenwyn, "what's your stake in all this? You didn't come here with them, so why help?"

Aenwyn looked over at Renna and shrugged, a slight smile on her face. "I don't have anything better to do. Besides, I know what it's like to be somewhere you don't want to be. And Renna here needs some help. Why would I leave now?"

"Because you don't know them, and they don't know you," Ferhani said, looking over at Braig and Renna. "Are you sure you trust her enough to let her help when you and your friend's lives are at stake?"

Renna glanced at Ferhani before looking back over to Aenwyn. "She already helped me once tonight. She could have done nothing like everyone else, but she put herself at risk. And if she's willing to help me again, I trust her. And from what I've seen her do, I think we have a better chance with her than without."

Shaking her head, Ferhani looked over at Braig. "What about you?"

Rubbing his hands over his eyes, Braig cleared his throat and took a drink of his tea. "I don't know her, so I can't rightly trust her. For all I know, she's got something to do with what happened to Faine and Skara, or to me in that alley. But I didn't see her there, and she helped Renna. And if Renna's putting her trust in her, I suppose I'll do the same...until I see something that makes me think otherwise."

Aenwyn turned her head, her eyes locking with Braig's. "I know you don't trust me, and I get it. I'm not sure I can trust you either. But this isn't my first time being in a rough situation, and I think you have a better chance of getting your friends out with me at your side. I know a thing or two that can speed things up a bit. And I give you my word that I'm here to help you. You can take that to heart. If I give it, it won't be broken. So," she said, turning back towards Ferhani, "tell us what we need to know."

"Very well." Ferhani took another drink and pushed her cup to the side, motioning at the nightstand behind Braig. "Open that top drawer and get me a piece of paper and a sliver of charcoal."

"So why are they there? Aside from the brawl, that is? You said a ship was coming for them," Braig said as he rummaged through the drawer.

"A ship will be here in a few days to take them to Ethilios. The Brothers of the Flame that you dealt with in Banrielle were working for someone there. The temple in Bright Harbor wants to see them made into an example. From what I hear, they're on their way to see the king. And no good can come from that."

Renna rubbed her temples and stared down at a nick in the table. "Then we can't let that happen. I know what they do to make an example. How do we get in?"

Setting the paper on the table, Ferhani grabbed the charcoal, sharpened it with her dagger, and began drawing on the blank sheet. "Here's Stonekeep. From what I know, your friends are being kept in the holding cell here, in the back corner. There are five towers, the central tower being the largest with the main gate and beds on the second level for guards. This is also where the only gate is to get inside. Around the outer wall on each corner is four smaller towers that usually only have a few archers. But there are also guards that walk the upper walls around the perimeter."

"There's no other way in aside from the main gate?" Renna said as she peered over the drawing.

"No. Unless you try to scale the walls, anyway. But you'd get shot down before you made it halfway. There are bars on the holding cell window, although I don't think there's any way to pull them off. We'd need a team of horses to even have a chance, but we'd never get close enough to even try."

Braig tapped his finger on the back corner of the drawing, pulling lightly on his beard. "And what about after we get through the gate?"

"The inside branches off from the main corridor. There are three cell blocks on the left, and two on the right, with the registry desk near the holding cell in the back. There's usually only one guard there at any time."

"And this empty back corner?" Braig said, pointing.

"That's the yard. There is a door that opens right in front of the holding cell, but there's nowhere to hide there, and you'd be spotted even if you somehow got in."

"So, you're saying the best way is through the front door?" Renna said, looking up at Ferhani.

"I'm saying that's the only way. I have a man on the inside that can let us in the front gate and get us a copy of the cell key. But getting past the guards is another story. And if we go in the middle of the night, we'll come across fewer guards. But even if we get inside, we still can't be seen. If one guard sounds the bell, the next guard will sound theirs until everyone's awake and flooding the cell blocks. We'd have no way out if we got trapped. So, we'll need a distraction."

Braig scratched his nose and shook his head. "What kind of distraction?"

"The flaming kind. We're going to attack the prison from the side with firebombs. We'll draw their attention."

"But doesn't that defeat the whole purpose? I thought we didn't want to sound the alarm?" Renna said, leaning back in her chair. "It won't work."

"But it could," Ferhani said, scribbling on the piece of paper. "We go into the woods, draw their attention to one side, and they sound the alarm. The guards will be rushing to the wall and falling into each other. It'll be chaos. You go in the front gate, take out the guard, and unlock the cell."

"And are we supposed to fight our way out if someone sees us and shuts us in?" Braig said, his voice gruff.

Ferhani set down her charcoal and looked over at Braig. "That's right. There'll be two wagons outside waiting for you.

Both leave at the same time in different directions. They'll take you to an alley where you jump out, run between the buildings and climb into a third wagon and head to the ship, while the other leads the guards away. It'll set sail the next morning to avoid suspicion. I didn't say there wouldn't be any risk. Death is a real possibility. You just have to ask yourself if saving your friends is worth it."

"Of course, it's worth the risk," Renna said, gritting her teeth. "But I don't want any of us to die trying. There has to be another way. We have no idea who's coming for them and why, or if this will even work."

Aenwyn cleared her throat and knocked on the table, drawing everyone's attention. "I have an idea that could work. It's still risky, but we won't have to worry about getting trapped in the prison. Getting shot with arrows from the wall, possibly. But not getting trapped."

"Oh," Ferhani said, tilting her head to the side. "What do you have in mind?"

Reaching for the charcoal, Aenwyn began to draw on the paper. "We go in the middle of the night, and you still cause a distraction. You hit the wall here," she said, drawing a large X on the side wall away from the holding cell. "But you wait for the signal. We want to sneak in, get into position, and then fire as I get them out. We'll keep them off guard. Then, we board two separate wagons waiting on the streets on both sides of walls: one on the front for you, Braig and your crew, and one on the side streets near the dock district for me, Renna, Faine, and Skara. Then we both head to the rendezvous point, the carriages split again, and we take a single wagon to the ship while the other two lead them away."

"And how do you think you're going to get them out by yourself...from outside the wall?" Ferhani said, a curious look on her face.

"I have some magic that'll do the trick."

"You're a mage?" Braig said, looking over at Aenwyn. "You don't look it."

"And what do mages look like? They're not short, bearded, and stocky like dwarves. We don't all have a certain look or wear flowing robes with golden runes embroidered on them all the time...we only do that on special occasions." Aenwyn said, flashing a smile at Renna.

"And do you think you can pull this off?" Ferhani said, crossing her arms. "If you start this and don't finish it..."

"I know," Aenwyn said, setting down the charcoal. "It'll work. When you hear the loud crash, fire the arrows and send in the fire-bombs. Let it cause some confusion so we can get across the clearing to the wagon. We'll only need a couple minutes to make it to the alley. Then we'll meet and take the wagon to the ship. And if it doesn't work, you'll be safely hidden in the trees."

"Then we'll wait for the crash. I trust it'll be something we can't miss. But speaking of the ship," Ferhani said, glancing between the three others sitting at the table, "we have the other side of the offer to discuss. I can have my people in position if we all agree on the payment. If not, you're on your own. But seeing that you don't have much of a choice, I think you'll find my offer more than fair."

"And what's your offer?" Braig said, crossing his arms across his chest.

"It's simple, actually. The wagon takes you to a ship as planned. But instead of taking the Wind Cutter straight to the Grey Wastes, you'll board my other ship—the Banshee."

"What makes you think we're going to the wastes?" Renna said, glancing over at Braig.

Ferhani sighed and glanced out the window before turning her eyes back to Renna. "I have ships, and I sail them. I was told you needed passage to Aerith, just north of Yonkai. And there's nothing north of Yonkai but the Grey Wastes. Now whatever you have planned there is your business, but it's my business to get you there. And to do that, you'll take the Banshee."

"And in return?" Braig said, leaning back in his chair.

"In return, you accompany my crew on a supply run."

"Why do you need us to go with your crew on a supply run? What it is you're picking up?"

Picking up the sheet of paper, Ferhani crumbled it, walked across the room, and tossed it into the fire. "My clients have certain wants and needs. Some items can be found around here, others can't. So, you'll be traveling with my crew south to Solis to pick up a load of herbs and other goods that need to get to a city outside of Yorkus. The wastes are on the way."

"You're a smuggler," Aenwyn said, nodding her head. "I hear there's good money in that."

"There's enough," Ferhani said as she leaned over the table. "And as such, it can sometimes be a bit dangerous. So, you'll be going along as extra protection. But the Banshee is fast, so she can usually outrun most ships. You also have the added security of a good place to hide should the ship get searched by any guards before we leave port. You should really consider taking the offer because you won't find anyone else willing to help you in such a short amount of time. And the longer you wait, the harder it will be to get your friends."

Renna pulled the flower out of her hair and tugged at the leather cord holding it in place. Shaking her head, she let it fall around her shoulders, tossing the flower onto the table as she looked over at Braig. "What choice do we have? Solis isn't too far from here, and whoever's coming for us won't know where we're heading anyway. I say we go."

Braig closed his eyes and took a deep breath, trying to calm the frustration welling up inside him. "Aye, we don't have much of a choice. But if I know that we need to head to the wastes, there's no telling if another prisoner they've been torturing could've cracked under the pressure and told them where to go. But it's been nothing but trouble here, and I suppose it's a risk I'm willing to take. The sooner we leave this shit-hole of a town, the better."

"Excellent," Ferhani said, standing up straight. "I'll have your gear loaded on the ship and ready for you. The ship is small, so you'll be sharing some tight spaces, but the trip should be quick. The wind favors the Banshee. Now, I suggest we get some rest. We have a long night ahead of us."

Moving to the window, Ferhani unrolled a dark piece of cloth, blotting out the bright morning light before strolling over to one of the beds. Falling wearily onto the mattress, she looked over at the three still seated at the table. "There's tea left in the kettle, and some dried food in a crate at the bottom of the stairs. I suggest you stay inside since there's a bounty for you. And if you go out or come back in, keep it quiet. I need my sleep."

"After the night we've had, sleep sounds like a good idea. I feel like I can barely think. You should get some rest too, Renna. They'll be out tonight, but there's nothing we can do right now," Braig said as he stood and walked over to the bed, not bothering to take off his boots before climbing in.

"I need some air," Renna said as she stood and padded across the room, heading towards the stairs.

"I'll go with you," Aenwyn said, following Renna down and out a side door onto the street.

Leaning against the wall, Renna took a deep breath and turned her head towards the rays of light shining between the building. The morning air was fresh, and the sun felt warm on her skin. It had been some time since she'd been to the ocean, and she wished that this visit was under better circumstances. What would happen they couldn't get Faine out of Stonekeep? Where would she go if something terrible were to happen? She had been traveling so long with Faine that leaving without him made her stomach turn. Of course, she would manage, she always did — but it would be harder without him.

"I don't know how you plan to do it, but I need you to know that it has to work. I can't leave them there," Renna said, turning to face Aenwyn.

"I'll get it done. I just need you there to watch my back. Maybe take out an archer or two if it comes to that. But I'll get 'em out of the cell."

Letting her shoulders relax, Renna moved closer to Aenwyn and ran her fingers down her arm. "I just want to thank you again for what you did back at the pub. And also for what you're about to do. I want you to know that you don't have to help if you don't want to. You'll be risking your life for people you don't even know."

Shrugging slightly, Aenwyn moved closer and put her hand on Renna's hip, picking at a small fray on the bottom of her bodice. "I risk my life all the time, so this is nothin' new. But look, I don't want to tell you your business, but I can be honest with you here?"

Pulling her hand away from Aenwyn's arm, Renna looked down at her fingers, bracing for what she thought would be an insult or a comment on her being part orcish. "Of course."

"Now, I don't know your reasons, but going to the Grey Wastes is a bad idea. The ruins there have some kind of curse on 'em. The place is abandoned and crawling with undead."

Letting out a small sigh, Renna looked back up at Aenwyn, her eyes catching the orange light of the morning sun. "We don't really have a choice."

"There's always a choice. About the only things around there are death and the old ruins of Q'bath. And that's been used for centuries by the worshippers of Ashkosh."

"I've read something about them before, but I don't remember much."

Aenwyn shook her head. "That's probably a good thing. I had to read up on history when I was studying in the tower."

"So, you really are a mage then? Not aberrant, as some like to call it?"

"Fully trained at a mage tower. But just because someone learned magic elsewhere doesn't make it mean any less than the spells learned in a tower."

Pulling her hair behind her pointed ears, Renna leaned in closer and lowered her voice. "So, what does it all mean? Why does the old cult still matter?"

"Because they're still functioning. Undead are drawn to the area, and I've heard that the followers of Ashkosh go there to die to better serve their master in death."

Renna tapped her finger against her tusk as she considered how to word her next question. "And have you heard anything about some kind of spell on the town? Or maybe read anything about something magical being left there?"

Aenwyn slid her thumbs under her belt and leaned against the wall. "And why would you ask something like that?"

"It's just a question. Usually, there's something more going on if a place is said to be cursed."

"Maybe," Aenwyn said. "But in this case, there's a story about something like that. It's just a story, though. It says that after the body of the daemon Quarb was found, the cult of Ashkosh tried to find out how to use his magic or blood for their own gain. They were hoping to make themselves pretty close to being immortal by siphoning the necromantic energy off him. The body was eventually taken back to Q'bath and resurrected.

"That's what caused the second undead war in Aerith. But before that, rumor had it that they were actually able to siphon enough energy to create a powerful stone. The legend says that it could turn anyone that died near it into a Denmol—an undead. It's still supposed to be out there some-where, showing up from time to time. Story has it that it moves from place to place on its own—like it knows where it needs to be for the right person to find it. But people have searched, and no one's been able to find it because it proba-bly doesn't exist. It's a story, just like the others."

Leaning away from the wall, Renna glanced past Aen-wyn and out onto the street. The shops were beginning to open, and the dockhands were making their way down to the boats to start work for the day. Seeing several people glance in her direction, Renna moved back closer to the wall, letting Aenwyn nearly block her from sight. "But do you think the stone may be there somewhere, waiting to be found?"

Aenwyn stood up straighter, her mouth slightly open. "So that's why you're goin' there. You're tryin' to find it."

"Keep your voice down," Renna said, motioning down-ward with her hands. "But, yes. I think that's why we have a bounty out. Whoever's following us knows we're looking for it and wants it for themselves. That's what started this whole mess. We just have to find it first."

"Did you not hear anything I said about the cult or how dangerous it is with all the undead roaming around?"

"I heard you," Renna said.

"You heard me but didn't listen. It's just a story. People have looked, and no one's found it."

"You said it moves on its own — and stories have roots in reality. Why else would someone be going through the trouble of trying to find us, and then sail here to take us back? They want what we know, which isn't much."

Aenwyn stood and shook her head. "We should think about this for a while. But for now, we need to concentrate on the task at hand. We have to get your friends out before you go anywhere. For now, let's head back upstairs and get some sleep, yeah?"

Nodding her head, Renna walked towards the door, letter her fingers lightly graze Aenwyn's hand as she walked past. "You're right. We should get some rest. It's been a long night."

FAINE PACED ACROSS the room, mumbling to himself as he turned his gaze from the window to the locked door leading to the yard across from their cell. His tunic was wrinkled and covered in dirt and blood, and his usually smooth hair had formed several small tangles and hung loosely over his shoulders. Scratching his slight beard, he moved over and sat next to Skara.

"You feel that?" Faine said, leaning in closer.

"Feel what?"

"The reckoning. We'll be getting out of here soon."

Skara laughed to himself and pulled his knees closer to his chest. His dark brown pants had several small tears at the knees, and his forest green tunic was spattered with dark stains that could either be blood, or something worse from sleeping on the mattress in the cell. Turning his head to look over at Faine, he let his head fall back against the wall. "I don't feel a damn thing. Are you alright? You don't seem like you're holding it together. I thought you've been in worse."

Faine sighed as he glanced over at the guard sitting at the desk a short distance away, his fingers rubbing his lips as he eyed a clay pitcher and several cups sitting on the tabletop. "I'm fine. I could use a strong drink right about now, though. But I'll get that soon enough."

"What do you mean?"

"Like I just said, we'll be getting out of here...tonight. We just have to hold it together until then and be ready to move."

Skara scowled as he turned his eyes towards Faine. "How do you know that? Unless you have a lockpick shoved up your ass, we're stuck here."

Faine rubbed his chin as he briefly turned his eyes up towards the ceiling. "Hmm. That's not a bad idea. But no, I can feel it. I don't know how, but I know. It's going to be fast and hard, but it's coming. I've known Renna for a long time, and I know she's already got a plan. Besides, Braig is with her, and he always seems to be looking for a fight."

"You don't know that. For all we know, they're locked up somewhere, too."

"Doubtful. Either way, whether they come or not, we'll be getting out. I have an idea if no one comes for us tonight. It involves the rancid broth, and it won't be pretty or smell very good, but it would work," Faine said, glancing over at Skara." But for both our sakes, let's hope it doesn't come to that."

Skara stared out over the nearly empty cell, hoping that Faine was right. He couldn't stay locked in here for very much longer. He had tried to squeeze through the bars and loosen stones, but nothing worked. This place was a prison, after all; and he didn't see how anyone could escape. The walls were thick stone, and the gates were solid iron. If one guard left, another would take their place. If no one came, he would do whatever it takes to escape or die trying. He wouldn't let himself be taken to Ethilios to be tortured for taking revenge on the brothers. There were too many things he wanted to see, and too many people that deserved a knife in the dark. "Let's hope you're right."

"Oh, I'm right. Sometimes you just have to have a little faith." Faine chuckled as he rested his arms on his knees. "A little faith," he said again, laughing a bit harder.

The Burning Man

Aenwyn kept her eyes on the patrolling guards, waiting for the right moment to make her move closer to the wall of the prison.

"What can you see? You think everyone's in position yet?" Renna squinted her eyes and glanced up at the towers, watching for any guards that might be looking in their direction.

"They've had enough time. Let's go."

Keeping low to the ground, Aenwyn darted from behind a bush near the road and ran towards the stone wall, pushing hard against it to stay out of sight. Torches burned on the walkway above them, dropping down sparks and embers as they flickered in the dark night. Creeping along the wall, they listened for any footsteps as they rounded the corner and made their way closer to the holding cell near the back wall.

"Why didn't we just come from the other direction?" Renna said, holding her bow and arrows on her back, trying to keep low to the ground.

"Too far to run across the gap without being seen. Now be quiet. We're almost there."

Nearing the back corner, Renna could see a small window covered with several bars. "This is it. But it's too high to reach."

Grabbing a few small stones from the ground, Aenwyn handed them to Renna and got on her hands and knees. "Step on and look in the window. If they're asleep, toss the stones to get their attention. But be quiet. Ferhani said there's a guard posted nearby."

Nodding, she stepped up onto Aenwyn's back and slowly peered into the window. The cell was dark, but she could see several lanterns burning down the corridor, and one on the desk to the left of the cell. She pushed her face closer to the bars but couldn't see if there was a guard nearby. Scanning the room, she saw two dark lumps huddled in the corner, one larger than the other. A slight smell of urine and vomit wafted between the bars, and she had to lean back to get a breath of fresh air before pushing herself forward to peer back in.

Tossing one of the small stones, it bounced off the floor, making a slight tapping noise before skittering into the wall. Holding her breath, she looked over towards the desk, waiting to see any movement, but everything was quiet. Breathing a small sigh of relief, she glanced back down at the mattress, but it was empty.

Hearing a grunt from Aenwyn as she stood on her toes, she leaned closer to the bars. Suddenly, a set of yellow eyes popped up in front of the window, the brief scare nearly knocking her backwards.

"What are you doing?" Skara said, peering around in the darkness. "We thought you'd come from the other way."

Still slightly frightened by the sudden jolt, Renna pulled herself closer to the bars, keeping her voice to a whisper. "Are you and Faine alright?"

"We're fine. But we have to get out of here. There's a ship coming to take us to Ethilios."

"I know. We're getting you out. Where's the guard?"

Adjusting his feet on Faine's shoulder, Skara glanced over to the commander sleeping at the desk. "He's asleep. But he won't be for long if we keep talking."

"I have a plan. But it could be a bit dangerous. I need you and Faine to get under your mattress."

"Why? What are you doing?"

Renna shook her head. "Being brash. Now do it. When we tell you to run, run!"

As Skara's face disappeared from the window, Renna climbed off Aenwyn and leaned back against the wall. "What's the plan, take out a section of the wall?"

"No," she said, a smile turning up the edges of her lips. "I'm gonna take down the whole tower."

Renna's eyes widened. "Why? We're supposed to be getting them out, not killing them."

"The tower has shifted in the dirt. If I just take out a wall, the tower could fall on us. So, I'm going to push it down into the empty yard. More chaos and time for us to make our escape."

"So much for an easy in and out."

Aenwyn winked at Renna. "Sometimes, getting into tight places needs to be a bit of a challenge."

Renna pushed herself closer to the wall, thankful that it was dark so that Aenwyn couldn't see her blushing. She really was beautiful. The light of the moons shined off her pale skin, and her red hair was like a flame in the darkness. Her leather armor and the sword hanging at her side hinted at her ferocity—like a wild animal that's beautiful to behold, but deadly if provoked. Taking a deep breath, she steadied herself and glanced up the length of the tower, setting her mind back on the task at hand.

"Now stand behind me. When the tower begins to break, get Faine and Skara and head for the wagon. I'll be right behind you."

"I can't leave you here," Renna said, her voice coming out in a harsh whisper.

"I have to hold the spell and push the tower. I'll be fine. Now, here we go, get ready."

Closing her eyes, Aenwyn began to mutter under her breath. Falling to her knees, she plunged her fingers hard into the dirt as the ground around them began to tremble. Soft green light pulsed from her hands as vines erupted from the soil and weaved themselves between the bricks, climbing higher towards the top of the tower. Growing quickly, the vines tightened around the battlement, cracking the mortar, and sending chunks of stone slabs toppling down, landing hard against the ground in the yard, dust and debris flying in all directions.

Sounds of bells and shouts rang out across Stonekeep as guards clamored over the walkways, running towards the collapsing tower, bows and swords in hand. Covering their eyes and standing clear of the falling stones, bright flashes and explosions sounded on the opposite side of the keep as small pots of burning liquid shattered against the outer wall, sending up plumes of black smoke as the guards began to fire arrows blindly towards the tree line.

Taking up her bow, Renna fired at the closest guards, keeping them off balance and sending them running for cover as they fled the flying arrows and shards of stone falling around them. "They're still in the cell—don't let the building come down on top of them!"

Taking greater control of the magic flowing through her, Aenwyn dug her fingers deeper into the ground as the vines twisted and split the mortar. Stone grated and buckled as the wall cracked, leaving a large hole into the cell, sending bits of broken stone crashing inwards as the tower swayed above them, held together only by the tangled vines.

"Now! Run!" Renna said, motioning for Faine and Skara to follow her.

Throwing the mattress off their heads, the two darted through the hole, covering their faces as the stones shattered around them.

"Follow me," Renna said, stopping to look at Aenwyn.

"Go, woman. I'll be behind you."

"Hurry," she said, leading Faine and Skara away through the open field.

Screams sounded across the keep as arrows flew from the forest, hitting the walls above or below the guards as they fired blindly into the dark woods around them, barking out orders. "To the rear, archers to the wall. The prisoners are escaping."

Clenching her teeth, Aenwyn's shoulders slumped, the strain of controlling such a massive flow of magic making her feel weak and heavy. Giving one last push, thick vines exploded from the open ground in the yard towards the upper section of the tower, wrapping tightly around it as they burrowed back into the cold soil, bringing the tower down with them.

Releasing the spell, Aenwyn stood, her legs weak and unsteady beneath her. Staring into the rubble of the collapsed tower, her heart dropped when she saw the commander of the guards stagger through the opening in the cell wall, his face covered in cuts and dust, his eyes fixed solely on her. Sliding on his helmet, he looked down at his broken longsword, throwing it hard onto the ground as he charged.

Turning to run, arrows buzzed around her as she sprinted across the field, hoping to avoid a strike in her back as she fled. Hearing the heavy footsteps getting closer, she ran until she was safely out of arrow range and turned quickly, throwing a ball of blue-green flame into the commander's chest, where it dissipated into nothing before making contact.

Pushing her arms out in front of her, a burst of energy shot from her hands, passing right through the commander instead of throwing him off his feet. Letting out a frustrated grunt, Aenwyn drew her sword and rushed forward, dodging the man's fist as she kicked him in the knee, dropping him down to one leg. Thrusting hard towards his neck, the man slapped her blade aside and smashed into her chest with his heavy fist.

Staggering backwards, Aenwyn gasped, trying to catch her breath as she held her sword out in front of her to fend off any possible attack. Mouthing the words of an incantation, she clenched her fist as vines shot out of the ground towards the man's legs, only to wither and fall to the ground at his feet.

"As long as my heart beats and blood flows in my veins, your magic is useless against me," the commander said, stepping closer.

Breathing hard, she could see several guards pointing in their direction as they scrambled around the sides of the keep, weapons in hand. Glancing over her shoulder, she saw nothing but an empty field and hoped that Renna and the others had made it into the dark alley between the buildings. Trying to buy them as much time as possible to escape, she lunged at the man, thrusting her sword hard towards his torso. Moving quickly, the commander raised his arm, catching the blade in one armored hand while gripping her throat with his other. Squeezing hard on her neck, he lifted her into the air, her feet dangling as she struggled for breath.

Electricity sprung from her hands as she reached for his face, punching and clawing, desperate for air.

"Pathetic. Without your magic, what are you?" the man said as he wrenched her sword out of her hand and tossed it onto the ground.

The world around Aenwyn began to go dark as she batted at the man's arm and chest, tearing at his fingers as she tried to pry them apart. Reaching to her belt, she grabbed one of her daggers, burying it deep into his arm as she twisted it from side to side. The man growled, dropping her hard to the cold ground as he pulled the dagger out of his flesh.

Crawling slowly across the dirt, Aenwyn choked and gasped as she reached out for her sword, the tips her fingers barely touching the pommel. Removing his helmet and throwing it to the side, the man stepped down with his boot, crushing her fingers hard into the rocky soil. Aenwyn winced as she looked up at the man, the sound of shouting growing louder in her ears as guards poured onto the field from the prison.

"This is a nice sword," he said, picking up the blade and rolling Aenwyn onto her back with his boot. "It's a shame you have to die by it. But know that I take no pleasure in it. The Order of Inethiel doesn't revel in killing. But the tenets were put into place to quench the fires of the wicked and I must to abide by them; lest the wor-"

His face twisted in pain as he dropped the sword and wrapped his hands around the arrow shaft protruding from his right eye. Another arrow struck him hard in the throat, its tip cutting clean through. Blood spurted from his mouth as he gripped the arrow shaft and dropped to his knees, staring blankly in the distance towards the archer.

Raising her head, she could see Renna and Faine running towards her, shouting to each other as Faine hoisted her off the ground and began to carry her across the field. Looking back over his shoulder, Aenwyn could see a faint orange glow flickering from the other side of the keep as Skara picked up her sword and dagger and leaped onto the downed man, stabbing him quickly in the neck with her blade before running to catch up.

Pulling out her knife, Renna cut a small gash into her arm, flinging the blood onto the commander's body. A dark mist spread from her fingers, falling like wisps of smoke that poured into his open wounds. The man's body twisted and writhed, its limbs bending unnaturally as it rose from the ground. Reaching out her hand, she concentrated on focus-ing the flow of magic, willing it into a small flame that sprung from her fingers. Keeping herself grounded, she took hold of the man's tunic, setting his sleeve alight.

The flames rose, spreading up to the man's torso and down his legs until his body was engulfed, lighting up the dark night around them.

"Keep us safe and return to the night around you when your body is ash."

The fiery creature turned from his maker and dashed to-wards the approaching guards, arms outstretched like a net trying to catch every man and woman on the field. Gut-tural growls poured from the creature's throat as the flames swirled around its body. The guards, frightened and enraged at what had become of their leader, struck hard with their swords, fighting for their lives and losing track of Renna as she ran; some screaming in agony as they were consumed by the embrace of the beast.

Faine and Skara watched the burning man dashing across the field as he wrestled with the guards, the fire on his body shedding light on the terrified faces around him.

"I didn't see that coming," Faine said, looking down at Skara.

Eyes wide, Skara shook his head as Renna ran full speed to the back of the cart.

"Get into the wagon," she said, climbing into the back with Aenwyn. "Everyone up."

Throwing the weapons into the cart, Skara stretched out his hand to Renna as he was pulled up and over the side, nearly landing on Aenwyn as she sat up, coughing and looking out over the scene in the field.

"Go!" Faine said, climbing onto the seat next to the Lutnar. "Or none of us will live to talk about what just happened."

"WHAT KIND OF SIGNAL are we supposed to be waiting for?" Braig said, moving farther into the small grove of trees on the outskirts of the prison.

"All she said was a crash. So, I'm assuming we're waiting for something to fall or explode. So, we'll just be ready for either."

Looking out over the expanse that stretched between the forest and the wall, Braig crouched lower and moved over next to Ferhani. "The distance is too far to throw anything against the wall. How are we supposed to get anything other than arrows even close?"

"This," Ferhani said as she handed Braig a large crossbow. "It was meant for arrows, but we dug out the slot and added a carrier for the fire-bombs."

Taking the bow, he shrugged and twisted it around in his hands, looking at it from different angles.

"You know how this works, right?"

"Of course, I know how a crossbow works! I've just never seen one like this before."

Ferhani pulled out one of the small clay pots and put it into the metal cup that was held in place on a greased metal groove. "You pull back the string, which is attached to the holding cup. Then put the pot in the cup, aim, and pull the trigger."

Braig grunted as he set the bow down on the ground, taking the small, corked pot in his hands. "And this is what I load?"

Ferhani's eyes shot open as she grabbed the pot out of his hands. "This," she said as she set the container on the ground a safe distance away, "isn't a plaything. It's filled with flammable liquid, and the clay is mixed with flash powder. When it hits the wall, or anything, the powder sparks and ignites it. So, if you drop it, you could be in some trouble."

"Then what're you carryin' 'em around for? I could've set myself on fire."

"But you didn't. I'm sure I could have found a way to put you out. Maybe I'd use one of my red potions."

Shaking his head, Braig picked up the crossbow and box of fire-bombs. "What's the plan when they start shootin' arrows at us? We have some trees here, but's it's going to be hard to see an arrow flying at us in the dark."

"We hide and shoot only when we can. Move from place to place so they can't target you. But stay low when you do. I'm sure that won't be hard for you to do."

Braig heard a slight laugh coming from the darkness beside him, and he felt his stomach tighten and his chest flutter. He had only known this woman for nearly two days, but in his heart, it felt like a lifetime. Moving into position behind a tree, he looked down at the box of clay pots, thinking about the flammable liquid inside them and how dangerous they were. But he wasn't worried about what they could do, because he felt as if his heart was already on fire.

Taking a deep breath to clear his head, he loaded a pot onto the bow and waited, eyes and ears open for any sign or sound. "Do ya hear that?"

"Hear what?"

"The cracking. Look, the top of the tower..."

Leaning her head out from behind the tree, Ferhani saw the top of the tower breaking into pieces, falling with heavy thuds onto the ground below. "Now, fire now!"

Taking aim at the wall, Braig pulled the trigger, sending the pot flying through the air, sparking as it hit the wall, sending up plumes of black smoke as the fire scorched the bricks. Placing his foot on the metal stirrup, he pulled hard on the string, locking it in place as he loaded another pot and fired.

Staying behind the tree, Ferhani fired arrow after arrow at the walls above and below the guards, trying to cause as much chaos to help Aenwyn and Renna without killing more people than necessary. Firing another arrow, she picked up her quiver and moved to a thick tree closer to Braig, catching her left ankle on a root and falling hard to the ground.

"Are you alright?" Braig said, lowering his bow.

"I'm fine. Don't concentrate on me, keep firing." Ferhani leaned her back against the tree, nocking another arrow.

"Get ready to run. The tower is about to fall, and there are four guards coming right for us."

Rotating her ankle, Ferhani winced in pain. Using her right leg, she pushed herself up the tree, bow and arrow in hand. "I can't run that fast. We have to get rid of them before more come."

Tossing down the bow, Braig grabbed his sword and shield and used the blade to reach around the tree and rustle the bushes. "I got their attention. Two comin' your way."

Putting as little pressure on her foot as possible, Ferhani wheeled around the tree, drawing her bow and firing in one smooth motion. The arrow flew silently through the air, striking one of the guards in the chest, sending him down in a heap. "I can barely see them from here. It's too dark."

Fumbling for the box on the ground, Braig grabbed the last fire-bomb, throwing it against a nearby tree as he grabbed Ferhani and moved farther into the woods, staying out of sight so the guards on the tower wouldn't be able to get a clear shot. The liquid poured down the tree as the flames spread up the dry trunk and onto the branches above, casting light in the small clearing as the fire spread.

"Give me some space," Ferhani said, pushing away from Braig.

"Are you sure you can take 'em."

"I can take one."

Banging his sword on his shield to get their attention, Braig stepped in the path of two of the guards and planted his feet, crouching low. As the first guard drew closer, Braig sprang forward, bashing hard with his shield to block the man's sword and drive him back, slamming him into a nearby cedar tree. The man grunted in pain as several small broken branches stabbed at his shoulders, bruising the skin beneath his gambeson.

Stepping quickly to the side, Braig narrowly escaped the swing of the second guard. Staggering backwards, shield tight against his body, he braced himself against the furious swings, his blade glinting in the orange glow from the burning tree beside them. Blow for blow, Braig parried and countered, keeping the two guards at bay as he looked for an opening to end the fight and make their escape.

Glancing occasionally over at Ferhani, he could see her spinning in the darkness, her sharp, straight blade piercing the man's leather armor as easily as a needle pierces cloth. Blood dripped from the man's wounds as he stumbled wearily, swinging high and low only to have Ferhani twist away at the last second and plunge her narrow blade into his soft flesh, dropping his body quietly to the red-drenched soil beneath him.

Growling under his breath, Braig pushed hard against his attackers, driving them back into a small clearing in the trees. Sweat beaded on his forehead as the fire spread through the canopy above, making it hard to breathe. Boughs of flaming branches fell around them, lighting up the nearby tree trunks as the smoke grew thicker, stinging his eyes. Straining his vision, he could see the remnants of a sturdy branch that had been split from the tree, its jagged edges visible in the burning glow behind the guards.

Swinging in wide arcs, Braig pushed the men farther back, keeping them in front of him. Nearing the tree, he dug his feet into the ground and charged at one the guards. Using his shield to push the man's sword to the side, he smashed into the man's chest with his shoulder, knocking the wind from his lungs. Pumping hard with his stout legs, he lifted the guard's body off of the ground as he ran as hard as he could towards the tree. Using all his strength, he lifted the man higher into the air, pinning his flailing body to the tree as the branch tore through his abdomen.

Dropping his sword, the man gripped the blood-slicked branch, his eyes wide with shock as he looked around frantically for anyone to help. Wiping the splatters of blood from his face, Braig could hear the shouting of more guards as they ran across the field, heading swiftly in their direction. Anger welled up inside him as looked over at Ferhani, leaning heavily against a tree, an ugly bruise forming on her face where the man must have landed a blow before being put down.

Throwing his shield to the ground, Braig picked up a heavy rock and hurled at the remaining guard. The stone bounced off the man's arm as he lifted it to protect his face, but that was all time Braig needed. Covering the short distance between them, he knocked the sword from the man's hand with a downward swing and drove his blade through his chest, severing the arteries in his heart. The man was dead before he hit the ground.

Breathing hard, Braig sheathed his sword and sprinted over to Ferhani, picking up his shield as he ran. The burning scent of cedar and pine filled the air as the smoke filled the clearing, stagnant in the grasp of the small, still grove.

"Are you alright? Can ya walk?" Braig said, coughing as he tried to wave away some of the smoke.

"I can make it. We have to move before we're burned alive."

Grabbing Ferhani by the hand, Braig pulled her low, leading her out of the forest towards the city streets. Moving farther away from the flames, the darkness hid them from the view of the guards as they began to spread out, searching the woodline and trying to avoid any falling debris from the burning trees.

"It's just ahead, I can see the wagon."

Climbing into the back of the cart, Braig pulled aside a thick canvas sheet and tossed their weapons in the corner. "Give me your hand."

Reaching down, he gripped Ferhani's forearms as he lifted, hurrying to get her to safety. Catching his heel on the side of his shield, he stumbled backwards into the cart, bringing Ferhani up and over the back before landing on his chest. Yanking the canvas sheet over them, he could feel the heat of her body against him as he banged his hand on the seat, giving the signal for the wagon to move.

The cart rambled down the cobblestones, bouncing hard as they made their way to the rendezvous point to take the next wagon to the docks. Ferhani's chest heaved as she stared down at Braig, not bothering to roll off of him. Her mouth hung slightly open as she leaned in closer. "That was close," she said, letting her body press harder into his. "I'm starting to wonder if you and yours are worth all the trouble."

Braig swallowed hard, his mouth slightly open, no words escaping.

"But I should hope you are. After all this, if I can't count on you take care of my ship, I'll have to kill you myself." Leaning her face closer, she let her lips hover over Braig's face, her warm breath blowing over his cheek. "But before then," she said, sniffing as she moved closer, "you should really wash your beard."

Braig's heart beat faster as she smiled down at him, her body bouncing on his as the wagon moved through the city, weaving between the streets, carrying them away from the destruction behind them.

A Parting of Ways

The wagon slowed to a halt in front of a long alley, giving them just enough time to climb off before it pulled away, leading any guards that might be following down a false trail. Moving quickly down the dark lane, Braig and Ferhani could see the cart waiting in the dim light of the street just ahead. A stained canvas tarp covered the back of the wagon, shifting slightly as the others moved beneath it.

Tapping on the side of the wagon, Braig helped Ferhani up onto the bench and climbed up after her, taking the reins in his hands. "Everyone back there?"

"We're all here," Faine said, peeking his head out from under the cloth.

Putting his hand on Faine's face, Braig pushed his head down and tucked the tarp back in place. "Good. Let's get moving."

Giving a quick whip to the reins, the horses trotted down the cobblestone road towards the docks, being kept at a steady pace to avoid drawing attention. The grinding of the wheels against the hard stone echoed off the buildings, making Braig's shoulders tighten as he watched the darkened windows of the shops as he passed. "I don't like being the only people on the road. By the stone! The roar of the wheels'll give us away if anyone's close enough to hear 'em."

"This way," Ferhani said, pointing down a narrow side-street. "Not much farther."

Handing the reins to Ferhani, Braig scanned the streets, keeping watch for any guards that might be heading their way. Turning down the broad lane that led straight to the dock, he heard the sound of hooves battering the streets in the distance, running hard as they followed the rumbling decoy carts away.

"We need to get the ship. It's not safe out here. And what about Gilly and Jutnar?"

Ferhani glanced over her shoulder as she gave the reins a quick snap, urging the horses to move faster. "They'll be fine. By now, they've jumped off the wagons and let the horses run. They're most likely back at the warehouse having a drink."

Taking a deep breath, Braig let his shoulders relax as he looked out over the harbor. Ships lined the docks, bobbing and swaying with the waves as they crashed gently over the shore. Beyond them was a vast expanse of nothingness that stretched out to the horizon, the water and the sky indistinguishable from the other. Aside from the glow of the moons rippling over the waves, everything looked empty and calm with nothing in the distance but darkness. He wasn't sure why he was comforted by this, but it made him feel more at ease than he had in months.

"Are we almost there?" Renna said. "It smells like piss back here."

"You try sleeping on that mattress and see how it makes you smell," Faine said, lifting the tarp flap once more.

"Be quiet," Ferhani said, reining the wagon to a stop. "We're here. When we pull the tarp back, hurry up and board the ship and head below decks."

"Aye, captain," Faine said, pulling the canvas back over his face.

Shaking her head, Ferhani climbed off the wagon and lowered the back gate. "Here we go," she said, lifting the back of the tarp.

Skara scampered down the back of the wagon and scurried underneath, watching for anything coming down the street as Renna and Faine helped Aenwyn out of the cart, her throat scratched and bruised where the commander's hand had held her. Pushing them along, Ferhani pointed them towards the ship as she led the wagon farther down the road and tied up the horses.

The lanterns on the deck of the ship lit the base of the two large masts and the crumpled burgundy sails that had been lowered while docked. Although she couldn't make out all the details, Renna could see that the ship was long and narrow, but large enough to store plenty of cargo and a good amount of crew.

"You can admire the ship when she's out at sea," Ferhani said as she strode across the narrow gangplank and opened a hatch leading below decks. "Down the ladder, and I'll show you to your room."

"Did you say room?" Faine said, taking a step down the ladder.

"Just get down the ladder," Braig said as he started climbing down, forcing Faine to move or be pushed.

Ferhani shut the hatch as she squeezed by the group and led them down the tight hallway. "We have several rooms off the main hallway. The galley is in the back left, the privy in the back right. You'll find a bucket and soap for washing in there and a barrel of fresh water. Be easy on the water and soap because it has to last until the next port. And if you think being under the tarp with Faine smelling like piss is bad, you don't want to be on a ship where the whole crew—yourselves included—smell that way. Now," she said, opening the door near the washroom, "this is where you'll be staying."

"And how are we all going to fit in here?" Faine said as he stuck his head inside the door. "There are five of us."

"That's about right. It's not much different for the crew. There's a bunk bed in the back, a bedroll underneath, and a hammock in the corner."

"It'll do just fine," Braig said. "Now I think it's time we all get some sleep. When do we set sail?"

"You'll leave a bit after sunup when all the gear is loaded. I'll be back down in the morning before you go to fill you in on the details and introduce you to the crew. Stay out of sight if you go up on deck. We should be fine here, but there are no guarantees. And if you hear anything out of the ordinary, there's a hatch through that crate near the bed. Open the top, lift the hatch and crawl in. It'll be tight for all of you, but it should keep you hidden. Now get some rest," Ferhani said as she turned and stepped out into the hallway, closing the door behind her.

Jumping up on the top bunk, Faine took off his shirt, smelled it, and tossed it to the floor. "At least this mattress is better than the last one."

"What about you, Skara, hammock, or bedroll?" Braig said.

"I'll take the bedroll." Untying the leather cord, he unrolled it under the bottom bunk and crawled inside, hiding his head from the lanterns burning on the wall.

"Well, that leaves the bed for you," Renna said as she looked over at Aenwyn.

"Can I talk to you up on the deck?"

Renna nodded her head and opened the door. Climbing up the ladder, the two moved to the bow of the ship, staying hidden in the shadows.

"I can't come with you," Aenwyn said, leaning against the railing as she gazed out over the dark waters.

Pressing her back against the rail, Renna looked over at Aenwyn and crossed her arms. "I just thought you wouldn't want to stay here."

"I'm not. But I have something I need to take care of before I go. And I've been thinking about what you said about going to the wastes. The shadow stone could just be a story, but it makes sense that something could have been created by the cult. And if it is real, I don't think that's the only one. There are old fables about powerful magic or stones from centuries ago."

"So, what are you saying?"

"I'm saying that if it's real, there's a good chance it'd be somewhere like the ruins—that place is full of death. But I'm also saying that even if it's not, there's a good chance you may not make it out. It's still a dangerous place."

Looking down at her hands, Renna picked at her nails, letting out a sigh. "You think I don't know that? Something's out there, and someone's looking for us because we helped Braig, and they were using him to find it. And whatever it is, it's powerful. It's the kind of thing bards write stories about."

"And that's fine, you can go there and search. I'm not going to try to stop you. I'm just telling you to be careful. I know the kinds of things that are supposed to be out there. Just stay low and quiet, keep your weapons out, and don't be afraid to use your magic if you have to. I saw the burning man out there on the field. I saw what you can do."

Renna turned her eyes down, staring at her fingers as she picked as her nails. "And that doesn't scare you, watching me bring a corpse back with dark magic?"

"It doesn't. I've seen things, done things. I didn't get these scars from doin' nothin'. We are who we are."

Turning towards Aenwyn, Renna reached out and pushed a strand of her red hair behind her ear, lightly tracing down the scar on Aenwyn's face. "Thank you for everything. We wouldn't be here if it weren't for you."

Aenwyn shrugged. "Look, I don't know how long you'll be out there, but I'll be leaving here in less than a week, and I'd like to see you again. I'll be heading to Ferridacci, which is on the south side of the mountains just east of the wastes. Keep going until you come to the river and find a place to cross, then follow the mountain range south. That should get you there. I plan on staying at The Evyresada Inn—it means The Riverside Inn. When you make it out, you should head there. I may have some more information about the stones for you. But be careful of who you talk to there. Some people don't like anyone a bit different. After all, Aerith isn't known for having the best history with anyone with orcish blood."

"And if I don't make it there?" Renna said, moving in closer to Aenwyn.

"Then it will truly be a sad day," she said, taking Renna's hands. "Take care of yourself, Renna Onthera. I'll be waiting for you by the riverside." Leaning forward, Aenwyn pressed her lips lightly to Renna's before turning and running across the gangplank and into the night.

Rubbing her hand over her eyes, she wiped away several tears as she walked across the deck and down the hatch, sagging wearily into her bed and thinking about all the things she'd lost along the way here, but all things still out there for her to find.

A loud knock sounded on the door the next morning, and with it, the call that breakfast was ready in the galley. Climbing out from under the bed, Skara picked up Faine's dirty shirt and tossed it up on the top bunk, landing over Faine's mouth. "Get dressed. It's time for something better than rancid broth and stale bread."

Faine coughed and sputtered as he threw the shirt back onto the floor. "C'mon! You know where that shirt's been. Why would you do that?" he said, picking pieces of hair off his tongue as he jumped down to the floor. "I don't even know where this hair came from."

Shaking Renna's shoulder, Faine stretched out his foot and pushed Braig, sending him rocking back and forth in his hammock.

"Do that again, elf, and I'll toss you overboard," Braig said, trying to steady himself before climbing down onto a box out of the hammock.

"Just testing your sea legs. The water was pretty calm last night. Just wait till we get away from the shore," Faine said, looking around the room. "Does anyone know where she put our bags? I don't really want to go to breakfast topless, you know?"

"Why not?" Braig said. "With no shirt and pretty blonde hair like yours, you might just get a bit extra."

"You know what, you might be right. Off to breakfast, then. You coming, Renna?"

Rolling out of the bunk, Renna stretched and trudged to the door.

"Everything alright?"

"It's fine. I'm just ready to eat and get moving."

Following Renna to the galley, bowls had been set out on the table next to a large pot of fish and leek soup. Several loaves of dark bread and a knife sat at the end of the table.

"Looks like I didn't need to flaunt myself after all to get a bit extra," Faine said, dishing out some soup into his bowl.

Hearing footsteps outside the door, Ferhani peeked around the corner before stepping into the galley. "Good, you're up," she said, looking over at Faine, eyebrows raised. "Trying something different for breakfast?"

Faine glanced down and shrugged as he took a bite of his bread. "I couldn't find my bag, so..."

"That's right. I'll have them brought down. Finish your breakfast, get changed, and meet me on deck in about ten minutes. I'll introduce you to the captain and crew."

"Where's everyone else?" Skara said.

"They've already eaten and are on deck making preparations. Ten minutes," Ferhani said as she walked away, leaving them alone to eat.

Finishing their meal, they heard several loud bumps in the hallway near the ladder. Sitting in a large pile were stacks of bags and weapons, spilling out onto the ground.

"At least they were gentle with it," Faine said.

Picking up their gear, they tossed it into their room as Faine hastily put on a shirt and followed them up the ladder into the salty morning air.

Up on the main deck, the eight-person crew hustled from stern to bow as they loaded supplies and prepared the burgundy sails to be raised. Stepping up on a crate near the captain, Ferhani shouted over the crew, drawing their attention.

"Everyone listen up. As I'm sure you've heard, the ship has four more aboard for half the trip. They'll be traveling with you to Solis and then taken to their drop point in Aerith. And although they are passengers aboard the ship, they have graciously volunteered to provide an extra set of hands should any disagreement arise while at port or out at sea. I think you'll find them more than capable of handling themselves in any given situation, and I expect you to treat them with the courtesy they deserve. Is that clear?"

The crew nodded, muttering to themselves as they went back to preparing the ship to sail south. Jumping down from the crate, Ferhani walked with a tall woman in their direction. The captain's light brown hair hung in a long braid over her beige shirt. Her sleeves were rolled up past her elbows, and tattoos of what looked like maps covered her arms. Her loose brown pants were tucked neatly into her black boots, each with several chains of jewelry wrapped around them that jingled as she walked beside Ferhani.

"Captain Lorsan, these are the boarders I told you about."

The captain, standing nearly a foot taller than Faine and Renna, moved closer to the group, looking them up and down. "How many of you have been on a ship before?"

"I have," Faine said, stepping forward.

"Well then, you know all about how bad it can be for someone's maiden voyage. I trust that you'll keep an eye on your friends while we're out."

Nodding his head, Faine rubbed his hands through his hair, pulling it back and tying it with a leather cord. "I will. It's been a while since I've been at sea, but I remember enough to make myself useful."

"Good," Lorsan said, eyeing the elf. "I'll make sure to re-member that."

"And just how bad does it get out there?" Braig said.

"I'm not gonna lie to you, the water near the coast of So-lis can be a bit rough. The sea is fairly calm on the way if we don't hit storms, but it can still make you green. And as Fer-hani said, you're guests on my ship. But if you get sick, do it overboard or in a bucket. Otherwise, one of your friends will be mopping it up. But we can deal with that when it hap-pens. Mostly, I expect you help when asked and do as you're told if we get caught in a bad situation; be it the weather or otherwise. And in return, I'll do my best to make sure you make it to Aerith in one piece."

Vaguely hearing Lorsan's words, Braig stared over at Ferhani as she smoothed down her deep blue tunic and adjusted her green and purple bodice. Her long black hair blew softly in the wind, and light specks of sea spray dotted her olive skin. The tattoo near her brow was an arcane symbol he didn't recognize, but it stood out boldly next to her eyes, drawing attention to their beautiful deep brown hue.

"Any questions for me, Braig?" the captain said, looking down, her eyebrows raised.

"Uh, no. I got it."

"Let's hope you do. Get settled in, we leave within the hour." The captain nodded to Ferhani and strode briskly across the deck, barking orders and checking knots as she went.

"That's a fine woman," Faine said as he turned towards Renna.

"No."

"What do you mean?"

"You know what I mean. The last thing we need is for you to get us all tossed overboard for doing something foolish." Renna put her hands on her hips as she squinted her eyes.

"Fine. You're no fun. I guess I'll just go coil some rope or something. Not like I'll be doing anything else for a while," Faine said, turning away and walking over to speak with a few of the deckhands.

Seeing several of the crew pointing out towards the horizon, Renna stepped over to Ferhani and leaned over the railing, watching as a large ship pulled into the harbor. Huge white sails billowed out from three tall masts, each accented in bright yellow trim with a white flag bearing the gold and red lion crest of House Egara.

Straining her eyes, she could see harpoons fastened to the dark brown ship, each fitted with long polished spears. The bow bobbed and swayed as the sails began to lower, and paddles emerged from portholes in the side of the ship, helping to guide them to the dock. Glinting in the sun at the bow of the vessel, a large bowsprit reinforced with metal rods and tipped with a bright yellow speartip stood out against the light blue of the horizon.

"What ship is that?" Skara said, moving to stand next to Renna.

"That," Ferhani said, pushing them away from the railing, "is the Sun Spear. It's a warship from House Egara. They use the bowsprit or harpoons to hold a ship in place to board it. And if you were supposed to be taken back to see the king, that's the ship that was going to take you there. No one should know you're here, but to be safe, hurry up and get back down below decks until we leave port. And take the elf with you."

Motioning to Faine and Skara to follow, Renna opened the hatch as she waited for them to descend before looking up at Braig.

"Wait," Ferhani said, grabbing his arm.

Shaking his head at Renna, he watched her close the hatch as he moved out of sight of the Sun Spear.

"I wanted to give you this."

"What is it?" Braig said, looking down at the bottle in his hands. "A bottle of your red potion?"

Ferhani shook her head and closed Braig's hand around the bottle. "It's one of my strongest. It can heal almost anything as long as you're alive to take it."

Squeezing the bottle, Braig put his hand over Ferhani's, looking up into her eyes. "Thank you for all you've done for us...for all you've done for me. I didn't deserve any of it."

"Sometimes, things happen whether we deserve them or not—good or bad. It's just a part of life. Now," Ferhani said, stepping back, "I want you to take care of yourself out there. I hope you find whatever it is your looking for."

"And what if what I'm looking for is somewhere else?" he said, looking up into her eyes.

Ferhani smiled as she turned and strode across the deck, glancing back over her shoulder as she stepped up onto the gangplank. "Then make sure to stay alive long enough to find it when you're ready."

Braig watched the shoreline growing smaller in the distance as the Banshee cut through the waves, gliding out onto the open sea. Climbing up from below decks, Faine, Renna, and Skara stood beside their friend as they looked back towards Mivara.

"Didn't I tell you it was worth seeing?" Faine said, clapping Skara on the shoulder.

Holding onto the railing, Skara gazed out over the water, his eyes wide. Behind them, the Sanguine Gulf stretched out to the shoreline, the soft, flowing red kelp garden moving below just below the surface, like drops of crimson blood shimmering in the clearest blue.

THE SUN SPEAR ROWED to the docks at the Mivara harbor, casting ropes to the dockhands below. Once the ship was secured, the crew lowered the gangplank, preparing to head to the shore.

"Stay close to the ship. We're here for business, not pleasure," Duelm said, tying on his white cloak.

"Yes, sir," several of the crew said, putting their fists over their chest as the commander walked by.

"Start loading the supplies before I get back. We put the prisoners in the brig, take a night to ourselves, and set sail for Ethilios in the morning." The commander smiled, pulling on a pair of black leather gloves. "You two, come with me to escort the prisoners."

Stepping out onto the dock, Duelm turned his head, searching for any of the guards from Stonekeep that should have been waiting to meet him. Moving farther up the pier, he waived to the dockmaster, drawing his attention as he weaved between workers and fishermen.

"Mornin'," the dockmaster said as he closed his ledger. "What can I do fer ya?"

"I'm here for several prisoners. I was told there would be guards from Stonekeep here to meet me. Have you seen them around?"

The dockmaster scratched his scraggly white beard. "No, can't say that I have. Last I heard they was havin' some problems up there at the prison."

Duelm clenched his jaw. "What kind of problems?"

"Can't say fer sure. Somethin' to do with a tower collapsin' or the fire."

Pinching the bridge of his nose, Duelm looked up towards the city. "And which way is it to the prison?"

"Eh, not too far from here. The dock district stretches out a good distance that way, but if you follow this lane up and that way, you should come across it. Large stone building in a big field, can't miss it."

"And I don't suppose you have any horses we could use?"

"Can't say that I do," the dockmaster said as he flipped open his ledger, making notes as he looked out over the ships.

Clenching his fists, Duelm strode up the side of the long street, pushing his way through the crowds of people that swarmed around the open-air stalls and shops. Stopping to ask for directions several times, he was led down several side roads before eventually seeing the wide stone fortress rising up out of the field just ahead of him.

Stepping into the clearing, he could see that only three of the four perimeter towers stood. The main gate was closed, and multiple guards and hired hands rushed around the fortress, hauling wagons of bricks and mortar as they cleared away the pieces of the fallen tower, using any salvageable stones to repair it.

Shaking his head in disbelief, he walked up to the main gate, glancing at the burned trees that still smoked a short distance away before banging on one of the wooden doors leading into the tower. Hearing the squeak of a small hatch opening on the door in front of him, Duelm leaned closer, waiting as a pair of eyes peered out at him from behind the door.

"What do you want? I already told you lot that you don't get paid until the end of the day. Now get back to work."

The small hatch slammed shut as Duelm looked over at the two guards he had brought with him from the Sun Spear. Banging harder on the door, the hatch flung open again, two narrowed eyes glaring out at him.

"What did I just say?"

Stepping forward, Duelm put his face up to the door and looked the guard in the eyes. "Close that hatch one more time, and you'll be cleaning up the rubble from another one of your towers. I've been sent here for two of your prisoners. Now open up this damn door before I break it down."

Closing the hatch, the guard opened the door, stepping out from the gatehouse. "Why didn't you say that to begin with, then?"

Scowling, Duelm waved his hand towards the keep. "What happened here?"

"We had a couple prisoners escape last night. They had a bit of help from someone outside."

"Who?" Duelm said, stepping closer to the guard. "Who escaped?"

"Just some drunk elf and a goblin, that's it. The tower fell into the yard, no one else got out."

"But you managed to catch them, right?"

The guard turned his gaze down and rubbed the back of his neck. "No. We chased them down the streets, but it turned out to just be a couple of empty wagons being pulled around."

Duelm slammed his fist into the wall next to the guard's head. "So, you're telling me that you lost the prisoners I sailed here to get because they had help from the outside. Tell me, how does someone bring down the tower of a keep, and fend off numerous guards?"

"They must've had magic. Vines just sprang up out of the ground and took down the tower and back wall. Fireballs and arrows came from the forest before it burned. We sent a few guards out into the woods last night, but whoever was out there killed 'em. They even turned our own commander on us."

"What do you mean?"

The guard stepped out from the main gate and pointed in the direction of the field leading to the back of shops in the dock district. "I mean that they set him on fire and sent him after us. We saw a few people running away, but we couldn't make out who they were. We were too busy trying to fight off that monster. Lost some good people here last night."

Stepping out onto the road, Duelm looked out towards the field. "How long ago did this happen?"

"I don't know...maybe six hours. We've had men out looking all night, but they haven't found anything."

"And where do you think someone could go if they wanted to get away in a hurry?" Duelm said, staring at the man.

"Most likely hiding out somew-"

"To the docks!" Duelm said, shaking his hands in the air. "Have you even bothered to check there yet?"

"We had someone ride by, but they didn't see anything suspicious there."

"And you wouldn't see anything if they were already on board." Popping his neck, Duelm looked at the man once more and pulled his gloves on tighter. "I'm leaving within the hour. If you have any more information, bring it to the Sun Spear down at the docks."

Walking swiftly down the side roads to avoid the crowds, Duelm made his way back towards the docks, waiving once more to the dockmaster as he approached.

"What can I do fer ya?"

"How many ships left port this morning?"

Flipping through his notes, the dockmaster ran his fingers across the page, his mouth moving silently. "Three out so far, two in."

"Have you seen any of the ships before today?"

"Course I have. They come and go from here every few weeks or so."

Duelm glanced out at his ship as workers loaded crates of supplies. "Any of them leave a bit earlier than usual?"

"Don't think so. One left early, but it happens sometimes if they're running a tight crew."

"Which ship was it?"

"The Banshee, I believe," the dockmaster said as he checked his ledger.

"The dark grey ship with the burgundy sails?"

"That's the one."

"Where were they headed?"

Closing his book with a clap, the dockmaster looked out over the ships bobbing in the water. "That's not really information I should be givin' out. They're fine traders just trying to run a business and stay afloat like the rest of us."

Reaching into a coin purse on his belt, Duelm pulled out two large gold coins. "These are gold marks. These can be broken into four pieces each, which is equivalent to around eight gold coins. You tell me where they're heading, and they're yours."

The dockmaster eyed the coins as he rubbed his fingers together. "And if I don't?"

"Then I take the book anyway and have you drowned for interfering with royal business. Now, what's your choice?"

"I'll take the coins," the dockmaster said, opening his book. "They're heading south to Solis. It doesn't say which port, but if I had to guess, I'd say the one on the northern point."

Handing the coins to the dockmaster, Duelm turned and walked swiftly down the dock, his white cloak billowing out behind him.

"How long until the supplies are loaded?" he said, stepping onto the deck of the Sun Spear.

"We should be ready to sail in less than an hour."

"Good. Send out a raven to Sonosa. Tell them the prisoners have escaped Stonekeep, and we're in pursuit. We'll send word when they've been captured."

"And where should I tell them we're heading, sir?"

"Tell them we're going to see the elves. Tell them we're going to Solis."

Shores of Solis

Skara clung to the bottom leg of the bunk as the ship rocked and heaved. Heavy waves pounded the hull as most of the crew hunkered below decks riding out the storm. His stomach rolled, and he felt as if he was going to be sick at any moment. The bucket Faine had brought down for them earlier slid back and forth across the floor, slamming against one wall before being thrown against another.

Above him, he could hear Renna moaning as she stumbled out of bed, keeping her arms outstretched for balance as she followed the bucket, quickly grabbing hold just as she became sick. The acrid smell of vomit filled the room as Skara closed his eyes and gripped the small antler necklace hanging around his neck. The rune carved into its surface was supposed to help protect him from harm, but he wasn't sure if its power would work against something as powerful as a storm at sea.

Rubbing his finger over the carving, he saw water dripping down from the ceiling as the waves crashed over the deck above, threatening to take anything not tied down back into the savage waters to be lost and consumed in their fury. A flash of his small home back in Banrielle pushed itself into his mind, and for a moment, he felt a pang of homesickness well up inside him.

Gritting his teeth, he tightened his grip on the bunk leg and tried to push the thought from his head. He couldn't go back there now, even if he wanted to. But despite everything he'd gone through so far, including the storm, he wasn't sure if he would change any of it. If he had stayed back in Banrielle, he would have still been alone, sitting night after night hoping that something would eventually change; hoping for some catalyst that would force him to do something different with his life.

And even though he would still be safe and comfortable, he knew he never would have left—or taken his revenge on the brothers and felt their blood on his hands. And sometimes, he thought, rubbing his fingers together, it was almost as if he could still feel it there, soaked deep into his skin, unable to be washed away. But he wasn't sure if that bothered him anymore.

He had been broken and remade into something different, something more. He was a shadow now, a knife in the dark. And although it nearly got him killed, he was glad that he stumbled across Faine in that cave. If it weren't for that, he wouldn't be here now. But given the current situation, he didn't know if that was for better or worse.

The crash of Renna being slammed into the bed pulled him from his thoughts. Scrambling out of the way, the wooden bucket slipped from her hands, splashing vomit across the room as it clattered to the floor.

"When will it stop?" Renna said as she climbed back into bed, the swaying of the ship pulling her back and forth.

"By the stone! It has to stop sometime. And where the hell is that blasted elf?" Braig said, holding himself tight against a crate in the corner.

Climbing out from underneath the bed, Skara pivoted around the vomit on the floor as he climbed onto the end of the bottom bunk near Renna's feet, moving closer to talk to Braig without having to shout. "He said he was going to stay up on the deck with Lorsan in case she needs a hand."

"That's what he says, but I think he's got more on his mind than that. I just hope he's not floating face down in the water somewhere," Renna said, her face a bit more green than usual. "I need the bucket. Someone get me the-"

Leaning over the side of the bed, Renna lurched, gripping the edge of the mattress as she tried not to roll off onto the floor. Her mouth hung open, drool dripping out onto the floor.

"I don't think you have anything left in there," Braig said as he turned his head away, trying to hold in his own breakfast.

A loud banging sounded down the hallway as the hatch to the main deck slammed shut. The wind howled outside as the boards creaked around them, water soaking their belongings.

"Who's out there?" Braig said, reaching for the bucket on the floor, ready to use it as a weapon if someone burst into their room looking for a fight.

The wooden door to their room flung open wide as Faine stood in the hallway, holding onto the frame for support. His white shirt was soaked and transparent against his skin, the dark tattoos looking muddled under the drenched fabric.

His blonde hair hung in loose strands, clinging tightly to his shaven face. Water dripped from his wrinkled skin as he steadied himself and tried to catch his breath.

Letting out a sharp laugh, Renna sat up in bed and stared at Faine. "You look like a drowned sewer rat," she managed to say before she coughed, nearly gagging and retching onto the floor.

"What's the word?" Braig said.

"We can see the coast of Solis in the distance. It's hard to see, but it's there."

"Thank I'Lurian," Renna said. "Are we going into port soon?"

Faine shook his head, water dripping from the loose strands of hair around his face. "No. We have to stay out at sea until the storm passes. If we get too close, the rocks'll rip the ship apart."

"Then what are we supposed to do, just float out here and risk being killed by the waves?" Braig said, gripping the hammock as another massive swell rolled into the ship. "Those'll kill us if we just stay out here doing nothin' but bobbing up and down on the water."

"Lorsan says we should make it. She's been at the helm keeping us above the water the whole time. She says that she's been through worse than this before."

Shifting around Renna's flailing feet as she laid back down, Skara looked up at Faine. "Did she say how long before we can dock?"

"It'll be a few hours at least, but she's pretty sure the storm will pass soon, and we can dock by evening. If not, it'll be tomorrow morning."

"And why can't we just dock as soon as it's over? Braig said.

"Too many rocks in the shallows. Hard to navigate in the dark."

Wiping the drool off her lips, Renna turned towards Faine. "And what should we do until then?"

Faine grabbed the latch on the door, pulling it closed. "Just hang on. We're almost there."

Several hours passed before the waters calmed, and the ship stopped swaying. Needing a bit of fresh air to help settle their stomachs, they made their way up the ladder and onto the deck. Black clouds sat on the horizon, the haze of rain pouring out from below them as streaks of lightning bolted from one cloud to the next.

The ocean had calmed, rocking the ship gently as Renna walked over to the railing and looked out towards Solis. The water around the coastline was littered with sharp rocks or ragged cliffs that jutted weather-worn stone in all directions. Vast sandy beaches cut into the mountains, creating hidden coves between the rocks that led into the dense forest behind them.

Massive evergreen trees dotted the landscape, their trunks as big as the ship was broad and reaching hundreds of feet into the air. A thick mist poured in from the water to the east, partially shrouding the moss-covered cliffs and tree trunks that overlooked the sea.

"I've never seen anything like it," Skara said, stepping up on the side of the railing.

"And you never will anywhere else," Lorsan said as she moved slowly down the stairs, her clothes drenched and clinging to her body.

"What do you mean?" Braig said.

"The large trees you see above all the others here only grow on Solis and the Mammoth Isles."

Skara glanced up at Lorsan before looking back towards the shoreline. "Why only here?"

Lorsan shrugged. "The weather, I suppose. Maybe something to do with the fog. The trees spread across the islands thousands of years ago. People say they can live for just as long, too. Some believe they were put here by the gods themselves, and that the first tree is still alive out there in the wilds."

"That's amazing," Renna said, her eyes wide.

"That it is," Lorsan said, clapping her on the shoulder. "And you're about to see them up close."

Shouting orders to the crew to raise the sails, Lorsan took the helm and steered the ship towards the coast. "Cabri, some wind if you don't mind. Get us to port before nightfall."

"Aye, captain," Cabri said as she climbed the ladder to the crow's nest.

As soon as the burgundy sails were fully raised, she lifted her hands to the sky, weaving them in tight patterns as she drew arcane symbols on the air around her. The sails slapped and pulled on their riggings as a strong wind blew from the north, swiftly pushing the ship across the water as it sped closer to port.

Running up the steps to the helm, Renna peered up at Cabri. "She's controlling the wind. That's how the Banshee can outrun other ships, isn't it? No matter the direction you steer, the wind is always at our backs."

Lorsan looked at Renna and smiled. "That's right. The winds have been with us so far this trip, and we haven't had to use her till now, but it pays to have a mage on board that can do that. Not everyone can. But it's not just the magic, the ship was built to cut through the waves."

"And she's got a great captain at the helm," Faine said as he moved closer to Lorsan, his hands resting on hips.

Rolling her eyes, Lorsan glanced over at Renna before looking over her shoulder at Faine. "Do you have a few minutes, sailor?"

A smile crossed Faine's face as he stepped forward. "Yes, captain."

"Good. After that storm, I'm sure we took on some water, and I need to know how bad the damage is. I need you to get down into the bilge and check it out. Really look for any leaks down there. Lots of rocks under the water around here."

The smile faded from his face as his arms fell to his side. "You want me to go down there and check? Into the bilge?"

"Is that a problem? Should I ask someone more capable?"

Straightening his back, he looked up at Lorsan. "No, captain. I'll let you know what I find."

"Very well. But be thorough. If there's a problem, we'll have to fix it when we dock."

Lorsan looked over a Renna, winking as Faine walked down the stairs and descended through the hatch below decks. "And that's how it's done."

"Like a drowned rat, indeed," Renna mumbled to herself, a slight smile on her face. "How long until we're at port?"

"Not long now. We're pulling into Ithren, which should only be a bit farther up the coast. The storm blew us off course to the south, but only slightly. We should be there soon. After you get yourself and your room cleaned up," she said, her eyebrows raised as she looked down at Renna," we should be about there."

Blushing slightly, she thought about how she had dropped her vomit bucket onto the floor and the mess that it had made when it hit. Nodding her head to the captain, she made her way back down the hatch to clean herself up and mop her room.

The sun hung just above the horizon as the Banshee lowered its sails and drifted slowly into the docks at Ithren. Buildings of smooth, white stone and deep red wood led up the hillside and into the mist-shrouded forest in the distance. The warm hues of the setting sun, slightly diffused, made the buildings and pathways glow red like they had been made of polished flame.

Lowering the gangplank, Captain Lorsan stepped onto the redwood dock and was greeted by two elves in natural woolen tunics and dark pants. Each wore a dark blue robe with an emblem of a tall tree that vaguely resembled a tower with a star above its peak. After a short conversation, Lorsan handed the elves a small pouch and motioned for the crew to follow.

Stepping in line behind the captain, the crew were led down a winding stone pathway past a sprawling two-story building with a spiraling tower that looked as though it had been made from white clay and twisted after it had been sculpted. Panes of stained glass in an assortment of colors and designs stood out against the bright, gemstone inlaid walls that rose up from the soft, green grass around them.

"This," the female elf said as she waved her hand, "is the college of Malumnae. Here, people of all walks of life come to study herbs, potions, and the interwoven relationship between sentient beings and the arcane aspects of the natural world around us."

Stepping out from behind Faine, Skara crossed his arms over his stomach and looked up at the elves. "And who's allowed to study here?"

The elves turned their heads and looked around the crew, focusing on the goblin. "Anyone is allowed to study here, provided they show aptitude. We don't turn away anyone with a desire to learn away, no matter the race. But it does come at a high cost. Anyone attending must follow strict rules of peace and be willing to put in the effort and risk the dangers that living in Solis can bring. Now, if you'll follow me, I'll show you to the inn where you may stay for the night. But you are always welcome to stay on your ship if that makes you more comfortable."

Looking around, Skara could see numerous races of elves, dwarves, men, and orcs, each of varying colors walking casually down the walkways. A small group of what looked like large, bipedal lizards with smooth scales nodded to him as they saw him looking out from the line of the crewmen behind the two guides.

"I spoke the truth," one of the elves said, seeing Skara's surprised look. "Anyone may study here. Now, this way, please."

Following close behind the elves, a dense fog began to settle over the forest as they made their way deeper into the city. The stone pathways became wide, smooth roads, littered with fallen pine needles and bits of bark that had been shed from the ancient growth around them.

Shops and homes were built around the bases of the trees, the stone and wood weaving together to create something that looked like it had grown from the very forest around them. Lanterns of bright red flame burned in decorative metal and glass orbs that lined the fog-soaked pathways beneath their feet, or spiraled up the enormous tree trunks, lighting numerous houses and buildings near the canopy, each connected by swaying bridges high above the ground.

"I can't believe what I'm seeing," Braig said, nearly tripping over Skara as he gazed at the structures built around the redwoods above him. "I never would have thought I would see anything like this in all my days."

Skara nodded his head as he stared wide-eyed at the sights around him. The forest he could see between the buildings was nearly black as the dark night settled in under the thick canopy above them. Small orbs of light darted between the trees, leaving fading tracers behind them as they moved around the towering trunks.

"What are those?" Skara said.

"They're called wisps. Something similar to a forest sprite. They're mischievous little things. So, whatever you do, don't follow them...or you could end up getting lost."

Watching the wisps as they walked, the elves led them to an inn nestled between a small grove of moss-covered trees. Ferns lined the pathway to the door, and Skara could see a roaring fire burning inside the hearth through the light blue colored window.

"Welcome to the Rock and Root. You'll find all the comforts you need inside, so make yourselves at home and rest for the night. Or, if you wish, explore the city. But be sure not to wander into the forest. There are kynnwulvs out there that could swallow you whole. Captain, if you'd be so kind as to follow me, we can finish our business and begin loading your shipment."

The elves nodded to the line of the crew as they began to walk back the way they had come, stopping briefly when they passed Renna. Leaning closer to look into her eyes, the elves exchanged confused looks.

"Excuse me?" the male elf said, waiting for her name.

"Renna."

"Renna. Beautiful name. My friend and I couldn't help but notice your eyes. It's a strange thing to see one so dark, and one so light. I can see by your ears and tusks that you come from two different lines, but do you know much about either, particularly your elvish heritage?"

Renna stepped back, her arms crossed over her chest. "I don't know much. I know my father was half-orc, and my mother was an elf. Why?"

"It just reminds me of some old stories that I've heard, that's all. You can tell a lot about someone from their eyes. But no matter, I just think they're beautiful."

A blush formed on Renna's cheeks as she looked down at the ground. "Thank you," she said as they smiled and continued walking down the path with Lorsan.

"You have such beautiful eyes," Faine said as he leaned towards Renna and puckered his lips.

"Ugh. Begone, arda."

"Heard that story from Skara, huh? No matter. Now let's go. It's good to have my feet on solid ground again, and I could use a drink."

"I bet you could," Renna said, following Faine through the door. "You have to do something to rinse the taste of that bilge-water out of your mouth."

"So funny tonight."

"Let's sit over here," Braig said as he walked over to a table near the fire. "There's a chill in the air tonight."

Taking a seat at a round table made from a solid chunk of a large tree, Faine waived to the barmaid. A plump elf with curly brown hair and dimples on her cheeks smiled and strolled over to the table, her green skirt flowing out behind her.

"What'll it be for you tonight?"

"Well," Renna said before Faine could answer, "we were told there were rooms available for the night."

"There are. How many will you need?"

"How many are available?"

"With the other guests, I have three left."

Renna tapped her tusk as she looked around the table. "We'll take two. Someone else might need the third."

"I'll put it in the books. Will there be anything else?"

"What are kynnwulvs? One of the elves outside said it could swallow us whole." Skara said.

"Oh, I'm afraid it could. A kynnwulv is a wolf bigger than a grown man. They live out in the heart of Solis near the wild elves. It's a dangerous place if you don't know where you're going. But you'll be fine if you stay in town. They don't come anywhere near us here."

Tapping his knuckles against the wood, Faine leaned forward, putting his elbow on the table. "Sounds scary. So, what's something I can only get here? Food and drink."

"I don't know about something only here, but we have fresh venison braised with red wine and herbs, poached pears, and soft bread with moonflower honey."

"And to drink?"

"I would recommend the gluwein."

Faine's eyes widened. "That sounds good. What is it?"

"It's a blend of our honey mead, sweet spices, and luminescent mushrooms. It's sweet, and the mushrooms make it glow and give it an earthy taste. I hear there are variations elsewhere, but ours is the best."

"Hmm. I think we'll take a bit of each," Faine said as he looked around the table and nodded.

As the barmaid walked away to gather their meals, Braig leaned in closer, keeping his voice low. "I know that this has been a hard trip for all of us so far. So if any of you want to stay here or turn back, I don't blame ya for it."

Everyone around the table shook their heads.

"We've come this far, why turn back now?" Faine said.

Skara nodded. "Some of us don't have anything to go back to."

Biting the edge of his lip, Braig looked around the room to make sure no one was listening. "I think I know where we need to go. I told you I had a dream about the stones and knew that one was in the wastes, but I wasn't sure where. Well, I think I know now. It started when we got on the Banshee back in Mivara. There was something strange about the nothingness out on the water, and it made me feel calm. It must've stirred something in me because I can feel it pulling at me."

"What do you mean, pulling at you?" Renna said, moving her hands off the table as the barmaid set down their food and drinks.

Taking a long drink of his wine, Faine waited for the barmaid to leave before leaning back in. "You mean like pulling you to the stone?"

"I think so," Braig said, pulling a piece of meat from the bone. "It's like a rope tied around my insides, tugging at me."

Faine shrugged. "Maybe it's just something you ate. I mean, how do you know it's the stone?"

"Because I've seen flashes of it. I see it, a dark shard in an old farmhouse. It's like there are eyes everywhere, but I can't see anything around me but the stone. It feels heavy. Like the air is alive and waiting to swallow me. I've been waking up at night covered in sweat, the image burned into my mind...and I just want it to stop. I don't know what's waiting for us there, but I think if I can get it, I'll know what I'm supposed to do."

"Aenwyn mentioned something about the stone to me before we went to Stonekeep. She said it could have something to with a cult or the Denmol, the undead."

"Then, why even go?" Skara said as he poured honey on a piece of bread.

"Because if we don't get it, someone else will. And I'll be damned if I let it end up in the hands of the brothers. Or worse yet, the hands of some king in Ethilios. And whoever took me in the first place has something to do with the king. Why else would we have seen the same Egara crest on a banner at the camp in Banrielle, and on the ship in Mivara? I'm sure the D.E. signed on the letter we found at the camp stands for someone from House Egara."

"And if we find it, what then?" Skara said. "Where would we go?"

Renna thought about the inn that Aenwyn told her she'd be staying at. Unsure of whether she'd be there or not, she felt it was best to leave out all the details until they had the stone and were looking for a way out. "We'll head east, inland towards the mountains. I've been looking at Faine's map, and it looks like our only option. There's nothing but more wastes north. But if we head east towards the base of the mountains, there's a village there that we might be able to find a ship at."

Wiping a bit of wine out of his beard, Braig looked around the table. "Do you believe that there's something people are meant to do?"

"You mean like being fated to do something?" Faine said.

Braig nodded as he chewed on a piece of venison. "Something like that."

"I normally don't buy into all of it. I think there could be any number of people working towards the same thing we are right now. To me, it's all like a game. We were put here for entertainment, like playthings. But I'll admit, things have been a bit strange. I don't understand what your visions are about, or where they're leading us, but they're pointing somewhere. Maybe it has something to do with your vision of Emin back at the temple, or maybe it has something to do with the cult and the stone. But either way, I think that there are things that we choose to do for whatever reason, not necessarily that we're meant to." Faine took a drink of his wine and shrugged. "But then again, I don't really know."

"I believe that sometimes we are," Renna said, reaching out to take Skara and Braig by their hands. "How else would we have come together? Skara was carried to us poisoned, and you were carried to us in a cage. Or maybe, Faine and I were carried to each of you by any number of the choices we made in our lives. But what matters now, is that we're all choosing to move forward together and see where this road goes."

"We are indeed," Faine said, picking up his mug of wine. "But before we go any farther down that road, let's drink our fill and chase some wisps. You never know what tomorrow will bring."

The Banshee

Faine awoke early the next morning, half-naked and lying face down on his mattress, a knocking sound beating in his ears. Raising his head slightly, he looked around the room, keeping his eyes nearly shut to try to block out the overly bright sunlight that poured through his window. Not seeing or hearing anything threatening, he buried his face back into the mattress, hoping it was still early enough to get a few more hours of sleep before he would have to drag himself out of bed.

In the hallway, Renna stood with her arms crossed, the sound of snoring drifting from the room. Banging harder on the door, she pushed it open, putting all her weight behind it to move Braig out of the way as he snored loudly on the floor.

"Gods, Faine. Put your pants on!" Renna said as she covered his lower half. "I don't know what you three got into last night, but you need to get up. The ship's leaving soon."

Faine moaned slightly, his lips moving just enough to form words. "Wisps. Like little balls of angry fire."

"Where... where's Skara?" Renna said as she glanced around the room, not seeing signs of him anywhere. Grabbing Faine roughly by the shoulders, she began shaking him, bouncing his body up and down. "Faine! Wake up. Where's Skara?"

Opening his eyes, he looked around groggily. "What? Did you check in the chest at the end of the bed?"

"No."

"Then check in the chest, woman."

Opening the chest at the end of the bed, Renna saw Skara curled up inside, bits of mud stuck to his face. "We don't have time for this." Grabbing a pitcher of water, Renna poured it on each of their faces, rousing them from their drunken slumber.

"Agh! By the stone," Braig said, sitting upright and wiping the water off his face. "Are ya tryin' to drown me?"

"All three of you get up. Grab your shit and get down to the ship before it leaves without us."

Faine stood up and stretched, the sheet falling off his waist. "And put on some damn pants!" Renna said, opening the door. "Make it fast. If you're not on the boat in fifteen minutes, I'll tell them to leave without you."

Standing on the deck of the ship, Renna watched as Faine, Skara, and Braig barreled down the hill, breathing heavy as they hurried aboard. Their clothes were wrinkled and covered in mud, and Faine's pants looked as if they had been set on fire at some point throughout the night.

Leaning over and gagging slightly, the three gasped for breath as the crew laughed and lifted the gangplank.

"Just made it," Lorsan said as she gripped the helm. Craning her neck, her amused smile fell from her face as she moved back and forth, running towards the side of the ship. "Get those sails raised! On the double!"

Men and women scurried over the deck, moving as fast as they could to raise the anchor and move away from the docks to reach open water.

"What's going on?" Faine said as he followed Lorsan's gaze.

In the distance, he could see large white sails accented in gold over a dark brown ship, sun glinting brightly off the speartip at the end of the bowsprit.

"It's the Sun Spear!" Renna said, moving out of the ship's line of sight. "Captain, what should we do?"

Spinning the helm, Lorsan began shouting for Cabri to take her post and to put her back into it. "We run, Renna. With all our cargo, there's nowhere big enough for all of you to go. Whether they see you or they don't, they'll search the ship and put us all in the brig."

"But won't they do that anyway if you run?"

"If we run and they follow, we can try to find a place to stow our goods or say we didn't see the Egara banner and fled for our safety against an unknown ship. Or, one of us won't make it out of the Boiling Sea. All hands on deck! Ready the ballista!"

A loud 'harou' sounded from each of the crew as they pried open crates, revealing several boxes of fire-bombs. Stacks of harpoons wrapped in thick canvas cloth were carried out of the captain's quarters and set near the masts. Flipping open a large hatch on the prow, several sailors heaved at two heavy ropes attached to pullies on two long posts. Rising from below deck, a ballista was locked into place on the bow with thick metal pins.

"Cabri, give it all you've got and keep us ahead of them—and if you can manage it, throw some wind in their direction to keep 'em off us for a bit. If they broadside us, that spear'll sink us. And get the whistle ready. Let's show 'em why they call this ship the Banshee." Lorsan said, guiding them safely out of the port.

Feeling a sudden jerk of movement, the sails billowed outward as the sharp keel cut through the rippling waves, keeping the ship just a short distance ahead of the Sun Spear.

"How is it moving so fast?" Faine said, stumbling up the stairs towards the helm.

"More sails to catch the wind. And I'm sure they have a mage or two on board. Now get down on the deck and help ready the harpoons. When they're loaded, tie a fire-bomb on tight to the tip. That goes for all of you. And don't drop one, or you could set us all on fire."

Rushing down the stairs, Faine reached for a coil of rope, pulled out a dagger, and handed it to Skara. "Cut it into lengths and separate the strands. Keep them straight and pile them up. When the harpoon is loaded, someone hand me a fire-bomb and a strand of rope, and I'll tie it on. But first, I'll go grab our weapons. I have a feeling we're gonna need 'em."

Watching as several of the crew set out longbows, Renna armed herself and stood close to the mainmast, setting her arrows in a line in the crook of a sturdy crate, steadying herself as the ship gained speed. The wind around her seemed to crackle with energy as she leaned closer to the railing, peering out over the water at the Sun Spear. Arcs of lightning sprang from the end of the speartip mounted on the bowsprit, spanning out like glowing tendrils across the water, growing closer to their ship.

Following Renna's gaze, Lorsan glanced over her shoulder at the Sun Spear, a scowl crossing her face. "Steady on," she shouted, adjusting the helm. "Make yourselves ready. Cabri, give us another push. We're almost there."

The ship creaked and shuddered as a burst of wind caught the sails, forcing the crew to hold onto something or risk falling overboard as they were thrust forward away from the shores of Solis, moving swiftly to the southeast around the coastline towards the Boiling Sea, crossing between the chain of rocky islands known as Kralorn's Maw.

Strapping his belt around his waist, Skara knelt down on the deck, gathered his bundle of rope, and ran to the prow. Stopping short of the ballista to squeeze himself between two crates, his eyes went wide as a looming grey haze twisted and writhed like a great beast floating on the water stretched out before the bow. The water churned and bubbled beneath them as a thick blanket of fog hung heavy in the air, nearly as wide and tall as the coast they had just fled.

Turning the Banshee headlong into the wall of mist, the ship faded from view, swallowed whole into the silver unknown. The dense fog swirled around them as bubbles of air rose from broken ridges deep beneath the water, popping and steaming as they reached the surface.

Riding through the mist for nearly an hour, the crew could hear the buzz of electricity or see the glowing arc of a fireball from the Sun Spear burning out as it hit the water around them. Barely keeping themselves at a safe distance, Lorsan motioned for Cabri to return to the main deck.

"Are you alright, girl?" Lorsan said, turning the helm hard to starboard, wheeling the Banshee in a hard loop to face their bow towards the broadside of the approaching ship.

Exhaustion clear on her face, Cabri nodded and knelt down on the deck, taking a long drink from the ladle of water one the crewmen brought her. "I'll be fine. I just need to catch my breath, is all."

Lorsan nodded as the ship bobbed in the water, quiet and still, waiting to see the crackling lightning through the thick fog. "Take a moment, but be ready to sound the whistle and get us out of range of the harpoons." Stepping away from the helm, she put her hand on Cabri's shoulder and looked out over the crew. "This is it. We can't outrun them any longer, and only one of us is going to make it out of here. I hoped we wouldn't be in this position, but here we are. We've all been through this before, and you know what to do. Hit hard and fast and move before they can hit us. No mercy. If we get boarded, fight for your lives and your family, or you'll leave nothing behind but widows and little bastards. Now, are you ready for some bloodshed?"

The crew let out a 'harou' and took their positions on the ship, manning the longbows and the ballista. Laying out several harpoons, Faine began tying fire-bombs onto the tips, being careful not to break any in the process.

Setting down the stack of rope strands, Skara crouched down next to Braig and Faine, his brow slightly furrowed. "You think we'll make it out of this?"

"I think we will," Faine said. "I don't think this is where we're supposed to die."

Strapping his shield tighter to his arm, Braig raised his eyebrow. "Thought you didn't believe in fate."

Faine shrugged. "I don't. But I don't think we're supposed to die anywhere. It just happens. But I trust Lorsan and the crew to take of the ship, and I trust all of us to fight for each other."

"And it's about time. This ship's been followin' us for too long. I say we just ram 'em and be done with it," Braig said as he stood and moved to the prow, staring off into the emptiness, watching for any signs of movement.

Skara shook his head and looked over at Renna as she stood with her head down, an arrow nocked and ready. Her dark hair hung loose, falling around her pale green face. "And if they do manage to board?"

Faine tied on another fire-bomb and glanced over at Renna. "We don't let them take us—and we don't let them take Renna. She wouldn't make it back to Ethilios in one piece. Whoever's on that ship would tear her apart. We do what we have to do to make sure that doesn't happen. You understand what I'm telling you?"

"I think so."

"When the fighting starts, we stay together."

A sharp buzz cut through the air as flashes of electric-blue light reflected on the mist around them. Waves of fire and sparks erupted from the deck of the Sun Spear as the mages fired blindly into the dense fog. The sails billowed as gusts of wind pushed the ship onwards, briefly clearing a path before the gloom of the Boiling sea rushed in, obscuring their sight.

Faine handed a harpoon to the crewman, keeping low as the Sun Spear pulled broadside to the Banshee.

"Now, Cabri," Lorsan said. "Sound the whistle."

A burst of wind blew across the deck and through the whistle near the crow's nest. A loud, shrill cry that sounded like the dreadful, soul-wrenching wails of a banshee pierced the silver veil and cut across the waves. Skara covered his ears against the shriek, briefly remembering several long nights he had back in Banrielle listening to those howls from deep in the forest.

Rubbing at his ears, he heard the soft thrum of the ballista as one of the crew fired a harpoon towards the Sun Spear. Flames erupted on the side of the ship, spreading up onto the main deck before being quickly extinguished by one of Duelm's mages.

"Get us moving and drop the metal lines!" Lorsan shouted, turning the helm hard to starboard.

Drawing on the magic in the air around her, Cabri broadened her gust of wind, filling the sails as the ship lurched forward, creaking under the sudden force. Boxes slid across the deck as Lorsan angled the Banshee away from the Sun Spear, trying to disappear into the mist around them.

Firing arrow after arrow, Renna picked off several of the crew, keeping out of sight to avoid being hit by any projectiles heading in her direction. Fireballs roared past the ship, deflected by the fierce wind that swirled around the Banshee. Electricity crackled around them as it struck long metal poles attached to the railing across the deck, each with lines running down into the water, diverting the lightning away from the ship or crew.

The Banshee turned and heaved, pulling away as it glided deeper into the mist, trying to outrun their pursuers. Shouting rang out across the water as the Sun Spear kept pace with the ship, running parallel beside them, firing arrows and spears across the expanse. The piercing wail sounded in the silver veil once again, and the wind began to falter.

"Cabri, get us the hell outta here!" Lorsan said as she looked over the helm onto the deck.

Cabri sat hunched over, her hand over her stomach, plucking at an arrow lodged deep inside her. Blood trickled from her mouth as she looked back up at the captain, panic spreading across her face.

Letting go of the helm, Lorsan ran for the stairs, narrowly dodging the arrows that sped across the deck.

"Everyone down!" Braig said, grabbing Skara as he held up his shield.

Slicing through the fog on their port side, a giant harpoon attached to a thick rope bolted towards their ship, ripping through the edge of the sail as it flew to starboard, narrowly missing the center of the mast.

Running over next to Cabri, Lorsan took her in her arms, pressing her hand over the wound. "Cabri! Wake up, girl. We have to go. We can't make it out of here without you."

The Banshee turned and shook as the rope attached to the harpoon was reeled in, getting tangled up in the sail and riggings as the Sun Spear pulled itself closer.

"The bastards are pullin' us in," Faine said as he ran towards the mast. "We have to cut the line. Skara, I need your help."

Curling his fingers together, Faine lowered his hands towards the deck and nodded up towards the rope. "I'll boost you up, but you have to catch the line and cut it."

Taking a few deep breaths, Skara gripped the hilt of one of his daggers and glance around the deck. Crewmen with swords and shields stood around Cabri and Lorsan while others loosed arrows and harpoons, or launched fire-bombs at the Sun Spear.

"Now, Skara! Before they pull us in or break the mast."

Dashing towards Faine, he stuck his foot in the palms of his hands and was thrown upwards, his fingers gripping the water-soaked line. Pulling himself up onto the tangled of ropes, he tried to cut the harpoon free, sawing at the strands until his blade struck metal.

"It won't cut. There's a solid line twisted into the rope," Skara said as he clung to the jumble of ropes hanging from the yardarm, pulling out enough slack to lower himself close enough to the deck to drop.

"Make yourselves ready," Faine said as he drew his sword. "It's about to get rough."

Keeping her hand over Cabri's wound, Lorsan glanced up, speaking to any of the crew that could hear her. "We have to get her inside and wrap her wounds. Seraph," she said, looking up at the sky, "don't take her. Not yet."

Pushing through the crew, Braig crouched down next to Renna, his mind turning in circles. "I have to help her, or we might not make it out of here—even if we sink the Sun Spear. I don't want to be stuck out here to die in the mists. There're things under the water here that I'd rather not see."

"And what can you do? The arrow is deep."

"I have a potion Ferhani gave me. If it works like she said it does, it'll save her."

Loosing an arrow, Renna ducked behind a crate and glanced over at Braig, lowering her voice. "And what if we need it?"

"Are you sayin' we just let her die?"

Renna sat silent, fumbling to nock an arrow as thoughts raced through her head. "No. They have mages on their ship. We're no match without her."

Nodding, Braig pulled the potion from his pouch and pushed his way through the small crowd, staying behind his shield as he ran. Kneeling down, he put his hand on Cabri's arm. "I have something here that'll help, but I have to get the arrow out. You need to brace yourself because this is going to hurt. Are you ready?"

Cabri nodded weakly as he pulled her body up into a sitting position. Snapping off the shaft near the fletching, he wrapped a strip of cloth over the feathers and put it into her mouth. "Bite down on this. And you," he said, glancing at Lorsan, "hold her here. Keep her close."

Putting his hand on the arrow shaft, he gave it a hard push, shoving it through her abdomen and out her back. A grunt of pain gurgled up from Cabri's throat as tears poured down her cheeks. Putting his hands around the point of the shaft, Braig pulled it through her body, dropping it onto the deck in a pool of blood.

"Here, drink this," he said, pouring the potion into her mouth. "This'll hurt a bit. I've heard it feels like your blood is burning, but it'll close your wounds. Until then, get her out of sight."

Several of the crew hoisted Cabri and took her to the captain's quarters, keeping low as the Sun Spear grew closer, reeling in the line as it rushed towards them.

Wiping the blood off her face, Lorsan stood up and sprinted up the stairs to take the helm. "Brace for impact and prepare to be boarded."

Turning the wheel, she angled the bow towards the approaching ship, protecting the Banshee's broadside from the spear-tipped bowsprit. "Aim for the deck! Aim for the crew!"

Harpoons hammered the Sun Spear, charring the timbers black as bolt after bolt ignited the flammable liquid before mages drew water up in a wave onto the deck, washing the liquid into the ocean to burn on top of the rippling waters.

Streaks of energy shot across the small gap between the ships, knocking two crewmen off the deck of the Banshee, sending the rest scurrying for cover. The harpoon line pulled tight as the soldiers formed a line behind Duelm, ready to rush onto the Banshee when the ships collided.

Looking pale and gaunt, Cabri stumbled out of the captain's quarters, sending out a burst of energy that sent the crew of the Sun Spear sprawling onto their backs to slide across the deck.

"Go now!" Cabri said just as the two ships collided, the port and starboard sides of the vessels scraping together, the spear on the bowsprit narrowly missing the Banshee's hull.

Leaping just as the ships crashed together, Braig landed on the Sun Spear and sprinted towards Duelm, striking down at the man before he was able to get back to his feet.

Rolling out of the way, Duelm threw a bundle of rope at the dwarf, knocking him off balance and giving him enough time to stand. "I have orders to take you back alive, dwarf. But they never said unscathed."

The sound of shouting and clanging metal spilled out over the silent waters as skirmishes broke out on each deck. Sword and axe cleaved wood and flesh alike as the shrill cry of the Banshee's whistle sounded in the billowing silver mist. Bodies fell and writhed, limbs and blood-red water sweeping across the deck with the waves.

Swinging wildly with her axe, Renna drove back two soldiers, disarming them as she channeled the stream of energy from the spilled blood around her into their weapons, turning them red-hot in their hands before kicking one man overboard and nearly beheading the second. The planks below her quaked and rattled as she turned to face a rushing soldier—only to see him sink into the wooden deck like quicksand as Cabri deftly slit his throat with her dagger, throwing spells as she passed.

Renna could see the strain on her face and knew that she was channeling too much energy at one time. And although arcane energy flowed through everything around us, it was easier to control a stream of magic rather than a rushing river that could tear you apart from the inside. At this rate, her soul could be washed away in the flow, and she'd be dead before the battle was finished—but she had to trust that Cabri would know when she had reached her limit.

Shattered bits of broken limbs slid across the deck in chunks as hammers blasted through the crewmen frozen by Duelm's mages. The ships grated and slammed together as the fierce, conjured winds and roaring waters shook the vessels, threatening to topple the masts and crush the hulls.

Jumping back across the gap onto the Banshee, Skara scoured the deck looking for the box of fire-bombs. Crates slid and crashed against the broken railing as the ships heaved, toppling them into the water, bubbling as they quickly sank below the surface. Peering over the rail, he could see pieces of the fire-bomb crates floating in the water, their contents swallowed into the depths.

Hearing the screams of the crewman being incinerated by Duelm's mages, he spotted the last of the harpoons still loaded into the ballista, a single fire-bomb still tied to the tip. Cutting the thin rope, he held it tightly as he rushed back across the deck and darted towards the stern of the Sun Spear, scurrying across the quarterdeck to flank the mages.

Keeping low behind several barrels, Skara crept to the edge, maneuvering himself behind them. Hurling the fire-bomb at the feet of the one the mages, the jar busted, sending flaming liquid up the man's legs and torso as bright orange flames licked at his face, bubbling his skin underneath. The mage screamed and clawed, batting at the fire and unable to concentrate long enough to conjure any water to put himself out.

Before the second mage had enough time to react, Skara leapt from the ledge above her, plunging both his daggers into each shoulder, piercing her heart and lungs as she dropped dead to the deck.

"Faine!" Braig said, hacking and slashing at Duelm, keeping the large man cornered between the mainmast and crates littering the deck of the Sun Spear. Blow after blow rang against his shield as he pushed forward, giving no room for the man to make an escape.

Pulling his sword from chest of the last standing soldier, Faine sprinted across the Sun Spear and jumped headfirst over the gap between the ships, landing in a roll on the Banshee. Dropping his sword to the deck, he took hold of the ballista and swung it towards Duelm. With a loud thunk, the bolt flew the air above Braig's head, slicing through Duelm's armored chest, pinning him to the mast.

Duelm's eyes went wide at the blast knocked him off his feet as the thick spear held him in place. Coughing, blood spurted from his open mouth as his hands clung to the shaft of the harpoon. Weakly looking over the carnage, he could see his soldiers lying in crumpled heaps below the remaining crewmen as they gasped for breath.

Braig dropped to his knees on the deck, a deep gash on his left bicep and smears of sweat and dirt across his face. Falling over onto his back, he stared up through the dull grey mist around him, briefly catching a streak of the blue sky before it was washed away out of sight. His chest heaved as he put pressure on his wound, gritting his teeth as he slowly sat upright and leaned against a nearby crate.

"Is everyone alright?" Renna said, rushing over towards Braig as she eyed Duelm barely clinging to life against the mast.

"I'm ok," Faine said, glancing down at the satchel Skara had over his shoulder, its bottom dragging across the deck. "But we took a hard hit. We lost five of the crew."

"We have to get to the wastes," Braig said, shaking his head. "Or this is gonna keep happening. Whatever's out there, the Egara's want it. And they're gonna keep coming till they get it...or we kill 'em first."

Staggering around the mast, Lorsan trudged towards Duelm, her saber covered in thick, clotted blood. "Why couldn't you just leave us alone when we left?" she said, staring at the man. "What was so gods-damned important that you had to follow us here?"

Duelm looked down at Braig, his eyes beginning to close. "We... do what we're told. A soldier's life sometimes isn't their own."

Lorsan's breath was hard and fast as she gripped her sword, the whites on her knuckles visible under the spatter of red. "That's not good enough," she said, raising her blade. "I'll be seeing you again in Thodun." With a few hard swings of her sword, she hacked Duelm's head off his shoulders and picked it up by the hair before tossing it into the water.

"What do we do now?" Renna said.

Lorsan's eyes narrowed as she looked down across the group. "We patch the sails, burn the Sun Spear, and get sailing. I want to get out of the mist before I give my friends their last rites. It's your fault we're here in the first place. If I hadn't told Ferhani I'd get you to the wastes, I'd leave you all here to burn. Now," she said, turning away, "gather your shit and get moving. I want you off my ship as soon as possible."

Unhallowed Ground

The Sun Spear drifted slowly away, lighting a path through the mist as it crackled and burned, falling in charred sections into the emerald water beneath it. Watching the ship until it had burned away and vanished beneath the waves, Faine, Skara, and Braig went back to their room where Renna sat hunched over sheets of paper scattered across the floor.

"Watch where you step," she said as they closed the door behind them. "Skara, you did good grabbing all these. After what happened with Lorsan, I didn't think we'd be able to get anything before she set the ship on fire."

Skara shrugged and tip-toed across the floor, dodging papers as he climbed onto the top bunk. "After killing the mages, I saw the door to the captain's quarters and just went in. I didn't know what they were, but I saw the stamp and took whatever was in the desk."

"Well, you got the right ones."

"What do they say?" Braig said. "Anything about me?"

"Not about you, specifically. But you're not the only one that Duelm bought and sold. From what I've read, he's under the command of Drasa Egara—D.E."

Moving to sit on a crate in the corner, Faine picked up one of the sheets of paper, glancing at it before letting fall to the floor. "Is that the king?"

"I don't know," Renna said, giving him an annoyed look. "But from what it looks like, Drasa is in charge. So, it could be."

"And what about the stones? Braig said.

There are more than one."

"How many more?"

Ruffling through the sheets of paper, Renna counted as she held up her fingers. "It looks like there are five. At least that's the number they have listed. It doesn't say what they do, it only says that's all they've been able to pull out of the other oracles so far. But from what I'm seeing, they don't know where they are. Maybe that's why they needed you," she said, looking up at Braig. "Maybe someone else knows what they are, but not where. Just like you can feel where one is, but not what it does. But I could be wrong."

Running his hand through his beard, Braig moved a small stack of papers and sat down on the bed. "All I know is that I can feel it out there. It's almost like it's calling me. I get this tight feeling in the pit of my stomach."

Leaning his head over the edge of the mattress, Skara followed the trail of papers with his eyes, pulling his black hair away from his face. "Was there anything in there about where they might be going next?"

"Not that I can see. There's a note in Duelm's log that says he should bring us back to Ethilios and that Braig is the only one that really matters. Well, that and one more person to make an example out of. But aside from trade logs, that's all I could find. Although it looks like they did make several trips to Elenath. Something about wanting to buy some black powder from the old mines. But it says the mines dried up a long time ago, and they haven't been able to find much since."

"Hmm, sounds familiar," Faine said as he jumped off the bed and pulled out his map. "Here it is. Right here in near the middle of Auren. Follow Marillia Bay inland, go past Rynlith and right into the city."

A soft knock on the door sent Renna and Braig scurrying across the floor, stacking the papers and hastily shoving them back into the satchel.

"Braig, are you in there?" Cabri said, knocking again on the door.

Hiding the satchel in one of the crates, Braig walked across the room and opened the door. "Cabri?"

Standing in the hallway, Cabri's skirt and blouse were tattered and stained with blood. Her face was sallow with dark circles under her eyes. "I know it's been a hard day for all of us, and I heard what the captain said to you. But I wanted to say thank you. You saved my life today."

Shaking his head, Braig opened the door wider. "But because of me, five others were killed."

"No," Cabri said as she stepped into the room. "They knew what they were getting into on the Banshee. We all do. It's part of the life. If it didn't happen today, it could have been any other time. And because of you, I'm still here."

"And how are you feeling?" Renna said, pointing to Cabri's stomach.

"The wound is gone. I just feel drained."

"You certainly look it," Faine said, getting a sharp look from Renna. "I don't mean it that way. I mean that you fought hard out there."

"I almost lost it. I tried to use too much magic and almost paid the price. It's like when you feel yourself slipping into sleep at night. You can hear that buzzing sound as you sink down into it. That's what it felt like...a slight tugging on my spirit like it was about to be carried off in the flow."

Suppressing a shudder, Skara sat up on the bed. "Sounds terrifying. Like being sucked away into the darkness."

A faint frown crossed her face. "Lessons learned, I suppose. But I won't keep you any longer. I just wanted to say thank you." Cabri reached out and put her hand on Braig's shoulder. "Without you, I wouldn't be here. And that's worth something."

Smiling, Braig put his hand over Cabri's, gently squeezing her fingers.

Turning to head down the hallway, Cabri looked back at Braig. "We'll be heading to the wastes tomorrow. We should make it there before nightfall. You should be ready to stay somewhere out there in the dark. The captain won't wait around for the sun to drop you off."

Giving her a quick nod, Braig closed the door. "Looks like we'll be walking at night tomorrow. Better get packed and rest up while we can. There's no tellin' what'll happen when we reach Aerith."

Working through the night, the crew made the necessary repairs to the ship, giving Cabri enough time to regain the strength she would need to summon the wind. Setting sail early the next morning, the Banshee cut around the northern edge of the Mammoth Isles, the sails full as they moved into the open waters of the Sanjal Sea. Once the ship was clear of fog, Lorsan had a small service for her lost crewmen, reading a short hymn before commending their bodies to Seraph, the goddess of the seas, praying for their safe passage into the afterlife.

Trying to avoid the crew, Skara stayed in their cabin as much as possible—playing cards with Faine or carving runes into the bedposts. It seemed that whenever he would make his way up to the deck, Lorsan would be staring, her eyes narrowed as she mumbled under her breath.

Trying not to let her glare bother him, he kept his eyes towards the horizon as he walked to the prow, looking out at the coast of Aerith and his way off the ship. Although he knew he wasn't solely responsible for the deaths of five of the crew, he wondered if she felt a pain akin to what he had felt when he lost his parents.

Pulling out a wooden pipe from the side of his boot, he packed it with a pinch of broadleaf and tamped it down with his finger. Picking off a sliver of wood from the railing, he opened the latch of a nearby lantern, lighting the end of the splinter and held it inside his pipe, puffing out clouds of white smoke before flicking the flaming wood into the water. Turning his head towards the sound of footsteps, he watched as Faine walked up to the railing, giving him a nod as he casually rested his arm on his head, smiling as he looked out over the water.

Pushing his arm away, Skara gazed out into the distance, the large mass of land growing closer by the minute. "We're almost there. Not much longer now."

"Less than an hour, I'd say," Faine said, putting his arm back on Skara's head. "Are you ready for this? The Denmol are formidable and focused. You've seen what Renna can do. I'm just hoping we can get in and out without being noticed."

Jabbing his fingers into Faine's side, Skara pushed him far enough away to avoid being his armrest. "I don't think we'll get that lucky."

Sighing, Faine leaned down onto the railing, listening as one of the crewmen shouted from the crow's nest about spotting a safe site to take the small ship ashore. "I don't either. But it's too late now. We can't stay here, and we can't turn back. Lorsan hates us, so it's dangerous either way. And with the looks she's been givin' us, I think I'd almost feel safer out there with the undead."

"Let's see if you still think that way later tonight," Skara said as he turned away, knocking the ash out of his pipe before heading back below deck.

Opening the door to their room, Skara saw Braig and Renna looking over Faine's map on the bottom bunk. Braig's wound was newly dressed, and their bags were packed and stacked in the corner. The smell of freshly cut herbs filled his nostrils as he was bumped into the room as Faine pushed his way in, closing the door behind him. The scent reminded him of the Green Cap and how he missed making his poisons. Most of the supplies of herbs he had were ruined on the trip by moisture or mold. He'd have to buy more in the next town or scavenge any he came across before he could make anything.

"Smells weird in here," Faine said, flopping down into the hammock. "What is that— snakeroot?"

"Snakeroot and maiden's lace," Skara said as he dug through his clothes in the sack, making sure they were all packed.

"That's right," Renna said. "I don't know how you can smell anything aside from the root."

Skara shrugged. "I've smelled it before. It's the vague sweetness that I remember."

Putting her nose up into the air, Renna sniffed, trying to smell anything sweet. "Hmm, I don't smell it. But Cabri gave us enough to make a poultice. She said she didn't want Braig's cut to get infected out in the wastes. It's looking better already."

Stretching out, Faine put his hands behind his head, keeping one leg on the floor to rock himself. "Hmm. Nice and astringent."

"So, what's the plan? By the time we get to shore, we'll only have a couple hours of light left. And if there's denmol around, maybe we shouldn't go that far," Skara said, cinching his bag closed.

Using his foot to stop himself, Faine sat up and looked over at Renna. "I agree. I think we should stay near the water and keep watch. It's too dangerous to go in when we can't see."

"Right," Renna said, pointing at the map. "We've been looking over the map, and the ruins are several miles inland, so it would take us a few hours to get there, depending on the terrain. It'd be best to wait."

Braig nodded his head and ran a hand through his beard. "And it'll give me a night to see where we need to go for sure. I know it's there somewhere. I can feel it."

The sound of the hatch closing echoed down the hall as the stomp of heavy steps stopped outside their door. "Captain says to get yer bags. This is where you get off."

"He's pleasant," Faine said, grabbing his bag and heading for the door. "Now, let's be off. Our carriage awaits."

Grabbing their belongings, they followed the man back up the ladder and onto the deck. A small dinghy bobbed in the water at the bottom of a rope ladder. A single man sat inside, oars in hand, ready to take them to the shore.

The crew was silent as Braig watched the others climb down onto the small boat. Climbing over the railing, he looked at Lorsan before glancing at Cabri, giving her a slight smile. "Tell Ferhani I'll see her again someday," he said, moving down the ladder.

Rowing swiftly towards the shore, the flailing oars splashed water into the boat, dampening their bags of clothing.

"By the stone, boy! Stop rowing so hard, or you'll crash us all into a rock."

The crewman didn't say anything but instead rowed harder.

"You have a way with people, Braig. I don't tell you that enough," Faine said, wiping water off his face.

The sun was just over the horizon to the west as they landed and were rushed out of the boat. The shore was covered in black stones that had been continuously washed up and down the beach with the tides, wearing them smooth and slightly polished. Tufts of beach grass sprouted from small dunes of black sand farther from the shoreline.

The setting sun cast a deep red glow on the groves and hills beyond the beach. Twisted, barren trees littered the hillside, reaching their skeletal branches towards the darkening sky. In the distance, the loud, shrill cry of ravens could be heard as they circled over the forest.

Moving up between the small dunes, they hunkered down between the rows of grass, sitting quietly for several minutes as the waves lapped up on the shore, softly rumbling like distant thunder.

"So... this should be a fun night. Who wants to take the first watch?" Faine said, fluffing up his bag like a pillow.

"I will," Braig said. "I wouldn't be able to sleep anyway. Should one of us look for some firewood?"

"Do you think we should," Renna said, leaning against a dune. "It might draw attention."

"We dig a hole and build a fire in it. Stack up a few rocks to help block it from view, and we can at least get some heat. We can't hide the smoke, but I think the wind should blow it away."

"Then let's go while we still have a little light. Skara, you mind gettin' the pit ready?" Braig said as he brushed the sand off his pants.

"I'll have it ready."

Digging a deep hole into the sand, Skara began stacking the rocks that Renna gathered from the beach in rows around the pit. As Faine and Braig carried back a few armloads of wood, Skara crossed one stick over the other as Renna lit the tinder with her fingers. The dried grass and driftwood sparked to life, warming them as the cool breeze from the water blew over the small dunes.

"Here, I picked these up before we left the Banshee," Skara said, reaching into his bag and pulling out a loaf of bread, two leeks, and a long slice of dried meat. "The bread's a bit soggy, though."

"That's fine with me," Faine said, tearing off a chunk of meat and bread before passing it around the fire. "I didn't even think to grab any food. But I did grab a bottle of whiskey if anybody wants some."

"Do you really think it's a good idea to be drinking here? You might end up getting shanked by an undead when you stumble off to take a piss." Braig said.

"Drink or no, that could still happen. And why deny myself a little comfort? Home," Faine said, raising his eyebrows, "is where you make it. And so far, this seems like a good enough place to be. Just listen. Can you hear the music?"

Braig turned his head, listening to the sounds around him. "What are you on about? Are you drunk already? I only hear the weeds."

"Exactly," Faine said. "That sound you're hearing is called night chords. They grow in clusters, and when the wind blows, the tops rub together and make a nice noise...like soft music."

Biting down on her last piece of moist bread, Renna stretched out over the sand. "Well, this has been fun, but I'm getting some sleep. I'll take the next watch if you don't mind. So that leaves one of you two for the third and fourth," she said, glancing at Skara and Faine.

"I'll take the third," Skara said.

Taking a sip out of his whiskey bottle, Faine put the cork back in and sprawled out next to the fire. "Then wake me up when it's time to see the sunrise."

Sitting behind a strip of beach grass, Braig kept his eyes on the dark hills and groves, occasionally throwing another log into the pit. His mind wandered as he listened to the crackling fire behind him and the rhythmic sound of the night chords just over the dunes.

His eyes began to lose focus as images flashed in his mind. Rubbing his palms over his face, he turned his head to look back towards the fire, but the beach was gone. In its place was a large field littered with corpses, the clumps of grass dark and dripping with blood. The tattered banner of House Egara fluttered in the wind, the red and gold lion torn and stained, the shaft broken and protruding upright from a man's chest.

Screams echoed across the open ground, coming from all directions. Shielding his eyes from the rays of light piercing the clouds, he could feel the ground trembling beneath his feet. Looking up to the top of the hill in the distance, a great army reached the summit, their horses lining the hillside. Above them, a banner flew in the wind, deep red with the image of a snarling black dragon in its center. The man holding the flag looked down on Braig, his smooth black hair blowing over his pale face.

Rising from behind the army of broken knights and fell creatures, a terrible shriek tore into Braig's mind, forcing him to cover his ears and cower at its sound. Powerful wings stretched out across the sky as a fearsome black dragon rose over the hillside and darted like an arrow towards Braig. The dragon screeched as its jagged teeth glinted in the sun, its gaping maw growing closer, ready to swallow him whole.

Letting out a scream as he felt a hand on his shoulder, Braig opened his eyes to see Renna standing in front of him, shaking him. The air around him was cold, and he could hear the ocean lapping on the shore behind him. The sun glimmered through the trees to the east, and he had to close his eyes to its brightness.

"What are you doing? You were supposed to wake me up," Renna said, her lips drawn back, exposing more of her tusks.

"I was in a field of corpses. Their armor was ripped and jagged, bodies charred beneath it. The air was alive, screaming at me, clawing at my mind. The flag of Egara was broken along with his army. And I saw it," Braig said, gripping Renna's arms. "I saw it on the hillside."

"Whoa," Faine said, holding up his hands to try to calm Braig. "Saw what?"

"I saw a man with pale skin and dark hair wielding a crimson banner with a black dragon. Beside him were legions of undead and fell creatures, their faces obscured in shadow. And then there it was, soaring over the hillside—a black dragon with scales like thorns coming to swallow me whole."

"It was just a dream. It doesn't mean it's going to happen. You said that yourself. It's not always what it seems." Renna said, glancing up at Faine.

Faine clapped Braig on the shoulder. "That's right. Look at where you are. A lot of bad shit happened here. It's no wonder you had a nightmare."

Braig shook his head. "It felt so real, so vivid. I thought it was over." Putting his head into his hands, he rubbed his face and looked up at Renna. "I don't know what's real or just a dream."

"It was a dream," Faine said as he pulled Braig to his feet. "The dragons stay in the mountains or under them. No one's seen one in a hundred years, especially not the black dragon. He's dead and frozen in stone."

Sighing heavily, Braig picked up the remainder of his loaf of bread. "You're right. It has to be this place." Taking a bite, he thought about his dream at the temple before they were attacked by the myrrow. That dream had been just as vivid—just as real. What were they trying to tell him? Could finding the stone be a way to keep his visions from happening, or will it help bring them to pass? Kicking sand over the firepit, he grabbed his bag and trudged along towards the forest, a sinking feeling forming in his gut.

Hours passed as they walked over the hills and fields, fertile soil beneath their feet.

"Why isn't anyone here farming?" Faine said, sifting the soil through his fingers.

"Aenwyn said something to me about a curse. People came to farm here, but the crops just withered and died. After a while, they just gave up and stopped coming."

Wiping his hands on his pants, Faine looked around at the leafless trees. "Makes sense. But where'd the people go?"

"What do you mean?" Renna said as she started walking.

"I mean, where did the farmers go after they left? Did they just head to a town somewhere?"

Renna scratched her head with a small stick. "I don't know. I would think they moved inland after nothing would grow. How long can you go without food?"

Stopping at the edge of a small grove that bordered a barren field, Braig motioned for them to get down. "By the stone! Maybe they never left at all," he said, pointing towards the remnants of a stone well near the end of the clearing.

Staggering out from behind the crumbling stones, a single denmol ambled over to a loose patch of dirt and crouched down, its bony fingers digging frantically until it pulled up a fat, writhing worm. The creature stared hollowly, its broken teeth grinding together as it gave the nightcrawler a violent shake and bit it in half. The worm struggled, falling from its grip only to be scooped up in a handful of dirt and shoved back into the denmol's gnashing jaws.

The darkened, leathery skin hung in flaps from the creature's naked body, bits of dried organs still clinging to shards of jagged bone. Thick, matted hair sat in a crusted heap on its head as its mouth chewed, the dirt and pieces of mashed worm falling through the nearly empty torso and back onto the ground.

Skara swallowed hard as he watched the creature shamble away, lifting rocks and eating whatever crawled underneath. "If it's already dead, how are we supposed to kill it?"

Renna paused, thinking about what Aenwyn had told her and stories she had heard traveling around with a caravan when she was younger. "They're held together by magic, so just cutting them apart won't work. You have to take the head or break the skull."

"How is that any different than cutting them up?" Faine said.

"Think of the skull like a closed chest or a reliquary. The energy swirls in the enclosed space, and when it's broken or severed from the body, it drains out. That's what I've heard, anyway. But I've never seen one that hasn't been brought back by a caster before."

"Then there's only one way to find out," Braig said, looking around the field to make sure there were no more roaming close by.

Tossing a stone to get the creature's attention, Braig stepped out from behind the trees and strapped his shield tighter to his arm. The denmol's eyeless gaze turned in his direction, a low gurgling hiss rising from its throat as it plodded closer. "What happens if it bites me?"

"I don't know," Renna said, grabbing her axe as she moved next to Braig. "So don't let it bite you."

Braig's lips tightened as the creature crossed the field, moving slowly on creaking bones, hands outstretched as its fingers gripped and clawed at the air. Charging forward, he slashed down, severing the denmol's arm, followed by the other. The creature pushed forward, broken teeth clicking together, inching its rotting jaws closer.

Crouching down, Braig used the creature's momentum against his shield to lift it over his head, flipping it onto the ground behind him. The denmol let out another hiss as it smashed headfirst into the dirt, cracking several ribs as it fell. Its rigid body jerked and trembled as it rolled from side to side, legs digging into the soil as it pushed itself towards Braig.

"Now watch," Renna said as she raised her axe.

Cleaving the creature's skull in half, a dark, shimmering vapor poured out of the split, dissipating as it blew away in the wind.

"Easy enough," Faine said, wiping a raindrop off his face. "We should really get moving though—looks like this weather is about to turn. How close are we?"

Thunder rumbled as Braig looked across the field towards the well. "My guts feel like they're in a knot, so we must be getting close. I think it could be just over the next hill. Looks like there's an overgrown road through the trees over there we can take. Might make passage a bit easier."

The rain grew harder as they made their way up the overgrown path, turning the hill to mud as the water pooled around their feet. Sinking up to their ankles on the wet road, they trudged to the top of the hillside, clothes soaked through as they looked down over the ruined village below.

Rotting wooden houses stood, some nearly collapsed, in the valley below. Barns and shops made from smooth stone and broken planks covered in green-grey lichen sat empty in the rain, doors and windows thrown open wide. Near the center of the village, black vines weaved themselves between the stone walls leading down into the stepwell, cracking the mortar as they tangled upwards. From its center, a slight mist rose from the stairway down into the caverns, drifting out silently over the rain-soaked village.

Skara wiped the water from his eyes and put his hand over his mouth. The air felt heavy, and the pouring rain made him feel like he was drowning. "We can't stay out here," he said over a rumble of thunder.

"No, we can't. But this is it. The stone is down there in one of the buildings," Braig said, setting his bag against a tree. "Take only what you need down there. We don't know what we'll find...and we may have to run."

"Wait," Skara said, rummaging through his bag. "Take these."

Pulling out three antler necklaces attached to leather cords, he handed one to each of them. Carved into the front were several runes and symbols, filled in with dark green paint. "I made these on our way here. The runes are for protection. It's worked for me—so far anyway," Skara said as he rubbed his chest near his heart.

Sliding the amulet over his head, Faine looked down at Skara. "I feel better already."

Braig and Renna agreed as they tied the cord around their necks. Taking only what they would need, they piled their bags of clothing against the trunk of a tree and crept down the hill, watching for any movement in the ruins of Q'Bath.

Drawing their weapons, they opened the door to the first house in a line of buildings that ran past the well and up to the stables near the barn. The door squeaked and broke from its rusty hinges, falling hard onto the wooden floors, echoing through the village. Stopping, they each held their breath, peering around the corner up the street, squinting through the rain to look for any movement.

"I don't see anything," Braig said as he stepped into the house.

The walls were bare, and the hay mattresses that were crumpled on the dilapidated beds were wet and covered in mold. Broken shards of glass littered the floor beneath the window, crunching as they stepped closer to a small dresser pushed into the corner.

Rifling through the drawers, Braig pulled out shreds of old clothing, throwing them to the floor as he searched. "There's nothing in here."

"I didn't see anything in the other rooms, either," Faine said, clenching his hands to keep the blood flowing through his cold fingers. "Let's check the next one."

Peeking around the corner, they scurried up the street to check the next house, trying to keep low and quiet, despite their feet making a sucking sound as they sank into the mud.

"Nothing here either," Braig said, pulling at his beard as he walked out the door and up the street. "By the stone, it's here somewhere! I can feel-"

"What is it?" Renna said, seeing Braig stop, his mouth hanging open.

"This is the house," he said, breathing hard. "The stone is in there."

Walking cautiously through the open door, they closed it behind them as they looked around the large room. Shelves stacked with water-soaked books hung on the splintered wooden walls with wide cracks that opened up to the cold air outside. Above them, rain poured through the sunken roof, dripping down onto the rotted floorboards that partially covered the mud below.

Breaking off into the room in the back corner, Skara pushed open the door and walked softly across the broken planks. A cold wind rushed in through the gaps in the walls as he climbed on a small, semi-sturdy table and began pulling books off a shelf. Noticing that some of the books were fairly dry, he flipped through the pages, catching a glimpse of something darting past one of the cracks in the wall outside.

Dropping the book, he jumped off the table and crept towards the wall, looking out into the small copse of trees behind the house.

"Denmol!" Braig shouted as they ran into the back room with Skara, shutting the door and barring it with the table and the shelves off the wall. "They're coming out of the well!"

Dashing to the window, Skara watched the horde of undead gathering in droves on the streets, their grotesque bodies stumbling through the copse of trees outside. The flesh and organs remaining on their bodies were bloated from the water deep in the well. Skeletal arms with sagging tissue in various stages of decay scratched and clawed at the broken wood of the bedroom, pushing the planks inward as they howled and bellowed, rough gurgles coming from mutilated throats.

"They're inside," Faine said, pushing himself against the small table blocking the door, struggling to keep it closed as rotting arms squeezed through the narrow opening.

The walls around them shook and groaned with the weight of the bodies pressed against them. Striking out at the arms worming through the cracks, Skara looked around the room, searching desperately for a way out. A wave of fear welled up in his throat as the door bent and shattered, falling to pieces as the undead pushed their way inside, limbs flailing and jaws clacking.

Braig, Renna, and Faine stood in front of the broken door, slashing and hacking as they tried to keep the horde from swarming the room as more undead scurried up the stairs from the well, flooding the streets around them.

Seeing a hole in the floorboards near the wall, Skara dove to his stomach and stuck his head into the gap, peering through the darkness for a way out. Turning his head towards the wall, he could see something sharp and black half-buried in the mud, the water dripping from above making its glassy surface shine. Eyes going wide, Skara plunged his hand into the wet ground, closing his fingers tightly around the stone.

"I found it, I found the sto-" Skara said, his voice cut short as a rusted shard of metal cut through his back, tearing through his chest and stabbing into the wood beneath him.

A muffled moan escaped his lips as he watched his dark blood pooling beneath him as it drained from his mouth and chest.

"Oh, gods...Skara," Renna said, dropping her axe and rushing to his side.

Turning him over carefully, she held him in her arms as her fingers scraped against the jagged metal protruding from his chest. Tears welled up in her eyes as she tore open his shirt to see the wound. His skin was scarred with runes that spanned his torso, the ragged metal cutting through the same symbol he had carved onto their amulets.

Ren...Renna..." Skara said, dark blood spurting from his mouth as he coughed, unable to swallow. "Don't...don't let me go. I'm not ready," he said, his grip tightening on the stone, its knife-like edge cutting deep into his fingers. "I'm scared."

"Skara, hold on!" Faine said as he swung and thrust, shattering skulls and severing heads. "Hold on. Gods-dammit!"

Blood covered Renna's hands and face as Skara sputtered, his yellow eyes slick with tears closing gently as the denmol beat at the walls around them, pushing their way through the cracks.

Renna's face twisted into a mask of seething rage. Her body shook as her fists clenched and opened, her tear-filled eyes darting around the room as her teeth ground against one another, her fingers rolling Skara's blood between them. Something lurched inside her, a sudden strength that clawed at her insides, making her blood feel like it was on fire.

"Faine," Renna said, her breath low and ragged. "Get Skara."

"I'm trying!" he said, his brow covered in sweat, his muscles aching as he and Braig held off the horde.

Writhing on the floor, Renna tore at clothing, ripping it off her body as she dug her nails into her flesh. Her bones twisted and broke as she screamed in pain, her flesh ripping as her limbs elongated and her face shifted and snapped into a large muzzle. Thick black and silver fur grew over her body as her distorted, grotesque form reshaped itself into a massive wolf, its back taller than Faine and nearly the length of the room.

"Gods, Renna," Faine said, falling back against the wall, pulling Braig out of the doorway as they stared, cowering.

Renna bit and snarled, her tongue quivering against the back of her teeth as she growled. Letting out a howl that made the house tremble, she glanced down at Skara's body and busted through the back wall, teeth tearing rotted flesh as she ripped her way through the mass of denmol that stood unflinching in the streets.

Pulling the metal shard out of Skara's back, Faine crossed his arms over his chest, picked up his small, lifeless body, and followed Renna and Braig into the pouring rain. Red teeth and streaks of silver fur flashed in the lightning as the wolf lunged, flinging bodies against walls and tearing off limbs and heads as they neared the edge of town, stopping at the rise at the top of the hill.

"What're ya stopping for, you dim-witted elf? We have to keep moving!" Braig said, glancing towards the forest leading away from the ruins before looking back at the approaching horde.

Pulling Skara's body closer to his chest, Faine stared back down the hillside, the massive black wolf behind him padding closer. Its dark fur was matted with putrid fluids and bits of torn flesh, and several deep gashes covered its long legs. The wolf's muzzle moved closer to Faine as waves of hot breath rushed over his face. Closing his eyes, he felt a low rumble through his body as the wolf growled, teeth bared as she stared down, towering above him. His heart turned over in his chest, and his legs shook beneath him. He knew that there was a part of Renna buried inside the beast, but he wasn't sure of how much control she had over her ferocity. Feeling her rough tongue scraping over Skara and his arms, he looked up at the massive wolf, her two different colored eyes gazing down at him.

"It is still you," Faine said, watching her charge back down the hill, taking her anger out on the denmol as she slated her thirst for vengeance, giving them time to escape.

"What the hell are you doing? We don't have time for this shit!" Braig said, roughly grabbing Faine's shoulder. "Take Skara and run I'll go back for Renna."

Faine looked out over the black and silver wolf below as the creatures closed in around her, her mouth gnawing and tearing them to shreds. "No! Leave her here. She'll find us when she's finished," he said as he turned and ran into the forest, blood dripping down his arms, the stone shard no longer in Skara's grasp.

The Shifting Darkness

The dark, dry soil shifted and swirled around Skara, stinging his eyes as he looked up into the blackened sky. Lightning flashed, cutting across the grey billowing clouds above him, lighting up a row of scorched trees with long black thorns and a small mountain ridge in the distance. Jagged rocks jutted from the ground in the field around him like sharp fangs in a waiting mouth, ready to consume him.

Laying his hand over his chest, he pressed his fingers into the deep wound running through him but didn't feel any pain or see any blood as he pulled his hand away. Feeling something sharp against his palm, he opened his hand and saw the shard of black stone he had found back at the farm still held tightly in his grasp. But where was he now, and why did he still have the stone?

Climbing to his feet, he ran his finger over the cut in his palm, wondering if the stone having direct contact with his blood somehow saved him, or transported him somewhere. He remembered being stabbed, but after that, everything went black until he was here staring up at the sky. Squeezing the stone tighter in his hand, he remembered Braig saying something about a dark place with blowing dust...about Thodun.

"I must have died," he said, coughing against the blowing dust, his body trembling as he gripped the stone.

Fear gripped his body as he held up his hand in front of his eyes and looked around the darkened fields. Although he wasn't sure of which direction to go, he knew that standing in the open in a place like this would only bring about more trouble. He needed to find a place to hide—or a way out if there was one.

In the distance, a glowing blue light on the horizon caught his eye as he turned to see a large, spiraling tower reaching into the sky, wreathed in blue flame. Stumbling forward over the crumbling soil, laughter rang out from a rock behind him, turning him on his heels as he reached for the empty sheathes on his belt.

"Who's out there?" he said, crouching down to pick up a handful of soil.

Hearing footsteps running up behind him, he turned and threw the dirt, hoping to slow the assailant. The fine dust struck the heavy-set man in the face, doing little to slow him as his thick fingers reached out for Skara, wiggling in the air in front of him. Rolling to the side, Skara sprang to his feet, running hard across the unsteady ground.

Moans and screeches sounded in the darkness around him as shadows fluttered at the edge of his vision. Focusing on the blue tower miles away, he pushed himself to move faster, trying to outrun the slow, deep laughter and heavy footsteps gaining ground behind him.

"Over here!"

Turning his head, he could see a pale man with long black hair motioning for him to follow him into a tight crevice between two stones. Pumping his legs harder, he could feel the large man's thick fingers grazing the back of his head as he turned, scuttling into the tight gap, leaving the man's obese arm reaching for him from outside the small cavern.

"Who are-"

"No time for that yet," the pale man said, grabbing Skara and pulling him deeper into the cave. "They'll be coming once they move him out of the way. We have to reach the other side and hide before they do."

Sprinting through the narrow stretch of stone, Skara followed the man, barely able to keep up as he darted around corners and slid underneath low overhangs. Hearing the rumbling thunder outside, he glanced up, expecting to see another flash of lightning, but saw nothing but rough stone. Although the cavern ceiling was solid, a dim light shone through the passageway, drowning everything inside and out in a soft, diffused haze.

"Here we are," the man said as he ran towards the mouth of the cave, stopping to scramble up a very tight passageway leading up to a hidden cavern farther up inside the cliff.

Shutting the trap door made from the black-thorned wood, he piled several stones on top to keep it closed before sitting down on the ground to look over at Skara.

"What good will that do?" Skara said, pointing to the thorny door. "I didn't think you could feel anything here in Thodun."

The man laughed, pulling his hair behind his pointed ears. "You figured that out easily enough. Some people never realize where they are. But you're wrong. You can most definitely feel pain here. You may not be able to feel your wounds from the plane of the living, but you'll feel any pain that happens here...you just can't die. So even if you're torn to pieces, you'll just come back together to suffer again and again."

"Who are you?" Skara said, moving farther away to sit against the wall. "And why did you help me?"

"I'm sorry about my lack of manners. A place like this has a way of changing someone. My name is Dreymon," the pale man said, putting his hand over his mouth as he rubbed his cheek. "And I helped you because I sense something on you that may be able to help us both."

Skara squeezed his fist tighter around the stone and glanced towards the trap door.

"But don't worry...I'm sorry, I didn't get your name."

"Skara."

"Well, Skara. You don't have to worry. I'm not going to take it from you."

"And how do you know about what I have?"

Dreymon took a deep breath and held his finger over his mouth as he heard scratching in the cave below him. Waiting until the noise had passed, he pointed to Skara's hand. "That item you carry gives off an aura. Before I came here, I was a mage. I spent the majority of my life studying magic and its flow between life and death. I think we can use it get out of here— out of Thodun."

Rubbing the back of his neck, Skara glanced at the door again before looking back at the man. "And how did you know I was even here? How much of an aura does this stone give off?"

"Enough to attract attention. If not mine, then surely someone else's. I'm going to be honest with you," Dreymon said, using the wall to help him stand. "Look at the scars on my body. I've been whipped and beaten here, torn apart and pieced back together more times than I can remember. I have to get out. I don't know how much more I can take before I become just another monster out there in the shadows. Trust me when I say there are things here that you couldn't even imagine...just waiting for their turn with you. And when you fell, it shook something inside me. I could feel the power that you carry, and I had to find you. "

A shiver ran down Skara's spine as he thought about the man that chased him into the cave. What would have happened if the man had caught him? Would he have been torn apart and eaten alive only to wake back up in this nightmare?

"And how would we get back? Is there even a way out?"

"Quiet," Dreymon said, holding up his hand as the thorn door began to move, shifting the stones. "We have to go. That stone you carry is drawing too much attention. Grab hold of this rope and pull open the door when I give you the signal."

Grabbing a rock from the corner, Dreymon positioned himself over the hole. The stone, although small, was covered in sharpened sticks tied on in different angles, capable of stabbing anything underneath as it fell through the opening below. "When I drop the stone to clear the way, we have to hurry. I don't know what's waiting for us out there, but I don't want to be trapped in here. Are you ready?"

Skara's hands shook as he took the length of rope, ready to pull.

"Now!"

As the hatch flipped open, Dreymon dropped down the spiked ball and pointed towards the opening. "Hurry, down the hole and out of the cave."

Scurrying down the hole behind the elf, Skara saw the pot-bellied man sprawled out on the ground with a long stick in his hand, the sharpened spikes of the stone sticking in his shoulder and head. The large man moaned, his fat fingers still reaching for Skara as he struggled to keep his eyes open.

Dropping off the rock wall and running out of the cave, Skara could see the deformed masses of bodies running in his direction, their limbs flailing as they reached out for him. Keeping a tight hold on the stone, he followed closely behind Dreymon, gnarled fingers tugging at his clothing as he darted away from the dark tide of bodies swarming towards him.

"This is it, Skara. You come with me now, or we both get ripped apart and get stuck here forever. Make your choice."

"I'll do it," he said, fear nearly choking him as the drooling and filthy shells of men and women surrounded them. "Use the stone."

Gritting his teeth, Dreymon ripped off a thick branch from a nearby tree, the thorns piercing his hands as he bashed a hole through the encroaching wave, ripping holes in the hungry creatures' skin as he wielded the staff. "Follow me to the tower. And keep up."

Running wildly around the sticks and stones, the two pushed farther into the desolate wastes, the tower growing brighter in the distance, the ethereal flames dancing across the crumbling tower, drawing them in like moths to the brilliant glow.

Circling the bottom of the tower to find the door, Dreymon dug frantically at a small gap in the blackened soil under the curve of an archway. Shrieks reverberated off the tower walls as the shadows gathered in the distance, following the pulsing stone in Skara's hand.

"Help me dig! The door is buried, and we have to get to the top."

Sticking the stone into his boot, Skara clawed at the soil, digging a gap just wide enough for one person at a time. Seeing the tortured souls nearly on them, Dreymon squeezed himself between the gap, struggling to fit as his back scraped against the sharp stone. Sticking his hands through the opening, Skara dropped to his back and grabbed hold as he was pulled through the hole. Grimy fingers and sharp claws scratched at his boots as he reached the inside of the tower, narrowly escaping one of the creatures as it clawed at the opening, trying to force its way in behind them.

"Quickly, up the stairs. Don't stop until you reach the pinnacle," Dreymon said, pushing Skara upwards.

The broken stairs wound around the inside of the tower, crumbling beneath their feet and sending chunks of stone plummeting to the bottom. Paintings hung on the walls, their images blotted away and ravaged by the elements, unrecognizable in their frenzy to reach the top. Broken flasks and bottles littered the floor around them as they ascended the stairs, glancing over their shoulders as they ran.

"How are all these things here? How is the tower here?" Skara said, following close behind the elf.

"The tower here is a mirror to the mage tower in the Grey wastes. The magic there is somehow connected to Thodun. That's how we're going to get back."

Pushing his fingers to his chest, Skara stopped and looked up at Dreymon.

"What are you doing?" Dreymon said, glaring back at Skara as he stopped. "We're almost there!"

Opening his shirt, Skara pointed to his wound. "I can't go back. My body is dead. There's nothing left for me to go back to."

Glancing up the peak of the tower, Dreymon clenched his teeth as he ran back down the stairs towards Skara. He knew that he needed to follow a soul with a body out of Thodun; otherwise, the spell wouldn't work. Although the body on the other side didn't need to be alive, if he used the stone, he could heal him. "Hold onto something," he said, putting his hand over Skara's wound, pinching it together. This is going to hurt."

Standing next to Skara, he held out his other hand. "Give me the stone."

"What are you-"

"I'm healing your body. But I need the stone. Quickly!"

Taking the stone from Skara in his free hand, he watched as a lanky creature with human limbs on the side of its body like spider legs rounded the staircase, scuttling towards them. As the creature bit at Dreymon's hand, he stabbed the black stone in its head, causing a thick liquid to drip from the wound.

Skara could feel the rush of magic coursing through his veins as Dreymon held his hand over his chest. A sharp burning sensation flooded his body, making his blood feel like it was on fire. He could see Dreymon concentrating, his eyes closed, and his teeth clenched as he drained the creature's dark energy, forcing it into Skara.

The skin and muscle on his chest shot across the gash, weaving it shut as Skara let out a grunt of pain, nearly falling backwards as his wound closed under Dreymon's hand. Pulling the stone loose, he pushed the lifeless creature off the edge of the stairs, watching it bounce as it plummeted to the bottom of the tower.

"Better?" Dreymon said, moving back up the stairs.

Feeling the tight skin across his chest, Skara rubbed the rune that he carved over his heart as he darted back up the stairs, trying to catch up to the elf.

Reaching the top of the tower, Dreymon held the stone towards the sky as he began speaking in a language Skara couldn't understand. Using its sharp edge, he cut four deep gashes in his arm, peeling away the flap of skin between them. Thick black liquid clung to the piece of flesh as he pulled it free and threw it down on the top of the tower.

"Give me your hand," Dreymon said, holding the stone like a knife.

Reaching out, Skara winced as the elf drew the sharp edge across his palm, spilling out a trickle of black liquid from the fresh cut.

"Now take hold of the wound in my arm," he said, looking up at the sky as the blue flames swirled around them, rising up to meet the dark, swirling clouds that dropped down, coiling together in a swirling vortex.

Wrapping his blood-covered fingers around the elf's wound, he could see him flinch as he squeezed tighter. Thunder roared above them as the wind whipped them back and forth, tossing chunks of brick off the tower onto the mass of dark shapes writhing below.

A heavy silence filled the air as the blue flames were pulled into the heart of the stone, making it vibrate with an energy that exploded outward in a bright flash of light, shattering half of the upper level into pieces, leaving the tower crumbling and empty with nothing but the rushing wind blowing across the fractured stone.

FAINE SLUMPED DOWN against a tree, exhausted and drenched from the rain. He had been running for miles to get as far away from the ruins as he could, his mind racing as he thought about what happened in the house. Looking down at Skara's body in his arms, he wondered if there was something he could have done to save him—or to keep it from happening in the first place.

"What do you think we should do?" Braig said as he sat next to Faine. "Should we bury him?"

"Not yet. We have to wait for Renna. I know she'd want to be here...to say something," Faine said, turning away from a Braig as a lump formed in his throat.

"There's nothin' ya could've done. There were too many of 'em. If it wasn't for Renna, I don't think any of us would've made it out of there. By the stone! I don't even know what really happened back there."

"We shouldn't have been there in the first place. Out looking for something we didn't even need to find. And because of it..." Faine said, letting his voice trail off.

Braig put his head down and focused on a patch of moss near his feet. "You're right. But there's no way I could've known that would happen."

"Isn't that what you do—see visions?"

Cursing under his breath, Braig scowled down at Faine as he moved farther down the trail to sit alone in the shelter of a pine tree. Keeping his eyes to the ground, he thumbed the amulet that Skara had made for him, occasionally glancing over at Faine as he sat in the rain, not bothering to find any shelter.

Hours passed as the two sat apart, keeping watch for Renna or any undead that may have followed them. The rain had stopped, and rays of sunshine broke through the trees around them, lighting up the small clearing.

Brushing the pine needles off his pants, Braig walked over to Faine and looked over towards the sun. "Only a few hours left before nightfall. We should try to make a fire, so we don't freeze to death. And," he said as he glanced down at Faine, "it'll give Renna something to look for in the dark."

Nodding his head, Faine carried Skara's body to a small patch of grass, setting him down in a ray of light. "The stone is gone. It was in his hands when I picked him up. He had a tight grip on it. It must have fallen out when we were running."

"I know it's gone. But I don't think it's on the trail behind us. I could feel the stone before we ever got to it. If it was still here, I'd feel it. As far as I know, it used its magic up raising those damned undead."

"Do you think that's what it was meant to do?"

"I don't know," Braig said, setting rocks in a circle for a fire. "It could be that those things were already down there waiting for anyone that came. And this time, it just happened to be us."

Faine looked down at Skara before he walked off into the woods, gathering any semi-dry sticks and pine boughs he could find along the way. Using his knife, he shaved off a few handfuls of cedar and birch bark before gathering a couple mushrooms from the rotting logs. Setting the tinder and kindling into the pit, Faine flicked a spark onto the crumbled inner layer of the fungus, adding the bark and thicker pieces of wood as the ember turned into a flame.

The sun had nearly set by the time Braig and Faine had built a steady fire and hung their clothes on sticks to dry.

"Do you think she made it?" Braig said as he warmed his hands.

"I don't think the denmol took down...whatever that was."

"I've never seen anything like that before."

"From the look of it," Faine said, "she didn't even know she could do that."

Hearing branches snapping out in the forest, Braig and Faine grabbed their weapons, standing back to back in their underclothes as they scanned the woods around them.

"Faine!" Renna said from somewhere in the darkness beside them.

"Renna? Where are you?" Faine said, dropping his sword and running to the edge of the light. "Follow the fire."

Hearing a soft groan, Faine turned to see Renna staggering into the light. Her thin tunic clung to her body, wet and torn from the branches along the path. Her mouth and face were covered in dark blood, and her hair was tangled and full of sticks and leaves. Dragging on the ground behind her were the four bags of clothing they had left near the ruins. Tied around her wrist was the amulet that Skara had given her, its cord broken from her transformation.

"Where's Skara?" Renna said, her breath coming out in fast clouds as she moved closer to the fire, her body trembling.

"Gods, Renna! You're nearly frozen," Faine said, taking the bags out of her hand and throwing them to Braig. "See if you can find her something dry."

Stripping off her clothing, he took the slightly damp tunic from Braig and slid it over her head. Laying down a shirt across a stack of pine boughs near the fire, he covered Renna's legs as she sat down, staring into the flames.

"Are you ok?" Braig said, glancing up at Faine.

"Renna," Faine said, crouching next to her. "Say something."

Shivers ran through her body as she stretched out her hands towards the fire. "I'm fine. I just don't...I've been walking for hours."

"How did you find us out here in the dark?"

"I could smell you," she said.

Faine glanced over at Braig and furrowed his brow.

"What happened back there?" Braig said as he moved closer. "Do you remember anything?"

"I remember everything. I need to see him," she said, throwing off the shirt over her legs as she looked frantically around the camp. "Where is he? Don't tell me he's already buried? Faine...where is he at?"

Holding up his hands, Faine walked over to a small space under the boughs of a pine tree. "He's here. I knew you'd want to see him," he said as he pulled off the branches covering Skara's body.

Tears filled Renna's eyes as she looked down at the corpse, his small arms folded over his chest. "Can you bring him into the light for me?"

Lifting gently, Faine set the body next to the fire as Renna knelt beside it, opening his shirt and running her fingers over the wound and arcane symbols that had been scarred onto his skin. Her shoulders shook with sobs as she put her hands over the wound and began slightly rocking her body back and forth as she turned her face up towards the canopy.

"I'lurian, great huntress who is both the wolf and the doe; both predator and prey. Please, cast your gaze upon me and find me worthy. I humbly ask you to return my companion from your kingdom in the Wilds." Pressing her hands harder over the wound, she raised her voice, yelling into the forest around her. "In all things, balance. In all life, struggle. In all death, renewal. I will send you deserving souls to be hunted in your forest, a feast for your wolves. I ask you to let your strength flow through my hands and return to me what was taken."

Renna's eyes shot open as she felt Skara's skin stretching under her hand as the wound began to close, the muscles and flesh healing under her touch. "Skara," she said, rubbing her hand over his chest where the wound had healed, "Wake up, Skara."

"Renna," Faine said, putting his hand on her shoulder. "Renna, he's gone."

"No! His wound is healed. He's coming back," she said, tears falling down her cheeks as she waited, gently shaking him. "He's coming back."

A loud crack sounded in the distance towards the heart of the Grey Wastes as a strong wind burst through the camp, shaking the canopy above them as the limbs bent and swayed. Covering their eyes against the blowing debris around them, a bright flash of blue-green flame shot across the sky as Skara gasped, sitting bolt upright, his eyes wide as his eyes darted around the camp.

"I don't believe it," Braig said, dropping to his knees.

"Skara," Renna said, wrapping her arms around him. "It worked. You're back."

"What happened?" Skara said, his body trembling and his breath coming out in white clouds.

"I was about to ask you the same thing," Faine said, touching Skara's shoulder, unsure if what he was seeing was real.

"I...I don't know. I remember going into the ruins and looking through the first few houses for the stone. But after that, it's all dark. What happened to me?"

Renna glanced over at Faine and Braig, her shoulders slumping as she turned her eyes toward Skara.

"You died," Braig said.

Skara frowned and looked up at Renna. "That can't be right. Then how am I here?"

"The goddess spared you," Renna said. "I pleaded with her to send you back. She healed you!"

Skara stared down at the cut across his palm and traced it with his finger. "I don't know...maybe you're right. Something inside me feels different. Not broken, but like I've been told a secret that I can't quite remember. There's a fog around my mind, but whatever's hiding there is waiting for me...waiting to swallow me."

Seeing the look on the faces around him, he pulled back his wet hair and rubbed his hands over his eyes. "Either way, I definitely feel like I've just come back from the dead."

"I bet. You look like shit," Faine said, a smile wide across his face.

Looking between his companions around the fire, Skara shrugged. "This coming from the three people sitting around naked in the dirt."

"It's good to have you back. You've missed a lot. But we'll have plenty of time to fill you in after we get out of here. I mean, the search is over. It's time to put this place behind us," Faine said, sitting back down on his pile of pine boughs.

"We can't just give up," Renna said, using a wet cloth to wipe the blood off her face. "Look what's happened here tonight. You can't just say that doesn't mean anything."

"Faine's right. We thought you were gone," Braig said, glancing over at Skara. "And there's something inside of you, Renna, that scares me."

"I never lost control. I knew who I was...what I was. I don't know how it happened, but it did. And if that magic hadn't clawed its way out, none of us would be here now. There are wild forces out there, and I have to look at it as a gift. It saved all of our lives tonight, here and in the town."

"I have no idea what happened, but there are forces at work here," Skara said, absently rubbing the cut on his palm. "And I don't think we should go back. We all made a choice to come here, knowing what could happen. We saw it in Banrielle, Mivara, and on the Banshee. People die...I died. Something is coming. It's like a shadow spreading across Hiraeth. I don't know what it is, but it's looking for the stones. And if we don't find them, I think that whatever happened here today is just the beginning."

The three nodded their heads as they looked to one another.

"At least we have one less stone to worry about. I think the stone here got burned up calling in all the undead. Or, it's just gone. If it were still here, I'd feel it."

"What do you think then, should we keep going? The letters from the Sun Spear said there were more out there," Faine said.

Renna tapped on her tusk and nodded. "Yes."

"Well," Braig said, running a hand through his beard, "I've never liked the thought of dying of old age warm in my bed anyway. I'm in."

"Then where do we go from here?" Faine said. "We don't even know where to start."

"We head east, to the Riverside Inn at the base of the mountains. We know that House Egara is involved, so that's a start. And I'm sure we'll find someone at the inn that can help us."

"I'll drink to that," Faine said, pulling the bottle of whiskey out of his bag and leaning back. "It's not every day you start making plans to kill a king, after all."

EMIN OPENED HIS EYES, the cold night air burning his lungs as he gasped for breath. Running his hands along the stone, he could feel the deep grooves beneath him filled with rain from the recent storm. Turning over onto his stomach, he sucked at the water in the cracks, catching a glimpse of his face in a shallow puddle. His flesh was thin and stretched like leather over his bones, his eyes dark and glazed. His cheeks were tight and split, rotted teeth showing through the gaps.

"I did it," he said, laughing to himself as he stood and shambled over to the edge of the mage tower.

Although he had made the journey through the veil with Skara, he had been preparing for that moment for hundreds of years. For centuries he had waited for the stone to find him, to make its way into across the threshold. And now, he had finally completed the ritual and ripped his soul in two, leaving half behind in Thodun, keeping him safe from death as long as it continued to roam the land of the dead.

Raising his hand in front of his face, his skin cracked like old parchment as he drew an arcane symbol in the air, trying to cast an illusion spell to appear how he once was before the shattering—but only a slight glow emanated from his fingertips before fading away into the darkness. Crossing the realms had left him weaker than he had anticipated, and he knew he would have to devour numerous souls before reaching his full strength.

Gazing out over the desolation of the Grey Wastes, Emin thought about all the long centuries he had spent trapped in that hell, waiting to reclaim the lands he had lost over a thousand years ago. And now, he thought, holding the Stone of the Denmol in his hand, the world was once again within his reach.